When They See Me

GILL PERDUE

PENGUIN BOOKS

PENGUIN BOOKS

UK | USA | Canada | Ireland | Australia
India | New Zealand | South Africa

Penguin Books is part of the Penguin Random House group of companies whose addresses can be found at global.penguinrandomhouse.com.

Penguin Random House UK,
One Embassy Gardens, 8 Viaduct Gardens, London SW11 7BW

penguin.co.uk

First published by Sandycove in 2023
Published in Penguin Books 2025

001

Copyright © Gill Perdue, 2023

The moral right of the author has been asserted

Penguin Random House values and supports copyright. Copyright fuels creativity, encourages diverse voices, promotes freedom of expression and supports a vibrant culture. Thank you for purchasing an authorized edition of this book and for respecting intellectual property laws by not reproducing, scanning or distributing any part of it by any means without permission. You are supporting authors and enabling Penguin Random House to continue to publish books for everyone. No part of this book may be used or reproduced in any manner for the purpose of training artificial intelligence technologies or systems. In accordance with Article 4(3) of the DSM Directive 2019/790, Penguin Random House expressly reserves this work from the text and data mining exception

Typeset by Jouve (UK), Milton Keynes
Printed and bound in Great Britain by Clays Ltd, Elcograf S.p.A.

The authorized representative in the EEA is Penguin Random House Ireland, Morrison Chambers, 32 Nassau Street, Dublin D02 YH68

A CIP catalogue record for this book is available from the British Library

ISBN: 978–0–241–99208–1

Penguin Random House is committed to a sustainable future for our business, our readers and our planet. This book is made from Forest Stewardship Council® certified paper.

For Jess and Sara

Prologue

Of course, I stand back to let her enter the shop. She's struggling with the wheel of the buggy — it's caught on the lip of the doorway — and I gesture for her to wait, bending quickly to free it and lift the contraption over the threshold. She stammers her thanks, not really looking at me; she's too busy trying to keep hold of her little girl with one hand, steering the buggy with the other.

'Thanks,' she says, over her shoulder, not making eye contact, moving further into the shop. 'These things have a will of their own.'

She doesn't wait for a reply. She doesn't even glance in my direction. They never do. And that's fine.

They never really see me until I will it. Until they are in my arms — cool blade pressed against their throats.

That's when I have their undivided attention. Yes.

That's when I am seen.

Wednesday

1

Laura

I turn my wrists upwards under the taps, letting cool water trickle over them, hoping this will magically get rid of the flush on my cheeks. Straightening up, I check the mirror to see if it's worked. Nope. No such luck. I dry my hands. It'll have to be make-up. I begin rummaging in my handbag, looking for foundation – did I remember to bring it? I could dab some over the worst of it, maybe – blend it in. No. Of course not. I picture it spilled out on the bathroom window-sill at home, the garish guts of my make-up bag – eye pencils, mascara, concealer – the arsenal I haven't used in months. Probably crawling with bacteria.

Stop panicking, I tell myself. This is an assessment, not an exam. She won't be trying to trip me up. Jackie called it a chat. 'Come in for your chat,' she'd said. 'Allow yourself an hour or so – we'll take it handy.'

Neither of us referred to the formal name for this chat – Fitness for Duty Evaluation. Or the fact that Jackie's appointed by the Garda Occupational Health Service.

It's a chat, Laura. A chat. Don't think of it as an evaluation. You're just stressed because you like to be the one asking the questions. Niamh's right. You're a control freak. I smooth my hair back – so long now that I've to put it in a ponytail – and turn to look at myself in the full-length mirror hanging on the back of the door. I'm wearing the charcoal trouser suit with a loose silk shirt. Mum would have approved. She always was a fan of tailoring. *Hides a multitude*, she'd say. And there's no doubt it's smart. I last wore it for months six and seven of pregnancy on Noah, and I'm not back in shape. The pleats on the shirt hide rock-hard boobs full of milk and about three kilos of post-baby belly.

A mummy looks back at me – edges blunted. Physically, that'll be the extra kilos. What stresses me is the fear that mentally I might be kind of blunted as well. Will I be up to this? What if she wants to go over the Cullen case? I feel my heart racing and I breathe, trying to control my thoughts. *You acted to preserve life, Laura.* If she brings it up, just keep saying that. *And don't forget to listen – pause before you answer, take your time.*

The bathroom is small and cosy, decorated in a beach theme – all faded blond wood, shells and smooth pebbles. Outside the door is a waiting room with a two-seater couch, a high-backed chair for the more on-edge client and the coffee table, on which sits a pile of *National Geographic* magazines. I could stay here for days – moving from bathroom to waiting room, reading the magazines, washing my hands in the creamy handwash. Since Noah was born nine months ago, this is the longest amount of time I've spent in the quietest space. It's warm. Vanilla-scented. I want to move in. At home, I can't even get five minutes in the loo on my own. *Noah needs you, Mummy! He's crying!* Katie berates me like a mini desk sergeant. *He's stinky! Are you doing a wee? Why are you taking so long?*

In the distance, I hear a door close. My watch reads a minute to 2 p.m. Here we go.

2

Laura

'How are you?' Jackie says, motioning for me to take the seat opposite her. Hard-backed chair for me; padded one for her.

'Great – good, thanks.' I smile, perching on the seat edge.

'There are no medals for suffering alone,' she says, looking up from my file. 'I think it's safe to say you learned that the hard way, yes?'

Jackie is a girlish-looking fifty-something, her large blue eyes and casual clothing – she's wearing a pair of jeans and a zipped hoody – belying an astute mind and a no-nonsense attitude. She would have no hesitation whatsoever in declaring someone unfit for duty. I can think of at least two from our unit who had to turn over their badges and head uphill to pasture following one of Jackie's sessions.

She takes off her glasses and begins polishing them slowly with a wipe, in a move I reckon she learned on a training course. It has the desired effect all right. I find myself kind of mesmerized by the action.

'I'll rephrase that as a question,' she says, her jaw tightening, and I'm reminded that I'm not her client here – An Garda Síochána is. 'What have you learned from the Cullen case, Laura? What would you do differently were it to happen now?'

The GSOC inquiry looms large and lumpen between us. Why did I think she wouldn't go there? Idiot.

I answer too quickly – gushing.

'Everything,' I say. 'There isn't a single aspect of – of, you know, what I did – that was okay – justifiable – on any level. I understand that now.'

She moves on to polishing the second lens and I try to slow myself down.

'And – I – even though I know it can't be justified – what I did – I was acting to preserve life, you see.'

The phrase comes out all wrong – with a pleading upward inflection. *Preserve life?* I sound like a child. From LA.

'Even so,' she swoops in, 'there's no tolerance for emotional or behavioural dysfunction when you're working as a detective. An armed detective –'

Those blue eyes lock with mine. She doesn't blink. *She doesn't know about the gun. No one does*, I reassure myself. *She can't hear your thoughts.*

She folds the wipe into a small square and puts the glasses back on. 'I don't have to tell you that the lives of others depend on you being fully functional.'

I hear the underlines on 'fully' and 'functional'.

'And if you have poor impulse control or an anxiety disorder that's running unchecked –'

My head is nearly falling off with the nodding and, in my mind, I'm doing the chant: *She can't hurt you. She can't hurt you.*

'Absolutely,' I say. 'I understand – I – well, you probably have it on file there? I did a three-month course of CBT and – I only stopped recently when I had Noah.'

'I see that.' She nods. 'That's good – Cognitive Behaviour Therapy can be very helpful.' She runs her pen down along the page and turns over to the next sheet.

'And what about medication? There are excellent long-term and short-term solutions for managing anxiety.'

'I'm still breastfeeding,' I say, shaking my head. 'So, I didn't want to –'

'Some of which can be taken when breastfeeding,' she continues. I say nothing, forcing myself to wait. *This is not an attack, Laura. It's just a suggestion.* Jackie sits back.

'Look, the bottom line is – well, let's face it. You'd be perfectly entitled – and it might do you no harm – to take some extended leave. Not a career break at your own expense, you understand what I'm saying? You were involved in a difficult case which brought up – your own issues. PTSD, anxiety. There's post-natal depression to think about, yes? After all, you've just given birth – recently given birth, rather. It's now March – I could write you off until Christmas – or the New Year? It's not weakness, Laura. Looking after yourself is your responsibility, no?'

I try to frame a response, but no words come. If she writes me off – so *I'm not a detective – working – a working detective, if I'm not that, who am I? Detective Garda Laura Shaw – or just Laura, mummy of Katie and Noah. Wife of Matt. The years of training, the years in the DDU –*

'You're long enough at this to understand the risks,' she's saying. 'And you do have insight into your –' She pauses, and we both run through the wordsearch – *illness/ condition/ weakness/ issues/ past trauma* – shimmering in the air between us. Her chair is higher than mine, and the desk rises like a wall between us. How I wish I was the one holding the file and asking the questions.

I make myself sit quiet, remembering that night – how I discharged a traumatized fourteen-year-old from the psych ward and basically brought her to the scene of her worst nightmares – the risks I took with her life, and my own. I still can't quite believe it. It's like it was a different time and a different me. Only for Niamh keeping quiet about the worst of it – the fact that Jenny got hold of my gun – the fact that she was intent on harming herself, or me, or both of us – only for Niamh's silence and for her watchful presence at the scene, it could have been a very different outcome. By rights, I should be out of a job. Disgraced. That's the very least I deserve. *You're a disaster. A liability.*

'GSOC were satisfied that you committed no offence and did not recommend that proceedings be instituted against you,' she reads, 'and you've demonstrated that you understand the seriousness of your behaviour.' She pauses again.

'And do you?'

My mouth opens, but she carries on before a sound emerges.

'Do you understand that, irrespective of the outcome – the fact that you saved a life, that you closed the case – none of that matters a jot, Laura?'

She flips back a page, looks at me.

'Your Commissioner's Medal can't help you here, not if you don't accept that you made a mistake – a grave error of judgement.'

A beat. I nod a slow nod.

'None of it. Because nothing justifies your reckless behaviour. Does it?'

I switch from nodding to shaking my head.

'No. Of course not. Absolutely.'

She waits another few seconds. I will myself to hold her gaze.

'How's the sleeping?'

'Oh, great,' I lie. 'Apart from the night feeds, of course. But – yeah – no problems there.'

She reads through more of my file, the only sound in the room the crinkling of the pages as she turns them. From outside, a gentle hum of traffic on the M50 overpass. As she reads, I have an insane worry that, somehow, she'll know I lied about the sleep too – that they could have access to my receipts from the chemist, where I've bought every over-the-counter remedy ever made in an effort to get some sleep. I've a path worn to their locked cabinet and the nice man jangling the keys. And at home, boxes and bottles in shades of navy and purple line the top shelf of the bathroom, all promising – but not delivering – calm, restful sleep. She reads on. I force myself to wait, trying to still my racing thoughts.

'Fine,' she says at last, leaning forward and taking off her glasses, folding them and placing them on to my now closed file.

'You're good at what you do, Laura. And from what I read here, you've got great support from your partner –'

'I do – yes. Niamh is brilliant to work with. She's –'

Another pause and a questioning frown. She tilts her head.

'At home?' she says. 'Your husband is most supportive, you've said?'

'Oh! Yes – sorry.' I feel myself flush. Idiot.

'Absolutely. Matt is great. I'm very lucky there.'

I hold the smile, my teeth clamped firmly on my lower lip to stop myself saying another word. Poor Matt, I think. The hell I put him through. His endless offers of help – the fresh start he longs for – he'd be second only to the director if he accepts the New York posting. And I know he'd love it. I think of the silence that yawns between us when we make eye contact, the things we both want to say drifting to the floor like ash from a bonfire.

'Right,' she says, breaking the spell. 'You'll get the go-ahead from me if you do decide to come back, but I'd strongly recommend –'

I exhale, adjusting my right hand infinitesimally – enough to hide the raw flesh on my thumb. A surge of adrenalin courses in my veins. I can come back! I'm good to go.

'What I mean is that you should also consider the career break option.'

I shake my head.

'I'm still discussing it, um, at home and – I –' I come to a stop, unsure what I want to say. The truth is, I hadn't envisaged this. I think I must have been expecting the decision to be taken out of my hands. Maybe I was expecting to fail this evaluation, and that would be that.

'Interesting,' she continues. 'I note you say "*I'm* discussing", as opposed to "*We're* discussing". Surely a discussion takes at least two?'

Her smile is tight. She leans towards me. 'Look – I say this as a working mum of three, you get me – as opposed to my professional opinion –'

I wait.

'I think a career break could be just the thing. Or – what about a step sideways – going for sergeant? More of a desk job, regular hours. Less risk?'

'You and Matt must be on the same team.' I laugh. 'And thanks – I'm – we – we're considering everything. Nothing's off the table. Career break, back to the unit, whatever. It's all up in the air. I've till Monday to decide.'

'Well, as long as you know – we've got to be certain that you'll ask for help if you need it,' she finishes. 'I'll be checking in with you, and I expect you to keep in touch. Yes?'

I fumble with the door handle on my way out, managing to lock myself in. Her face creases into a smile.

'Other way,' she says, laughing.

3

Niamh

'Jush ring the bell already!' Amber's voice peals like a little bell in the chilly night air, rising over the constant hum of Ranelagh traffic. I have the key against the lock, but with Amber hanging out of me, her movements made clumsy by the rake of vodka and slimline followed by a ridiculous number of espresso martinis, I keep on missing the keyhole.

'Drothery – Dror – Dor-oh-thee – Dorotheeee wone mind,' she giggles, tilting her head back to gaze up the three storeys to where the black-slated roof meets the navy night sky. Spying a square of light at the very top of the house, Amber inhales, ready to shout.

'Sssh! Don't yell – don't – Amber!'

Amber has had years of vocal training – she has to, for her job – and I don't doubt that she could easily make herself heard by Dorothy, my landlady – or indeed by half of south bloody Dublin. She could probably get them to hold the Luas for her from here.

'Sssh! Sssh!' I pull her closer against my shoulder and try once more and – thanks be to Jaysus – I finally get the key in the lock and shove the door open, shuffling the pair of us inside my basement flat.

I prop her against the wall, holding her steady with one hand while I shove the door closed with the other. She rests her head on the exposed brick, her blonde tresses fanning out so that she somehow manages to look like something from a fashion shoot, rather than a twenty-eight-year-old wannabe actor, too drunk to stand. On the wall beside her head – a bit too close to her face, actually – hangs the gift she gave me when she slept over for the first weekend. Her phrase – *our first sleepover*. It's a key-holder made to look like a rabbit hutch with two little front doors side by side. Two rabbit keyrings came with it. I hang up mine, noting that one hutch is empty. Yeah. In theory, Amber lives in the nice apartment her daddy bought her in Sandymount but, in practice, she's been more or less permanently living here for the past five months.

A heavy truck trundles by – Dorothy's house is right on the main street of Ranelagh, opposite the pharmacy she owns and still runs, though she's in her eighties – and all the front doors rattle – ours and the rabbits'.

Amber's eyes fly open. In the dim hallway, she looks like a teenager, her eyes enormous and dark against her pale skin. She's wearing a grey blazer coat thing, with a silky white shirt dress underneath and a ridiculous pair of black thigh-high boots. The effect is as if she's wearing her big brother's school uniform – or half of it.

'So, does – does –' She frowns, closing her eyes momentarily, then tries again. 'Do – do you think your friends like me, Nimmi? 'Simportant.'

She opens one eye, blinks, then with tremendous effort opens them both.

'I wan them to like me. Laura, too. I wan her to like me.'

She nods, then with a lurch moves to a standing position and begins tottering along the corridor towards the bedroom, steadying herself with her fingertips on either side of the wall. She attempts a strut – bless her.

'I wan them to like me,' she says, 'even though we have *nothing* in common – you know, and I –'

'They do like you,' I say, following behind her, my hands poised either side of her tiny waist, ready to catch her if she falls. 'I know they do. They like you a lot.'

'Laura doesn't,' she says. 'And don' say I'm wrong because I know – I know she doesn't like me.'

I open my mouth, about to speak – but there's no way I'm going there at this hour, when she's like this. Laura only met her for about two minutes, when we called up with a present for the baby. And Laura was up to high doh.

'Laura doesn't know you yet,' I say soothingly. 'But we'll go out some night – like tonight – like we did just now – and we'll have fun and they'll – she'll definitely love you.'

She sways.

'They all loved you,' I add.

'Yeah, and – I made them laugh, didn't I? When I was telling them about the kissing –'

'Haha, you surely did.'

She'd had them in stitches, in fairness, describing the woeful kissing technique of one of our upcoming leading men. They'd been filming a trailer for a short movie – it might be her big break. Amber told them he licked her face first, *Like a spaniel, I swear! Just like a spaniel.* Liath, Shauna, Ruth – the whole lot of them – were falling around laughing, and Amber was in her element.

She staggers towards the edge of the bed, turns and flops dramatically back on to it, only just missing cracking her head against her jewellery box she left there earlier. There'd been much debate about what and how much to wear of everything – make-up, clothes, jewellery.

'Are they *all* camogie girls?' she'd whined. 'Like, will they be wearing jerseys and stuff?' This was before we left the house. Before any drink. Before Amber with a capital 'A', theatre Amber, movie-star Amber, showed up. She was nervous.

I'd told her that camogie girls were just like other girls – and that, no, they wouldn't be wearing their jerseys.

'Shauna's a doctor, and Liath works in Google, for God's sake! And they're going to love you.'

Encouraged and pacified, she'd settled on the white dress and long boots.

Now, the silky dress is being pulled up to expose her tanned, flat stomach, and higher, so I get a glimpse of the lace bra. She reaches up her arms, blinking at me as though trying to focus.

I've been kind of blinded by Amber since we first hooked up, to be honest. She's sort of – she's pure dazzling. I've never been with anyone so – so ridiculously good-looking, I suppose. And I'm not imagining it. Sometimes when we meet people together, I see them look at us – comparing. And I come up short.

I smile, watching her try to blink me into focus. She points at me, her finger swaying from side to side.

'You – you know you're a ride, don' you?' she slurs.

'Is that so? And which of us do you want to ride?' I grin, sitting down on the bed beside her and getting to work on the boots. They sort of roll down, like mad leather socks. Her hands flop to the bed and she wriggles.

'Me or the other me?'

'Bothayouse,' she mumbles.

'You're wasted, Amber,' I say. 'I'd be taking advantage.'

'Nimmi! I am not! I just want – do you – what's wrong with me?' There's a catch in her voice. Christ.

'Here,' I say, finally getting the second boot off, then whooshing her properly into the bed and pulling up the duvet. 'There's nothing wrong with you. You're –'

She's hiccupping. I have about thirty seconds. I sprint into the bathroom, grabbing the basin from under the sink, then into the kitchen for a pint glass of water and the kitchen roll. I tie her hair back and kneel on the floor beside the bed, waiting.

'You're beautiful,' I say, as she starts retching.

The secret is not to be greedy and not to leave a mess – to wear gloves and to clean up after yourself. The secret is to spread it out by hundreds of miles, so there's no danger of the police making the connection. The secret is to deny yourself for months and keep up your regular routine at work and home – looking forward to it the way some men look forward to their annual ski holiday. They'd like to be indulging their pleasures more often, and so would I – but needs must.

What is one life worth? What value do you put on your own life?

In my line of work, I see so many different types of people – the ones who cling to the world and their place in it. They're fierce. They've got the last space on a lifeboat and they're going to prise the fingers off anyone who tries to scramble aboard. These people feast on life, sucking the marrow from its bones. They'll trample over bodies – living or dead – if they have to. Whatever it takes to survive. Mother was like that. Greedily gorging on being alive.

And then there are the others. Floating about like thistledown on the wind. Dotting their 'i's and crossing their 't's, blending in, seeking permission, cringing, and smiling – a speck in your glass of wine, nothing more. They don't deserve life. The most useful thing they could do is die and let someone have the use of their organs. They're nothing.

I like the ones that fight. I respect that. And yet it's intriguing – interesting – to take a life from someone who doesn't care, someone who, through terror or despair, has given up. I'm doing them a favour.

Yes. Both interest me.

But one is far easier to kill.

Thursday

4

Laura

Go and check on them. You should go. Katie could be crying right now — maybe she had a nightmare and she's crying, too scared to come in, in case you give out to her like you did earlier. You snapped the head off her. And what about the baby? Why hasn't he woken yet for a feed? Are you sure you put him lying on his back? You need to raise the end of the cot. You were going to do that, weren't you? Why haven't you? Go and check on them.

I know about these thoughts. I know what they are, and I know what you have to do. They're not real. Beside me, Matt sleeps on. He's no idea about this ritual — the nightly orgy of evaluation, recrimination and self-flagellation that has to happen before I can sleep.

I try to summon Sam, the counsellor I went to see in my early twenties after the assault, when the panic attacks started. I think about his study — the muffled silence of that room, like a carpeted vault. Green light splintered by the old chestnut tree by the window. The distant clang of Cora clattering things in the kitchen.

Challenge them, Sam tells me. *Sit with the thoughts. They're not real. You don't need to check them because this is not real. The kids are fast asleep. They're asleep. Do not give in to the compulsion to check them.*

I move my arms away from my chest. My breasts are heavy, and part of me wishes Noah would actually wake looking for a feed. Christ! And I could check Katie when I go in to get him. The chant starts. Maybe if I just do four of them. Four times: *Nothing will hurt them. Nothing will hurt them. Nothing will hurt them. Nothing will hurt them.*

How's the sleep? Jackie had asked. *Oh, grand.* Yeah. I'm kicking myself – why didn't I answer truthfully? I could have got help – she could have arranged counselling hours or a psych referral. Hell, I know this isn't right, and it seems so much worse in the small hours of the morning. Why am I putting myself through this? Why wasn't I honest with her? I could be off on paid leave – never mind a career break. But instead, I'd laughed and lied. Habit of a lifetime. Laugh. Lie.

I sigh, opening my eyes, automatically scanning the room. That's another one my warped brainwaves give me – the night assassin. He's a hunched figure wielding a knife who dispatches the kids first, severing the arteries inside their little throats – the blade plunging into pillows of flesh – then he comes for us. Or, in the worst scenario – he doesn't take us both. He kills the kids. He kills Matt. And I'm left alive. Why would I think like this? How can I stop myself?

I sigh and turn over on to my back, clasping my hands together to still them. What do I want? What should I do? When I told Matt about Jackie advising the break, he was ecstatic.

Well, first he was pissed off that I hadn't told him anything about the meeting in the first place.

'Jesus! Why are you so bloody secretive, Laura? Seriously! I'm your husband, not your boss. But as usual, I'm shut out!'

But after that. Afterwards, he was delighted.

'So, she can sign you off for a career break? Two years? You can take up to two years, can't you? We could go to New York and make a go of it – a proper go of it.'

He'd taken a step closer and, yeah, for a split second I'd

thought he was going to kiss me. The full-on cradling my face, like he used to –

'So, you'll take the break?'

His hands fell away, one reaching to the back of his head to fiddle with his hair, in that gesture he does. It's a self-comforting thing. That's my curse – to understand the psychology but still not be able to influence or change my behaviour. In the silence between us, he'd dialled it down.

'Okay – not New York. Just the break, then. That's what we decided – we – both of us, we decided, didn't we?'

He's right. We had talked about it, and it makes sense for me to take a break. I told him I'd no intention of going for sergeant. It would mean a transfer and more training, and a year back in uniform in another district.

'So, take a career break,' he'd coaxed. 'We can do it – and the kids –'

I'd shushed him then. Not wanting to hear how happy it would make the kids to have me home, how happy it would make him, knowing I was with them.

'And it would be better for you,' he'd urged. 'With your – the anxiety? You said yourself that stress makes it worse. Well, this way, you'd be home with them. They'd be with you all the time, so you wouldn't be worrying about them. And with the –'

The pause told me what he wouldn't say. We're still trying to negotiate our way around the assault – the rape, Laura. It was rape. After Jenny's case, I'd finally spoken to him about it and, initially, there was this huge sense of relief. I'd felt seen – naked and vulnerable – but understood. But there's a massive problem when you finally face the elephant in the room, and it's this – once you've seen it, you can't see past it. *'Can't go over it, can't go under it, can't go around it –'* the refrain of Katie's storybook, *We're Going on a Bear Hunt*, chants in my brain. The jagged, dense shadow of that night when I was nineteen, when time fractured into Before and After, when everything that I was going to be was ripped apart and thrown back at me in tatters – that shadow looms between us, blocking the light, so we can't see our path towards each other.

'It doesn't work like that, Matt.'

'*Gotta go through it*,' that's the next line.

How do I tell him that I feel like an imposter in my life at home? That the only place I feel real is in work – grilling someone in an interview or blue-lighting it in the car with Niamh on the way to a callout. Work – the adrenalin, the risk, the urgency – or maybe it's the brutality; I don't know what it is – but I know it distracts me from the compulsions; and I'm not sitting at home, trying to be a perfect mum, sorting feeds and fights and picking up Lego. I didn't tell him that the only reason I'd gone for the assessment in the first place was based on the need to know where I stood from the work point of view. If I wanted to go back, would they take me?

I don't know – no one tells you what to expect when you have kids. Not really. It's all about how exhausting it is and the knowing smiles about how tired you'll be and how you'll never have a minute to yourself. Nobody tells you that you will now live in terror of something happening to your child. That the world is no longer sunny and bright, it's filled with risk; with rapists, abusers, paedophiles, murderers. And nobody tells you about the loneliness. Nobody tells you that a thousand times a day you're faced with the worst aspects of yourself. Your flaws and failings magnified a thousand per cent. How in the name of God I thought I'd be able to manage when I'm tapping and counting and shredding the skin of my fingers till they bleed, with my lists and my imperatives and my overthinking.

And the daily terror you live with – the risk of injury and

death. It feels like you're a hair's breadth from fatality all the time, like we're running through a hailstorm of shards of glass. Anything could happen. They could fall; they could choke. I could crash the car with them in it. They could suffocate on a sofa cushion or a stray plastic bag. Katie could hurt him without meaning to. He could ingest one of her Sylvanians and die from a bowel obstruction. The buggy could roll out into the road. Katie could shove the buggy on to the road. I could shove it. I could – what if I'm the biggest danger in their lives? The daily terror of being alone with them – responsibility, risk, harm. On and on and on. It's so ludicrous, it should be funny. Except it's not.

Light from the landing outlines the chest of drawers, the dressing table on which Matt has left a teetering pile of holiday brochures, even though I've told him I don't want to go anywhere. More risk. Swimming pools. Planes. Airborne diseases. Snakes. Venomous spiders. But for Matt it's so simple. A family holiday followed by Mummy taking a career break. Then off to New York for a Fabulous Adventure. His suit jacket is hung neatly on its hanger in readiness for the morning, the trousers over the bannisters to keep their creases sharp. This is how Matt lives.

There's complete stillness in the room. In the silence, I can hear the distant plunging of water over the weir. That's another one – the buggy being tipped into the weir – or yeah, let's honestly admit what I see. I see me tipping it in. I watch it sink. I watch the little hand stretch up and up until it's gone. Why am I like this?

It's 4.40 a.m. Christ. I've got to get some sleep or I'll be useless tomorrow. My body is seized by a yawn, which turns into one of those double and triple yawns. I'm exhausted.

The silence in the house roars on in time with the rolling water. Matt twitches and then sighs. I must have had some sleep — mustn't I? Could I have been lying awake since eleven, or whenever it was I went to bed?

I must have slept. But what woke me? I heard something — a click or a rap on the door — something. I rewind mentally. Yes — it was a click. The lock on the front door clicks like that.

It was the front door closing softly — as though someone guided it gently into the frame and held on to the snib as it clicked. And, while I've been lying here, they could have crept up the stairs and into the baby's room — or Katie's room. They — he — it's a 'he' — it's not the assassin. It's the guy who — the kidnapper for the paedophile ring. He's lifting Katie out of her bed, his hand over her mouth so she can't make a sound, the other hand scooped underneath her sleep-slack body, her bare feet bobbing in time with his steps and now — now he's taking the stairs two at a time with Katie in his arms and he'll be outside and into his car in a matter of seconds.

I know this is nonsense. I know I must check.

5

Niamh

The Irish coffee was a mistake, I think, rolling over, trying not to snag Amber's hair, fumbling for my phone. Laura might be up – last reports of Noah were that he was still demanding night feeds. I stalk her 'last seen at' on Whats-App. Yes! Last seen at 4.30 a.m.

Well? The dots appear after a few seconds.

Feeling

Feeling what? I text back, settling myself against the pillows, my body angled away from Amber in case the light from the screen wakes her. Which is unlikely, seeing as how there were tears following the puking, then more puking. Then I got her to drink a glass of water and, mercifully, she fell asleep. The basin is still on the floor by the bed, just in case. Espresso-scented snores waft towards me. I stroke her hair while I wait for Laura to reply.

Feeding abd texting leftjsand, Laura texts. Then there's a pause before she hits me with my own version of 'how are you?'... *Well?*

Ah, nothing really, I text. *Had a late one with A. Off tomorrow. All good. You go on with the feed. Kiss the babas from me. Can't wait to see you Monday.*

I wait, but no dots appear.

I click out of the app and settle down to sleep, jaded but still wired from the coffee.

No work tomorrow, so no need to set the alarm. Through

the blinds, I can just make out the blackness of tree branches against the slatted pieces of night sky. The soft hum of traffic — and the occasional truck.

It's so different from home, where the silence is as thick and heavy as treacle. There's a timeless quality too, from the ancient red bricks and the brass doorknobs. From the wrought-iron gates and from Dorothy herself. I'm mad about her. She's like something you'd grow in a lab to go with the house. The day I moved in, she gave me the quick tour like a sergeant major, all clipped sentences and no nonsense.

'Rather plain decor — agent's suggestion. For professional types,' she'd said, studying me, as if my outfit held clues to what decorating style I might like. 'Not very much in the way of — ah — cushions and suchlike —'

I'd cut her off, assuring her that it was absolutely perfect. Dorothy — tall, spare and practical herself — awkward as anything but eager to do the right thing by her new tenant. One thing I knew for sure after I first clapped eyes on her was that the flat would be spotless. She had that scrubbed-clean look and she smelt of old-fashioned soap — Imperial Leather or something like that. Later, she'd insisted on bringing me upstairs to her part of the house — the sparse, high-ceilinged sitting room at the front — where she tried to stuff me full of her home-made biscuits.

I'm glad I'm the one renting from her, though. She's a pet. What if she'd got some dickhead student and his ten pals crashing on the sofa bed and the floor? Partying all night. It's near town and a short walk to the Luas. And Dorothy's happy for me to park the car in the tiny space in the front.

We left it that I was delighted with the flat as it is — that I won't be needing any cushions or a man to come and paint the dark furniture, and that I'm to go upstairs once a month or so and she's going to teach me how to bake. Tomorrow — today,

I suppose – the first lesson is lined up for my day off. Bakewell slices. 'Easiest thing in the world,' Dorothy says. I asked her if Amber could stay over a few nights a week, reckoning she had a right to know who's in her property, and she was grand about it.

'Nice for you to have company,' was all she said. 'Lovely girl.'

The 'lovely girl' rolls over, muttering something in her sleep, and I'm on high alert in case she's about to throw up again. But she's just trying to get comfortable. Once again, she looks like something from an ad – the tousled hair, the thick eyelashes shadowing that heart-shaped face. Face it, I think. I'm still playing catch-up. I've watched her in plays and ads, I've dried tears after auditions and helped neck the champagne after triumphs. I've even met her platinum mum – a tinier, more silver version of Amber, who lives in a mansion on the Vico Road in Killiney. I've never been with anyone remotely like her, and I can't help feeling that, any minute, it could all fall apart.

Finally, I feel my shoulders relax and I take a deep breath, luxuriating in the silence, the house, the calm. It feels like the end of a perfect day – well, apart from the puking. We'll go to Brother Hubbard's tomorrow, I think, get some great hangover food.

I've had what feels like about an hour's sleep when my work phone rings. I nearly jump out of my skin trying to get it before it wakes Amber. McArsey's tone is formal as ever.

'Good morning, Darmody,' he says, 'the inspector was looking for you. He wants us both. Can you meet me up at the Military Road? I've sent you the location.'

On cue, my phone pings.

'There's been a fatality. Or, rather, a murder.'

He hangs up.

6

Niamh

The clock on the dash reads 7.32 when the flashing blue lights strobing the bend in the narrow mountain road let me know I've arrived. Three squad cars are parked in the layby beside a blue 18 D Passat which I presume is the hillwalkers' car. The tech unit van is further up, mounted on a hillock of grass. I pull in behind it and park. Crime-scene tape flickering in the breeze tells me that the scene has been cordoned off, and I spot two uniformed officers who will have been logging every visit to the scene since the first responders arrived. One of the tech guys – Byrne, I think, by the height of him – is taking photos with a drone. That's good, I think, spotting Senan – how the actual fuck is he here already? – *marshalling the troops*, as he likes to call it. He checks his watch before nodding in my direction. Typical.

Ignoring him, I sign the scene log and show my credentials, then go straight to Byrne, stepping carefully on the foot plates, so as not to disturb anything.

'Morning, Byrne.'

He nods without taking his eyes off the drone.

'Did you get shots of the layby – before half the force parked on top of the tyre tracks?'

He moves the control stick and the sound of the drone changes as it drops lower.

'I did,' he says. 'Good to see you, Darmody – although this is bloody grim. She looks about fifteen.'

I look towards the body, not wanting to get closer until Byrne is finished. From here, I can see a pair of bare feet poking out from a covering of branches and leaves. My stomach lurches – her feet are destroyed – the bare skin is torn and scraped raw.

'Christ! Did he make her do a barefoot pilgrimage before he killed her?'

Byrne makes a *tssk* sound between his teeth, concentrating.

'Sorry.'

He rotates the lever again, causing the drone to circle and rise up above the body.

'You're grand. I'm nearly finished with this anyway,' he says, 'but, yeah – her feet are in bits.'

'Detective Darmody?' says Senan, marching over towards us, his North Face puffa zipped up to his little chinny-chin-chin. Senan McArsey – human version of one of those swimming-pool noodles – and just as insubstantial, makes up for his lack of heft with a muscular devotion to the rule book. Jaysus, I don't know why he annoys me so much – is it the rules? The fast-tracking through the ranks? Maybe it's the priestly air, or maybe I'm just jealous of his foot on the property ladder and the way he's tipped for promotion. He's from home as well – not that you'd ever know it. It's like he's ashamed of his roots; he never mentions it. Oh yeah – and I'm a bitch – so it's probably that.

'Well.' I nod, turning away from Byrne and walking to meet McArsey, aware that I'm breathing in deeply in preparation. Only a couple more days of this. Suck it up and smile, bitch. He doesn't outrank you – he only thinks he does.

'Morning, Senan.' He winces at the familiarity, and I prepare myself for the rebuke, but he's got other things on his mind.

'The team from Rathfarnham was on. It's possible this is the missing au pair.' He makes a little beckoning motion right under my nose – another one of his priestlike habits that make me want to punch him – indicating that I'm to follow.

'She was reported missing from the Clonchapel area yesterday – went to pick up the child from playschool, didn't return.'

The wind is whipping my hair all over the place, so I stop to tie it back. Senan waits, a look of long-suffering patience stamped on his pale pink features. He nods his approval when I finish. I want to punch him again. What is *wrong* with me? I've managed nearly ten months – I can manage the last few days.

'Dr Parminter is on his way – should be here any minute.'

He picks his way over the tufts of grass and heather in his hiking boots. How the hell did he know to wear hiking boots when he got up this morning? We stop some metres away from the girl, waiting as she's photographed by another tech guy.

Most of the body is covered by branches; only the girl's shoulders and her poor feet are bare. It's almost as if he was trying to cover her modesty. A killer with opinions about nakedness? A religious zealot? I step a bit closer – her dark hair is smoothed – maybe even slicked back; it looks wet. From here it's hard to tell if her darkened lips are oxygen-deprived, or if she's wearing heavy lipstick.

'Not your average look for an au pair,' I say. 'Are you sure it's her?'

'Clearly, we won't know for sure until a formal identification's been made,' says Senan, as though I'm a complete idiot. I take a step away from him, not trusting myself.

'I'll go and have a word with the couple who found her,' I say, indicating the shook-looking pair – her still clutching her walking poles – talking to one of the uniformed gardaí who is taking notes.

'Good idea,' says Senan.

Jaysus!

Before I reach them, the garda breaks away from the hikers and starts making her way towards me. She's tiny, and her stride is too short for the foot plates, so she has to gather herself and leap forwards at each step, as though she's playing hopscotch. Eventually, she arrives. I check her shoulder number – one of ours. She must be new.

'Hi – Detective, eh, Darmody – I'm Wilson, I'm new in the unit.'

She blinks rapidly – tears from the wind, or –

'They're wondering if they can go. Like – not hiking – they were meant to be hiking.'

'In the dark?' God! The things people do when they could be home in bed.

'Yes – they – they wanted to see the sunrise. From the top, and – I think they're in shock, actually. Do we let them go home or what?'

She blinks again, adding an anxious throat clear, and I remember the first murder scene I attended. I was terrified.

Her hair is pretty much nailed into the proper regulation bun and tucked under the cap, but I can tell by the freckles standing out against her pale skin that she's a redhead. She reminds me of a squirrel – the darting movements.

'Hell, no, Wilson!' I snap, 'Of course not! You'll have to take them in for questioning – they could be suspects. Go and cuff them.'

Her mouth opens.

'What? Sorry –'

I wait a beat, then I grin. She almost wets herself in relief. Her whole body relaxes.

'So –'

'So, you have their contact details and you've checked them out?' She nods, starting to take out her notebook. I shake my head.

'Tell them they can go.' She thanks me and turns away.

'Actually – maybe you should go back with them, yeah? See them into the house, do the whole cup of tea thing – that will calm them down. Tell them we'll be taking statements at some stage this morning and then head back to the station, okay?'

Her smile of relief is priceless. She scampers off, bounding across the tiles. I watch her progress, feeling old. She exchanges a few words with the couple and waits until they start the engine. Before she can get into her own car, I spot McArsey. He summons her over to him with that beckoning finger, then bends over her in his creepy way, saying something. What's he doing? Is he giving out? It looks as if he's imparting some of his legendary wisdom – he's nodding and smiling like some benign overlord. Patronizing dick.

Dr Parminter, the state pathologist, arrives. Mournful persona – check; doleful stoop of his shoulders – check. Dr Death himself. Under the protective clothing, he will be wearing a hand-stitched three-piece Italian suit and, though he's actually a chirpy enough type of personality, let's just say his appearance suits his line of work. He looks like a carrion-feeding bird – a buzzard or a vulture.

'Detective.' He nods at me.

'Morning, Doctor.'

Senan bustles over.

'This way, Doctor.' He does a bit of semaphore indicating the tent, which is now fully erected. I want to tell him that, in fairness, I think Dr Parminter is capable of working out where the body is. The big white tent thing is a bit of a give-away. Then I remember – only a few more days.

We leave him at it and get on with searching the scene, along with Byrne and the rest of the tech team. We're looking for a weapon, a scrap of clothing, hairs snagged on twigs – anything at all that could be part of the jigsaw. At this stage, we don't know if the girl was already dead when she was left here or if the cold expanse of the Dublin mountainside was her last sight on earth.

I look around me. We're about three hundred metres above sea level on the exposed bogland that is the Military Road. The winding road snakes up from Rathfarnham, casting off houses, traffic, people, vegetation – civilization, I suppose – with every metre climbed. Even with the bit of spring sunshine attempting to peer over the top of the mountain, it's easy to see this as a place of execution, a place where you'd hide a body. Everywhere is brown and grey – too early for any flowering of yellow gorse or purple heather.

I sigh, hit with a sudden longing for home – the fields and stone walls, the rolling hills and, feck it, the different shades of green. The song doesn't lie – there *are* forty shades. But let's face it, will we, Niamh – as we're here – it's not the fields of home or the farm or the stone walls of Tipp I'm missing. It's the idea of home. The concept of a place where you're loved and accepted, your roots entwined through the bricks and the roof slates, your name crayoned (and later scrubbed off) on the exposed bit of wall behind the bedroom door. The place where you ate, slept, fought, cried, laughed, did your homework, thumped your brothers – *that* home. Even after ten years in Dublin, when I'm falling asleep I sometimes listen out for the thwack of Tom's sliotar hitting the gable wall. Five years my senior, Tom was allowed stay up to what I reckoned was midnight but must have been only about nine o'clock. For all Tom's practising, it was Rory who eventually made the county team.

The last time I went back was September – overtime put paid to any notion of Christmas at home – but I was relieved, to be honest. The things Mam said – yeah, and me too, I suppose – they can't be unsaid. I sigh, butterflies squirming at the thought of bringing Amber home next week. No backing out now.

'Detective? Did you hear me?'

I start – comically it would seem, because Byrne snorts with laughter.

'You got a hangover, by any chance, Detective? Big night out for the boggers, was it? Did someone win the Sam Maguire?'

'Feck off. What?'

'Thought you were gonna draw your weapon.' He laughs. 'Lightning reflexes, Darmody.'

'What is it?' I seesaw my gaze around the scene. A group of tech lads are lifting the wrapped body on a stretcher, bringing it over to the van.

'Dr Death's gone on. They're bringing her to the mortuary. He'll get cracking on the post-mortem, he says.'

'Right, thanks. Here, listen, did you get close-ups of her face? Was that lipstick or –' He's nodding.

'Looks like it, yeah. You'll see when you get the shots. A really dark red colour. Now' – he inhales noisily – 'I'm heading back to look at these. You should talk to Barry – get him to show you the drag marks.'

He points towards a heavy-set bald guy tiptoeing with surprising daintiness around the perimeter of the tent. 'Looks like he couldn't make up his mind where to put her.'

Byrne frowns, adjusting the strap of the bag containing the drone as though it's suddenly become too heavy.

'Could explain the state of her feet.' He pauses. 'This job,' he says, turning away.

'Yeah,' I reply.

Barry shows me the tracks. They zigzag across a central patch of bare, muddy ground, disappearing where the terrain becomes stonier or covered in scrub grass.

'Did we get his footprint?' I point to a deeper impression in the ground.

'You wish,' says Barry. 'Nothing we can use.'

He hunkers down, using a biro to show the circular shape of an imprint. 'It's like he did a full circle here – changed his mind about where he was dragging her.'

'You reckon she was dead already?'

I ask – hoping he'll say yes.

'Or out of it.' He nods. 'There are no footprints for her. She didn't try to run – didn't stand anywhere here, that's for sure.'

We both straighten up. Barry points back to the layby.

'Let's say he parked back there – we've a few tracks to check out. So, he could have parked and – I dunno – they could have walked a few metres before he knocks her out – or – or they're going for a stroll, but they have a row and –' He stops. Shrugs. 'Speculation's your job, thanks be to God. I'll stick to finding evidence.'

'If she was already dead, or out of it, he could have carried her from the car?'

He nods. I carry on, glad to have someone to bounce ideas off.

'But either way, you're saying that from here' – I point to where the stony path opens out into the clearing – 'from there onwards, she was dragged – unconscious or dead?'

'Looks like it,' says Barry.

No wonder her feet are cut to ribbons. Bastard.

'Darmody?'

Senan is summoning me with his Beckoning Finger. Christ on a bloody bike!

Barry raises his eyebrows, nods.

Seventy-two hours, I tell myself, making my way towards him. He's standing talking to one of the uniforms on duty. They'll be here day and night, preserving the scene, taking note of anyone who comes in or out, until the tech team have got all they can. He makes a show of lifting the tape to let me underneath. I get it. I'm a giant. I've about eight inches on him.

'We should get back to the unit,' he says. It sounds like he's telling me to leave.

'Yup,' I say, 'I'm on my way.'

I point at my name in the logbook so the uniformed garda can sign me out, adding a smile to show I'm friendly – that it's only Senan who's pissing me off.

'And one of us should –'

I stop.

'Look, Senan, I know what I'm doing, okay? I'm going to go down to the station, see what's happening with the incident room, check in with the SIO – as in, see what Cig wants me to do – how he wants to play this. I'll handle this.'

I start walking and he hops over to walk in step beside me.

'No "I" in "team", Darmody.' He smiles, revealing small, cream teeth. 'There's a whole lot of I – I – I in what you've just said. Last I heard, we were a partnership, working together.' His head tilts as he waits for my response.

'Not for much longer,' I say – shite – out loud. Then – hanged for a sheep and all that – I blunder on: 'Shaw is due back on Monday. She might even start a few days early – that'd be tomorrow.'

It's like exchanging the first shove of the match. A relief. Honesty at last. But Senan is looking at me strangely.

'Oh! So, you don't know then?'

'What?'

'Right.' He nods slowly, like he's pondering the third secret of Fatima. 'I suppose Cig told me first because he'd so much trouble getting hold of you this morning.'

A sympathetic blink is added to the head tilt.

'Last I heard, Detective Garda Shaw has applied for a career break.'

I stop walking.

Senan puts his hand on my shoulder. Seriously? He adds a sympathetic squeeze.

'So I guess you're stuck with little old me.'

7

Laura

Of course, I woke Noah when I checked him. Now I'm still feeding, stuck in the front room, wrapped in a rug, and he's latched on finally, eyes rolled back in his head like a junkie, covered in a pale, translucent veil, as though even his eyeballs are milk-coated.

I try to get more comfortable, leaning back in the seat and tilting my head towards the headrest. Immediately, his eyes focus and a frown gathers on his brow, as though someone pulled the drawstring on a hoody. He releases my nipple and – shit! No! I watch in dismay as the milk continues to pulse and squirt on to his reddened cheek and down into the creases of his neck. Noah roars his protest.

'Yeah, you're right, I shouldn't have moved,' I say. I could weep. He's going to wake everyone now, and then Matt will be narky, or worse – patient and long-suffering – and Katie will be cranky, having lost sleep. I adjust my position and try again, pressing the nipple against his mouth, willing him to take it, and after some angry headbutting, he does, and settles.

It's a seesaw of emotions, not a rollercoaster. It's going well and you're up, then a night of colic or high temperature, or a stomach virus, or a nappy that leaks and you're stripping a howling baby in the early hours, trying to wash shit off his back and belly without waking the house, in the depths of despair. Now I'd welcome a rollercoaster – at least that way you'd have a prolonged bit of good times before the downward plunge.

He's always gulping – frenzied – as though someone's going to take it away from him. Then he gets colic. Music sometimes works to keep him feeding calmly. Gingerly, with my free hand, I take out my phone, noticing with a lurch of guilt that I never replied to Niamh's last text. I click on the radio.

'Gardaí in Seskin West are appealing for information in relation to the discovery of a body in the Dublin Mountains. The identity of the deceased – a young woman – is not yet known. Anyone with information or who may have been travelling in the Military Road/Glencullen area in the past twenty-four hours is asked to contact the Gardaí at Seskin West Garda Station on –'

Jesus! Another one! And on our patch. It can't be more than a year since they found that girl's body in the woods beyond Bray. I try to think, measuring time in pregnancies – the new normal for me. More than a year it must have been. Because I had Katie but I wasn't pregnant on Noah. The girl had been out running. Late twenties, a teacher in a local school – Charlotte? Caroline? Yes – Caroline. By the time they found her she'd been missing more than a fortnight, her body hidden in dense undergrowth. Wildlife had been at her, so they, the Wicklow unit, had nothing to work on. No DNA evidence – absolutely nothing. As far as I know, they still don't have anyone for that.

I tap out of the radio app and – almost by reflex – press 'N' for Niamh. She'll be on this. Her face appears on the contact information, squashed into the circle, curly hair and big grin, fingers in a 'V' sign in front of her cheek. I'm just about to press call, but then I stop. Noah is completely peaceful, his soft features arranged into a beatific smile, like a little pope.

I exit rather than call. Live in the moment, Laura. It's probably your fault the child has colic. Stop thinking about work. Work, which you are about to quit – remember?

When Baby sleeps, you sleep was the advice of the saccharine-soaked district nurse on an early visit. *You're not to be worrying about the house or the baby weight or anything,* she'd said. *Time enough for all that when he's running about the place,* she'd added, her head tilted to maximum Patronize angle, waiting for the nod of assent. Up till then I hadn't been thinking about the fecking baby weight at all. Thanks, Nurse MakeyoufeelShite, as Niamh christened her when I told her.

And his name is Noah, is it? Well now, imagine! Her face had said it all. It said something along the lines of *Look at you and your notions – what class of an eejit calls a child Noah?*

Luckily, Matt had stepped into the breach at that point. You can't fault Matt's ability to schmooze. He'd come into the room, making a big deal of carrying the tray with tea and chocolate biscuits. Then he'd reached into the cot, gathered up the grizzling Noah and popped him on to his shoulder, having made sure the muslin square was already in place, like a pro.

'Let's leave the ladies to chat, will we, big fella?'

As he left the room, Nurse's ear nearly reached her shoulder as the head tilt changed from Patronize angle to Ah-God-your-husband's-gorgeous-isn't-he? angle.

I think back to the Cullen case, which even now hits me with shivers of dread when I think of what could have happened – how badly it could have ended for Jenny, who was only fourteen when she tackled her abusive stepfather. But we got him. And Jenny's evidence ensured that the bastard was locked up for a minimum of eight years. We'd all gone out to celebrate, the whole team on the beers; even Cig stayed for one. The gang – the whole lot of them – stood and cheered when I waddled in (less than two weeks to go and I was ginormous). They all offered to buy me pints, knowing full well I was on the ginger ale, and I stupidly told everyone that it was a boy this time. Loads of names were suggested, most of them ludicrous. But when I came home, Matt was waiting up to look after me, I remember, with a lurch of nostalgia for the good times. He'd got three separate pillows arranged down the bed to prop the bump and my knees on, a packet of Tayto in case I got the salt craving, and the glass of water to follow – all perfect. Katie was fast asleep in her big-girl bed, thank God.

We'd lain side by side or, rather, him crammed along the rim of the mattress to leave room for my giant belly, and talked names. He'd been the one to suggest something left field; Elijah was one – and Elvis. I said Noah and – I'm not misremembering this – he definitely was on board. Until he changed his mind.

You mean, like a guy who saw it coming – the end of the world?

No, that's not what I mean. I mean a – a sensible bloke, calm and organized – like you. It sounds nice. It sounds strong.

Whatever Mummy wants.

I'm sure that's what he said. And he'd kissed me then – a sweet 'you're the mother of my children' type of kiss and – just for that moment – it all made sense.

Six weeks later, when it was too late to change our minds, with Nurse MakeyoufeelShite's cloying perfume – a mixture of dirty nappies and baby powder – still clinging to the curtains, we had our first fight in ages. Pregnancy truce is well and truly over.

You said you were on board with Noah! You definitely agreed, Matt!

Look, it doesn't matter – it's whatever you want, he'd sighed. *I'm just saying we can – maybe we don't have to stick with it. I just don't want him to get teased in school and stuff.*

So, we left it at that. And he backed down. And now, his resigned expression when he looks at me and, sometimes, the *way* he looks at me now – tiredly, like it makes him tired just to cast his eyes in my direction – it chips away another flake of something every time he does it. The opposite of bedding down strata of rock. A layer of certainty pared off. Or confidence. Or something.

I stand up carefully, hoping to put Noah down before waking Katie for school, but immediately he wakes and starts wriggling and wailing. I try 'Cool the jets,' one of Niamh's. 'Cool-the-jets! Cool-the-jets,' I chant, patting and jiggling him up and down in time to the words as I bring him to the changing table. It works. I imagine telling her he speaks Bogger – when I see her –

But I won't see her anytime soon. If I go ahead with the career break, our paths will diverge. Sure, she'll call over now and again and we'll message each other with plans for a session we'll never have. But it's not the same. And if we do go to New York – well, that's the end of everything. All they're waiting for now is the signed form. Jackie recommended I do it. The Chief Super said she wouldn't pressure me either way. I still haven't signed it.

A surge of longing hits me – for Niamh's too-loud laugh, for the two of us sniggering like sixth-classers at Cig, for the slagging and the noise and even the shit coffee at the unit. I close my eyes, bending to touch my lips to Noah's soft hair. May as well declare the day started, I tell myself.

'Right, let's wake your sister.' I ignore his grizzling and head for the stairs. 'And your mummy is going to go to the chemist today to get us both sorted – colic drops for you and a shedload of antihistamines or something for me.'

I hear the slam of the bathroom door as Matt heads into the shower and the thud as Katie clambers out of her bed and down the little ladder.

Another day in babyland.

8

Niamh

Not gonna think about it. Not now. I arrive ahead of McArsey in the incident room. He said something about calling to Clonchapel. Already, it's buzzing. A shaft of sunlight spears the greyness, lighting up the streaked dust on the windows and the outline of Denise's hennaed hair, making her look like she's on fire.

'Well, well, well,' she says, grinning, juggling between two phones.

'How's it going?' I nod.

Mairéad is half hidden behind a computer screen, inputting all the jobs to be done, and at the top of the room Inspector Don McNeil, SIO – the Cigire – is pacing. I'd say like a caged panther, except his large gut puts paid to that image. Pacing like an old, tubby spaniel. That's more the image.

My phone vibrates in the pocket of my jacket. That'll be Laura. Keeping my eyes on Cig, I end the call. I sigh.

'Darmody, am I boring you?' says Cig, a flush of anger appearing near his collar – or it could be a shaving rash. A snort of laughter to my left is swiftly turned into a cough. I don't turn around. It's Alison, the press officer.

'Sorry, Cig – no. I was –'

He carries on as though I hadn't spoken, which is no harm. I was only going to come up with some shite anyway. I'm distracted. And it's not just the poor girl lying cold and dead on the side of the Featherbed, whose tattered, bleeding feet I can't get out of my mind. It's Laura. I can't believe she didn't tell me – that I had to hear about her career break from the uptight lummox that is Detective Garda Senan McFeckingArsey.

Cig is still talking.

'It's most likely the au pair – reported missing yesterday at Clonchapel. Mia is her name. Denise took the call. A FLO's gone down to the girl's host family – they'll have to do an interim ID of the body.'

He inhales as though we're not going to like what comes next.

'And I don't want any cock-ups or cack-handedness. This has got to be done – everything has to be done – right. The host family are the Nairns – as in Tom Nairn Senior Counsel. The wife is Rosa and the child is Carly. So, don't – just mind your bleeding Ps and Qs, right?'

There's a shifting movement in the far corner, where Larry 'Sniff' MacDonald sits, like a bear waking from hibernation. He wheezes with a 1950s chain-smoker's rustling, his face compressed with a grievance so old no one knows who did what or why it matters any more. Only that someone pissed him off way back and he's not about to let it happen twice. He sniffs one of his trademark sniffs.

'Shower of shites,' he says. 'Think they can get away with anything.'

Larry's like one of those tattered lions with chunks out of him, moth-eaten and weary but still dangerous. He scans the room with an air of disgusted laziness. 'The Silks. I've never met one that could be trusted. And he's as crooked as any of them.'

I haven't had the pleasure of a cross-examination from Tom Nairn, but Laura has. It was relentless, she said. He leaves nothing to chance. This is the guy who made sure the date-raping dickhead from UCD never served a day of prison time. He does defamations, false imprisonments and assaults – *alleged* assaults – by Gardaí as well. So, needless to say, we don't exactly love him. For a low-key kind of guy, he manages to do a fair bit of damage to his opponents. I make a note to find out where he and Larry crossed paths. There must be something.

'Save it,' says Cig, shooting a glare across, and Larry stares him down for a couple of seconds before settling back into his folds. Cig eyes the clock. 'It'd be good if that gets done in the next hour –'

'Isn't he defending in the murder case that's running now?' I say. 'The drowning?'

I don't add the rest of the sentence. None of us needs to hear it out loud. A mother is accused of drowning her little boy in the bath while the dad was out with their twins. The case is all over the media. Cig nods.

'Yes – that's him.'

Christ. It takes a moment for me to collect myself. I got such a fright when the news broke on that one. I'd been so worried and, just for a split second, Laura had popped into my brain. I know she'd never hurt Katie – but – but all the same, she was in bits after the Cullen case and she's so tightly wound and she's so – I don't know, damaged? It was around the same time she'd had Noah and, because it was a child victim, identities were protected and details were scarce, but still and all, I can't deny it. For an instant, I'd wondered.

'Do the au pair's parents know?' says Denise, breaking into my thoughts.

That'll be another job for the FLO. Another reason to be glad I'm at the detective end of things. Especially in a case like this. They'll have to get in touch with the police over in Spain, or wherever she's from, arrange for them to call to the house and somehow inform them of their worst nightmare. When they can, they drip-feed it – describing first a serious accident, telling them they need to prepare themselves. That gets them as far as the airport. They'll help with arranging flights, pick them up from the airport and basically hold their hands through the whole shitty, heart-breaking process. Christ.

'Not yet. We need the ID confirmed first.'

He pins a photograph to the centre of the board – bare now, but pretty soon it'll be covered in photos, notes and scraps of paper as we build a picture of the victim. Victimology – the starting point. From three desks back, I can see her tattered feet.

'Get me up to speed about the scene,' Cig says, turning away from the board and reaching for a folder on the desk in front of him.

'It's sealed off completely. Parminter's been and gone. The body's on its way to the mortuary.'

The clock is showing 9.40.

'Should be there by now. Tech were there when I left, doing a fingertip search. They got aerial shots of the body and what could be a partial tyre track. She may have been dead already – or drugged – when he got to the mountain. He dragged her around a bit – like he couldn't make up his mind, or –'

I nod towards the photograph.

'Her feet.' Cig holds up a hand to stop me talking.

'Speculation.'

The inspector is not a fan of speculation. I know this. Rookie error. I clamp my mouth shut.

'Press?'

'Yeah,' Alison says, tilting the phone towards me so I can see. 'Ours, and this – BODY OF A YOUNG WOMAN FOUND – is the screeching line from a site called MyLocalNews.ie. They've shots of the screened-off scene: tech lads crawling over it like grubs in their white suits, the barrier tape, the tent, the uniformed officers on duty – the whole shooting match.

Cig pushes a stubby finger around the inside of his collar, as though trying to make space. He sighs, then turns to Alison.

'What are we running?'

She scrolls on her phone and reads: '"Gardaí in Seskin West are appealing for information in relation to the discovery of a body in the Dublin Mountains. The identity of the deceased – a young woman – is not yet known. Anyone with information or who may have been travelling in the Military Road/Glencullen area in the past twenty-four hours is asked to contact the Gardaí at Seskin West Garda Station on"' – she looks up – 'and then we have the freephone confidential number.'

'Leave it at that' – Cig nods – 'until Parminter gets back to us.'

Alison clicks out of the message.

'And we'll do a press conference – yeah? Set that up, okay?' Cig scratches his ear, leaving his pudgy finger inserted and swivelling his head rather than the other way round. It's another of his 'I'm thinking' tics.

'Right, Cig.' Alison scurries off.

Cig beckons me.

'Can you get down to –'

'Mc— Carthy's already there.'

He stops dead, glaring at me.

'You know what I'm going to say, do you, Darmody?'

'No – sorry, Cig.'

'A bleedin' mind-reader and a detective combined, are you?'

I see Mairéad and Denise exchange a look. Somebody should have warned me – he's worse than usual. Maybe he's back on the no-carbs thing. I put up two hands, miming, *I surrender.*

'Really sorry, Cig.'

'What I was *about* to say was, I want you to get across to the mortuary. Link up with the FLO – it's Denny – when he gets there. Make sure the whole thing is as smooth and painless as possible. And fast. So Denny can contact her parents.'

'Yes, Cig.'

I turn and begin heading towards the door, and I know it's a bit of a gamble, but the thought of being shackled to McArsey has me feeling reckless. I stop.

'Cig?'

'Detective?' He turns wearily, with a look of 'what the hell now?' plastered across his face.

'Is Shaw – I mean – I thought Shaw was coming back on Monday. Next Monday, her maternity leave ends. I was wondering, would it not make sense for us to – like, you could call her in early, so we could make a start on this together?'

'Shaw put in for a career break,' he says. 'She met with Occi Health and her request was granted. It's up to her now.'

He shrugs, flipping over one of his large red paws.

'She has until Monday to decide but, if she's any sense, she'll decide to stay away. I know I would.'

A flare – no, smaller, a spark – a tiny spark lights inside me.

'So, she hasn't definitely decided yet?'

Cig's pouchy face assembles itself into a pitying look.

'I didn't say that, Darmody. I'd say she has decided all right, but maybe she hasn't made it official. And, for some reason, she clearly hasn't told you.'

He strides the length of the room towards me, indicating with a nod that he wants to talk to me outside. We move to the corridor and he closes the door of the incident room.

'McCarthy is an excellent detective,' he says.
'I know –' I nod, getting ready to reply, but he silences me.
'Shaw –'
'Shaw's brilliant, Cig, you know that.'
'I have the highest regard for Detective Shaw,' he says, 'but this is not primary school, Darmody! Yes, you two were a good team and you did some great work, but if Shaw's not ready to come back, then she's not coming back. And if she doesn't come back, then you work with whoever I put you with. In this case, that means Detective McCarthy.'

He watches me closely – like the cute hoor he is.

'I don't have to remind you about the Cullen case, do I? Shaw was lucky GSOC didn't apply sanctions.' He waits. I know he's right. And if they ever found out what really happened, we'd both be in the shite. 'It happens, you know. People burn out –'

I can't let that go.

'She's not burnt-out – she was stressed –'

'Or people decide to put their family first,' he continues. 'And who could blame them?'

I'm so angry I could deck him. There's no way he'd say that about a man. I nod, buttoning my lip. Years of practice on the pitch means that sometimes, just sometimes, I know when to shut up. He sees me do it.

'Go and do your job, Darmody. Get to the mortuary and we'll take it from there. And lookit' – he shakes his head – 'do not make contact with Shaw. Do not pressure her into a decision you both might regret.'

On cue, my phone vibrates again. I let it ring, not trusting myself to take it.

I like a woman to look smart and, above all, elegant. Of course, if it came up in conversation in work or socially, I would never say that. I know perfectly well how it would sound to any women who might be present. The patriarchy. Now, they're all full of the right to dress comfortably — why should they dress to please men? Et cetera.

I imagine my mother's horrified reaction to that concept! I never saw her in a flat shoe — not once. Her early training in ballroom dancing left her with a love of glamour, I suppose. She dressed with a certain formality — skirts or dresses, or little suits. In summer, when other women wore sandals or flats or even flip-flops, she would change to a lighter shade of court shoe. She had one pair that I adored — sling-backs with kitten heels made of soft suede with snakeskin trimming around the top.

Yes. My mother dressed smartly. Even pruning the roses or clipping the wisteria that grew over the porch saw her wearing a blouse or cashmere cardigan, an A-line skirt cut to the knee, below which tapered her shapely legs (encased in tights — mink was the shade she preferred), and her black, everyday court shoes. Anything lower made her feel clumpy. And Mummy was never clumpy. My mother was light on her feet. She walked with a bounce in her step, as though puffed along by small gusts of wind, her elegant arches always on display, like the dancer she was.

She and I both took pride in her beautiful feet. After all, it was I who wielded the blade. We soaked them first, then she sat in the low armchair with her legs outstretched, feet resting on a towel, wiggling her toes while she waited. I carried the basin carefully with two hands — up high against my chest to keep it steady. I was determined to do everything right, to preserve our closeness, as this was the closest I got. I clutched the

edges of the ⟨…⟩
or spill. That ⟨…⟩
mistake again.

My favourite p⟨…⟩
them in my lap on ⟨…⟩
against the back of th⟨…⟩
held her feet, and her le⟨…⟩
knees were no longer on ⟨…⟩
leading from the edge of her ⟨…⟩
a slice of fabric in shadow ⟨…⟩
puzzle over, trying to identif⟨…⟩
ancient and subterranean.

I would bend forward and gra⟨…⟩ ⟨…⟩ and setting it down precisely — and the he⟨…⟩ ⟨…⟩ my groin. A towel and newspaper separated them ⟨…⟩ ⟨…⟩, I felt the weight.

It is so important for a woman to pay attention to these things. They should never be neglected. The hair, also, should be sleek and swept off the face to reveal the features. In her thirties, Mother pinned hers up in a neat chignon. Later, a chic, short, swept-back style which suited her delicate neck. Locks of long, unkempt hair make me shudder.

With the au pair, it was the first thing I had to address.

Laura

Time to collect Katie. I drive the two kilometres. The baby weight will just have to stay on for now. Noah grizzles in the car seat, but without much conviction. With any luck, there'll be a parking space outside, so I don't have to take him out. Then I can pick up Katie and we can have a bit of what she calls 'Just Us Two Girls time' – she's clinging on to the title of being my special girl. At some point I must get her to stop telling Noah that he doesn't matter because he's only a boy – not yet, though; another conversation I'm putting off.

I've got to talk to Niamh. I wait at the junction for the right-turn filter, flexing and releasing my fingers against the steering wheel. I've got to tell her – now – today. Thursday. As soon as I get the two of them settled for the afternoon, I'm telling her.

Matt assures me she'll understand – that she'll be glad for me. But the closer it gets, the more certain I am that she'll be – I don't know – angry? Hurt? And now?

We'd gone through it again – for the millionth time – last night.

'I feel like I'm betraying her.' I'd cried then – into his shoulder, for Christ's sake. Breastfeeding hormones.

'She's your friend,' he'd said, stroking my hair, a gesture usually reserved for when one of us is sick. 'Of course she's going to want whatever's best for you.'

'But she's been waiting. I – if I was going to take a

break – I should have discussed it with her. I feel so shit about this, Matt,' I'd snapped, pushing his hand away.

Matt changed tack. He stood up abruptly.

'We've been over and over this, Laura. You – you were the one who said, by your own admission, that you were cracking up. Remember? You said you were glad to be at home – glad that it was just us. You were even glad about the lockdown – remember that?'

He'd turned on his heel and paced the length of the room, turned back. 'It's just a career break, for God's sake. You'll be able to see her properly now – when you're not working. Won't that be better? You can enjoy her friendship properly as a friend – not a partner. I'd have thought this was a dream come true for you.'

He'd put his arms around me, then I'd allowed myself to be held, comforted, as though I was a delicate thing, as though I might shatter. A fleck of something sour floated through my subconscious – like gone-off milk in a cup of coffee: *he loves me most when I'm weak*.

I squash that one back down smartly. Breathe in. The lights change, and I take the turn and head up the hill, glad I'm not pushing the buggy. Matt's right. Breathe out. It's just a career break – it's not the end of anything.

There's a space just inside the gate – fantastic. I pull in and switch off the engine, hoping the sudden silence doesn't wake Noah. He sighs but, thankfully, doesn't wake. I crack open the windows a couple of centimetres then get out, closing the door in slow motion. A small group of mums, childminders, au pairs, grandparents and one dad have formed one of those bizarre social circles. That's weird – they must have changed the queueing system since yesterday. I zip up my coat – it's nippy – and make my way over. I haven't made friends with any of the other parents or grandparents yet – another thing to look forward to during my career break. Matt reckons it'll be good for me. One or two faces swivel in my direction, but most remain fixed on the speaker – a smallish woman with short dark hair and a sleeping baby strapped to her front.

The two people on the edge of the circle shift and pull aside to make space for me.

'It's unbelievable,' she goes on, covering the baby's head as if to protect him from hearing her words.

'I heard she was taken on the way home from here – they never arrived home.'

'Jesus Christ!' says another. 'What? Taken – abducted – from here? Yesterday? Here at the school? Oh my God – what about the child?'

'No – I think it was on their way home. He – they – didn't take the child, or maybe he did and then changed his mind. She – the child – was found in the afternoon in the laneway at the back of Wellington Park.'

'Are you sure?' says an older woman I recognize as the granny of one of Katie's pals. Before she can reply, a strangled sob bursts from a tall, striking girl whose youth must mean she's an au pair.

'Oh no! No! I ring and ring Mia all last night and she never reply, and this morning – and now –'

'The body,' whispers the woman beside me, a tall Australian woman who I recognize from the local café. 'Christ.'

She steps across the empty space and places her hand on the girl's shoulder, pulls her into a hug. There are murmurs and head shakes of sympathy.

'It's Tom Nairn's family, I think?' says another woman, head to toe in Lululemon – either just finished or just about to hit the gym. 'The little girl is Carly. The mum is Rosa? And you're sure Mia's her au pair?'

I'm stunned. Carly is one of the names Katie bandies about after school – she's a little doll of a child – and everyone knows the Nairns. Tom's defending that murder case – the mum who's accused of killing her little boy. A shaft of horror goes through me any time I hear about it. I've been avoiding following it; it – it's too close to home in every way.

The au pair nods. It looks as if the Australian woman's arm about her shoulders is the only thing that's holding her upright.

'Yes.'

One of the young women is scrolling through her phone, shaking her head.

'No names yet; nothing about the little girl – Carly. Same statement as earlier on RTÉ and LatestNews.ie. But now it says Gardaí are treating this as a murder investigation.'

The au pair surrenders to the embrace in earnest now, burying her face in the Australian's jacket. At the mention of the Gardaí, I watch to see if anyone looks at me. I haven't told anyone my job, but Clonchapel is a small village.

The door of the school opens and Joanne, the head-teacher, comes out on to the step, eyes tinged with red.

It's definitely Mia so.

Joanne sees the waiting parents and minders, takes in the tearful au pair, and nods. In the hallway behind her, toddlers and carers gather ready for the handover.

'We're – we don't have any definite information yet, so I won't, sorry, I can't discuss anything. I'm sure you understand. We –'

'Will the school be open tomorrow? Should we stay home –'

Joanne begins passing the children out to their respective parents, grandparents and minders. Many of them are holding pictures – daffodils made with the painted centres of egg-boxes, tissue-paper tulips. She smiles at the children, her training so ingrained that the cheerful positivity doesn't falter for an instant. I see Katie behind her, clutching her daffodil, and my heart contracts. Her little pink schoolbag with nothing in it, her runners with the bits that light up when she stamps her feet, the tragic innocence of her open smile. I clamp down the urge to tell her not to smile like that.

'We'll contact you – we'll be advised by the Gardaí and let everyone know tonight,' she says in her breezy voice, as if she's announcing an end-of-term event. 'I cannot stress enough,' she goes on, her voice dropping, 'that this is not to be discussed in front of little ears. At. All.'

We nod like toddlers.

I take Katie's hand and bundle her into the car. I've got to talk to Niamh.

10

Niamh

It's turned into a bright day. Sunlight glints on the barrier at the entrance to the car park behind the mortuary. I park in a patch of sunlight and make my way to the door on the side of the building, where the families enter. The post-mortem room is at the far end, on the ground floor.

The small hallway is empty. Where the hell is Denny? I'm just about to text him when I hear voices outside. I retrace my steps towards the car park.

'You're not leaving, are you, Darmody?' Denny, the FLO, looks stressed off his head. He makes eye contact with me over the roof of the car as he goes around to open the door for the occupant, who seems to think he's her personal driver. A platinum-blonde woman in her late thirties, wrapped in the folds of a satiny black trench coat, emerges stiffly, with the gait of the injured or bereaved. She's wearing designer shades – like she's summoning the ghost of Jackie Kennedy – and she's brittle-thin like her too. Her head is by far the largest part of her body.

'Thank you, Garda,' she nods, as though dismissing him. Denny gestures towards me.

'This is Detective Darmody, one of the investigating officers, and' – he pauses, waiting for her to move – 'we'll head in, will we?'

'Not until Tom arrives,' she says, spitting the words like pips as she rummages in a quilted handbag which even I recognize as Chanel or something. Taking out her phone, she stabs at it with a manicured fingertip. As she puts the phone to her ear, she scans my face vaguely and gives a small nod, as though pleased that I'm remaining in place, waiting. I return the nod, my eyes travelling the length of her, taking in the coat, an expensive bracelet, leather trousers, black heels – on a weekday, at this hour. Something in her manner – the way she holds herself like bone china, shiny and impermeable – reminds me of Laura. It's an act. I wonder if, like Laura, she's terrified underneath.

'Rosa Nairn.' She nods, her eyes drifting away from my face, scanning the scene.

'Tom, I'm at the bloody morgue – mortuary – whatever it's called,' she snaps. 'This is' – she pauses, rummaging for a sentence – 'I'm not doing this alone. Get here.'

I eyeball Denny, wondering which of us will tell her it's a time-sensitive situation; that the sooner we get the ID, the sooner Parminter can get to work on the post-mortem. And not even that, I think, with a spurt of annoyance. If it is Mia, we need to tell her parents, get them on a flight over here. Shit.

'Mrs Nairn.' I take a step towards her. 'It would be most helpful – obviously, the sooner we can get this done, the better.'

I move as though to usher her through to the entrance.

'Don't worry, it's not like on TV. You won't even have to –'

'Wait.' She holds up a finger to stop me, like a referee. Christ! Even more annoying is that it works – I stop talking.

We all turn to watch as a taxi pulls up and a man gets out. It's Tom Nairn. He's dressed in a long grey coat over a black suit, and I can just make out the pair of white tabs worn by barristers. He's not who you'd cast for a top Senior Counsel, the barrister of choice for a certain type of client. The type with money. For the guy who's supposed to be our nemesis, he's sort of disappointingly insipid-looking.

'Tom Nairn, SC,' says Denny, in case I didn't recognize him.

Denny steps forward to greet him, but Rosa moves away to stand on the entrance step, waiting for her husband to catch up. When he does, they exchange a look – flat and empty of warmth. She's got to be twenty years younger than him. I think of the au pair living with this couple, trying to visualize her, a Spanish teenager living in South Dublin with Tom and Rosa and their child. I try to imagine her arriving from Spain into Dublin – grey Dublin – and meeting them for the first time. Was she scared? Shy? Homesick for Spain or ready for adventure? But I can't see her laughing. I can only see her torn feet and her little rounded face.

I step forward and introduce myself. Nairn looks closely at each of us, his expression blank. When he speaks, his tone is low, formal.

'Thank you, Guards. I – ah – appreciate this.'

He takes hold of Rosa's elbow – one of those guys who steers you around the place – and the sleeves of his coat and jacket slip backwards to reveal a glinting gold watch – antique, I'm guessing – bright against the dark clothes. We go into the hallway. Denny does his thing – reassuring and efficient.

'Follow me,' he says. 'Unless anyone would like to use the facilities?'

He points to the toilet off the hall. Nobody says anything and we follow him into a small room with a couch and a table, sparsely furnished but tasteful – modern. Though there's enough seating, no one sits.

'Right, in a few minutes we'll be going into the ID room. I'll escort you, don't worry. You'll see a curtained window along one side. That will be drawn back, and you'll be able to see the body.'

'Thank you, Guard,' says Nairn.

A sudden noise – an exhalation – comes from Rosa. Is she about to faint? We all turn to her.

'Not doing this.' She shakes her head, her mouth clamped into a tight line. Her husband reaches for her, but she turns away.

'Why don't we go outside?' I shoot Denny a quizzical look. He nods.

'Yes – thanks – Mr Nairn, could you –'

Nairn finishes the sentence for Denny. 'I'll do the ID, of course.' He smiles, an appropriate one for the circumstances, small and tight.

We wait outside, Rosa inscrutable once more behind the shades.

'Mrs Nairn,' I say, 'am I correct in thinking that you'd already contacted the Gardaí yesterday, when this was – when Mia didn't come home?'

'Yes! I tried to file a missing-person report,' she snaps. 'I was beside myself! She must have got into a car with someone – a man – they both – she put Carly – oh! I told them all of this. My child was actually in the car too, and only that whoever took her decided he didn't want a two-year-old and put her out –' She pulls off her sunglasses in an angry motion, glints of tears visible in the corners of her eyes. 'Maybe if you'd done something then? If an emergency call had gone out – did you think of that?'

I count three for an in-breath. Four out. I didn't know that the child had been in the car. Missed that memo. Who the hell was on the desk yesterday in Clonchapel? And why hadn't I heard about this? Shit.

'I understand. I know you're upset. But Mia is over

eighteen. She got into a car with a guy and went off. This time yesterday, that was something that none of us could have known was a risk. Adults – young adults – this is something they do.'

'They're not allowed to go out overnight – and she was working! That's why I knew it was bad. Mia would never have done anything to risk Carly. She's – she's – she was actually a lovely girl. And an excellent au pair.'

She shakes her head as though ridding herself of that comment. When she speaks again, she's calmer.

'She was a wonderful person. It's a tragedy. But I can't believe – she had Carly in the car too! She – they – they left Carly at the side of the road!'

Nairn and Denny emerge from the building, Nairn buttoning his coat with one hand, phone in the other. The process couldn't have lasted more than a couple of minutes. Denny gives me a nod. No one needs to say it aloud. It's definitely Mia. I turn back to Rosa.

'Garda Denny will bring you both back now. I'll be down later. In the meantime, can you make sure none of Mia's belongings – that nothing is touched? Her room needs to be sealed off. Did she have a laptop? Phone? Can you give me her number?'

'I understand. Yes, she has – had – a laptop. I – I think it's in her room.'

She sweeps the glasses on to her head and reaches into her bag to retrieve the phone, angling it so I can see Mia's contact details. I punch them in and press send so they can start pinging it straight away.

'And her phone – she always had it with her. I – we – insisted. For safety.' She breaks off and looks at me. I can just make out her eyes through the tinted glass, and they're scanning mine in hurried little sweeps, left/right/left/right.

'Oh my God. Her poor mother.'

I feel a tiny stir of sympathy for her. There it is – the first piercing.

'What do you do now? Please Jesus don't tell me I have to call her! Can the agency – oh! Someone will have to contact Hannah at the agency – they knew she was missing. They'll be –'

'See you, then.' Nairn's voice reaches us from midway down the path. He ends a call. Rosa stiffens.

'You're not going back to work, are you? Seriously?'

He continues walking towards the road, where a taxi is approaching. At the door, he stops, turning back to look at his wife.

'I'm in the middle of a case,' he says mildly, carefully pocketing the phone. 'It's already underway. There's nothing I can do. I'll get back as early as I can.'

Christ. He's just identified the body of his murdered au pair. And he's cool as you like. Her face is pure venom. Denny steps into the path of their mutual glare.

'If you'd like to come with me, Mrs Nairn, I'll drop you back home first. Then I'll be contacting Mia's parents and the agency. I'm presuming you have all the contact details at home?'

She nods, and they make their way to the car, while I walk back into the building, checking my phone. Missed calls from Senan and about twelve WhatsApp photos from Amber. Shit! I haven't time for this now.

I pocket the phone and enter the office. The secretary, a neat woman in her fifties, looks up from her screen.

'The post-mortem will get underway soon.' She pauses. 'You've time to get a cup of tea or –'

She stops, changing tack.

'It's very sad,' she says. 'I've a girl the same age. She's

travelling in –' Again, she stops, collects herself with a shake of the head.

'Her poor mother.'

'Yes,' I say, because there's nothing I can add. 'I'll take myself off now, thanks,' I tell her. 'I'll be back about four – for the debriefing?'

'Make it three thirty,' she says. 'He's starting in the next half-hour.'

I nod my thanks.

In the silence of my car, I scan Amber's texts.

Thanks for last nite. Head not too bad. Making myself useful lol, xxx and a trowel emoji – underneath a selfie of her in a pair of wellies and gardening gloves.

Hi ho! Hi ho! – and a photo of a massive pile of weeds and dried twigs. Next, there's a photo of a bemused-looking Dorothy at the upstairs window, smiling down at her. The text is perky – yeah – I bet she's weighed herself and lost weight. That'll be it. If she's lost even half a fecking pound, she's euphoric.

Thanks for putting up with me, Nimmi. See you later. Doing a spot of gardening for Dorothy instead of the cake-baking. Did you forget? Puzzled emoji there.

Shit! I did forget. Dorothy was going to show me how to do jam tarts or biscuits or something.

Doh! I text, adding a slap-forehead emoji. *Tell her I'm sorry – we'll rearrange for another time!*

I throw in a shedload of kisses and hugs. Then I sigh. At least Amber's not too hung over. But she's not finished.

You don't like the shorts? Sad face. Ah crap – I never commented on the tiny shorts. Amber says she could wear a plastic bag and I wouldn't notice. Seeing as how I'm a couple of feet away from a beautiful young girl in a plastic body bag – a girl only a few years younger than her – I'm not exactly feeling it. But I reply – purple devil plus peach emoji. That should keep her happy.

Detective Garda Senan McArsey has left a voice message.

'I decided to head to the Montessori school – as no doubt you have matters in hand at the mortuary.'

Patronizing git. 'Suggest we link up in an hour at the unit, touch base – and head to the house – she au paired for Tom Nairn, Senior Counsel.'

Yes – thank you. I toy with the idea of sending him the 'Doh!' emoji. Stop it. It's only because – it's all down to Laura, I realize. I've got to convince her to come back – and not take the leave. Simple. I text him a thumbs-up – that will annoy him. So I add the praying hands.

11

Niamh

'Yep. Yep. Right, Cig –'

'I mean it,' he repeats. 'Every parent, every babysitter, every auntie and uncle – the au pairs and the older brothers and sisters – you're to get a list of every single person who has ever crossed the door of that crèche – Montessori – whatever.'

'Yep, will do.'

'And get it to the team. I want it done yesterday. And where are we with other hall users? I want us all over that building: the car park spaces, who rents them? I want everyone and –'

'Anyone. Yeah, got it, boss. Are you sending anyone –'

'Denny's been in touch with the parents. He's sorting them out.'

Rather him than me. The thought of it – meeting them at the airport, trying to manage them, shepherding them through the airport and the press, helping them find somewhere to stay, being their point of contact in this whole nightmare – gives me the shivers. I can think of nothing worse.

McArsey has been listening. He looks over at me, then directs his gaze back to the traffic ahead.

'The Montessori teacher says Mia collected the girl at the usual time yesterday – twelve thirty,' he says.

I wait. But he adds nothing. I press on.

'And? Was that it? Anything else? Did she notice anything about her?'

He turns his head a fraction, furrowing his brow.

'No. Well, nothing that she mentioned to me anyway. She said it was raining, and she noticed that Mia didn't have an umbrella, so they offered her one of the school ones.'

He shrugs.

'But Mia didn't want one, apparently. They're very bulky. Like golf umbrellas.'

Jaysus, I think. Now he's going to tell me the measurements of the fricking umbrella!

'The au pair – Mia – was wearing a jacket, and Carly had a raincoat, so they went off.' He pauses. 'That's it.'

Inwardly, I heave a sigh. Great input, knob. Thanks.

We cruise to a stop at the traffic lights by Tesco. To my left the Dodder – swollen with yesterday's heavy rain – rolls in glossy brown eddies and swirls, a moving frame along one side of a picture. Laura says you can now walk the whole length of the river from here to Dundrum – they've built a walkway. I imagine it's jammers at weekends, the young and cool of Dublin tramping along on their quest for a flat white. Kids on those wooden bikes or scooters, Bichons Frises and Cavachons straining on their leads. I shrug to myself. Give me either the city or wide-open fields – the extremes. I can't be doing with this halfway-house suburban shite.

The silence is broken by McArsey's fingers tapping in little rippling movements along the steering wheel as he waits for the lights to change.

'Are you stressed?' I say. It seems he wants me to notice.

Maybe this is a good time for my plan. I have an idea. It's in two parts – and the most important part is that Laura changes her mind about the career break. But that still leaves McArsey.

'Ah no, a bit tense, is all,' he says. 'I did my firearms training last week, and I'm always itching to get back, to do better.' He inclines his head in a small gesture, like a coy little girl, 'Although I did well. There's always room for improvement, isn't there?'

I sigh inwardly. We've to do the training a minimum of twice a year, and then there's the FATS – firearm training simulator. McArsey probably falls asleep watching the video. Some people – and clearly McArsey is one of them – go to the range for target practice like others go to the gym.

'Do you know, it's notoriously difficult to shoot so that you disable your opponent, rather than finishing them off altogether?'

'Oh yes,' I say, deadpanning it, because of course I know that. Everyone fecking knows. 'I had heard that.'

He ripples the fingers again. Nods to himself.

'I must get back – have another session. I suppose I'm a perfectionist.' He sighs.

Beside him, I nod and murmur assent. Ah yes, I think. The classic. *My worst fault is that I'm a perfectionist.* Idiot. He grips the wheel in the ten-to-two driving position and takes the car into a leisurely left turn.

'Did you do the specialist driver training as well?' I say innocently, although I know full well that will be another one he's up to date on. There's a pause as he wonders, with some justification, if I'm taking the piss.

'You drive well.' I turn back to look out the window, maintaining the innocence.

'Ten years in Dublin, and I still don't like driving in the heavy traffic.' I sigh.

There's a tiny lift in his chest, a preening, like a robin all puffed up.

'Ah, it's not difficult,' he says. 'Not when you're driving in rush hour every day.'

And there it is – the little reminder about the house in Saggart. Less than half an hour outside Dublin, corner site, right beside the Luas. Who at our age can buy a house like that? On a garda salary?

'Did you win the Lotto or something?'

He sort of simpers.

'Hah, no, a lucky inheritance.'

Typical. The road unspools as we head towards the next junction. McArsey inclines his head to the left.

'The school is up there,' he says, 'on the left. And the girl was found at the other end of town, up at Wellington Lane, about a mile away. The far side of Tesco.'

'So, what are you saying?'

'Just that they could have come along this route, unless they went up via Rathfarnham –' He peters out.

I look up at the lamp posts, hoping there'll be traffic cameras. Nothing.

'I'll talk to Mrs Nairn,' he goes on. 'Rosa. You might try seeing what you can get from the child? It makes sense.'

I nod. It does make sense for me to talk to the little girl, but, if it was Laura, we wouldn't even need to discuss this in advance. We'd go in, judge the mood and the lie of the land, sort of blend in and see where we're at. McArsy's so – so bloody uptight. '*You might try.*' He's some dose.

'Yeah,' I say. 'Good idea. Look, just before we arrive, can you turn up here?' I point to the road leading uphill from the junction. It's worth a try. He blinks in surprise but indicates and makes the turn.

'There's a garage in on the right. Can we pull in?' I clamp my hand across my middle and emit a groan. His rippling fingers clamp the wheel in terror.

'What is it? Are you sick?'

'Ah no' – *moan* – 'it's just' – *another moan* – 'you know, I get desperate monthlies – cramps, spasms, nausea, the whole shooting match.' *Moan.* He's pulling into the forecourt, still clenching the wheel between his fingers. I may be imagining it, but I think I see a sheen of sweat gathering at the edge of his sandy temple.

'I've such a heavy flow, yeah. I probably lose pints.'

Senan swallows.

'But you've never – I mean –'

'Oh yeah, I was on the pill before, but you know – side effects and all, and well –' I break off and put my hand on the door handle as though I'm about to get out, then I double over again.

'You wouldn't mind – I mean – you're okay with all this kind of stuff, aren't you? You'd never be an angel and go in for me, would you?'

I hold out my cash card and he accepts it, swallowing. His hand is sweaty.

'Ye—yes. Certainly – of course. No problem. What do you need?'

'Well, if they have Tampax Super Plus, without the applicator. Actually, no, it doesn't matter, either will do. Or Lil-lets.'

'So, eh, T—T—Tampax or, or the other ones? With – eh – with applicator, or not?'

Ah! This is cruel. I groan again, wave my hand around.

'Whatever. Either. Both. Oh!'

'Sorry, and S—S—Super Max, was it?'

'Just the biggest ones you can find!'

He begins scrambling from the car.

'Thanks, Senan, you're an angel,' I shout after him.

While he's in the shop, I check my reflection. I look hale and hearty – what my dad would call *in fine fettle*. This would be easier if I was a foot shorter. Then again, there might be a danger of him falling for me. I have a feeling he likes to think himself the big man.

No – this is my best bet. My hormonally challenged femaleness will do the trick. I make a mental note to discuss orgasms another time. Female ejaculation might be the clincher.

Mummy said it was being on her feet at work that gave her the corns, that it had nothing to do with the high heels she wore for practising her dancing in the studio.

Our garden backed on to a laneway beside the river where we had a garage and, beside it, a purpose-built dance studio that Father added on shortly after we moved in. The builder that Father engaged tacked the studio on to the side of the garage facing the laneway. A narrow, two-storey block, it consisted of the practice room itself with a wall of mirrors and a ballet barre, off which there was a small kitchen, a walk-in closet and a bathroom. The dance floor was sunk a foot into the earth. I remember it took them two days to dig it out. The gardener had to help. As you enter the building, you can go straight ahead into the practice studio or up the staircase on your left which brings you to a mezzanine area. The mezzanine has a window overlooking the river on one side and, on the other, a balcony from where I would watch Mummy twirling far below. Looking out the front windows, you'd see people making their way along the river path, thinking they couldn't be seen, never knowing that I was watching from my hiding place, far above them. More often, though, I watched Mummy on the floor below. She would whirl and glide, lost in her own glamour.

Father did not dance. Above all things, Father loved quiet and order. He did not like parties, and he did not like dancing. When he wasn't working, he liked to sit, reading. Or he would disappear down to the garage with the soft cloth and spend hours polishing the silver Mercedes, his other great joy.

Father liked cleanliness too. After all, cleanliness is the natural partner of order. At home, surfaces were required to be free of dust and dirt. At work, even more so. Windowpanes, mirrors, the glass fronts of cabinets were wiped with cloths rinsed in hot water and vinegar, then polished to a shine with squares of old newspaper. I lost track of the cleaning ladies who were taken on, only to be let go following the discovery of a cobweb in a corner or a fleck of fly dirt on a windowpane.

Likewise, he was a man who imposed order on the human body. He believed in the power of medicine to annihilate infections, regulate excretions and shrink inflammations. Tonics were taken and tablets were ingested. He believed in a pill, literally, for every ill. Even the most routine run-of-the-mill childhood injuries and illnesses were addressed. A patch of dry skin required the application of a salve; a strange, peach-coloured ointment would be produced. A grazed knee meant sitting up on the kitchen counter, wincing as a cork stopper dipped in iodine was printed all over the torn skin. He especially enjoyed the graze plus grit combination – this meant the full treatment. I would have to lie down fully on the counter and the Anglepoise lamp was brought over, plus the magnifying glass. Father took some tweezers and extracted every particle of grit – plinking it all on to a saucer to show me later. His touch was fastidious and gentle, yes. That's a memory I will keep. His touch was gentle.

Father believed that the female body, in particular, required constant vigilance. Or perhaps only Mummy's. Sundays were her special days. After Father brought her up the tray of special medicine, Mummy came downstairs in her dragon robe, with bare legs and only a pair of heeled slippers on her feet. She looked strange, her skin waxy and a bare look around her eyes. I glimpsed odd mounds and bumps rippling under the silk. Mummy, I should add, was a young woman then, and so very jiggly under the shining silk.

Father waited like a cinema usher to show her to her seat, and she floated across the room, coming to rest on the towels he had laid out on the low chair. She put up first one foot, then the other, on the footstool and closed her eyes. She was always so sleepy for this part. I was still too young to help – and certainly I was never allowed to take the scalpel to her feet at that stage, but Father let me pour the bubble mixture into the warm water and fluff it up to make foam. I knelt beside him as he performed the ministrations, marvelling at the endless variations of keeping Mummy beautiful. There were hair tints and face masks, though the hair was only done every few weeks. Father brushed the strong-smelling brown paste into her temples and along the centre parting with a stumpy black brush, then wrapped her hair in a clear plastic bonnet, beneath which condensation would begin to form – like a chemical experiment.

'Your mother needs this,' he would say, concentration furrowing his brow as he bent over her. 'It's important.'

I wonder when it started, this strange ministering to Mummy. At what point in their courtship did it become the norm for him to do these things for her? Things that I know now are performed by beauticians and therapists. And how strange the air between them. Mummy should have seemed vulnerable, exposed and weak, yet those hours saw her at the peak of her powers. A queen in the hive, fat and fertile. Sleepily, she tolerated his devotion, his need to minister. She allowed his worship.

And his face bore a kind of religious zeal on treatment days. Father was old, I knew – much older than Mummy. Once, outside the school gate when Mummy had come in the car to pick me up, I'd heard two mothers talking about her. They were huddled under an umbrella, watching her in the car. Mummy drummed her fingers against the steering wheel, her slicked-back hair and slash of red lipstick exotic, thrilling and bright even through the rainy windscreen. She wasn't like the other mothers in their shades of grey and kelp.

'A bit much for the school run,' said one. The other sniggered.

'You know he's over fifty?' the first woman whispered. 'He wouldn't do it for me anyway.'

I thought they were jealous, then. And now, I wonder if that could be true. A dangerous current ran between them. It was as though Mummy ruled the galaxy – she was the burning sun around which Father and I orbited. On Sundays, she was our high priestess. No – she was our goddess. It was as though she had birthed us both and we must forever worship.

Sometimes I got the job of massaging her hands with scented creams or brushing her dark hair with the silver brush. She lay back in the low chair, her feet propped on the stool or in Father's lap, with her eyes closed.

Father began with her feet and worked his way upwards. I was allowed to spray the sausage of foam along her shining shins and watched with a shivering horror as Father assembled the blade with which he shaved her legs. The razor came in three parts which sat in a neat plastic box, alongside the little package of blades. Father took apart the head of the razor, inserting the blade like the filling in a sandwich, then screwing it in place with the small handle.

A strange squirming wriggled in my private parts as I watched him draw the blade along her skin. I knew I could never tell either of them about this. I knew it was shameful. And besides, I enjoyed it. Now, I realize, I was being swept up in the same current. Mummy was goddess and sacrifice combined. She had all the power, and we were her lowest slaves. Yet Father wielded the blade and, if he had wanted, he could have sliced her apart. With every stroke, she relaxed into soft folds of flesh.

Sometimes, at the end, when she got up, I was allowed the treat of applying her lipstick. Carmine was her favourite – the deep red of insides.

'Go on,' she'd say, her lips pulled taut across the scaffolds that were her teeth. I twisted the stick up, but not too high or it would break. I moved closer, closer, closer, and I breathed her in – her scented message that told me who she was. Vanilla and lemon and the black parts of toast. Coffee and the brown stick she smeared on her face. And lipstick and sweat and sometimes the smell of onions. I had to be quick, because already, so soon after Father's work, bits of Mummy were leaking. Tiny sequins of moisture sat in the creases of her upper lip. More nestled in the cosy shadow between her breasts.

When Mummy was finished – smooth and gleaming, her dark hair swept back and every bit of her dazzling and beautiful – she went upstairs to put on the dress. Father and I went down the garden and in the side door of the studio to wait.

We climbed the stairs of the mezzanine and waited, looking over the low rail like churchgoers in a gallery, as Mummy – goddess and superstar – entered the ballroom below. Father's face spoke of worship, and he would tilt towards her, a tiny movement, a little rocking motion. Mummy moved as though borne on currents of air, her arms holding an invisible partner. She smiled at the unseen audience behind us, far away. Father's breathing grew deeper – then deeper still. The rocking stopped.

I knew then that it would be time for my lie-down. Father gave me the same medicine in a little plastic cup with lines along the side saying 5ml, 10ml, 15ml, 20ml. There was no 25 figure, but if you filled the cup to the brim, I knew it would be 25ml. Father filled it to 10ml and watched as I drank.

Sometimes I lay down and slept on the couch in the landing but, more often, I watched them through the crack, drowsy and confused, not sure if I was dreaming. Mummy would be lying on the velvet sofa below, tired from all her dancing, and Father – it looked like he was whispering secrets to her or checking that everything was working. He climbed on top of her, and he lifted up her giant skirt so he looked like a blind worm crawling across a beautiful flower. He began with the rocking, but then – then his hips would move angrily, brutally, as though he was punishing her. It was the ugliest thing I'd ever seen, and it had no place in Mummy's beautiful world.

Poor Mummy. Always light on her feet like the dancer she was. Until she wasn't.

12

Niamh

There's an in/out system on the driveway, and an automatic gate. If McArsey is impressed, he stifles it. I make a big deal of battling through pain as I get out of the car and – yep – he steals a sneaky, terrified glimpse at the seat, checking for stains. Rosa lets us in. There's a double-width front door leading into a glassed-off interior hallway in which sits an antique wooden chest full of shoes. Why would you keep shoes on display? I wonder, before realizing that, of course, we're meant to take ours off and put them there. Two ends of an eejit!

The glass doors separate – no mention of shoe removal is made – and we enter the hallway proper. Double height – stuttering Jesus! – the ceiling's higher than the church back home. Mam would love to hear about this place. I feel like I'm in a magazine; Denny's not wrong there. Everything is white – the floor, the walls – even the giant painting over the white console table is a study in white. I'm aware suddenly of the jeans I'd hastily pulled on this morning. Are they stained? I'll surely have dropped food on them – I always do. I pull down my jumper a bit lower. McArsey checks his reflection in the (white-framed) hall mirror we pass on our way through to the living room. He's surrendered the puffa jacket to the hall cupboard and he's even skinnier than I remember, narrow and bony, in navy trousers and sensible fleece. For some reason, he's wearing a buttoned shirt plus tie under the fleece.

Rosa ushers us past the breakfast bar (some kind of white marble with white fibreglass stools) and the kitchen table (more white stone, and chairs that match the stools) through to an L-shaped seating area with – yep – white leather couches. There isn't as much as a teaspoon sitting out on any surface.

'Tea? Coffee?'

'Lovely. Tea, please,' I say, intrigued as to where the kettle is kept, as much as wanting to observe her manner.

'Tea would be great, thanks.' Senan settles himself on the edge of the leather couch.

Rosa makes her way towards the sink, presses the edge of a drawer and begins taking cups and a teapot out.

'A teabag is fine,' says Senan.

Rosa puts the teapot away and begins filling the cups directly from the tap. She notices us watching.

'This is one of those hot-and-cold taps,' she says. 'They're absolutely brilliant – I'd recommend.'

I imagine my mother's face if someone made her a cup of tea with water that never saw sight of a kettle. She'd freak.

'Actually, could I use your toilet?' I flash what I hope is a girlie-coded tampon-needing look. She gets it.

'Oh, yes. The – the bathroom's out there, to the right of the hall where you came in.'

Bathroom. Of course. I head back out into the hall, find the toilet and enjoy that moment of escape when you've locked yourself away from everything just for a minute. My sister Siobhán has three kids and there isn't a centimetre of space in her house that the little feckers haven't penetrated. There'll be a crayon in a corner, a half-finished bottle on a mantelpiece, a piece of Lego lurking in the carpet; schoolbags, coats, apple cores, drawings pinned to walls – the works. Her toilet is the worst. Sometimes you have to fish out the special seat that's inserted so their little arses don't fall through – and try not to fall over the plastic step they use to reach the washbasin.

The toilet – no, bathroom – in Mrs Nairn's house is not like Siobhán's. Pristine stone, gleaming white loo and sink, fluffy hand towel, scented hand gel with matching moisturizer and sanitizer. I flush, then wash my hands. The hand basin rises out of a sleek vanity unit with a frosted glass door. I open it. Spare toilet rolls fill the lower shelf and a quilted make-up bag lies on its side beside a comb on the top shelf. I unzip the bag. Inside, there are two tubes of lipstick, one in a coral shade and the other more of a bronzey-brown, and a little pot of concealer, in a pale shade. Not Mia's anyway. Likewise, neither of the lipsticks looks like the shade Mia was wearing. The comb is immaculate. It looks brand new.

Before I leave the toilet I open the box of Tampax and take one out, hiding it in the zipped inside pocket of my bag. Then I replace the opened box at the top in my handbag so it's visible. McArsey's a pain. But he's not a fool.

When I go back in, he's taking notes and Rosa is picking her manicured fingernail. It seems to be hitting her.

'Your daughter?' I say, pointing to the only thing adorning the walls in this part of the room, a huge black-and-white photograph of a beautiful toddler in an old-fashioned dress, her face a portrait of wonder as she gazes at a soap bubble.

'Yes, that's Carly. We had it done – that was a few months ago.'

Again, I think of home – what's wrong with me today? – of the assorted photos arranged or, rather, not arranged, on the wall behind the door of the good room, which is never used. Siobhán, angelic in her First Holy Communion dress, Tom at his Confirmation, GAA team photos of him and, later, Rory, when he made the county team. There's one of me in Senior Infants with a vicious fringe Mammy inflicted on me, and a small one of my Communion, bursting out of the dress Siobhán had worn at the same age eight fecking years earlier. And little Martin – he only gets two photos – his christening and one of him in Daddy's arms, pointing at a tractor. He was obsessed with them. Poor little divil never even made it to Junior Infants.

This photo must be four foot square. The child sees herself in a giant photo every day when she's eating her Rice Krispies. *That'll do more harm than good*, says Mammy in my head. *It'll only give her notions.*

'She's gorgeous.' I accept the cup of tea, noting with a twinge of disappointment, but not surprise, that there are no biscuits to go with it.

'Lovely,' McArsey agrees.

'Where is she at the moment?'

'My neighbour is minding her – sorry – you hardly expect to – you don't need to talk to her, do you?'

Well, actually, I do, I think. But – it'd be better to do that when Laura's back, I realize, so I give a little smile.

'Not now – but we will. Your daughter is – she might be the only witness we have, you understand? Perhaps you could take us through the events of yesterday? We'll start there.'

She sighs, placing her untouched coffee cup on the tray. The movement changes the angle of the tray – it had been perfectly aligned with the edge of the table – and she adjusts it before replying.

'So, Wednesday – I do a Pilates class at ten on Wednesdays and I'm not usually back till eleven forty-five or midday.' She gestures towards her right shoulder, giving an apologetic little sigh.

'I've an old injury – a broken collarbone when I was a

child – and if I don't do my regular physio exercises and Pilates at least three times a week, well . . .'

She looks to McArsey for sympathy. He nods.

'It's –'

'It's a disaster,' she finishes. 'I had to leave my job – the pain?'

'What did you do?' Fair play to McArsey for sticking to the script.

'All day at an easel, bending over and –'

'Are you an artist – an architect?'

She smiles at him, enjoying this.

'Oh, no! No, I'm – I was – an interior designer.' She waves a hand, her thin wrist describing circles in the air. 'This type of thing – this is all me. I designed our house – obviously, not the building work, but all of this.'

'You were telling us about yesterday,' I prompt, missing the cue to tell her I'm impressed with the decor.

That was such a Laura thing to do, I realize. I tease Laura all the time about her chess moves – the strategic questions. I'm always telling her to let the conversation flow naturally, but – Lord! I wish she was here. We'd be halfway finished by now. A bit of sucking up is always good – don't knock it – but Jaysus, Senan is full-on puppy eyes. She's wearing a high-necked silky blouse tucked into the leather trousers. The platinum bob looks as if it was blow-dried this morning.

'Yes. Right. So, Mia walked Carly to school – you know, the Montessori up in Clonchapel?'

'Tiptoe something?' I try to recall the name. She nods.

'Tippy Toes Montessori.' She does a little shrug. 'Sweet.'

We nod. Senan is taking notes, I'm watching her.

'That would have been about nine thirty. And I went to Pilates and – we'd a quick coffee afterwards, so I'd say I was back here by about twelve at the latest. Yes, because I had a shower – I wanted to have my shower in peace before they came back for lunch.'

She pauses, the words 'in peace' hanging in the air.

'And what about Mia? What does Mia – what did she do between dropping Mia to school and – I'm presuming it was Mia who also did the pick-up?'

Rosa nods.

'Yes, they walk. It's – it's not far, and it's – good for the environment, and health and –'

'Absolutely,' says McArsey. *It was pissing rain*, I think.

'So, after Mia drops Carly to school, what does she do?' I prompt.

'She comes back and, you know, she does – did – a bit of light housework. They don't have to clean or anything. Not like – well. She used to, you know, put away Carly's clothes and toys, arrange her room, tidy up a few dishes, light chores – that type of thing.' She notices a tiny splash of coffee on the leg of her trousers, frowns and blots it with a hanky she withdraws from her sleeve.

'And that would take how long – an hour? Half an hour?'

'Oh, not long. Maybe forty minutes. And then she'd be free, so she might meet another au pair or a friend, or maybe spend time on her English lessons or, I don't know, maybe Snapchat, or . . .' She trails off.

'Actually, I don't know what she did,' she says. She looks at McCarthy, stricken. 'I'm so sorry.'

13

Niamh

'Don't worry,' says Senan. 'This is all very helpful.'

'It is,' I agree, 'but let's just get the timing checked, will we? So, usually Mia has some free time after the school drop and after her chores –'

'Light chores.'

'Of course – her light chores. And then she – she walks back to Clonchapel to collect Carly at what time?'

'Yes, she prepares the lunch for them – she usually leaves it ready, a salad and pasta or something, you know – and then she leaves the house about ten past twelve to walk up to the school.'

'And that's the regular routine?' I say. 'Every day?' She shakes her head.

'Thursdays are later. Carly does a full day and then stays on for the after-school club. Mia picks her up at six thirty on Thursdays.'

My face must betray what I'm thinking, which is *Jaysus, that's a long day for a two-year-old.*

'She loves it. Joanne says she wolfs her dinner.' I'm not imagining the defensiveness so. I smile. *I'm not judging.*

'Right,' I say. 'But yesterday was a normal early day, so you'd have seen her yesterday. You said you got back from Pilates at about twelve?'

'Oh, yes, well, I did. I was.' She shakes her head. 'But she'd already left. The lunches were out – Mia must have left a bit earlier. Sometimes she meets up with one of the other girls – there's quite a few au pairs at Tippy Toes. They've a WhatsApp group, I think.'

I make a note to get access to the WhatsApp messages.

'So,' I say, trying to picture the scene: Rosa arrives back from her class, presumably has a shower and gets dressed. I'm guessing she does the full blow-dry and make-up, which I now know (since Amber moved in) can take anything from half an hour to an hour and a half. 'So, you must have been very surprised when they didn't come back. Presumably you'd expect them back by about one at the latest?'

Again, she shakes her head. It's more of a flick of the hair – nervy, as though flicking aside a troublesome thought.

'That's the thing – I didn't realize. I – I had no reason to suspect anything bad or untoward – I wasn't here when they came back. When they didn't come back.'

She looks to McArsey, a pleading, little-girl look.

'I had a lunch appointment at two, so I wasn't even going to be there when they got back. It's sometimes easier that way –' She breaks off then adds, 'Do you have children?'

I ignore the question, but McArsey shakes his head regretfully. He can't be more than thirty-five, I think. It's hardly the regret of a lifetime. She carries on.

'Sorry, I – well – the whole separation anxiety thing. I mean, that's why we got a nanny – au pair. I find it's far easier to leave them at it for the day. Carly interacts with Mia during the day, and later on – the evenings – she has me to take care of her. And Tom, of course – although he's rarely home before her bedtime.'

'Right,' I say, 'so you're saying that even if they had come back for lunch at one, you wouldn't have been here. Which is why –'

'Which is why I nearly died of shock when the guards

phoned me, saying they had Carly – that she'd been found alone – alone! In – in some – wandering in some estate where she could have been abducted or – or knocked down by a car! Thank God for that woman.'

'Go on,' says McArsey. 'The woman?'

'A woman walking her dog along the lane – she found Carly and of course knew something wasn't right. She brought her to the guards in Rathfarnham, and Carly still had her schoolbag – she likes to think she's a big girl – and there was a note from Tippy Toes in the bag about an activity next week. So, the woman rang the school and –'

'Did you get her name? The woman?'

She sits back, clasping her hands under her breastbone, pressing against her chest.

'No – yes, I – I think I heard it, but I can't remember.'

I make a note to check the details in the log for yesterday. They'll have got it all.

'Are you okay? Do you need a glass of water?' McArsey is ready to leap into action, but she shakes her head.

'Sorry. I'm fine – it's just when I think what could have happened, I just –'

'And what did Carly say about what happened?' I ask, determined to keep this moving.

Rosa's head shake has turned into a nervous twitch.

'Did she say anything at all about being in the car? About why – why did he put her out?'

'No! Jesus! Mostly she wanted to talk about the dog, for goodness' sake! She was so excited to be allowed to hold the bloody lead. She – she –'

'Take your time, Mrs Nairn,' says McArsey. 'It's important that you try to remember her words. Her exact words.'

'I don't know,' she blurts. 'I mean, I was beside myself when the guards arrived. To think –'

'Well, she must have said something – let's go back a bit. Did she say anything at all about why they got in the car in the first place?' It comes out more sharply than I'd intended. McArsey frowns at me.

'She said, let me think – she said it was raining and, and her shoes were all wet, and the nice man –' She looks up at me, nodding. 'That was it – her words were that "the nice man" gave them a lift.'

McArsey looks up from his notes. 'Did she say exactly that – did she use the phrase "give us a lift"?'

'No – I don't know. Maybe, maybe she said –'

She looks at us in turn.

'She's not even three,' she says. 'All I remember is she talked about a nice man and the dog and that she sat in the car.'

'And then, later, he put her out of the car?'

She doesn't reply. She dabs at her eyes with the hanky, nodding. 'And she had a red mark – tiny – a tiny mark on her cheek. It's gone now. She said she hurt it in the car. That's it. All I know is that she was in a car and she said her face "hurted" – that's what she says when she has a bump or something.'

'It must have been awful,' I say.

'It was – and of course, I couldn't reach Tom – he's in the middle of this case and, oh dear no – if the world was ending, you couldn't interrupt one of his cases!'

She eyeballs me, angry tears glinting.

'You know he ran a case on the day of his mother's funeral? His own mother's funeral? I mean, I know they didn't get on, but it's not natural. I swear to God, we could drop dead or be raped and murdered and I don't think he'd –'

She halts. The words hang in the air.

'He was an only child – maybe that's it – he's not used to

thinking about anyone except himself. Or maybe – maybe it's the job. You need to be cold to do what he does. He unpicks people – like – it's like he dissects them. He cuts you open and shows you what's inside.'

She stops, trying to contain herself. I'm sorry for her then – just a bit. What's the point of the big house and the magic tap and the beautiful child – and the lifestyle of classes and lunches and shite like that – if you can't enjoy it? If you resent the person who provides it? Because, I'm beginning to realize, Rosa is a woman consumed by resentment.

'You had to deal with it yourself.' I nod. 'That can't have been easy.'

The sympathy unravels her. She begins to cry in earnest, tears staining her silk shirt. McArsey gives me a terse little nod, obviously wanting me to drop it. A thought occurs to me.

'Do you have a current photograph of Mia, Mrs Nairn?'

She dabs her eyes with the hanky, swallows.

'Yes, I –'

I wait as she gets her mobile phone from the island. She opens the screen and hands me the phone.

'That was – we went to the playground a couple of weeks ago,' she says, pointing at the picture. 'The playground behind the castle – Carly loves it.'

Blonde, pink-clad Carly is perched at the very top of a slide, held in place by a laughing girl with long dark hair – Mia. She's so young. Christ. She doesn't look nineteen – more like sixteen. About five foot four – petite in her build. I can't help it – I look at her feet like I need to see them in better days. She's wearing chunky ankle boots, dark leggings or tights, a bright red skirt – it looks like corduroy – and a black denim jacket. I frown. The girl in this picture is fresh-faced – no make-up, her hair plain and natural.

'How long ago was this?' I'm wondering if something

happened – if she started seeing someone and changed her look.

'Not that long ago. Wait.' She checks the date.

'Saturday two weeks ago – the twenty-seventh, it says.'

'Did she change her hairstyle? Does she wear it shorter now?'

'No,' Rosa says, shaking her head. 'That's what she looks like – long hair, sweet, unsophisticated – a pretty girl.'

'And if she was going out – if she was meeting someone? Did she wear lipstick, make-up?' I say, thinking of the slicked-back hair and the red lips – incongruous and harsh against the earth tones of the mountainside.

I forward the photo to my own phone, then hand it back to her. She takes it delicately, as though not wanting to touch it after I've been holding it. She places it on the counter. Instinct tells me she's going to wipe it down before using it again. Maybe it's the post-Covid world – or maybe she'd be like that anyway.

Again, Rosa frowns.

'No, actually, well, not lipstick, certainly. Perhaps a little bit of eye make-up? She's – she was very natural-looking, not like – compared to – you know the way they're all bright orange with fake tan and the dark eyebrow thing? I definitely don't remember her wearing lipstick.'

She pauses, her head at an angle. 'Is it important? I mean, now I think about it, I'd say yes, she – maybe she wore eyeliner – but I couldn't even swear to that.'

I drop it.

'I'd like to have a quick look at her bedroom,' I say, getting to my feet. 'Mia's?'

She stands too. Her body language is tense; everything about her says no.

'If you prefer, I can get a warrant, but –'

'Of course,' she interrupts, turning and gesturing for us to follow. 'It's fine.'

The stairs rise in a column of glass and marble from the rear of the hallway. We pass another huge window on the return, which looks out over the foliage in the back garden. It's as though we're climbing into a glass treehouse. We reach the first floor, which spreads into a long corridor, off which I count one, two – two doorways to the left and another four to the right. One door is ajar – what must be the master bedroom. A vast double bed with thick mahogany posts at the corners dominates the room and, to the left of it, a delicate dressing table with one of those angled mirrors with smaller mirrors either side. I glimpse expensive-looking bottles of perfume and one of those little jewellery trees, from which I can see beads and gems dangling. Rosa steps in between us and closes the door.

'This way,' she says. We follow her down the corridor, our footsteps muffled by a central runner of carpet set into the wide oak beams. She pauses outside a door towards the rear of the house, where there's less light.

'Mia's room?' I put on gloves, and McArsey does the same.

We go inside. Smaller and darker, it's hard to tell if the fact of Mia's death is what makes it gloomier or if it's just a dark room. Grey walls and white paintwork make it clean-looking but stark. By the window, there's a desk and a chair, with a laptop perched precariously on the books that are scattered in small piles over the desk. They look like school textbooks. A single photograph – black and white – of a bunch of lilies takes up much of one wall.

Mia had obviously tried to cheer the place up. A bright rug in stripes of green, blue, red, yellow and turquoise is spread out over the end of the bed.

'She brought that from Spain,' says Rosa from the doorway,

seeing me notice it. 'Actually, it was a gift for me from her mother,' she amends, 'but I –'

I can't picture it anywhere else in the house.

'I thought it'd be nice for her to have it here,' she finishes.

The en suite bathroom is tiny. In the shower cubby, no fewer than five bottles of shampoo, conditioner, balms and treatments for curly hair vie for prime position. To the right of the mirror, there's toothpaste and an electric toothbrush, a pack of wipes for removing make-up, a bottle of toner and a tube of moisturizer, a pot of concealer and a smaller bottle of a skin treatment for spots. All are regular brands, the kind you'd buy in the supermarket or your local chemist. A small wicker container sprouts eye pencils, like a desk cactus, in shades of charcoal, black and purple. No sign of any lipstick.

'So,' says Rosa, clearly ready for us to leave.

'Thank you,' I say. 'I'd just like to –' I open the tall wardrobe beside the bed. Inside is a carnival of colour; not just the clothes – bright T-shirts and trousers or skirts, which are hanging or stacked in the cubbies – it's the photographs. The entire inner surfaces of both doors are covered in photos. And I thought people didn't print them off any more. Many of them are from home, family scenes, a couple of boys who must be brothers – the resemblance is strong. A photo of Mia hugging a middle-aged man – must be her dad – and a self-conscious one of Mia and her mother dressed up as if for a formal event. On the top right are newer photos, Polaroids with the retro white edge. I recognize the cobbled streets and an ice-cream parlour in Temple Bar. There are groups of laughing students and, in particular, several shots of a tall fair-haired guy, maybe in his early twenties. He's standing on a wall, he's raising a pint of beer, he's posing on top of a rock, he's got his arm draped over Mia's shoulder. In that one she looks like she's pure delighted.

'Do you know who this is?'

Rosa peers at it, shaking her head.

'Sorry, I —'

She's on edge, like she can't wait for us to be gone. I wonder if she's always like this — nervy — or if she's hiding something. I reach into the wardrobe and carefully peel off the more recent photos, the ones of her friends and the boyfriend. McArsey, I see, records it in his notebook. I place them in an evidence bag.

'And did she go out much? Who would she meet up with, do you know?'

Rosa shrugs.

'They — the students — they have their weekly classes at the language school on Thursday mornings and so they hang out, you know, in town, on Thursday afternoons. I — I don't know names. You know the arrangement, it's not like we're in loco parentis or anything — you know that? I'm not responsible — I can't be responsible for her —'

'Quite,' says McArsey. 'No one is suggesting that.' He shoots me a daggers look.

'Of course,' I agree. 'Sorry — I'm not for one minute suggesting that, Mrs Nairn. I'm just wondering if you know of anyone Mia might have met up with? I suppose what I'm saying is, there's a possibility that she arranged to meet this person. Perhaps it's someone she knew — after all, she got into the car with him. Isn't that what your daughter said?'

'I —' Rosa nods. 'Yes — yes — she said it was raining and they — look —' She stops abruptly. 'This is pointless. Carly is two and a half. I haven't a clue — what I mean is she was mostly talking about the dog — and if she was upset at all, it was because Mia didn't say goodbye to her.'

She examines her gold wristwatch. 'And I've got to go and pick her up – she's with my neighbour. I said I'd get her as soon as I got back. I'd better –'

I nod. McArsey is virtually bent double in a bow.

'Thank you very much, Mrs Nairn. You've been very helpful. The team from the technical bureau will conduct a thorough search later,' he says.

'Yes – thanks,' I agree. 'I'm going to take her laptop in the meantime.' I wait for McArsey to kick off. But he says nothing.

'We'll be off now.'

'Yes, we'll head off,' parrots McArsey, the knob.

From the vaulted hallway, I glance back into the kitchen, wondering which of the eight-foot-high gleaming presses contains the vodka – or the herbal tea – or the slabs of chocolate, wondering what is Rosa's go-to solace. McArsey is tying his shoelace. Eejit. If Laura was here, she'd be questioning and I'd be watching. Or the other way around. Either way, we'd get it done.

We move closer to the hall door.

'So, the technical team will be back shortly –'

She's nodding, keen for us to be gone.

'And I'll need to talk to Carly –'

Her face falls.

'But how – I mean, where? There's no way I'm bringing her to a garda station! She'll be terrified.'

'Mrs Nairn,' McArsey soothes, 'I can assure you there's nothing to worry about. Detective Darmody here is a trained SVI – a specialist victim interviewer.'

The word 'victim' seems to make her worse. I step in.

'And of course, we won't be bringing her to the station. Don't worry, what happens is it's done really informally, here at her home. She could be playing with her dolls or whatever and I'm there just as a visitor – a friend of her mammy's – who is playing too.'

There's a pause. Rosa's paler than she was when we first came in. There's a bloodless look to her mouth. Her lips are grey.

'Look, Mrs Nairn, Carly might be the only person who saw Mia's abductor. She's been in his car. You understand – I have to talk to her?'

She repeats the head twitch, pressing her lips tight so they fill with blood on release.

'Fine,' she says.

14

Laura

'I'm big – I'm a big girl – I can do it!' Katie bats my hands away angrily, turning back to the buggy. It's a rear-facing, supposedly all-terrain buggy which, in theory, I could use on the 10k runs every young mother does. Katie's too short to see over the hood part, so it's like she's driving blindfolded. Noah, bundled up in layers and, thankfully, not crying – yet – seems to enjoy the vigorous joyride as she crashes him down on to the path from the doorstep, batters the buggy into the gate, then rides roughshod over every pothole, stone, dip and rise along the narrow footpath. I'm trying to steer as well, without her knowing I'm doing it, petrified she's going to career straight into the path of an oncoming car or ram the buggy against a gatepost or kerb and upend the whole thing. But every time I touch the handle she goes nuts.

Why did I think this was a good idea? The kitchen is a state after their lunch, peas and half-chewed clumps of rusk under Noah's highchair, chocolate smears everywhere – I gave in and let Katie have the last chocolate finger while I tried to call Niamh again. It went straight to messages.

I long for them to be asleep. I can't believe I'm actually fantasizing about them being asleep or occupied or, I don't know, out of the way, so I can clean the kitchen. I've reached a new low – the point where all I want to do is have uninterrupted time to clean. Meanwhile, I hope to God we don't meet anyone, because both of them – actually, all of us – look a state. Katie's hair is in two bunches she insisted on doing herself, with the result that they hang lopsidedly and asymmetrically, one from the middle of her forehead ('like a unicorn, Mummy') and one over her ear. Her cheeks are red from the brisk wind, or maybe – maybe she's not well. Could she have a temperature? She was complaining of a sore ear earlier. Noah is plastered in Liga over the lower half of his face, with matching clumps in his dark curls. And I'm wearing my pregnancy coat, a baggy parka-type thing in a shade of teal I'd never choose for myself. Matt's Christmas gift. He was trying to be nice and it's some expensive German brand that his mother wears, so it probably cost hundreds – but it's teal, with mustard contrasting strips along the pockets and lining the hood. It looks like a sleeping bag. At least the capacious hood hides my own questionable hair, grown out of the bob and manky.

A car approaches, turning down from the main road. Our road is a cul-de-sac, so it's likely to be a neighbour or someone doing a U-turn. Shit. It's Kay. Kay lives opposite, her house situated at three o'clock, if the roundabout was a clock, which gives her maximum opportunity to keep an eye on the comings and goings of the neighbourhood. She knows everyone. She knows everything about everyone, and their parents before them, and their grandparents before that. Illness, unexpected deaths, cancer and now Covid – especially young people struck down by the disease – are her specialist subjects. Matt tells me to avoid her. *Give her a wide berth, like I do – you know she's only going to make your anxiety worse.* Yep, because I go around looking for things to make me worse. Thanks, Matt. Me and my anxiety waiting for you at home to ruin your life. Easy for him, as he's out all day.

I think she waits – she can see our front door from her

house – and by the time I'm at the gate, she's there in her coat. *Lucky I caught you, I was just going out myself. Look at those lovely children!*

She spots us and comes to a gear-grinding, jerky halt, already winding down the window so she can talk to us. Katie, no fan of Kay and the long, grown-up conversations punctuated with mouthed words and whispers, speeds up. The cross-terrain dual wheels of the buggy must have somehow ended up facing the wrong way, because they lock and the buggy comes to an abrupt stop. Katie stumbles while keeping hold of the handle, tipping the buggy upwards and almost – almost – catapulting the now screaming Noah out of it.

'How are you doing?' Kay shouts at me, oblivious to the mayhem she has caused. I yank Katie to her feet with one hand, righting the buggy with the other. Luckily, Noah was strapped in. But I'll have to take him out now to settle him.

'Hi, Kay,' I manage. 'I'm just – that's fine, Katie, he's all right.'

Katie is wailing, 'I'm sorry, I'm sorry, Muma – it wasn't my fault,' all pretence of being a big girl gone. 'I'll be good, Muma! I'm sorry! I'm sorry!' The crying turns into a wail. Jesus! I kneel on the path, hugging them both to my chest. Noah's little cold cheek is pressed to mine and I feel myself being coated in a slimy mixture of runny nose and tears. Katie burrows her head into my neck on the other side, crying hot gusts of self-hatred into my collarbone.

Still kneeling, flanked by crying children, I look at Kay. I don't think she's even noticed them.

'Did you hear? I was just in the chemist's, and everyone's talking about it. Oh, sweet Jesus! What a thing to happen! And you know he took the child?' Her eyes slide across me, landing on Katie.

'He must have – she was found about two miles from the school. Thanks be to goodness, she must have a guardian angel. Somehow, she got out, or maybe the girl put her out, or – who knows what was going on. You'd need to be sick. Evil and sick to do something like that, isn't that right?'

Her voice drops to a mouthing whisper. 'Murder!' She shakes her head. 'Right here in Clonchapel.'

I begin to straighten up, having been nodding and shaking my head at the appropriate times. 'I know. Imagine! It's desperate! Yes.' I don't tell her about the drug deals, burglaries, assaults and abuses that are constantly taking place in Clonchapel and all over the country, the backdrop of crime she knows nothing about. Two cars are now stuck behind her – neighbours as well – so it's all very civil and no horn-blowing.

'I'd better not keep you.' I point at the cars.

Kay's hands fly up to her hair in a panic. 'Oh! Yes! Goodbye, dear. Mind yourself now.' The car lurches forwards, but she's not finished. 'And keep an eye on the little one' – she nods at Katie – 'she's coming down with something. Watch out it's not –' She mouths, *the Covid*.

Thanks.

I put Noah back in the buggy. The crying has tired him out and he goes straight to sleep. A chastened Katie makes no attempt to push it. Instead, she steps up on to the buggy board and does her Joan of Arc impression, staring bravely straight ahead, her little chin quivering with unshed tears. She thinks I'm still cross with her. She hates making me angry, disappointing me in any way. I don't think I give out to her much; if anything, I hide my anger. Why is it so hard to find the balance? I don't want her sobbing and being a little tear-stained saint full of self-loathing! I just don't want her killing her brother.

I pat her head and she looks up at me, delighted with the affection. What sort of a bitch mother am I? Have I made her like this?

'Am I your best girl?'

'Of course you are.' I smile.

'An' you love me every little bit?' Our family mantra.

'I surely do,' I chant like a robot. 'Come on, we'll go for our walk while Noah's asleep. You can be the queen and I'll be pushing you along in your fancy carriage.' She nods.

'I'm the princess and you're the queen, but you're a good queen, not a evil queen.'

That's good, then, I think – trying not to cry. I'm grateful to be the good queen. Christ.

We've almost made it as far as the junction where the cul-de-sac meets the main road. I check the time – almost three. It'll be time to change Noah when we get back, then I'd better clean up the kitchen – oh, and hang out the wash. And then it'll be time to get their tea, and then I'd better start thinking of food for us, and – I close my eyes. *Fuck this shit* – Niamh's expression – pops into my head.

The thought of her is accompanied by the lurch of guilt. I've got to talk to her. Maybe Matt's right, and she'll understand. I can barely hack it as a mother – and that's when I'm not even working. I'd implode if I was trying to juggle an investigation and the kids and the house and – I stop. What the hell?

One of the unit cars is coming down the hill from the 'good' part of Clonchapel, the golf-club end of the town. It's the white Prius, the one Niamh and I often used and – shit! That's McCarthy and – and Niamh. Of course! They must have been up at the house.

I stand there, tracking their progress as they sweep down the hill, through the junction, and start heading uphill towards

Rathgar. Or no, they're turning left along the river. They must be going back to the unit. It's like a slow-motion shot. God, McCarthy looks as though he's – he's delighted – the proverbial cat plus cream. But it's Niamh – the sight of Niamh – I literally experience a lurch inside, like when you're in an elevator and it drops suddenly. She's laughing, her face turned towards him like a spotlight.

I can imagine – no – I don't need to imagine, I can remember that feeling, written all over her face. She's excited. They both are. It's the start of a big case and you're pumped, especially in the early stages when you're uncovering stuff and all the information is new. You can't get to it fast enough.

A little whiney voice in my head goes, *But Niamh doesn't even like McCarthy – she's MY best friend.* What am I – six? I tear my eyes away and focus on Katie.

'Hold on tight now to the handle, we're going to cross the road.'

'Here, you look like you could do with a hand.'

A male voice by my right ear causes me to leap in fright. Where did he materialize from? He's middle-aged, stocky, dressed in track gear for someone a decade younger, someone about to run a marathon, judging by the hydration pack. There's a whiff of sweat from him – and it's not fresh *I just ran 10k* sweat. I flinch, gripping both the handle of the buggy and Katie's hand more tightly.

'No – no, thanks,' I stammer. 'I've got this, thank you. It's –'

He smiles and turns away with a little shrug, making his way towards what must be his car.

Another over-the-top reaction, Laura. Are you proud of yourself? Just an older man offering to help, as opposed to an axe murderer slash kidnapper. Idiot.

'Come on,' I say to Katie, hurrying us all across the road.

In a few minutes, we arrive at the footbridge beside the park and Katie gets down off the buggy board. Suddenly, she bolts off in the direction of the parked cars, squealing.

'Katie!' I'm instantly panicked – what the hell? 'Katie!' I scream. Then I see where she's heading. Niamh is hunkered down on the pavement with both arms wide, waiting for Katie to run into them. She must have spotted us and got McCarthy to pull in. There's hugging and more squealing – Katie is transformed. After a few moments, Niamh sets her down, telling her to go and collect twigs to drop from the bridge. She peeps in at Noah.

'Asleep,' I say, unnecessarily.

'Fair play,' she says. 'Well?'

Niamh takes a step back to look at me. I'm aware of my dirty hair, the dried slime coating my right cheek, the food-stained clothes. More than anything, I'm aware of the disappointment in her eyes.

'I – I –'

She waits.

'I tried to ring you?'

'I was at the scene, then interviews. You know how it is. We're heading to the post-mortem debriefing now.'

I nod.

'Is there anything you want to tell me?' she says, walking towards the bridge, holding the twigs Katie gives her. She turns back to hold up her fingers – mouthing, *Five*, at McCarthy. He's on a call, but he makes eye contact and gives a little nod of assent.

'Dick,' smiles Niamh, softly so only I hear.

'Look – I – I was going to tell you. I did try to ring –'

'Today.'

'Eh, yes, earlier today.' I scramble for the right words. 'I'm sorry – I hadn't, I hadn't made up my mind completely and

I – I just couldn't decide, but then we talked, Matt and I, and he thinks – I mean, we think – it's best if I take a career break.' I don't mention New York. It's not going to happen anyway. I know that much.

'I know,' she says, giving Katie a thumbs-up. She's crowing because her stick won.

'What?'

'Oh yes, McArsey informed me this morning at the crack of dawn on the Featherbed that I get the great honour and joy of being partnered with him for this case and – and who knows? Maybe I'll get really lucky and he'll be my partner for ever and ever.'

She sighs, turning towards me and searching my face. 'Same as ever, Laura. At least you're consistent.'

'I'm sorry, I –'

'Your left hand doesn't know what your right hand is doing you're that switched off, Laura.'

She begins walking back towards the car. McCarthy's fingers are drumming along the outside of the driver door.

'I'm being summoned.' She nods. 'Wanker.' Then loudly, 'There in a tick, Senan! Thanks for waiting!'

She turns back.

'It's always the same with you' – she shrugs – 'you tell me nothing. Even after all the time we've worked together, it might as well not have happened. Look, I know last year was tough and that, you know, that whole thing – Jenny's case – really took it out of you. But did you ever stop to think that even in the middle of whatever post-natal shite you were going through, and your own trauma from the past – don't wave it off, Laura.' She puts her hand on my elbow and leans closer, peering at my eyes as though she's trying to see into my brain. 'You said yourself you had your own demons. But what I'm saying is that even with all of that, you still did the right thing. And we nailed the bastard. So now, you make your choice however you see fit, but don't forget you're bloody good at what you do.'

She steps back, puts her hand in her pocket. 'Thing is – and maybe I need to work on my own issues,' she says, layering on the sarcasm, 'I still think of us as a team. Our own unit.' She nods. 'Yeah – and I forget that, for you, it's not like that.'

'Ah! Niamh! That's not fair, and you know it. We're friends – we –'

She stops a couple of feet away from the car. Noah has begun whimpering, so Katie 'helps' by rocking the buggy to and fro along the path. We have about five seconds before he begins wailing.

'Look,' she says, more kindly, 'if I thought it was what you really wanted – needed – whatever, I'd be right behind you.'

She tilts her head, looks me up and down. 'But this – Jaysus, Laura – is this you? Really? That's the problem with you, you don't know how good you are, do you? Ever hear the phrase "play to your strengths"?'

She bends to hug Katie then straightens up and speaks softly.

'There's a nineteen-year-old girl – someone's daughter – lying dead on Parminter's slab. Somewhere in Spain her parents are being informed of their worst nightmare. I've a killer to catch and a two-and-a-half-year-old witness to talk to. The child was in his car! In the actual bloody car! This is your area – this is what you do best. Christ's sake, Laura! You and me – we could do this.' She turns, shrugging. 'Just think about it, Laura. I'm asking you. Not what Matt wants, and your mother-in-law – Justy, or whatever her name is – wants, and not what the kids *think* they want. What do *you* want? Really?'

15

Niamh

As soon as we arrive at the mortuary McArsey is in like Flynn. Of course, he wants to watch the post-mortem. There's a viewing room for the detectives, the tech lads and people involved in the case – he's not out of line or anything – but I usually prefer to get a cup of tea and wait for Parminter's debriefing after. But no, if he's watching, so am I. The sisterhood or something. Maybe it's because she's so young or, I don't know, far away from home, and the feet – I'm back to the feet again: they're getting to me.

She'll be lying on the cold steel, only a sheet between her naked body and the eyes of us watching. There'll be Parminter, the exhibits assistant and the anatomical pathology technician (APT) whose job it is to assist him, and the group in the viewing room. Parminter will be wielding his scalpel like he's an artist tracing patterns on her chilled flesh; the APT taking notes, recording Parminter's findings; the exhibits assistant being handed the evidence, which will be brought to the forensic science lab in the Phoenix Park for analysis; and, in the viewing room, Senan creepy McArsey and the others. One of the girls from the camogie team, Audrey, she's always talking about the male gaze. I'm sure there's a whole theory about it I haven't got to grips with and, in fairness, I don't live in the land of the straight girl and maybe I'm more immune. Even so, I know what she's on about. You're judged from when you're a child, from before the first swelling of your little sky-high boobs. There's a – a sort of quantifying look that happens. An assessment is made.

I think of the aul fellas hanging over the high wall of the mart as the beast is brought in, eyes raking her from hoof to tail, checking the heft, the muscle tone, the look of her. The decision is made in a few split seconds. Likewise for us – you're in your little bubble in the corner of the bar or at a table in a restaurant and the guys come in and you're strafed in a glance, like they're scanning your barcode.

What's that game – Ride, Marry, Murder – where you laugh about your options? It's real enough is all I'm saying. Every girl knows what the lads are thinking – they're asking themselves, *Would I?*

Yeah, well, I don't like post-mortems, but I'm damn well diluting the male gaze today.

'I thought you'd prefer to get a cup of tea.' McArsey is all concerned. It seems I've buttered him up nicely – a bit too well.

'Ah, no, I'm grand now.' I shrug. 'It's just the first couple of hours – the shedding, you know? By the afternoon I tend to be a bit better.'

He swallows, his top lip curling as though smelling something unpleasant.

'Good.'

The exhibits assistant is a woman. Parminter introduces her as Elaine Hynes, and the three of them – Parminter, Hynes and the APT – move in a strange, quiet dance around Mia's body. First, it's all about looking. We watch in silence as the girl's limbs are lifted, lowered, set to one side then the other, revealing dark bruising on her shoulders and ribs – and under the armpits. He sweeps aside her dark hair, checking the scalp, the back of the neck. Tape lifts are done on her mouth, the lipstick still vivid against her pale skin.

Shit! I should have got a photo of the lipsticks at the house. I make a note to get the lads to ask for them.

Parminter snips, prods, lifts more tape from her fingers and toes, makes his incisions, delving into the body with surgical dexterity, producing samples like a magician pulling rabbits from a hat. The APT distributes them with care, holding them flat on his palms like religious offerings before placing them on slides or inside plastic bags and giving them to Hynes. Notes are made and labels are stuck on jars and bags, and all the while the stack grows on the countertop. While this is happening, Parminter is talking, noting his findings.

And all the time I wish Laura was here with me, bearing witness to Mia. She should be here. We should be sitting here like big sisters, watching over the girl, searching for a way to nail whoever did this.

Almost two hours later, mournful as ever, Dr Parminter enters the briefing room, the mark of the mask straps still visible in his sallow skin. The charcoal-coloured suit he's wearing probably cost more than I've spent on clothes in a decade. And the shine of his shoes makes me think he does them himself. It's probably how he relaxes.

'As you know, I work on Locard's principle that every contact leaves a trace,' he says. 'Sometimes it's the smallest and most insignificant injury that reveals most about a death, and remember – each injury tells a story.'

He consults his notes before continuing. The screen behind him flickers into life, revealing a diagram of a female body with shading and arrows indicating injuries.

'In this case, we have a healthy female of nineteen, with good dentition, a strong constitution and no evidence of natural disease. She was not pregnant and there is no sign of sexual assault. Her death has come about as a result of a penetrating neck injury, namely complete spinal transection. That is, the severing of her spinal cord. The site and precision of the stab wound' – he points to a spot on the back of the neck – 'strongly suggest that the perpetrator knew exactly what he or she was doing. One might consider the possibility that the perpetrator has, therefore, some medical expertise. He would also – apologies – the killer would also require a fair amount of strength to wield the blade. It fractured the C5 vertebral body completely.'

So, we're looking for a knife. McArsey turns to me.

'It could be a doctor, or a medical student,' he whispers. I nod, not opening my mouth in case the words *No shit, Sherlock* emerge. Parminter adjusts his square-framed glasses, lifting them a minute distance, then replacing them exactly as they were.

'Onset of rigor is temperature dependent, slowed in low temperatures and speeded in high temperatures, as you may know. Last night, the temperature in the South Dublin area was a chilly four degrees, therefore it is reasonable to conclude that she died a few hours before midnight and that she was dead when she was placed at the scene.'

I think of her feet. Hoping to God she was already dead when he dragged her across the stony ground, deciding where to put her. That's something.

'Perimortem bruising – that is before, at the time of, or shortly after death – can be seen in the blood vessels and on the skin of her feet. Tape lifts have been done on the top of her feet and on the toes. These are being sent for analysis, but it seems that some contain earth and grit from outdoors; others are tiny wooden splinters which may be from a different location, possibly indoors.'

He pauses and, beside me, McArsey bristles to start asking questions – the type designed to reveal the brilliance of the questioner, no doubt. But Parminter either ignores him or doesn't notice.

'Interestingly, there are no similar abrasions on the heels of the victim nor on the soles of her feet, so it is unlikely that she stood or walked upright at the scene. This strengthens my opinion that the victim was already dead when they arrived at the side of the mountain.'

He points to a diagram showing the layout of Mia's bruising, around the wrist and torso.

'Extensive bruising can be seen here' – he points to an area under the armpits – 'here' – the side of the right breast – 'and the ribcage, in particular the lower-right ribcage.' Parminter regards our nonplussed expressions.

'This suggests that she was possibly carried by her assailant with one arm – the right – circling her body, leaving his left hand free.'

I try to picture it. So, he's left-handed? And strong. Perhaps he held a torch in his left hand and hauled her across the stones with his right – it would have been pitch dark in those early hours. I make a mental note to check how much of a moon there was last night. Or maybe the bruising was done earlier – perhaps he held her like that to deliver the fatal stabbing? As usual with Parminter's debriefings, questions multiply tenfold as each fact emerges.

As though he heard my thoughts, Parminter continues.

'It's possible that he held her in this position when he severed the spinal cord, then continued to hold her, to transport her to wherever he next wished to place her. It would explain the extent of the bruising – he would have had to grip her very tightly, applying a considerable amount of pressure if the body was limp and lifeless.'

How heavy is she? How much bigger and stronger would the killer need to be if he's going to haul her around with one hand?

'Now, to disappoint you,' says Parminter. 'The killer clearly knows something about DNA evidence. We found traces of sodium hyperchlorite all over her body, including under her fingernails. It seems he wiped the body down, possibly with disinfectant wipes. You know the type – they're widely available.'

A little click of something – recognition, maybe – happens in my brain. The body in Wicklow, that was the same. Her fingernails, skin – everything had been wiped with bleach. And everything else was got by foxes and the weather.

Parminter shakes his head with a rueful expression. 'In fact, due to the lack of fibres, hairs, skin cell samples, semen, it's a strong possibility that the killer wore protective clothing of some sort. PPE is, of course, widely available now.'

More gifts from Covid. Feck it. Now we have murderers with a degree in biology – in full PPE.

'Also, the victim was wearing a considerable amount of make-up,' says Parminter. 'A heavy coating of foundation on her face and, as you'll have seen, the red lipstick. Her hair was coated in some type of hair gel and at the time of death it was worn short – shorn, really – and slicked back. All of this means that it will be more difficult to get clean samples of skin cells and fibres which the killer may have shed.'

What is going on with the hair?

In the Q&A bit at the end I let McArsey take centre stage. He asks about toxicology and Parminter gives one of his melancholy sighs.

'We've sent blood and urine samples to the state labs for testing. This may take a few days.'

'So, we don't know if he drugged her or if she took something?' The biro McArsey's holding hovers above his notebook. In fairness, it's a good question.

'Classically, tranquillizers, benzodiazepines, opioids – the so-called date-rape type drugs – are slipped into drinks and taken orally. They're cleared from the body within hours, although traces may be found in the blood for some days afterwards.'

He raises his hands in a 'who knows?' gesture, his pale, long fingers like a saint's, then sits back as though finished. I envy him in a way – he's done his bit. He's found answers to how Mia died and when she died. He knows about her dental hygiene habits (good) and the state of her womb (not pregnant). He even knows what she ate for her last meal – oat-based cereal and bread. Some chocolate. But every fact he feeds us brings another question. We're only getting started. We need to find out why Mia died. Who killed her? Where is he? How do we catch him?

An image flashes in my mind – the photo of Mia and Carly at the playground; her long hair.

'Dr Parminter?'

He nods at me. 'Detective?'

'Can you tell us anything more about her hair? Was it recently cut – would that be something you could tell on examination?'

Parminter considers the question, flicking back through the notes, already shaking his head.

'There would be no way of telling when it was cut, no. At the time of her death all I can tell you is that Mia wore her hair short – to the jawline, approximately – and slicked back with gel.'

'I see. And could you tell if it had been cut professionally or if she'd cut it herself?'

McArsey is looking at me like I've six heads. But Parminter has spotted something in his notes.

'I see I've used the word "shorn" here. Perhaps' – he adjusts his glasses again, thinking – 'yes, it did strike me as – now that you bring it to my attention, I think it was uneven – blunt. Yes.'

We file out of the briefing room. I tell McArsey to go on

ahead and I nip back to catch Parminter. I have the weirdest notion that he's finding a cool, damp place to sit in silence. Like a nocturnal animal.

'Doctor?'

He turns – waits in stillness as I approach, my phone extended like a gift.

'This is Mia just a few days ago – I thought your technician might want to see this? I mean' – I hesitate – 'this is who her parents will be expecting to see. Not the whole lipstick and slicked hair?'

Parminter nods vigorously and I feel ridiculously pleased at his approval.

'Of course,' he says. 'I'll see she gets it. Most sensitive and thoughtful. Well done.'

'Great. I'll –'

'Yes, thank you, and we'll get it printed off. Thank you, Detective – Darmody, isn't it?'

I'm impressed he knows my name and, I suppose, chuffed. Hundreds of gardaí file in and out of this building.

'And another thing, could you ask her – the technician who'll be getting Mia ready – could she check her hair, the way it's been cut. Could she venture an opinion as to whether it was a professional or if Mia did it herself?'

'Certainly. Are you thinking –'

'I don't know.' I pause, aware that I haven't fully thought this through. 'I just want to explore all the angles. If a girl – if a person – is running away, you know the way in movies, the first thing they do is stop at a gas station and cut their hair.' I shrug. 'It might be nothing. Maybe she felt like a change.'

'It might be something,' he says. 'Every contact leaves a trace. I'll ask Ella and she'll get back to you.'

Friday

16

Laura

'Is it birthday time, Muma?' says Katie, her eyes round at the sight of me elbow deep in a bowl of butter and sugar. Damn it! I thought I'd get these in the oven before she came down. I reckoned she'd take a good twenty minutes putting her Disney-princess hairclips in place – all eight of them. She plonks her little schoolbag on the floor by the fridge and dashes over to the kitchen table, rolling up her sleeves in readiness.

'I can help! Is it Christmas soon?'

'No, not today, lovey.'

'Why are you making cakes then?'

So much for me being earth mother stay-at-home goddess. Niamh would break her heart laughing at that.

'You can help with the next bit, okay? I just need to get this in the oven. Tell you what, you get down and wash your hands lots and lots –'

'Germs – I remember,' she chants, clambering back down off the chair and running into the bathroom. I hear her running the taps, already humming with delight. There's a full bottle of scented hand gel – I have another three minutes, maybe. A twinge of guilt pings – that's all it takes to make her happy. A bit of organization, a bit of time doing something creative with her – why can't I do this every day? Matt has gone into work early and Noah took an early feed – both boobs – before six, so I could bake with my daughter, clean up the kitchen, maybe look at a picture book and help with her pre-reading skills – I could do it. I could be that mother, couldn't I?

Yeah. I pour the mixture into the baking tray and fire it into the oven, then wash and dry the bowl. When Katie comes out, I've the flaked almonds and sugar all ready for her to mix together for the topping.

'When these are cooked, we're going to put them in a nice tin and bring them up to Carly's house,' I say, brightly.

She frowns.

'What about school?'

'No school today – Treena is sick – no! Not sick,' I amend, looking at her stricken face. Christ. 'Treena's car won't start, so there's no school today. And Carly – your friend Carly – she's a bit bored at home, so I thought it would be lovely to go and see her – cheer her up.'

Katie pauses in her mixing – which involves spraying almond pieces all over the table – and looks closely at me. She frowns.

'Carly's only little. She's in the baby class.'

'I know that – I know you're much bigger. You're a big girl, but it's a kind thing to do to visit someone when they're feeling sick –'

'Carly's not sick. You said she –'

The bloody third degree from my daughter. *She didn't lick it off a stone*, Niamh would say.

I try another tack. Honesty.

'I want to talk to Carly's mummy,' I say, 'about grown-up things. And you could help by playing with Carly. You'll be like – it will be like we're working –'

'Like you and Niamh?' Her eyes shine.

'Exactly,' I say.

17

Niamh

I wake before the alarm and before Amber, who lies, curled like a kitten, facing away from me. It strikes me that she always sleeps like that – so I'm the one who has to unfurl her.

The spring sunshine and the whole 'help the elderly' role she'd been playing yesterday had put her in great form. That and the calories burned by all the gardening. It was after ten by the time I got back, and I was worried she'd be in a bit of a sulk – I was meant to be off today – but she was in her pjs, wrapped in the duvet, sipping her smoothie. She'd cleared a pile of stuff in the garden, then gone to her rehearsal, which had also gone well. I make a note to ask her all about it later. There's talk of a TV series – I think they may have even filmed an episode.

'I saved your ass with Dorothy,' she said, shaking her head at my waywardness. 'How did you forget the baking arrangement?'

Easily, I felt like saying. What with the murdered nineteen-year-old and bloody Senan McArsey breathing into my ear and Laura not coming back.

'Work,' I shrugged. 'Mental.'

'Anyway, I went upstairs – wow! Can you believe the stuff she has up there? It's like a museum? The house must be worth a fortune.'

She's right. Dorothy inherited the house from her parents, which means she's lived here all of her eighty-four years. It's an imposing house all right, with the stone steps rising up to the pillared thing that shades the front door. Inside, a lifetime of rugs, vases, paintings, clocks, books, occasional tables, mantles, mirrors and floral sofas compete for your attention in the front room. Her kitchen is tiny, a narrow space on the return of the landing above our flat, with painted wooden cupboards and two gas ranges, one that works and one that doesn't. Back in the day when the house was built, I'm presuming the kitchen would have been where we are – in the basement – and it would have had staff. Dorothy's up – I can hear her pottering about. I should call in and apologize before leaving.

'I'd better get going,' I say, softly. Amber stirs and opens her eyes, and I lean in to kiss her. She pulls away, and I remember the new rule – no kissing before toothpaste. Instead, I plant it on her neck, inhaling her morning, grassy smell, which I love. At home we'd often have a sickly lamb by the range during lambing season. Daddy would put it in a box and shove it into the corner, out of the way of Mammy and the tramping feet of us kids. It's a similar smell. I don't tell her, though. I'm learning that Amber is mostly at war with her body – what goes into it, what comes out, its smells and secretions. And most of all, how much of it there is. She doesn't like to be reminded of any of it.

'You will be back in time for a drink, won't you? Kenneth says we need to honour our time together.'

I'm not sticking to the shift times anyway, not while the investigation is ongoing, so I should be able to make it. We're meeting up with her new work friends.

'Yes indeedy,' I say. 'Looking forward to it.'

I throw my bag on the front seat of the car then run up the main steps towards the front door. Dorothy opens it before I can ring the bell. She's pure legend in the looks department, in fairness. She wears her grey hair short like a little cap, framing her strong features. One of her many hand-knitted jumpers is worn tucked into the same black corduroy skirt that she always wears, although I suppose she could have two and alternate them. The skirt ends below the knee and beneath that she's wearing woolly tights and laced brogues. There's a vaguely military air about her – that no-nonsense bearing. This morning, though, something's off – the set of her jaw, the lack of sparkle in her eyes. She's angry.

'Dorothy, you've no idea how sorry I am about yesterday. I –'

She tries to smile, struggling for forgiveness.

'I was really looking forward to the baking, honestly. I – I didn't forget. Well, in fairness, I'm sorry – I did forget,' I amend. You can't bullshit Dorothy.

'But even if I had remembered, I was caught up in a case –'

She holds up a hand to stop me. She's shaking her head.

'Niamh, stop, it's not that.' She frowns. 'It doesn't matter a jot about the baking, for goodness' sake! Why on earth would you think I'd be angry about that?'

I wait, confused.

'But Amber said –'

'Look, I was in two minds whether or not to tell you, and Amber clearly didn't, so –' She breaks off and seems to gather herself together. 'And in the light of the case – that poor girl – I presume it's that one?' She holds her hand up once more. 'You probably can't discuss it. I understand.'

'Well, no, but yes, that's part of it, you're right – but what happened yesterday? Amber told me she helped out – that you and she did gardening or something?'

She sighs. 'I feel terrible saying this – she means well. I know she does. She raked up a load of leaves and she did a bit of weeding, and then she said she'd hose the driveway, get rid of the moss. I hate using that power washer – it has a mind of its own – so I was delighted that she was going to do it. I must confess I was also a bit surprised – she's such a little scrap of a thing and so dainty. I wouldn't have thought gardening was her thing at all.'

I nod. I know what Amber's like when she's in a role. Fully committed. Lucky Dorothy doesn't have a bloody flame-thrower; she'd have been all over that too. I look at the granite steps, dreading what I'm going to see. Maybe they cracked or something. But they look fine, glinting in the morning sun.

Dorothy looks up into the corners above the pillars. She sighs again. 'It doesn't matter –'

'What? Dorothy, look, I'll pay for any damage. Has she damaged something?'

'Nothing like that, no. It's just that she hosed them away – the nests. There've been swallows' nests in that portico since I was a child. I tend to get them cleared every ten years or so because – well, I could be imagining this – but they say the same birds come back to the same nest for years. They look unsightly, of course. And then there are the droppings and suchlike – oh! I wasn't going to say anything. I spoke severely to myself this morning and told myself I'd say nothing. Although, just so you know, there's only certain times of year you can remove them.'

'They were empty, though, weren't they?' I say, thinking, *Please God let her not have power-hosed baby birds*.

'Yes, yes – thank goodness. They haven't arrived yet – it's usually mid-March.'

She puts her hand, freckled and planed by the years, on my forearm and squeezes.

'I never cry,' she says. 'And I'm not going to shed a tear over this – not when you're dealing – not in a world where young girls are murdered. And I don't want you to say anything to Amber. What good would it do? It's too late.'

'I'm so sorry, Dorothy,' I say. 'Jesus, that's terrible, and Amber, she wouldn't have a clue about that. Maybe they'll come back? Is there anything –' I put my hand on top of hers. 'I'm really sorry,' I say.

She draws me into a bony hug and releases me, patting my arm.

'There – I got it off my chest, and I hope – I hope I haven't ruined your morning, have I?'

I shake my head. 'I'm just so –'

'Off you go to work. We'll say nothing more of it. Best way. Least said, and all that.'

After soaking Mummy's feet, it would be time for the pumice stone. Slow strokes – over, back, over, back. On and on, until the pinkened flesh was revealed and you could clearly see any bumps or corns that lingered. Then you prepared the blade.

Father was pleased at my first operation. I held her foot steady with my left hand. It was flexed upright like a plank of wood and I used the smallest blade, my fingers low and close to the edge, so I could get the angle right. I was like a carpenter – no, more like a sculptor. I planed the blade low and smooth across the sole of her foot. It didn't hurt her. The skin is already dead.

In my line of work, I see people at their worst. Hazard of the job, I suppose. Nothing surprises me because I know – I know that people are capable of anything. 'You'd have to be a monster, to do what he did,' they'll say. 'It's inhuman. Barbaric.'

And I want to remind them that no, it's not inhuman. It is the very essence of humanity, and it could be any one of us. That any one of us is capable of the most appalling, cruel or reckless act if the circumstances dictate. And they should know that pain begets pain.

My mother suffered a stillbirth. She birthed or – rather – miscarried a deceased baby boy two years before I was born. He was almost eight months in utero. She told me all about it, at a time when I was perhaps too young to understand. She described the birth in culinary terms, or maybe I merely thought of it like that. Because when she told me he wasn't ready, I could only think of a sagging sponge cake that was taken from the oven too soon.

'He wasn't finished. And he was too weak to survive,' she said. 'When that happens, the baby comes out with a lot of blood. And it dies.'

Everything became jumbled in my head. The baby boy covered in blood. The exposed flesh. The sharp implements. I imagined Blood Baby – red and slick and shining wet – being prised out of Mummy's body. Fat clumps of blood quivered and glistened like jam on his head and dripped over his grinning face. In that picture, Mummy held the blade. Mummy prised him out of her own belly because he was too weak to live.

But I was completely wrong about that. I found out, as I grew up, that my mother was devastated by the loss of that baby. Because Blood Baby was going to be everything. Everything good and strong and brave and true, with smooth skin and golden hair. He was going to be a prince and she would have loved him. For him, she would have been capable of love.

18

Laura

The daffodils are out in full force, clustered around the stone that marks the entrance to our cul-de-sac. Vying for space and light are bunches of the little purple flowers whose name I can never remember – something that doesn't sound like what they are. It's one of those spring mornings that hold a promise of long days. I have Noah strapped to my front in the sling, so there'll be no battles over the buggy, and I'm holding the hand of my skipping daughter. My shoulder bag contains the tin of traybakes – pretext for our visit. This is the feeling – when it's all coming together – this is what I thought it would be like. This is how it should be.

'Daffodils – see them, Mummy?' Katie stops to examine them like a botanist. 'And the little ones are called crocuses.'

'That's right!' I grin at her, doubly delighted. Why couldn't I remember? 'How did you know that?'

'From school!' She looks at me as if I'm from another planet. 'Treena taught us the flowers, and she says we're going to plant our own seeds so we can grow our own flowers as well.'

We walk along the river, turning at the arch. I can't pass it now without remembering Jenny. That's where they found her. *At least that bastard is in prison*, I tell myself. *You did a good thing.* And last I heard from Megan, the social worker assigned to her case, is that Jenny's doing really well. She's in Transition Year and has apparently been asking Megan if she'll take her for work experience. That's something. Sam would tell me to pay attention to the small victories. Mum would say take your bow when you get the chance. The thought of Mum hits me with a pang of loss that's so sharp – so intense – I can feel it in my chest. Like someone reached in and tore off a long, bloodied stripe of heart tissue.

People die, Laura, I tell myself, disgusted by my inability to move on. *You're not unique there. Parents die before us, and that's the way it's meant to be. She was ill. She died. End of.*

'And that's cherry blossom.' Katie points to the beautiful tree on the corner of Clonchapel Drive. 'And the big, sad ones by the river are weeping willow. Did you know that, Mummy?'

She grabs my face to make me look. The chill of her little hands brings me sharply into the present.

'I did not,' I say, glad to have been distracted. 'Actually, do you know what, Katie?'

'What?'

'You know way more about flowers and trees than I do. You're an expert.'

She's delighted.

'And today I'm helping you, amn't I? We're being you and Niamh, Mummy, aren't we? We're working together?'

'We sure are.'

She squeezes my hand and squares her shoulders, lengthening her stride in a passable imitation of long-legged Niamh.

Beside her, I heft Noah a few inches higher and brace my own shoulders, sticking my chin out. I used to be good at this. I used to be a bloody good detective.

19

Niamh

When I arrive in the unit, McArsey's there ahead of me – of course. He's having a little confab with Cig over by the scanner. They both look at me when I come in. Maybe he's asking not to be on the case – could it have worked that fast? Something is agreed, because they nod before breaking apart. Cig calls us to order.

'Right, everyone. As you know, Mia's parents ID-ed the body last night, formally. They'll be here for a few days. There's a memorial service in Clonchapel tomorrow afternoon and they'll fly the body home for the funeral next week.'

He tilts back on his heels as though rocked by an unseen gale, then forwards. A self-comforting thing, maybe? He may be a cranky git, but I've seen him with Leonie at matches, hugging her and ruffling her hair. He's a big softie. This will be getting to him.

A murmur of sympathy ripples through the room. It's everyone's nightmare, and there's nothing you can say to make it okay. McArsey arrives at my elbow, gives a little priestly bow of greeting.

'Press conference this evening, in time for the six-o'clock news. The Chief Super will be leading it,' says Cig. 'I need hardly tell you that time is of the essence. Seriously, I want officers all over the Dodder and up in Terenure. Follow the route she took with the child. Short cuts. Alleys – there's a river path below the road near the crossroads, isn't there?'

Nobody says anything.

He sighs. Makes eye contact with Senan.

'Detective McCarthy interviewed Mrs Nairn yesterday,' says Cig. Beside me, McArsey does a little ripple of preening. 'Are you going back there today?' He addresses the question to McArsey.

'I'm going down to talk to the child,' I butt in ahead of him. 'Might be able to get something from her – a description of the car, maybe?'

'And I'm –'

But McArsey has missed his moment. Cig continues.

'What do we have from Tech? Anything from the Nairn house?'

Byrne rustles pages.

'We've checked out her laptop – nothing useful has come up so far. Emails from home, from the language school, friends – no substantial leads.'

He looks up.

'If she arranged to meet someone, she didn't do it by email. We've pinged the phone.' McArsey flips a page in his notepad, shaking his head.

'Nearest mast – and last place we can locate it is in Terenure, close to the school.'

'So, she could have switched it off and taken out the SIM card if she didn't want to be found,' says Byrne. 'Or, if she didn't, her abductor could have.'

There's silence as we consider a killer with a plan – not a random act. A killer with a blade capable of severing your spinal cord, who knows about phone triangulation, who wears PPE, who wipes away DNA evidence.

'Right. And I want to extend the search where the child was found,' Cig goes on, checking his notes. 'Wellington Lane. Check cameras on the lane – there must be something.'

'I'm heading down there,' interjects McArsey. 'That's what I was –'

'Good,' says Cig.

'And I'm going to track down some of her friends,' I say, pointing to the photos I've pinned to the board. 'Maybe a boyfriend thing?'

'Right,' he says. 'Start close to home. Makes sense. Off ye go. Darmody – a word?'

Beside me, McArsey stiffens. Is it my imagination, or is he looking guilty?

'Later,' he says, slinking away.

'Look, there's no fancy way of saying this, so here it is,' says Cig when the room is cleared. 'Detective McCarthy has asked – he's brought it to my attention that there have been certain –' He pauses to clear his throat, sticking a chubby finger between his shirt collar and neck as though loosening a noose. I wait, still hoping that McArsey has asked not to be on the case. That'd be some fast work.

'Inappropriate remarks,' Cig continues, delighted to have found a word. He looks at me. 'We don't have time for this, Darmody.'

'What do you mean, Cig? I haven't a clue what you're on about –'

'Inappropriate remarks – innuendo – you know full well what I mean, Darmody. He's saying – alleging – that you're inappropriate with him. Behaving inappropriately.'

'Ah! That's bull – that's ridiculous, Cig! I don't know what you mean, seriously.' I stand there, shaking my head. 'Do ye mean to tell me he thinks I *fancy* him, like?'

Cig starts shuffling pages together, picking them up off the desk and inserting them into a manilla file – clearly embarrassed.

'He said he felt uncomfortable – that was the word he used.'

'Uncomfortable with what?'

'With the level of intimacy – he talked about maintaining professional boundaries.'

'Oh, sweet Jesus!' I splutter. 'Cig –'

He's standing with the file in front of his chest like a shield, feet planted wide apart.

'Inspector McNeil,' I amend, 'with respect, I'd like to assure you that I'm capable of maintaining professional boundaries with Detective McA— McCarthy and that he is safe from my – he's safe with me. You've no idea how safe.'

Cig raises an eyebrow in warning. Am I imagining it or is there a tiny hint of a smile?

'It's possible that – that I was too casual, I'll give him that. You know, banter and – but that's all it was, a bit of banter. Perhaps he – has he asked to transfer to another case?'

Cig's expression clouds over.

'No. He's asked for a different partner on this one. He's asked that you be transferred.'

Shite and shite! That wasn't the plan.

'Cig – oh my God, what? That's ridiculous. Apart from anything else, he's going to need – the case needs an SVI to interview the little girl. That should be me and Shaw! Or me, anyway.'

'Garda Hennessy is available,' he says.

Bloody Edel Hennessy! This is a nightmare. I struggle to hide my mounting panic, although I reckon it's written all over my face. I'm about to lose my rag. Damn it to hell, McArsey! I take a deep breath. Two can play at that game.

'Actually, I'm glad you raised this matter, Inspector. McCarthy is not the only one with an issue here. I – I have felt undermined and belittled by him – yes. And – and –' I take a breath. In for a penny in for a pound –

'And I think this may be motivated by prejudice.'

Cig stares at me.

'Prejudice? What – against people from Tipp?'

In fairness, that's funny, but I'm on a roll and I don't give him the satisfaction of a smile.

'Anti-gay prejudice, Inspector. I am a gay woman. It's not a secret, but it's never arisen as an issue before. Perhaps it's an issue for McCarthy?'

If Cig is surprised, he doesn't show it. He sighs a long, luxurious sigh – the sigh of a man wishing for retirement.

'I need hardly tell you that if it *is* an issue for him –'

Cig stops me with a hand sign.

'I'm glad we had this discussion, Detective. Leave it with me.'

I stand for a moment longer, wondering if now is a good time to ask again about Laura. Cig has turned his back. He's leaning against the desk on splayed fingers, as though the smooth plastic might give him magical powers.

'No,' he says, without turning his head.

20

Laura

Thank goodness for Carly. Rosa Nairn is guarding her front doorstep as though I've come begging. A woman with a baby strapped to her front and a toddler by the hand can be many things but, hopefully, in this situation, not threatening.

'Tatie!' squeals Carly, leaving her position clutching Rosa's leg and tottering forwards to Katie with her arms out. It's sweet. Katie bends her knees as though she's an adult, mimicking her teachers perhaps, and squeezes her into a hug. Carly is still in pyjamas – a frilled pink two-piece with teddies on the front.

I smile the conspiratorial smile of motherhood – or what I hope resembles it – at Rosa.

'Hi, Mrs Nairn. I'm Laura Shaw – our kids are in Tippy Toes together? This is Katie. We brought you some traybakes, thought you might like some company?'

Her face relaxes. She's wearing a soft cream lounging hoody – cashmere, I reckon – with matching soft-woven joggers. On her feet are cream short Uggs. Her haircut – a jaw-skimming bob in a shade of ice blonde – is immaculate. She wears no make-up except for a slick of neutral lipstick and her face has that puffed-up look of someone who has been crying. Or it could be fillers.

For a fleeting moment, I'm grateful to Justy and Dermot for the years of training they've given me. I know how to behave around money, old or new. Rosa herself, though, appears to struggle. She's dwarfed by the giant doorway and the expanse of property rising behind her. It occurs to me that Rosa did not come from this.

'Oh – oh, right.'

She steps back into the hallway. Glass doors separate behind her with a swish. 'Come in, of course. Please excuse the state of us – we're not dressed yet.'

Spotting the shoe container, I kick off my trainers and pop them inside.

'Shoes, Katie,' I say. Katie plonks herself on the floor and opens the Velcro, copying me.

'I apologize for arriving so early,' I say, looking at the oversized station clock on the kitchen wall. It's not even ten. 'It's just Noah was asleep – this is his mid-morning nap time – so if I was going to pop over it had to be now.'

Her eyes drift to the sling, where Noah is still sleeping, mercifully. We perch on the stools at the kitchen island, and the tin of traybakes sits between us – gaudy-looking in shades of blue and red – on the white marble expanse. Katie and Carly have settled themselves kneeling among the toys in the corner of the L-shaped room. A low table is a riotous jumble of pastels and primary colours in the all-white room. Some crayons and sheets of paper are already laid out on the table – good. Maybe Carly was already drawing. I've positioned myself so I can see them, although I long to park myself right beside them and start 'playing'. You learn more in those playing sessions with kids than hours spent in interviews.

'How are you doing?' I say. 'It must be so difficult for you – I hope you don't mind us dropping in like this. Katie missed Carly at school yesterday and we live just a short walk away, down in the gardens. You know the cul-de-sac that backs on to the park? Clonchapel Gardens?'

'Yes.' She nods vaguely. 'I –'

'Opposite the kiosk shop?'

'Of course – lovely,' she says, as though reassuring one of us.

There's a beat of silence.

'So?'

I'm just about to answer that when the doorbell chimes.

'Excuse me.'

'Of course.' I nod, adding a smile. Niamh always says I'm so focused on the information I forget the niceties. As Rosa passes, a waft of Jo Malone washes over me. She's so elegant – the pristine lounging clothes, the hair, the gold glints of watch and bangle at the wrists, the diamond engagement ring. And yet there's something not quite right, something that fails to convince. Rosa Nairn has secrets. Or – I discard that thought – it's not that she has secrets, it's more like she's acting. The whole thing seems like an act – the house, the clothes, the colour scheme. It's like Rosa is worried she doesn't fit in her own life.

Noah stirs against me – I've been sitting still for too long. I stand up and walk over to the girls. If this is a neighbour calling in, I'll have to clear out anyway.

The girls have discarded their dolls and are busy drawing. Katie looks up.

'This is me and you, Muma.' She points to the figures. I can clearly see myself – she's given me a scribble of brown hair with elaborate curls. Must get my hair cut. And she's drawn herself on a swing. She's busy adding flowers all around the edges.

'That's lovely. Is that us at the playground?'

'Yes, and Noah's not there cos it's just you and me at the swings.'

I hear the murmur of voices in the hall. Female.

'And what are you drawing, Carly?' I smile, peering at the

page. Carly has been copying Katie – she's drawn two figures. 'Is that you and your mummy?'

Without looking up, she shakes her head.

'Is that one you?' I say, pointing at the yellow-haired figure.

'Yes.'

The voices are coming closer. I'd better hurry.

'Is that Mia – your minder?' I say. 'I'd love if you could draw Mia for me. Do you think you could?'

She points to the taller figure – in a red dress with large hands that look like flowers.

'Is Mia,' she says.

'Carly, do you think you could draw Mia's friend with the car? Did Mia meet a friend when she picked you up? What does the friend look like?' Immediately the little girl bends towards the page. I feel the thrill of possibility.

Then something shifts and I break off, aware of a sudden stillness in the air.

'I was just – this is Garda –' Rosa's words are drowned by Katie.

'Neeeevee!' she squeals, springing from the floor up into Niamh's arms.

'How are you, chicken?' says Niamh. 'I didn't expect to see you here.' The sentence is laced with meaning. She cocks her head in my direction.

She grins. You take it from here, she's saying. I know that look.

'Sorry – what – what's going on?' says Rosa.

21

Niamh

The day Daddy walked out of Mass I was ten years old. I remember because it had been my birthday the day before and my mind was still blown at the notion that I was now in double figures. We were sitting in a row near the back so, luckily, he didn't have to walk the full gauntlet of the aisle – but people stared all the same. Daddy is a shy man – it must have cost him a fair effort to do it. Especially as Father Stephen had started preaching, so everyone was quiet.

I suppose the real memory of it has been altered by my adult version. I was sitting beside Daddy – he was uncomfortable already; he had been sighing and shifting, like he was confined against his will. He was – is still – a giant of a man. That morning, it was as if he was trapped in a cage – a bear in chains.

The priest began to speak. Daddy sat back. On he went, and Daddy shifted to one side, then the other. He sighed. At the other end of the pew, Mammy leaned forward to look at him, a question in her eyes. He didn't look at her. Father Stephen went on for another few seconds, and I saw Daddy inhale then place both hands on his knees – braced. His fingers were splayed to the edges of his thighs, white discs in the centre of each nail with the pressure. I waited.

Then his fingers crunched into spiders as he pressed hard and rose to his feet. He said nothing. He stood up, turned his back on Father Stephen and walked out. Siobhán was having a heart attack of mortification, her head whisking from Mammy to Daddy and back again. A red flush crept up the sides of Tom's neck and Rory began tugging at my sleeve, whispering, 'Are we going?' Mammy ignored us all, sitting with her hands clasped together in her lap, face tilted, a devoted acolyte of Father Stephen, as though nothing had happened. After a moment, Siobhán did the same.

'That's called voting with your feet,' Daddy said afterwards. 'I didn't agree with what Father Stephen was saying, that's all. And so I voted to leave.'

'But Mammy says —'

'Your Mammy has her own mind.' He smiled. 'And she decided to stay — and that's fine.'

Years later — around the time I came out at home — Daddy told me what Father Stephen had been preaching about.

'It was all about sin,' he said. 'And I've no time for that — all that guff about wickedness and sin, how sin will keep you out of the kingdom of heaven. Pure rubbish. I don't know why it got to me that particular day. Or maybe I do. It was a beautiful sunny morning and I wanted to be out in the field — I'd a fence to repair — instead, I was listening to that little fecker droning on, making us feel bad, and he — ah! Sure, it's long ago now, but I'd just had enough. Enough. My feet decided for me.'

He gave a sheepish grin.

'Your mother's devoted enough for the pair of us — for the whole family,' he said. 'We'll leave it at that.'

He's right too. None of us bother with it now, except Mam and Siobhán, who I think does it for the kids. Siobhán's three made their Communion and all go to the Holy Faith School, where we went. Tom and Nadia were married in a civil ceremony and never darken the door of the church, which he reckons will be handy for when he takes over the farm.

They've Rocco's name down for the Educate Together school in Roscrea. And Rory is too busy, with the hurling and the shop. Sunday mornings see him training or on his way to matches now he's on the county team. In fairness, Dad didn't stay away. He still goes the odd time, just to keep Mam happy. But that day, I learned what voting with your feet meant.

Now, it seems Laura has voted with her feet — she's back at work. And I'm pure delighted. I set Katie down and she runs over to get her picture to show me. Laura stands there with Noah strapped to her chest, one arm curved underneath him for support. He must weigh a ton. Why did she not bring the buggy? She's standing in front of Carly, who is intent on her own picture, as though trying to obscure our view. I know that stance. She's playing for time.

'I was just about to show you.' She fumbles in the pocket of her jeans and brings out her ID. 'I mean, what I was just literally about to tell you, Rosa — I mean, Mrs Nairn — is that as well as being a mum from the school and your neighbour — the fact is — I mean —'

She pauses for a second, pressing her lips together as if trying to moisten them, and is about to continue when Katie interrupts.

'Mummy is a garda,' she says, carrying on with her picture, not looking at us. 'And so is Niamh. Niamh, I'm putting you here in my picture too. You can be on the slide in the playground.'

'I was literally just about to tell you, Rosa,' says Laura. 'Honestly.' She pushes her hair back behind her ears and straightens up, trying to look more professional. Rosa's face is a stretched canvas.

'Well, you might have —'

Shit, this is blowing up in our faces. She glares from Laura to me and back again, her mouth a scrape of displeasure.

'You're not who you said you were,' she says, stepping back so that she's behind the gleaming marble breakfast bar. She places her hands on the back of one of the tall chairs, knuckles tightening around steel.

'I thought you were another mum, a friendly face from the crèche. That's why I let you in. You lied. Where I come from, we call that lying.'

Her chin tilts – defiant. 'I think you should leave.'

22

Laura

'Mrs Nairn – Rosa –' I jiggle Noah up and down to stop the grizzling.

'I've done nothing wrong – we – I've done everything the guards have asked. I was interviewed yesterday, was I not?' Rosa spears me with the same glare she's giving Niamh.

'Why treat me like I'm an idiot? Or worse, a criminal?'

She inhales deeply and seems to decide something. 'You could have simply arranged a visit, instead – what is this? Are these even your children, or is it all part of the act?'

'I –'

'You should leave,' she repeats.

Noah starts wailing. Katie clamps her hands over her ears and runs back to the play corner. Carly copies her, shrieking.

Niamh steps into the breach, ramping up the Tipp.

'Ah here!' she guffaws. 'Of course they're her children. Christ! Plainclothes don't go as far as hiring kiddies for props!'

Rosa remains defiant.

'I don't – it's – it doesn't change anything. Why – why would you appear on my doorstep with your children? And – you brought traybakes for goodness' sake!'

I'm drenched with sweat, suddenly, as though I've been plugged into the mains. I'm trying to shrug myself out of the sling without dropping Noah. He's still roaring.

'Sorry, can I just –'

In desperation, I lift Noah upwards, the sling still clinging to both of us. His foot is tangled in the folds and it's still tied around my neck. Bloody hippie sling. I should have got the one with the plastic clasps.

I don't know how it happens – perhaps once you've had a child you're forever programmed to respond to the crying, but next thing, Rosa steps forward and takes hold of Noah, lifting him out of the sling and on to her front, where she holds him with one arm, peeling away the fabric that's hooked around his little foot. The surprise of being held by someone new works like magic – he stops crying.

'Thank you,' I say simply. 'I – I'm so sorry –'

I stop. Niamh is signalling something. And then I feel it – the let-down. Initiated by the crying, my boobs have decided to give up the goods. Flowers of sodden fabric bloom across my chest. I'd chosen a pale blue shirt this morning in an attempt at smartness. It's not a good colour for breastfeeding. I look down. Drenched in milk, it appears black.

Something clicks in Rosa. Or maybe it's between the three of us women.

'The bathroom is in the hall,' says Rosa, stepping aside to show me the way. 'If you want to take off your wet things, I'll get you something – I have something that will fit. I'll go get it?'

'Thanks.'

I'm mortified. But not in a position to waste any time. Milk is still throbbing its way out of both breasts.

'Will he be okay with me?' says Rosa, inclining her head towards Noah, who is peering over her shoulder. 'I'll just nip into the laundry room.'

'I – yes – thanks.'

She puts him on to one hip and hurries out of the room.

'Fair play to you,' breathes Niamh as I scurry to the bathroom. 'Good move!' She grins.

'Yeah,' I say, returning the grin. 'I planned that.'

There's no further talk of kicking us out. In a few minutes, Niamh and I are sitting on the Nairns' sofa, me wearing a plain linen shirt of Rosa's, soft and freshly laundered, while Noah feeds. It seems a truce has been called. Rosa has made tea, set out the traybakes and poured cold drinks for the girls. Before she sits down, she fills a glass with chilled water and hands it to me.

'It makes you really thirsty,' she says, nodding at Noah feeding. 'Doesn't it?'

I don't get a chance to reply. Carly has scrambled to her feet and is thrusting her finished picture at her mum.

'I drew Mia,' she says. 'An' me.'

Rosa takes the picture without really looking.

'That's lovely, darling.'

Katie joins us – not surprising, as all the action is now centred around the coffee table. She stands behind Carly, studying her long, baby-blonde hair. A hand reaches out to touch it meditatively.

'I want long hair, Muma,' she says. 'Why can't I have long hair too?'

But I'm not listening. I've spotted something in the picture.

'Can I see it, Carly?' I say, holding out my hand. 'I'd love to see it.'

She takes it back from her mother, scrunching the corner in her grasp, and thrusts it towards me, her eyes focused on Noah.

She frowns.

'What's it doing?'

I barely register the question because I'm studying the

picture. Carly has drawn two figures which I'm guessing are herself and Mia and a blobby shape with smaller blobs underneath it. It could be – yes – it is. She's drawn a car.

I'm dimly aware of Katie speaking.

'That's my baby brother, and he's having his feed.'

The girls study Noah sucking and swallowing, a feeding blister rising on his top lip. I tilt the picture so Niamh can see it.

'What?' says Rosa, anxiety in her tone. 'What is it?'

'Who are these people?' I say to Carly, keeping my tone light and even. 'You've drawn them very well.'

She doesn't turn her head, still fascinated at the sight of Noah feeding.

'Carly?'

'That's me, and that's Mia,' she says crossly.

'And this thing – what's this?' I say, holding the picture so Carly can see my finger on the blob shape.

'Daddy car,' she says.

23

Niamh

'Tell me more about this,' she says.

And we're off. Tell. Explain. Describe. She's in full clarification meeting mode.

'Who's this again?'

Carly sighs with exasperation, sounding not unlike her mammy. Laura's pissing her off.

'That Mia!' she says, pointing to the taller figure. She's drawn Mia's hands like flowers — a central circle with smaller circles attached representing fingers. Hands are important to children — adult hands lift, hold, give food, stroke foreheads, rub sore tummies — or slap, squeeze, restrain. They're the interface of action between adult and child. It makes sense that children notice them too because they're at a child's eye level whereas the face is floating somewhere up in space. I think someone wrote a paper once, suggesting that abused children draw adults with bigger hands. Or am I inventing that?

'Great,' says Laura. 'Is that her long hair?'

Carly nods.

'Like mine,' she says. 'A princess.'

'I like her red dress.'

'That a skirt,' she corrects sharply.

'What's going on?' Rosa's tone is anxious. Laura ignores her. She's in the zone. With kids this young, you only have seconds before they're off, and you lose the moment.

'And this is you?'

Carly points to the top corner of the page. She's drawn a small figure surrounded by green slashes of colour.

'This is you?' Laura repeats. Carly nods.

Laura points to the big oval shape in the centre of the picture.

'And what's this? I've forgotten – silly me!' smiles Laura, adding a head shake. Carly responds with a giggle, enjoying the fact that only she can decode her picture.

'What did you say this is?'

'Daddy car,' says Carly.

'I see. And you've drawn Daddy's car in this grey colour – is Daddy's car grey? Were you and Mia in Daddy's car?'

Carly considers the question, then discards it. She reaches out to touch Noah's head.

Laura doesn't even notice.

'Did Mia go in Daddy's car?' says Laura softly. 'Yesterday – after Mia picked you up from school? Did you go in Daddy's car?'

Rosa is not one bit happy. The emotional temperature has plummeted. I'd thought there was a mammy bond going on between the pair of them and that we were home and dry, but this has changed everything. Or maybe it's the look on Laura's face – hungry and intense. She's strategizing. She hasn't even noticed that Noah's fallen asleep and stopped feeding. So, she's sitting there with her left boob half exposed.

That's a shocking sight. Not the sight of a breastfeeding boob, but this is Laura. Laura of the immaculate wardrobe – the smart little jackets and suit trousers. Laura of the sharp bob, the neat shoes – everything about her is tidy, organized and neat. She'd been bundled up in her coat yesterday, so I hadn't seen her properly but now I realize how far she is still from her usual self – her work self. I thought she was back – but now I'm not sure.

Rosa stands up, snatches the picture from Laura's grasp and places it on top of the fridge, as though confiscating it from her.

'Thank you for the traybake,' she says.

She turns to Carly. 'Say goodbye and thank you, Carly.'

'Thank you.'

'Now you run upstairs and start getting dressed. We're very behind. I'll be up in two minutes.'

Carly makes no move to go.

'Mrs Nairn, we need to talk to Carly,' I say, trying to sound reasonable. 'It's just –'

Rosa turns her body so she's angled towards the door. Piss off out of here, she's saying. There's a panicked look, a little flicker – a widening or something behind the pupils. It reminds me of a startled horse. Laura tries again.

'Was it Daddy who gave you a lift yesterday?'

'Enough!' snaps Rosa, her face closed down. 'This is ridiculous. I've indulged it long enough and' – she stiffens, as though finding her mojo – 'I'm not an idiot. I know you're – this is highly irregular. I could report you both!'

'Mrs Nairn, you're right. Of course you're right.' I smile, still hoping to win her round. Laura only needs another couple of minutes – we're so close. 'But if you could just –'

I get to my feet, one hand up as though I'm calming a frightened mare. Laura has just noticed the boob. She flushes and starts fumbling with the shirt buttons.

'How about I finish chatting to Carly now, while Katie and Laura gather up their stuff. Come on, Katie,' I say. 'You help your mammy, okay? Go and get your stuff.'

I give Laura the nod and she takes the cue. My turn.

'Carly,' I start, 'after playschool yesterday, did – who gave you a lift in their car?'

But the moment is well and truly gone. Carly is chasing after Katie.

'Carly!' Rosa's tone is shrill. 'Go to your room at once!'

It's Katie who freezes first.

Rosa inhales a deliberate and long breath.

'Sorry, darling,' she breathes out. 'Mummy is very busy. I've to meet with Mia's parents later,' she says, directing the second part of the sentence at us, 'and you can imagine how stressful that is going to be. This interview – or *whatever* it was – is over.'

She motions her two hands in a wave, moving us towards the hallway, ushering us out. Laura takes the sling and moves as if to start loading Noah into it.

'We'll go in the car,' I say.

'Do you have baby seats?' says Katie. 'All children *have* to sit in their special seats when they're in the car,' she chants, mimicking an adult tone. 'And they have to be good.'

Shit.

'I'll sort something,' I say. 'Come on, chicken.'

In fairness to Rosa, she doesn't beat about the bush. We're on the doorstep when she calls it.

'If I am to be questioned again, I'd appreciate the courtesy of a phone call and an appointment. I will come into the station. I don't want you in my home again.'

'Thank you for your help, Mrs Nairn,' I say, desperate to keep it professional. If she reports this – the questioning from Laura when she's not even officially back – we're stuffed. But Laura has the bit between her teeth.

'We need to talk to Carly,' she says. 'Properly. What she said about the picture, the car she drew –'

'Oh, for goodness' sake!' Rosa's tone is scathing. 'Carly thinks every car is her daddy's! Or mine. She's not even three yet. If you ask a three-year-old to draw a car, what do you expect? And anyway' – she folds her arms across her stomach in a protective gesture – 'like I told you, Tom works every bloody minute of every bloody day! He's never home. He'll have been in court yesterday – on that case. Or don't you read the papers? Why don't you check the court listings first, instead of tormenting my child?'

She stares at us from the extra foot of height the doorstep gives her, framed in that giant doorway, bracketed by granite and landscaped garden. She's putting us right back in our boxes.

'And, you may be assured, I know my rights. I know a fair bit about the law, actually. So how about this? How about you go and find whoever did this? Do your jobs. How about that?'

Rosa Nairn turns on her heel and walks back into the house, still clasping her elbows to her stomach. The door closes with an expensive-sounding click.

We talk Katie into getting into the car without car seats 'just this one time and never ever ever again'. The drive to Laura's house takes less than three minutes, during which we fall into our routine.

'I'll make the call now – straight away,' she says. I can't hide the smirk. She elbows me. 'Anything to shut you up.'

'Good to have you back, pardner,' I say, shoving her.

'Can you –'

'Court listings? On it.' I nod towards my phone, ready to search. 'The case opened on Tuesday, I think.'

'Great.' She nods.

Outside the front door, I hand over the changing bag while Laura manhandles Noah on to her hip. Katie hangs out of her leg trying to get the key into the lock. Jaysus.

'Well?'

'I'll make the call now, I swear,' she says.

'Class!' I grin, hugging her with one arm. 'Good to have you back, Detective.'

My parents had very little time for me. My mother, in particular, was always busy, or distracted, or on her way out the door. Any interaction I had with her was, it occurs to me now, entirely on her terms and usually performing a service for her. If I wanted to be near her — and I did — I knew I would have to be silent — so quiet that she wouldn't know I was even there.

And so, I learned stealth. I learned how to disappear. I learned that it is to my advantage to be underestimated. This works in both my professional and my private life. People drop their guard when they are unthreatened.

I wasn't a normal little boy. I remember Miss Sullivan — kind, smiling Miss Sullivan, my teacher when I was in infant school. I couldn't have been more than six. I remember her watching me as I studied the box of hatching eggs that lived under the heat lamp in the corner of our classroom. She knelt on the floor beside me so that both our faces were level with the edge of the container. She was so close I could see her freckles and smell her lovely smell of sugar and biscuits. 'We'd never do anything to hurt the chicks, would we?' she said. 'We never hurt a living thing.' And I remember wondering how she had looked inside my head and seen me crunching the eggs one by one, my fingers slick with yellow beaks and feathers.

Miss Sullivan always wanted me to play with the others and run around with them and talk. She wanted me to share, and that meant letting them — the other children — touch my things. She wanted me to hold hands when we made a circle and that meant letting them touch me. She got angry if I pinched or hit anyone. She got scared when I pinched myself. I wished, many times, that Miss Sullivan could be my mother, though I hated myself for the treacherous thought.

Slowly, however, I learned how to fit in. I read a lot, a quiet pastime that pleased my parents equally, although the story world I entered was anything but quiet. The stories I loved featured two brothers, Hal and Roger. Hal was the older one. I looked them up the other day — you can still get them. The whole boxed set on Amazon for less than twenty euro. But I didn't click. It wouldn't be the same.

Hal and his little brother got a year off school so they could help their father capture animals for his collection of rare species. There were rescues from man-eating lions, scuba-dives to collect specimens from an undersea city; there were gorillas and snakes, panthers and exotic birds. How my blood raced! How I longed for adventure and risk and thrill. And a brother — more than anything, I longed for a brother.

I thought a lot about Blood Baby. If Blood Baby had lived, he would be older than me, and we would fight, as brothers do — but with no malice. He would be my friend and adviser. He — he would explain — no — I knew that wasn't true. I knew that my mother defied explanation. I knew from the other boys in school. I'd been in Geoff's home once, watched as his mother rummaged in the cupboards to find crisps and biscuits for us. She was small and pretty — on her way to work; I can't remember at what — and she flung our snacks on the table in the exact same way she tipped dry food into the dog bowl. Then she ruffled Geoff's hair and dashed out the door. 'Be good,' she said, grinning.

I've seen mothers at the side of rugby pitches — I didn't play, but I supported the team — I've seen them in cars at the gate, waiting to pick up after school. None of them were like mine. If I had a brother — Hal — if Hal was my brother, he would be my witness and my best friend. I felt as though there was no one to witness my life and I had no friends. Mummy made sure of that.

But, if there had been two of us, it would all have been so different. Two boys getting into mischief, playing, climbing trees and kicking a ball around. Me and my big brother — Hal. Hal would have made her take notice.

24

Niamh

Five o'clock, and I'm in the biggest conference room in Seskin County Hall. Feeney is briefing the press. Flanked by a sorrowful Cig on one side and the grim-looking Murtagh on the other, we're left in no doubt as to how seriously they're taking this crime. The front three rows are taken up by press and, hidden at the back, maybe at their own request, are Mia's parents, Renata and Alfonso Ruiz. Christ! The sight of them would crack your heart. Renata stares at Chief Superintendent Feeney dry-eyed, her back ruler straight as though willpower alone is what's keeping her upright. Her husband is crumpled against her side, clutching her arm at the elbow with both his hands, as if they'd linked arms but now he can't let go. Conversation stops as the three take their seats. Feeney launches straight in.

'Mia Ruiz was nineteen years old. She'd been in Ireland since last September, attending a language school in the city and working as an au pair.'

Feeney looks up from the typed page in front of her, squaring her shoulders for the rest. There's a chorus of clicking camera shutters. Feeney is one of only a handful of female Chief Supers. Maybe it's the glass ceiling, or maybe it's the long journey, but women in the top ranks are still like fricking hens' teeth. Her hair is cut severely, greying at the temples, and she wears the uniform like a suit of armour. I see she's taken to wearing glasses – round and silver-framed – giving her an owl-like look. Not so much the fluffy wise owl, more the nocturnal hunter. Feeney's a woman who doesn't tolerate bullshit, who wouldn't hesitate to take down one of her own. My last run-in with her was all too recent for my liking, when she questioned me about Laura's role in the Cullen case. I think she knew way more than she let on – but somebody was on our side. Laura was cleared of any wrongdoing.

I do a quick scan of the room – no sign of McArsey. Maybe I've got rid of him. And anyway, Laura's back. Soon it'll be just us – back to normal.

My eyes rove over the assorted crowd – the good people of South Dublin. I spot a group of five tearful girls – whispering and crying, tissues clutched to their faces. They must be from the language school. There's a young guy – he's maybe nineteen or twenty – dressed in a navy coat and a pair of mustard chinos. The guy in the photos, definitely. He's groomed and gym-buffed, with a sweep of blond hair that's cut to look messy. He's two rows behind the students – that's weird. Why is he not with them? They all looked pretty cosy in the photos.

'Mia went missing from the Clonchapel area on Wednesday afternoon, on her way home from picking up the child – a two-year-old girl – in her care,' Feeney continues. 'Their route home would have brought them along Terenure Road towards the bridge then left for Clonchapel Drive. This would have been approximately between 12.30 and 12.45 p.m. It was raining. A witness has told us that Mia may have accepted a lift from a person driving a silver or grey car. We don't know who this is or the route taken. But the child was found – unharmed – near Wellington Lane at around 1 p.m.'

There are murmurs and whispers as people digest the information.

'Gardaí in Clonchapel were alerted and were able to find where the child lives and bring her home.'

With a look towards Renata Ruiz, the Chief Super carries on.

'But Mia never returned home. Early on Thursday morning, the body of a young woman was found on rough ground on the Featherbed, near the Military Road. Gardaí were alerted and the scene was sealed off for forensic examination. The body was found to be that of Mia Ruiz and a postmortem was carried out by the state pathologist, Dr Parminter. Following the findings of the post-mortem, a murder investigation has been launched. We extend our deepest sympathies to Mia's parents and the wider family on the loss of their daughter, sister and friend. A family liaison officer has been appointed to assist them at this time.'

She presses her lips together, jaw set for a fight.

'An Garda Síochána is determined to bring whoever is responsible for this shocking crime to justice. Mia was a bright young woman – still in her teens – who came to this country to learn a language and widen her experience of the world. For this to happen is an outrage. Her parents have lost a loving daughter, her siblings have lost their beloved sister and Mia's life has been stolen from her.'

Her gaze rakes the room, roving along the lines of reporters and friends. She ignores the clicks of cameras.

'We would like anyone with information to come forward. Were you in the vicinity of Terenure or Clonchapel on Wednesday last at the time in question? Did you see Mia and the little girl? Did you see a silver or grey car pulling in? Did you notice anyone getting into a car?'

At this point the photograph of Mia appears on the screen behind them and it tears me up, the knowledge that this photograph – smiling, gentle Mia – will be the latest addition to the big, bloody book of murdered girls and women, trapped in time, skewered like butterflies on steely pins. Their innocent smiles – why are they always smiling? – the tragedy of those smiles and of us, looking at them. Knowing what we know and they don't. Yet.

'Mia was wearing a red skirt and a black, hip-length jacket. Some time later, the child was put out of the car on Wellington Lane. Are you a resident of Wellington Lane? Did you notice anything suspicious? Mia's phone was last used in Clonchapel, and we will be conducting searches across the area and in Terenure. We ask that the public cooperate and come forward with any information.

'Likewise, if you were in the vicinity of the Featherbed or the Military Road in the early hours of Thursday morning, please contact Gardaí at Seskin West Garda Station or Clonchapel.'

She raises her head, removes her reading glasses and places them on the papers in front of her. Then she rests her forearms neatly on the table, one lying on top of the other. She spots me standing near the back and makes the smallest nod of recognition. I respond with the same. Her eyes seek Renata Ruiz, and she directs her closing remarks directly to her.

'The Gardaí are determined to find whoever committed this shocking crime and to bring them to justice. Our full resources will be brought to the case.'

The room erupts into whirrs, clicks and questions.

'Is it true that your chief witness is a two-year-old girl – the child Mia was minding?'

'Was the child harmed in any way?'

'Do the Gardaí believe that this could be connected to the attempted abduction of Julie Widera last year in Oldbawn?'

The reporter who asked that is a young woman – she's

maybe in her late twenties – with a dark complexion and braided hair. The badge around her neck reads '*Seskin Echo*: PRESS.' I don't recall seeing her before. I spot Cig lean in towards Feeney and whisper something. Feeney nods and gathers up her papers.

'I have no further comments at this time,' she says, getting to her feet. Cig and the Super do the same. They're out the door in seconds, to a soundtrack of camera clicks.

25

Laura

I'm outside Tippy Toes crèche and Montessori, waiting to talk to Joanne. If I'm going back, Katie will have to do two full days to allow Sylvia – our childminder – to work around Noah's naptimes. I just hope Joanne has room for her. The evening pick-up is different. People come and go – on their way home from work. I see only two au pairs, whispering urgently in Spanish, and various parents and grandparents take turns to buzz the intercom and call out their child's name. I spot a granny and a guy who could be an older dad or a young grandad, at the side of the building. There's no sign of any Lululemon yoga gear, no tennis whites. I check my phone: it's 6.35 p.m. Behind me, a sigh. Irritation? Sympathy? I turn, readying a comment, something like, *It's all go, isn't it?* Or *There's not enough hours in the day*, something bland yet accepting. This is our life – ha-ha. There's another world of despair, grime, cruelty, greed, poverty, in the dark, deep slime at the bottom where no one is wondering if they've got enough green veg for the kids' dinner or trading phone numbers of party entertainers – but the woman hadn't intended it for me at all. She's messaging someone.

I hate when I'm like this. *Judgey bitch*. It's not their fault they live on the surface and, maybe, Laura – did you ever think that maybe some of them are like you, but they've chosen to live in the bright water? Maybe they work hard at it – and you don't have the monopoly on the dark side, I tell myself.

Because it's all okay, nobody can see the churning inside and, like I said, you don't have the monopoly on hidden pain. Put it behind you and be grateful. Get back to work and get your shit together.

These are the post-work collections. A curly-haired woman who must be the mother of Katie's little pal Ava – the curls give it away – stands just ahead of me. Both she and her son, a boy of about ten or eleven in his football kit, are on their phones. She seems to be wrapping up a work call.

'Cool. Cool,' she says, her eyes raking over me without seeing. 'Tell him – yah – cool. I'll call him first thing, tell him. Cool.'

She hangs up and focuses her gaze on mine, giving a tiny shrug of complicity – a sort of 'What can you do?' shrug. I smile back, just a second or two late, envying her sharp business suit. I'm still in the grubby parka.

The woman nods, her dark curls bobbing, then turns aside, telling the boy to put his phone away. The grandad or older dad smiles at her in approval, does a little eye-roll, as if despairing of the younger generation. She matches the gesture, as he intended, and it occurs to me, idly, how easy it is to bond with people over children. Older dad is smartly dressed too and I feel even more tatty by comparison. Something about him reminds me of Matt's dad – maybe it's the old-school men's shoes, polished to a brilliant gleam. The boy pockets his phone obediently and leans into his mum.

'Good lad,' says the older dad.

This earns an open smile from the mum.

Note to self, I think. Smile more. Smile wider. Jackie's right. We're all in this together.

The door opens and the line begins to move as people collect their various charges from the entrance of the crèche. One au pair collects twin boys and the other a very young baby – it can't be more than six months old. Seeing that, an even younger baby spending the entire day in the crèche, pares away a shaving of mother guilt. Like I'm pleased there's a worse mother than me. That's not how I think, really – it isn't.

And yet, somewhere inside me, the judgey bitch thinks exactly that. I sigh.

Older dad stands aside to let the curly-haired woman and her son go ahead, and she lifts Ava on to her hip, mouthing a thank you. They make their way to the car park and she smiles in passing.

'Not enough hours in the day, hey?'

'It's all go,' I reply.

26

Niamh

If you want to catch a killer, study the victim – that's one of Laura's pearls. *You've got to get the victimology right, or you haven't a hope.* Another reason I want Laura back is her psychology background. She knows her stuff – she did Psychology in Trinity before switching to train as a guard. When I arrived in the unit first, I thought we'd be doing psychological profiling and in-depth analysis of personality types – the hardened criminals, drug lords and gang members, the murderers. We'd get to know them, see what makes them tick, study the wiring of their particular DNA until we got to know them like family. Is it a misfit loner we're looking for or a charming sociopath? Is it the guy whose brother was gunned down in front of his three children or the one with the mansion in Mallorca? What motivates them, and how do we catch them? And, in fairness, all of this is important. But that's not where we start – not in a case like this. Laura says start with the victim.

'Tell me about Mia,' I say to the group of language students. 'Did you know her well?'

I direct the question to them all but particularly to the one whose eyes are swollen from crying. I introduce myself.

'I'm Detective Garda Niamh Darmody. I'm investigating Mia's murder.'

The girl swallows. Sniffs.

'I'm Gloria,' she says. Then, still clutching a damp tissue, she sweeps her dark hair off her face, leaving a moist trail on her cheek. I rummage in my bag and hand her a clean one.

'Thank you.' She attempts a watery smile. I gesture towards a cluster of armchairs around a low table. 'Could we – have you five minutes to talk to me about Mia?'

They murmur agreement, and I get their names, seating myself closest to Gloria, who seems to have known Mia best. Two girls are huddled at the end, one with short hair and glasses and the other in a brown leather jacket who looks like she can't be more than sixteen.

'Did Mia like it here? Did she like the work – the college?' I ask.

Gloria's English is good, and she's the first to answer. The short girl, who introduces herself as Tina, translates for the other girl. The consensus is that Mia loved Ireland and she loved Carly. She was looking forward to going home in the summer to take up her place in college.

'What course, do you know? What was she going to study?'

'Bioinformatics,' says Gloria, a question in her voice. Tina nods in agreement.

'Is – it's a mix of science, biology and, you know – computer science. She – Mia's very smart,' says Gloria. A fresh wave of tears washes over her.

'I'm sorry,' I say. 'I don't mean to upset you. This is – it's very helpful, what you're telling me. I need to know what Mia was like, who she was friends with, what her hobbies were – that type of thing. Can you think of any reason she would have got into a car with someone? Did she have any friends – a friend, maybe – anyone who had a car?' A heated burst of chatter blurts from the other two.

'What?' I say. 'Do you know anything – anything about the car? Or a friend with a car?'

Gloria turns back to me.

'They're saying she would never get into a car with a stranger.'

'Nev-er,' parrots the girl in the leather jacket. 'We all know this from when we are babies.'

I nod.

'But it was raining heavily –'

'Even if it is raining, she know this.'

'Okay,' I say, thinking aloud. 'So, you're all in agreement that Mia must have known whoever was driving the car?' There's a chorus of yeses.

'What if someone tricked her? Maybe they told her that Mrs Nairn was in hospital or something – they could pretend to be a neighbour?' I wait for this to be translated.

'Even if this is what the person say, even still, Mia would not get in the car. She would call the mother?'

'She'd call Carly's mother?'

She looks at the others, shoulders shrugged into a question mark. They agree.

'Right, thank you,' I say. 'This is good to know. And did she have any hobbies? Did she go to a gym? Was she a member of any clubs or anything?'

Tina's expression suggests that's the most stupid question she's ever heard, but Gloria narrows her eyes, remembering something.

'There is a tennis club – it's cheap if you play early. It's in the park.'

'Bushy Park?'

She nods.

'I don't think she plays now, but when she first came she played before she bring Carly to school.'

'Okay, and who did she play with? Did she have lessons?'

'There's a guy – they just played,' Gloria says, shaking her head. 'I think his name was –'

She pauses, looking at her friend, says something in Spanish. Tina also shakes her head.

'Sorry,' says Gloria. 'Can't remember.'

I jot down 'Tennis/Bushy P/early mornings' then turn a new page.

'Okay, thanks. I'll check that out. But, one last question, was there anyone special in Mia's life here? A friend? Maybe a boyfriend?'

A look passes between Gloria and Tina. I can't work it out exactly. It's as though they're deciding something. I wait. Sometimes it's best to say absolutely nothing and just wait. Tina speaks first.

'His name is Marcus. He – he was here.' She points towards the conference room we've just left.

'The guy with the –' I mime the fringe over the eyes sported by the boy in the mustard trousers. They nod.

'He's her boyfriend?'

'No, not now. He was,' says Gloria. 'Before Christmas.'

'I see.' I make a note. 'Marcus?'

'Harding –' says Gloria, trailing off.

'So, he's called Marcus Harding?'

'He has two names – double –'

'Double-barrelled?'

She nods. 'I think it's Blake – Harding-Blake.'

'Thanks. And Mia went out with Marcus before Christmas, yes?'

'Almost straight away,' says Gloria. 'Marcus' – she stops as Tina buts in, 'Marcus goes with every girl, when they first arrive. He always moves in, he –'

'We told her he does this,' says Gloria. 'I've already been here six months when Mia arrived and I – we both told her not to go with him, but –' She shrugs. I recall my impression of Marcus – he's a good-looking guy.

'So, Mia and Marcus dated for a few months and – who broke it off? Who ended the relationship?'

'Mia did,' says Gloria. She leans forward and makes a move as though to pull me aside.

'He cheated on her with Abril,' she whispers, eyeing the girl in the brown leather jacket.

'This girl is Abril?' I incline my head towards the girl; she knows we're talking about her. 'And Mia found out?' I whisper back, thinking I've landed up in some weird teenage soap opera.

'I told her' – Gloria is defiant – 'and then she break up with him. It was not Abril's fault – it's him. He lies.'

I'm nodding wearily. Yes.

'And is Marcus in your college? How long has he been here?'

'Marcus lives here,' says Gloria. 'He's Irish. He's in college but he works part-time in the bar we go to in town. He's always there.'

Tina nods in agreement. 'Looking for new girls,' she says, a look of disgust on her face. Yes, I think. I know the type.

'What's the name of the bar?'

Tina answers for them, 'The Caged Bird.'

'Right.' I know it. Near Essex Street. My phone buzzes. That might be Laura. 'Thanks, girls,' I say, handing Gloria my card. 'Ring me if you remember anything else, okay?'

Sitting in the car, I check my phone. It wasn't Laura. It was a long lovey-dovey text from Amber. I fire off some hearts, then send a text to Laura. She'll have had time to ring the Super by now. This will work – it has to. She's dying to come back. It's written all over her face.

There's a boyfriend. See you tomorrow morning? Room 3

She doesn't reply, but that doesn't matter. She's back.

I check the courts services website for the listing of Nairn's case, just to be sure, although I know the case is up and running. There it is – the listing for Wednesday last: 'Sitting at the Criminal Courts of Justice, Parkgate Street, Dublin 8, before The Hon. Ms Justice Catherine Parker in Court 9 CCJ at 11 a.m. DPP v WJ in Court 5.'

That's that then. All we have is a two-year-old's picture of Daddy's car. Bugger all. I reckon the boyfriend is more likely. Definitely.

I scroll through the other messages and missed calls. There's one from the mortuary, with a voicemail.

'Hey, Detective, this is Ella from the state mortuary. Dr Parminter asked me to give you a call – you asked about the hair? Whether it was professionally cut. Anyway, the answer is no. It was a hack job if ever I saw one. You couldn't really tell at first, what with the gel and everything. We brushed it out. Thanks for the photograph – I did my best to re-create her look.'

She pauses, and there's the sound of rustling paper.

'Anyway, you can call me back if you need more info. I'm in tomorrow from half eight. Oh, and the lipstick was a nightmare to clean off. Heavy-duty brand, I'm guessing – almost like stage make-up. Hope this helps.'

27

Laura

The moment Niamh left I rang the Super and told him I was coming back and that I'd decided not to extend my leave into a career break. I had to – to cover the unscheduled visit to Rosa. And for all of about ten minutes, I was euphoric. It all knitted together. Joanne has plenty of room in Tippy Toes for Katie to do the full day, and then Sylvia screamed – actually, squealed – in delight to hear she was being offered her old job back. She was ready to come down straight away, but I told her Monday was fine. Decision made.

I ransacked the wardrobe upstairs, spreading out my work clothes across our bed. Katie watched as I tried on one, two – four pairs of trousers before giving in and putting on the maternity pair I'd worn from months five to seven. I got a jacket on, not the nice grey short one but the black linen. It was tight at the biceps and across the chest, but I could wear it open.

'You don't look like a princess,' said Katie doubtfully.

'Princesses aren't all they're cracked up to be,' I said, thinking I was giving her a life lesson. 'Little girls shouldn't just want to be princesses,' I went on. 'They should want to be – I don't know – doctors and lawyers, or scientists and inventors.'

'Or teachers?'

'Or teachers, yes, and guards –'

'Like you an' Niamh.'

'Yes. Or, they can be whatever they want to be, Katie – dancers, teachers, captains of ships, astronauts – anything.'

She picks up a bracelet from the china dish of dust-covered jewellery on the table near the mirror, putting it on her arm and drawing it all the way up to her shoulder.

'Or they can just be mummies.'

I'd sighed then. Will this ever be over?

'No mummy is ever just a mummy, Katie. They – we – we all have things we used to do and things we need to do. And things we will go back to. Like work.'

'And that's why you're going back and I'm having Sylvia?'

I remove the black jacket and put it on the hanger for tomorrow.

'Exactly.'

Yeah. Less than two hours later, Matt and I were bickering.

'If it's all arranged, then why are we even having this discussion?'

Matt sits at the end of the kitchen table, a selection of empty breast-milk pouches, containers, rings and teats of different sizes spread out in front of him. He looks at them unseeingly, waiting for my response.

'I just think – I think it will be better for all of us, if I go back. I – I can't do this.' I wave at the paraphernalia on the table, the pile of ironing spread over two kitchen chairs, the toys crammed in the cubby between the fridge and the door. 'I can't be this perfect mother!'

'You're a great mother,' he says, tiredly. 'And you *can*. You know I want what you want – what's best for you, don't you? I only – the only reason I was pushing the career break was because I thought it would be less stressful. I –'

He gets to his feet and comes towards me. I'm sitting with my boobs out, trying to fit the suction cup from the breast pump over my right nipple. The sight of my flesh, the blue veins and dark nipples, fills me with loathing.

'I feel like a fucking heifer!' I snap, pulling the suction cup away. 'And I can't do this either!'

He takes the cup from me and sets it down on the table, then comes to stand behind me, placing one hand on my shoulder, kneading a knot of muscle. With the knuckles of his other hand he traces a gentle line from my jaw, down the side of my neck and over my collarbone, down and down, across the swell of my right breast. His fingers stroke the red weal left by the suction cup.

'Ssh,' he whispers. 'It's all going to be all right.'

More than anything, I long to rest my head back against him and close my eyes. But I don't.

'It's not all right, Matt. You just don't know what it's like.'

Some nights he doesn't get home till after eight, not even getting to see the kids. Earlier this evening, he'd arrived to find them both in bed – Noah actually in his own cot – and me unpacking the breast pump. We'd high-fived.

'Go, Muma!' he'd said, grinning. 'You're smashing it.'

Before he could start planning the holiday which would kick off my career break, I'd broken the news. How quickly it all unravelled.

'Laura, I'm trying to help,' he says. 'But I don't know what you want. And it looks to me like you don't either.'

'I want to be – I want to do a good job,' I say. 'I want to be back in my job, doing it well – is that so much to ask? But I want to be – I want to be a good mum too, and I need you to –' I sigh and start afresh. 'I want to do something right – Jesus! Either wife or mother or garda or friend – one of them.'

The tears start welling up. He edges one foot out the door – Matt hates the tears.

'Clearly, I'm not helping,' he says, his voice resigned. 'I'll be on the bike – call me – look, you know where I am if you need me.'

'But are you okay with this?' I say. 'With me going back? I mean –'

'I don't know why you're asking me this.' He sighs. 'You were always going to go back, Laura. You're the only one who didn't know that.'

Very occasionally, my mother deigned to notice me. As soon as I was tall enough to partner her, she taught me to dance. She had rekindled her love affair with ballroom dancing and begun attending classes in a local parish hall, and she bought me a smart black suit and showed me the ballroom hold. Now, on treatment days, with Father watching from the gallery, I danced with her. Under my fingers, I could feel her softness and, beneath that, the curved bones of her ribs. She pulled me close — close enough to breathe in her scent — and I felt her breasts against me. I sometimes remembered the worm and the flower, and the strange feeling rose within me — thick and ugly like the blind worm. Then Mummy's fingers would squeeze mine sharply and she'd arch away from me, head turned as though posing for an unseen photographer. She didn't seem to realize that my arms were her cradle and that, if I wanted to, I could just let go and watch her crumple to the floor.

I wondered if Father was rocking.

Cancer ate away at Father for most of my fifth year in secondary school. He shrank and shrank, even as I grew bigger and bigger — taller and broader than both of them. He refused the oral chemotherapy offered for his glioblastoma and turned his pale face towards the approaching end. One evening, less than a month after his diagnosis, they arrived home, Mummy carrying a little case filled to the brim with medication — the end-of-life care pack.

We nursed him, but he went downhill very quickly. He lost the ability to swallow, or move, the sight in one eye and, finally, the ability to speak. Mummy filled syringes with morphine, and it was my job to turn him over — an easy task, like preparing a turkey for the oven — and then inject the drug. It's intramuscular. You need to take your time and keep your hand steady. I varied the injection sites. I kept my hand steady. I did a good job.

One week after his funeral, on Sunday morning, I brought Mummy her breakfast tray. She was deeply asleep, lying on her side so the rise of her shoulder and hips formed a 'V' shape under the blankets. The strap of her nightie had slipped and her breast lay like a fat teardrop against the crook of her elbow. A stripe of grey hair gleamed along her parting and her nail varnish was chipped and worn. A festering smell hung in the room – ripe and heavy, with a tang of rotting seaweed and old medicines.

'Time for your treatment, Mummy.'

If she was surprised, she made no mention of it.

Dancing nights, competition nights – they were the best. She needed me. Up the stairs we went, Mummy leaning against me, unsteady in her heels, her head on my shoulder, the hair brittle with dried gel. I brought her to the bathroom and helped her find her toothbrush, which I'd laid out, all ready for her with toothpaste on. While she brushed her teeth, I unzipped her dress and helped her step out of it, hanging it carefully on the hanger on the back of the door. Mummy's dresses cost hundreds; they couldn't be discarded on the floor.

While she used the toilet I waited outside like the perfect gentleman, her tray of medicines at the ready. A glass of water. Two paracetamol for her head. And 20ml in the measuring cup. I made sure I had everything I needed.

She was getting sleepy and leaned against me, still in her underwear and high heels. I escorted her to her bed – the way a ballroom dancer escorts his lady to the dance floor – and eased her on to the sheets. My breath became shallow. Soon. Sssh.

'Sleep well, Mummy,' I said, taking her shoes off. As each shoe was removed, she sighed a little, murmured something. 'Let me rub your tired feet.' I sat on the bed, lifted them into my lap. Her eyes were closed, and her breathing steady. Slower and slower.

'Ssh,' I said, stroking her feet, my thumbs pressing deep into the arches, pressing myself against her, shifting, squeezing. 'Ssh.'

When she was deeply asleep, I still had work to do. I brushed out her hair with the soft silver brush. I wiped her body with the washcloth that had sat in a bowl of hot, lavender-scented water, waiting. Competition nights are tough work and sometimes it took three or more wipes to get rid of the smell of sweat. I thought of Father, then, and the battle he had waged against the vagaries of the female body.

I once — one time — I came so close to removing her underwear. I had hooked my fingers around the elastic at the top, and I tugged, driven by a compulsion I couldn't resist. I'll just make her comfortable, I told myself. And then she ruined it. Through her sleep, with her eyes closed and without speaking, she made plain what she wanted. She shifted her hips towards my hand — helping.

I let go as though I'd been burned. That's not how it works. The man is in charge.

The classic ballroom hold is called the Closed Hold. Man and Lady stand facing each other, Lady slightly to the right of centre of Man, light contact between them. Man's left arm is raised so the elbow is slightly lower than the shoulder, bent sharply and sloping upwards and slightly forwards. Lady places the fingers of her right hand between the thumb and first finger of Man's left hand. Man's fingers then close loosely over the side of Lady's right hand. Lady's left arm is placed comfortably on Man's right arm with her left hand resting lightly on Man's right arm, just below the shoulder.

It doesn't say anything there about Lady pushing her hips against Man.

28

Niamh

'I was only trying to be nice,' says Amber, stirring her drink with the little glass stick. She looks up at me through dark lashes, working the cute factor. 'Actually ' – she draws out the *ah* so it sounds like *aaaaah*ctually – 'Aaaahctually, I was covering for you, if you remember. I did all that for you. So Dorothy wouldn't be disappointed about the baking.'

It's after ten and we're in the trendy tapas place down the road from the apartment. Her friends are due any minute. If I hadn't observed her getting-ready routine over the past few months, I'd be fooled into thinking Amber was casually dressed. She's wearing a little black strappy vest with cream cords and a chunky pair of boots. There's a short jacket slung over the back of the barstool – we're at a tall table around which are clustered five stools. The jacket is glossy, lined with a bright, satiny fabric. Huge, square earrings dangle from her earlobes, mostly hidden in the swathes of blonde hair. Just a T-shirt and jeans – preceded by tan, blow dry and no-make-up make-up.

A tiny sigh escapes me, but it's a sigh of relief, or pleasure or something. Amber looks good and she's in good form and pleased with me. She nudges against me with a little rippling movement, her bare shoulder against mine.

'"Thank you, Amber," is what you say.' She plucks the lime from her glass with her dainty fingers – I forgot that: add an extra ten minutes' prep for the nails. Beads of liquid sparkle on her varnished fingernails and her fingertips squeeze together around the fruit as she sucks the lime juice and alcohol combined.

'Nyummy.'

She leans her head on my shoulder, not even needing to look at me to know the effect she's having.

'"Thank you, Amber, for saving my ass with Dorothy, and for –"'

'Thank you, Amber,' I parrot – tucking away the memory of Dorothy's lined and sorrowful face this morning. I looked it up. You can buy actual nest boxes for swallows in the hardware stores. I'm going to get her some. It will be okay.

It's all going to be okay, I realize. Laura is back. McArsey's gone. It's all gonna be grand.

'And for?' says Amber, straightening up.

'For being the finest, most beautiful little bitch in the whole world – will that do?'

She tilts her head, considering.

'And you love me,' she says.

'Absolutely.'

'And your mom and dad, they're going to love me too?'

I know better than to hesitate – I'm getting good at this.

'They'll *adore* you,' I croon. 'How could they not?'

I picture her – us – at home. I can just about manage it – picture her – in the sitting room on the good couch or leaning back against the dresser in the kitchen with a mug of coffee in her hand. She'll entertain them. I know she will.

It's when I try to imagine her walking around the yard or up in the fields – nah, I just can't see it. It's like she's assembled in the wrong colours or something – Amber's palette is all squeaky-clean gleaming pastels, whites, pinks. I just can't see her against the backdrop of greys and greens, the brown stubble, the stone walls. But it's happening. Mam rang me last week, said she's making up the twin room. That's a big step for Mammy. And I appreciated it – I do still.

'And you're going to be nice to my friends – don't make them feel like – don't do your whole garda thing and make them feel bad –'

'Of course,' I say. 'I'll be on my best behaviour. I won't arrest anyone.'

She sighs happily.

'I've booked us in for a dance workshop next Sunday. Seven till nine.' She giggles. 'We can leave after that, can't we? So, we're there for the whole day Monday.'

'I –' Shit! Did she mention this? I'm racking my brains.

'You're giving it to me for my birthday – it's a surprise.'

'Dance? Ah, here now –'

'You do remember it's my birthday next week?' Her brows leap towards each other in a scowl.

'Of course!' I lie.

'Well, I know you won't have had time to get me anything, and I want – you know I have to be able to do basic ballroom for my job – for work?'

'Ballroom?'

'Yes.' She's shaking her head at me, tapping the stirrer in her drink in time with the shake. 'Yes-es-es. Actors need to be – I could be in a period drama or something – and I need basic tuition. I thought it'd be fun to do together?'

A coy tilt of the head announces the clincher.

'And if we ever got married' – she giggles cutely – 'we'd be able to, you know, waltz around. We'd be so fab!'

I know when I've been outplayed.

'Sunday.' I nod. 'Great!'

The friends arrive a little high already. Or maybe that's just actors – they function on a different plane. Siún I recognize from a long-running drama on RTÉ – she plays the twelve-year-old daughter of a drug lord; and she looks about twelve herself. She's a tiny scrap with scruffy blonde hair, cropped short.

'Don't you have to have it long for the show?' I say, remembering a two-foot blonde ponytail.

'Hair extensions,' she says. 'And the ponytail is clip-on.' The others, Lucas, a Brazilian bartender, and Polly, are also actors. Or maybe dancers – or maybe all three. Lucas is about twenty-four and the most beautiful boy-man I've ever seen. Polly is the quietest of the three; she's from New York. It crosses my mind to wonder why Amber has no friends from school that she sees – or from home. Is the distance too great?

The talk is ninety miles an hour, there's squealing and in-jokes about courses attended and horrible vocal coaches, adverts and auditions, voiceovers for government information campaigns, dance and theatre workshops. The drink flows. They do shots. I stop drinking after my third – there's no way I can have a skinful and be on the case early tomorrow. I feel another burst of excitement. Laura's back – so we can get to it and find this bastard.

I spoke to Denny this evening, before I left the unit. He was grey after the extended session with Mia's parents. After the press conference, he'd brought them back to their hotel, the soulless red-brick just off the motorway. And earlier they'd had the meeting at the house. We discussed how it had gone, how Rosa Nairn was with them.

'They're still kind of out of it with shock,' Denny had said. 'They sort of shuffled around that giant mansion. Himself wasn't there, of course. But Mrs Nairn, she did her best. The girl's bedroom was sad – she'd filled an entire wardrobe with photos from home, her ma and da and brothers. Jesus wept. When they saw that they kind of fell apart. Even Mrs Nairn.'

I order a Ballygowan and another round for the children. Not going to think about that now. Tomorrow we're back on it, and we – me and Laura – we are going to find him. We have to.

A cheer goes up at the sight of the tray of drinks. I settle in, give them a few Tipp stories, stuff from 'back home' and the farm. I steer clear of work.

'I love your accent,' says Polly. 'And the way you say *"in fearness"* – is that a play on the word "fear"?'

'In *fair*-ness!' Amber squeals. 'Ask her to say "anyway".'

'What's wrong with how I say *"annie*way"?' I play along.

They roar laughing. Amber smacks her palms together like a child. I'm clearly a hit.

The night unfurls in a mash-up of voices, clinking glasses, laughter, the clatter of plates being set down and cleared away, the happy faces of people who don't have to look at dead girls' feet. Stop it. Even though I'm now sober, I'm swept along in the tide. Amber's having fun. Her friends like me. All is good.

They tell each other about work, the highs and lows of selling yourself. Amber sits back, setting her drink down with deliberation. There's a little settling of her shoulders, an intake of breath as though puffing herself up in readiness. She's been looking forward to telling them this, I realize. If it all goes to plan, Amber will star in the next big TV drama. She thrusts her palms into the centre of the group, halting the conversation. Her fingers spread wide as though miming, *Wait for it*.

'And guess what?' she breathes softly – such a consummate actress is not going to shout this.

'What?' whispers Lucas.

'I did a pilot!'

In the moment's silence that follows – before they start

congratulating her and asking for details – I do a *fear* amount of damage.

'That's something you might want to keep to yourself, love?'

She never gets the crowd back.

'You couldn't let me have one moment, could you?' she says, her voice flat and slightly slurred. She's standing at the mirror taking off her make-up, forcing the flesh of her face into strange contortions, pressing and pushing as though at war with herself. She throws the used cleansing pad in the bin and grabs another. 'You know what's wrong with you –'

I wait, inhaling a deep breath. I deserve this.

'At least I'm honest about myself – at least I know and admit I like attention, that I want people to like me. But you –'

She bins the pad and begins patting moisturizer around her eyes with dainty fingers, peering at her reflection, searching for flaws.

'You – with you it's all "Oh don't mind me sure, amn't I just a lovely garda, salt of the earth, begorrah!" When all along . . .' Her voice trails off. I remind myself she's pissed and angry and hurt.

'I'm sorry,' I say. 'You're right. I'm sorry.'

She comes into the bedroom in her little silky pyjama shorts, weaving unsteadily through the furniture towards the bed.

'You're – I thought you were different,' she finishes, drawing back the duvet and folding herself into a little package of hurt. 'But you're just the same.'

I move to hug her, but she twists further into her awkward pretzel.

'I'm sorry. I was only – I was just messing, Amber. I swear.'

I lie awake for another hour, listening to her soft breaths. The digital clock reads 03:20 when I remember that she's going to wake dying of thirst, so I get up and fill a pint glass with water and place it by her on the chest. I don't do a lot of self-analysis. It's a load of shite – all that picking at yourself, scab by scab – it's like taking apart a knitted jumper. Pull a thread here, remove a dropped stitch there until – until you're left with nothing. I thought I was just being funny. I thought I wanted Amber's friends to like me for her sake – not mine. I was socializing when what I really wanted to do was work on the case – there's loads of stuff I could have been doing. I could have been getting an early night. Or I could have spent the evening with Dorothy making the bloody biscuits and making up for Amber hosing the bloody baby swallows. I was doing something nice for her. Wasn't I?

Saturday

29

Laura

I arrive at the unit before eight and check in with Sarge – Declan – who'd surprised me by posting a card and really cute baby gift a couple of weeks after I had Noah. Always chirpy, with a boyish look even though he must be well into his forties, he's a difficult one to read and he keeps his home life quiet. It was a Dublin jersey – I wonder did he choose it himself? He did well on the sizing, twelve to eighteen months, so Noah has time to grow into it.

'So, the rumours are true!' He laughs. 'How're ya doing, Shaw? I thought you're not on till Monday, though?'

'What can I say?' I laugh too. 'I'm keen to get out of the house.'

Before we can exchange any further chat, I hear Cig's voice in the hallway behind me.

'A minute, Shaw?'

He jerks his head towards his office, and I follow him in.

'Close the door.'

I close it, swallowing down my nerves. You never take your welcome for granted with Cig.

'I – was on my way into you, Cig. I got the go-ahead from Occi Health –'

He raises a hand to stop me and motions for me to sit. Towering piles of paper, files and photos lean against each other in various stages of messiness on his desk. Behind it, his private life is arranged in out-of-date, crooked framed photos. Him and Linda somewhere sunny and historic – Rome, maybe – long before they had Leonie, and when Cig had a full head of ginger-toned hair. One of Leonie's christening, I'm guessing – she's in a long robe and they're outside a church. One of Cig and a group of three other men I don't recognize, at a rugby match, clutching pints. I reckon I'm looking at more than thirty years of service.

'I don't give a toss about that,' he says. 'You could tell them anything.'

'I know – and I –'

Once again, he holds up his hand. Then he picks up a plastic pocket from one of the teetering piles and shuffles the photographs out of it on to the desk in front of him face downwards so I can't see them. He rests the fingers of one hand lightly on top, tapping them meditatively.

'Another body's been found,' he says, eyeballing me. 'Another one – for Christ's sake! And it looks like it could be the same guy and so –' He raises his shoulders, then releases them with a huge sigh. 'Yeah. We need all hands on deck for this one. We could do with your input.'

I'm nodding, waiting for the chance to speak. I can do this. I know what we have to do. But his dark eyebrows are knitted together in a look that stops me butting in.

'But – and this is a bloody big but, Shaw – if you're not up to this – and don't start with that jabbering about how well you are and how many courses you've done and whatnot – you can't bullshit me, Shaw. I know you. I've *known* you since you were a wet week out of Templemore and, trust me, I know a bullshitter when I see one. And you forget that I have a kid and a wife and a life outside, so I do know what it's like to try to balance the two.'

He pulls out his own chair and sits, resting his chin in his hands as he studies me, creases of sagging skin draping themselves between his fingers. He looks desperately tired.

'If you're not up to this, then you have no right to be here. And you're only jeopardizing everyone else.'

He glares at me, his eyebags crosshatched in thin purple lines, like a grid. 'You are bloody sharp. That can't be denied. You have a way of unpicking things. And your interviews – they can't be faulted. When you're on form, Laura' – there's an echo of a smile – 'no one can touch you. But you cocked up mightily on the Cullen case.'

'I don't deny that, Cig.'

'And there's no shame – seriously – there's no shame at all if you want to get out of the unit. If you want to transfer to the OPIU, I'll back you all the way.'

'The OPIU?' I parrot idiotically.

I'd heard all about the OPIU, of course. The unit is based in Harcourt Street. They investigate organized crime linked to the sex trade. But – what the hell?

'I don't want to transfer,' I say, deciding on simplicity. 'I want to come back and do my job. Catch this guy.' I nod towards the photos under his fingertips.

He tilts his head, his grey eyes catching the light from the window behind him. They're watery, like the eyes of an old man.

'I wasn't going to say this – but sure – yeah.' A pause in which I shuffle a hundred things he might not want to tell me: I've been reported, or there's a complaint against me, or I've done something awful. He continues, 'If I had people in high places watching out for me, ready to give me a hand up the ladder, well now, I might just take it.' He blinks.

What the – I haven't a notion what he's talking about. From my expression, that must be obvious.

'If I had people backing me – people who are high up in legal circles, say, and if they – well, if they were friendly with other people who are high up in Garda circles, then I might be inclined to take a little sidestep. With people looking out for you, it's only a hop and a skip to the top. No one would judge you, Shaw, if you –'

I can't believe what I'm hearing. Except, of course, I can. This will be Justy. Justina Thompson, senior partner in Stonehouse, Flynn, Mortimer – top law firm. Top mother-in-law. She's not interfering – not in the clichéd interfering mother-in-law way you hear about – she'll be helping. Like one of those snowplough parents, clearing the obstacles ahead. She means well. But to think that she – she must have spoken to – Christ! I think she's friendly with the bloody Chief Commissioner, Mary Wallace. They're on some committee together.

I am mortified to think of her discussing me, and of it filtering down, down – through the Assistant Commissioner, to the Chief Super and the Super, and now to Cig. I feel a flush of embarrassment, or anger, gather on my chest and I'm glad of the buttoned-up shirt.

It's my turn to interrupt.

'Anything like that is going on without my knowledge,' I say, 'and without my consent. Cig, I'm back here, ready to do my job. Can we –' I nod at the photos, staring him down.

The angle of his head shifts barely a degree, and he blinks a slow blink – like a blessing.

'Right,' he says, his words slow and emphatic, still pressing the photos on to the desk face down. 'You're back – and I'm glad to have you.'

He turns over the first photograph.

'Hope you didn't eat breakfast.'

The rest of the team are in by the time I make it to the incident room. There's a friendly chorus of *Welcome back! Did the dole not work out for you? Could you not get a transfer, then?*

Detective McCarthy stops in my path, his hand extended. We shake – it's a firm but clammy experience – and he bends towards my right ear.

'Never got a chance to say this earlier,' he says, 'but congratulations on the birth.' He avoids Niamh's eye and slides away.

'What did you do to him?' I whisper when he's out of earshot.

'That would be telling,' she says, a smirk nestling at the corners of her mouth.

A loud 'Right!' calls us all to order as Cig comes in. He clicks on the screen.

Enlarged on the TV monitor in the incident room, the photos look even worse. There's a murmuring and a few expletives as the first appears onscreen.

'Female, young – between twenty and thirty – discovered partially buried about half a kilometre further along the trail where Mia was found,' says Cig, turning so his body blocks the lower half of hers.

'So, he dug a grave for this one?' Beside me, Niamh is taking notes.

'Seems so,' says Cig, 'and the lower half of her body was protected from the elements. But here' – he turns and points to a badly decomposed knob of flesh – 'the shoulder, her face.'

I've seen this photo, and I don't need a second look. I watch the revulsion ripple through the room. You need a strong stomach for this job.

'Either he didn't finish and he left her upper body exposed, or maybe he misjudged the size of the grave, the depth he'd need.' Cig pauses, his face expectant, waiting for input.

'Or he was disturbed?' This from McCarthy. 'Or the wildlife got digging.'

'Yeah, or he just got tired. If it is the same guy, he's strong. This one was a good bit further along the trail,' says Cig. 'Dooley, want to fill us in?'

St Bernard – Bernard Dooley, the dog handler – shifts in his chair, checking his notes. 'Yeah, Solo found her at 9.32 yesterday evening, not far from the first body. Obviously, this is an earlier victim – couple of months ago. To be confirmed when Dr Parminter checks her out. The marks you see there' – he nods towards the scrape marks on the ground around the shoulder and head of the victim – 'that's not Solo's digging – something else discovered her. Foxes, badgers – whatever. They've been helping themselves.'

'Fair play, St Bernard,' says Niamh. 'That's a great find – well done, Solo.' She turns to Cig.

'Have we an ID?'

Cig shakes his head.

'We have not. Dr Parminter is doing the PM today. We'll know more after that. I want Missing Persons checked – you know the drill.'

'On it,' says McCarthy.

Cig passes his hand over his face like he's hoping to reveal a fresh one underneath.

'Well, I want some answers appearing soon,' he says, frowning. 'Because this is shaping up to be a shitshow of the highest order. Two bodies – and no leads.'

'And we should look for any links with the girl from Bray last year. Caroline?' I say. Cig nods slowly.

'And I'll check out that attempted abduction in Oldbawn.' Niamh flicks a page in her notebook. 'Guy tried to stuff her into the boot of his car.'

'Christ. We've a guy on a bloody killing spree,' says Byrne.

'Technically, it's not a spree if the killings are spread out over a longer period,' says McCarthy. 'It's a series – so we're looking for a serial killer ...' His voice trails off into the silence.

We wait for Cig to blow, but he dials it down. It strikes me that McCarthy is well thought of on the team. It's only Niamh who's taken against him.

'Interesting, Detective McCarthy, thank you.'

He clicks off the monitor.

'Have we anything – anyone else in the frame for Mia?'

'There's a boyfriend to look into – and a tennis coach.' Niamh looks up from her notebook. 'I'm going to check the tennis coach. Her friend mentioned him. Apparently, when she first arrived, Mia played early mornings – in Bushy Park.' She shrugs.

'Tough job – but someone's got to do it,' Dooley sniggers. 'Checking out the tennis coach,' he adds, in case no one got the joke. McCarthy frowns at him.

'Right.' Cig interrupts before it can go further. 'And now the fun part – the Super wants Nairn brought in.'

'As in, arrested?' I can't hide my shock. 'On the strength of the child's drawing? We can't seriously use the drawing. It –'

He gives a little *tsk* of irritation.

'No, not arrested. Interviewed under caution, helping with enquiries – you know the drill. Every line of enquiry must be followed, every avenue explored, and Nairn is not exempt. There's no reason why we should go any easier on him because of who he is.'

'That's for bloody sure,' mutters Bernard.

I nod, but I'm none the wiser. This is so heavy-handed – and premature. And even I'd be the first to admit that Carly's picture is not evidence of anything. Besides which, Cig clearly hasn't heard about the case.

'Also, he's in the middle of a case,' I add. 'He was in court on the day of Mia's murder. His case was running in the CCJ. Niamh – Detective Darmody – checked the listings.' I turn to Niamh, who nods.

'Right. Interesting. Well, that might change things. All I know is there's no love lost between Murtagh and Nairn, I can tell you,' says Cig. 'Nairn – he's good at what he does, and –'

'Wouldn't trust him as far as I could throw him,' Larry interrupts, 'and just because it's listed doesn't mean he was actually there.'

'Yeah, it seems like the Super is in agreement with you, Larry,' says Cig. 'Let's say he wants to flex a bit of muscle. Darmody, talk to the tennis coach. Get the boyfriend in. And Nairn. Make sure he comes in. Shaw, welcome back. You'll be interviewing.'

30

Laura

'I see you've been honing your driving skills on the school run.' Niamh grins, grasping the edge of her seat with one hand and the overhead handle with the other.

'It's not me – that's a sharp bend,' I protest, although I ease off the accelerator coming out of the turn where Killiney Hill Road joins the Vico Road. We're on our way to talk to Marcus but, finding ourselves flanked on our right by the silver ribbon of Killiney Bay glinting through the greenery and by ancient deciduous trees and shrubs rising up like sentries – guardians of the good life – on our left, there's more of a feeling of a day trip – like we're on holiday in Italy or somewhere. This is a million miles from the grey grime of Seskin West DDU.

'Jaysus,' Niamh breathes.

'I know,' I say. 'What a place to live.'

She doesn't reply. Sunlight strobes through the canopy overhead, as though teasing us with the promise of more, and then suddenly we emerge from the partial shade into full sunlight. Shards of silver shimmering on chill blue water, everything blue and green and golden. We pass some parked cars and a pair of elderly women sitting on a viewing bench overlooking the sea.

This doesn't feel like work. I feel a guilty lurch of joy – no kids for a whole day. No wheedling, cajoling, distracting, mopping, wiping, feeding. And no time to obsess over stuff

I've no control of. I slow down and pull in outside the house, the satnav telling us we've arrived at our destination. On our right.

'Look at you.' Niamh laughs. 'It's like escape from Alcatraz!'

The house. It's built into the slope, so that almost every room has a view of the sea. The entrance is unassuming; stone pillars flank a short gravel driveway leading down to the main building.

'Mammy's probably swimming?' she says. 'Or walking the Labrador?'

'I think you'll find it's *Mummy*.'

She rolls her eyes. We crunch our way across the gravel and stand looking up at the house – the large porch, the balcony that sweeps across the front and around the side to make the most of the sea views and, below us, terraces and what looks like a tennis court. We wait almost a minute after ringing the bell and, just as I'm about to press it again, the door is opened by a tall, dark-haired woman in her early fifties. She's wearing jeans and a knitted jumper. Hand-knit linen-cashmere mix, I'm thinking. Behind her, I glimpse a black-and-white-checked hallway filled with light and, beyond, a room with chintz curtains, white woodwork. The hall is dominated by a big circular table on which sits a massive vase of flowers and greenery, fronds trailing across the polished wood.

Mummy is not walking the Labrador. And Mummy is not impressed at the thought of Marcus being interviewed.

'This is not an arrest,' Niamh assures her. 'We'd simply like Marcus to assist us with our enquiries. He can come in with us – we'll conduct the interview at the station.'

'Is this about the girl?' Her face is drawn. 'Dreadful. But, all the same –'

Marcus appears behind her, clearly having just got out of bed. He's wearing a hoody, jeans and bare feet. He looks younger than in the photos I've seen.

Mummy turns to him.

'They want you to go to the station for an interview,' she says. 'Answer some questions.'

'What? Oh, yes, right,' he stammers. 'I'll – I'll just get my shoes and stuff.' He disappears behind the door. We're still on the doorstep.

'Should I be there? I – I don't know –'

'You can come if you want,' I say, 'but you won't be able to be in the room with him. You can wait, of course.'

Something seems to occur to her.

'Does he need a solicitor? I mean, should I be contacting our lawyer?'

'He's entitled to have a solicitor present,' I say, my tone colder than intended. Niamh takes pity on her.

'We just want to talk to him,' she says. 'Find out a bit about his relationship with Mia.'

There's a stiffening in her face.

'I wasn't aware he had one,' she says. 'Now, if you don't mind waiting outside.' She goes to close the door. 'He'll be out in two minutes, and we'll follow you. Thank you.' We're dismissed.

A few minutes later, I turn off the Vico Road, heading back towards Dalkey Castle, deliberately keeping my speed down so that Mummy can follow in her Lexus Hybrid. Niamh jerks her thumb towards a terrace of Victorian villas – last batch of opulence on this amazing road.

'Amber's parents live there – well, her mam – mum – whatever.'

I turn to catch a look at her. She looks sheepish.

'Really?' I turn back to concentrate on the road ahead.

'You never said that before. Have you met them? Have you been in the house?'

She shifts in her seat, sighing.

'God, no! It's – it's –' She pauses, turning to look back at the sea. 'I don't know. The whole thing with Amber – it's complicated. We're – we're from different worlds.'

'Well, yeah. If you're telling me Amber lives here, or grew up here, it sure is a different world.'

That explains a few things, I think. I've only met Amber once – we couldn't do a christening for Noah because of the restrictions, but they dropped around with a present one Saturday afternoon a couple of months after I had him, and I – I feel guilty even admitting it to myself, but I didn't much like her.

'It's more than that. It's – I've never been with anyone like her,' Niamh is saying. 'Ever. She's so – it's like she's this precious, delicate, rare – I don't know – she's like this glittering piece of crystal or something. And I'm so lucky to have her – and –' She sighs again, shaking her head. 'Ah God, this sounds pure stupid, and I know you'll think I'm thick – but when I'm with her, it's like I'm being really careful all the time, every moment – I want everything to be right for her.'

Wow. I'm careful to say nothing for a couple of seconds. What do I know? One short meeting on the doorstep. High-maintenance was my first impression. The highlights, nails, brows, tan – everything about her looked like it took time and cost money. Even her teeth – white and even, straighter than you'd believe possible. I know her type, though. I've faced girls like her on the hockey pitch, sat beside them in lectures. Backed by generations of money, property and privilege. At the time, I kicked myself for being judgey. If she's right by Niamh, then she's right by me, I told myself. But all the same, in the short conversation, she didn't endear herself to me. Her eyes skidded over Noah and me to the hallway behind, then across the small yard at the front of our house, like she was appraising the property. And she made Niamh wait in the car while she fixed something on her sunglasses, then got in the passenger seat as though it was a taxi. She's young, was what I thought. And spoiled.

In the end, I just do some uh-huh-ing.

'Yeah,' I say. 'I know what you mean. But –' I stop, annoyed with myself. Now is not the time.

'What?'

Niamh's tone is defensive. 'Go on – you can't leave it at "but".'

I hesitate. There's a beat.

'Nothing – I just mean that it's a bit like with the kids sometimes. Sorry, I don't mean Amber's a kid,' I amend hastily, seeing her expression.

'It's just that, you know, sometimes I've seen this with Matt, that the more he tries to please Katie, the more he does to keep her happy and – I mean, it's not just him, I'm sure I do it myself – but I've noticed that the more he does for her, the more she demands. I'm not saying Amber is like that, I'm just saying –'

There's a silence that stretches on and I concentrate on merging on to the M50, waiting.

'If she makes you happy, Niamh, she's good enough for me.'

She doesn't reply.

31

Laura

For the first time in almost a year I'm facing someone across the desk in an interview room. Marcus has recovered some of his swagger. It's as if, having left Mummy in the hallway a barefoot boy, he came back downstairs girded for battle. The hoody has been replaced by a shirt – button-down, open-necked – with a jaunty but not too garish stripe, a casual jacket in a heavy cotton, navy chino-type trousers and lace-up shoes. Smart young doctor about town is the vibe. A young man with nothing to hide.

Interview Room 3 is the smallest of the rooms at the unit. It's basically a Portakabin tacked on to the main building. There's no view outside beyond the white slice of sky visible along the line of windows set at ceiling height. A bit claustrophobia-inducing. There's only space for the large table; a couple of chairs and the recording equipment are set against the back wall.

My heart is battering in my chest in a way it hasn't since – since the last interview with Jenny and the showdown that followed. At the same time, I can feel this energy like a – a flame, burning through my body. I'm nervous. But yes, I'm psyched.

He stands when we enter, the model of a well-mannered young man, and we take our places. Niamh will do the notes and recording. I study his body language as we go through the procedure, identifying ourselves and noting the date and time of interview. He's nodding, his hands cupping his spread knees as if at any moment he might spring to his feet to perform a task we require. Everything about him speaks of the desire to be believed, to be liked – he's helping us with our enquiries, his pose says. And nothing is too much trouble.

A tremor at the ankle, his foot jigging ferociously up and down, up and down, is the only tell of his fear. It stops at the caution.

'You are not obliged to say anything unless you wish to do so, but anything you say will be taken down in writing and may be given in evidence.'

We remind him that he's entitled to have a solicitor present. He waves away the notion.

'I've done nothing wrong,' he says. 'Why would I need a solicitor?'

Spoken by a young man with generations of privilege behind him, I think. The words of a boy who probably has pints with his trainee solicitor or doctor friends or spends a day fishing with some lawyer pal of Daddy's – or Mummy's. There's a push/pull going on in my brain. I look at him – so young, so educated, so confident of his place in the world – and I feel like slapping him. At the same time, I realize that everything he has – the confidence, the bravura, and yes, even the sense of entitlement, is what I want for my two. I look at him and think this could be Katie, or Noah, in a few years.

I get started.

He's happy enough for the first few minutes. I lull him along, trying to establish a rhythm where I ask and he replies – the lobbing of tennis balls over a net.

Yes, he knew Mia quite well. Yes, they were close friends, not exactly a couple, but they dated for a few months, yes. He pushes back the unruly fringe – earnest.

'Look, it wasn't serious,' he says, sitting forward. 'I mean, I know where you're going with this –'

'I see,' I reply. 'And where am I going with this?'

'You're going to ask how long we were together and who broke it off, and you're going to wonder if I'm – you know – a seething mass of resentment because she finished it –'

I give him a little smile, as though impressed.

'And are you?'

He bats that away with an eye-roll.

'Mia finished it, as you say. Tell me about that – about when Mia broke it off.'

He shrugs his shoulders, palms up.

'I reckon the others – they probably put her up to it. I don't think she'd have ended it herself,' he muses.

'Who are "the others" and why would they put Mia up to it?'

'The girls in her class – Gloria and the group – they – well, they told her about Abril and, yeah, I'd say they sat her down and told her not to tolerate, eh . . .' He trails off, suddenly seeming less sure of himself.

'Don't stop,' I tell him. 'Give me the fast-forward version, like you did earlier.' I soften the words with another smile.

'Yeah, well, I'm not proud of it but, yeah, I cheated on Mia. Just once. I hooked up with Abril. It was nothing. Like, there was drink and a party and –'

He sits back, shaking his head. And I think, there it is, like a neon sign above him: *A guy at the mercy of his passions. Couldn't help himself.*

I feel it stir – the grub that I've buried deep. It feeds on anger. I breathe a cleansing breath. It settles. The silence continues.

'So, Abril meant nothing?' I say.

'Yeah – no – I'm not saying Abril meant nothing. It's – I mean, what we – the fact that we slept together meant nothing.' He looks at me. 'You're twisting my words. You're making me sound like a dick.'

I don't reply. He decides to try again.

'I slept with someone else. It was a mistake. It meant nothing to her and nothing to me. We'd agreed to – we were both going to keep it secret, but somehow Gloria found out and told Mia. I didn't get a chance to explain myself to Mia. She ended it. End of.'

'I see. Thank you. And how did Mia end the relationship?'

'We met up in Bushy Park. It's where we used to go sometimes.'

'Where in the park did you meet? Actually inside, or did you meet on the road outside and walk in together?'

I'm thinking of the car park and the new bridge which brings you to the lower part of the park – the woods, beloved by generations of Clonchapel and Rathfarnham teens with nowhere to go. There's a ruined summerhouse, still with shells stuck into the old plaster, where we used to hang out. Same illicit goings-on.

'We met at the bridge. It's where we always met. And before you're, like, imagining us smoking weed and necking cans in the woods, give me a little credit, will you?' He looks pained.

'I'm twenty. Mia's – Mia was nineteen. We went for a walk around the duck pond. Sat on a bench, and she ended it. It was very civilized.'

It matters so much to him what people think, I'm beginning to realize.

'And how close were you two?'

'Close enough – but it's not like we were, you know, moving in together or anything.' I think of the sheaf of photos taken from Mia's wardrobe door. *Close enough.*

'Were you sleeping together?'

He looks affronted. Waits one beat. Another.
Eventually, he answers.

'Yes. I mean – not often. You know they're – well, they're treated like children – the au pairs. Some of them – with a curfew and everything.'

'And Mia?'

He shakes his head.

'She couldn't get away much. She had – she was off from nine thirty on Thursday mornings till the pick-up.'

'The twelve-thirty pick-up?' He shakes his head.

'No, the little girl stayed on in school till six thirty on Thursdays. It's like the au pairs' day off – they have a morning lecture in town, and they all go out after. Mia went too – but she always had to be back by six thirty to pick up the girl.'

I nod. That figures.

'I see. So, Mia is off on Thursday mornings and so, if you – when you and she –' I'm aware of Niamh watching me – aware, too, that I'm enjoying myself.

'When you and Mia wanted to "be alone" and enjoy each other's company, ah – Thursday was the best day.'

He looks embarrassed.

'Yes.'

'And where would you meet up on these occasions? The park, or Mia's house or –'

'I have my own – there's a separate apartment at home – to the side of the house. It has its own entrance and –' He stops himself from saying, *everything*. 'We went there – it wasn't even that many times, actually.'

I nod. His own apartment off the main house. Nice.

'So, what you're saying is that when you and Mia were seeing each other – and all was going well, of course – the two of you went to your apartment and – how did you get there?'

'In my car – I picked her up.'

'I see.'

I let that sit. He nods.

'And you were free on Thursdays too? That's convenient. You're in college, aren't you? What are you studying?'

'Medicine. I'm in third year.'

'No lectures on Thursdays for third years?' I say, innocently. He leans forward towards the bottled water on the table. I pass it to him and he snaps the seal on the lid, puts it to his lips.

'No, there are. I mean, yes, there are lectures. On Thursdays. I don't – didn't always go and – well, anyway, it wasn't every Thursday that we met up in any case. It was just –'

He doesn't finish. I decide to drop the Thursday thing, for now.

'Were you upset when Mia ended the relationship?'

He swallows three big glugs of water, places the paper cup on the table and smooths back his fringe again, his palm flat, in a soothing gesture.

'Upset? Define "upset". If you mean, was I troubled or unhappy – I suppose, yes. No one likes being rejected. I was a little unhappy about that.'

The water seems to have revived him. That and the fact that I've dropped Thursdays. He gives me the full wattage of his boyish grin, back on solid ground.

'My mum would tell you I'm an egotist. *Mea culpa*, and all that.' I nod, letting him enjoy himself a bit more.

'But if you mean upset as in angry and wounded enough to abduct and murder my former girlfriend, then, no, I was fine.'

He clearly thinks he's rested his case. And that's when I realize that in all of this, he hasn't once spoken of Mia with affection, with any real regret for cheating on her, at the realization that she's dead. It's as though she only exists in relation to him.

'Where were you on the afternoon of Wednesday last – from about twelve thirty onwards?' Again, the shrug.

'I was – I've lectures on Wednesdays. So, I'd have been in town – and at twelve thirty' – he pauses, frowns – 'I'd have been – I was probably in – where did we go on Wednesday? – sorry – I reckon we went to the Buttery and got a sandwich.'

'We?'

'My, eh, group, I suppose. A few of us hang about together.'

'I see. So, you got a sandwich with your group of friends, and then what?'

He's nodding vigorously.

'Yes! I even remember where we sat and – I didn't have a sandwich. I had the soup. You can ask my friends – Josh, Ellie and Francie – they were there. I remember now.'

'And then?'

'Then my next lecture, biochemistry – it starts at one. So, you see?' he finishes. 'I couldn't have been in Clonchapel at half twelve.'

He waits, clearly expecting a response.

'I never said Clonchapel.'

'Yes, but everyone knows –'

'Never mind. You have a biochemistry lecture that starts at one and, though you're clearly an intelligent young man, you can't bilocate.'

He doesn't laugh.

'I had lunch with my friends – you can check that,' he says, sulkily. 'And then I went to my lecture. At one.'

I nod. 'Presumably, Josh, Ellie and Francie will attest to the lunch,' I say smoothly, 'but we already know that you don't always go to your lectures.' I make a small hissing sound through my teeth, as though I'm concerned.

The gloves are well and truly off now. He's stopped trying to make me like him.

'The thing is –' He stops. 'I did go. I was at the lecture. But – well, I'm only telling you this because you'll find out anyway, which should prove to you that I'm – I'm being honest, but my name mightn't be on the register. Some of the lectures are massive – that one is full of science students as well. There's up to two hundred in it. So, they don't always bother with a register.'

He sits back. Swallows. And seems to think of something.

'You know, I think – yeah – I'm here voluntarily, right? So, I'm free to go – aren't I?'

Niamh and I exchange a look. There's the tiniest of eyebrow raises. Yes, I think she's right. We've done enough for now.

'True. You're not under arrest. I just have one last question, Marcus – what car do you drive?'

He's getting to his feet.

'A silver Golf.'

32

Laura

'I've been fielding phone calls and issuing statements like a blue-arsed fly for the past three hours. Every sighting of a silver car is being rung in. People are getting antsy. And why is that?'

We know better than to answer. Cig's face is more creased than it was this morning, as though he's been dragging it between his fingers himself. Which he possibly has.

'Because we've got what – oh yeah! Nothing – no evidence, no murder weapon, no suspects. The people want arrests – they're scared. Every day that goes by is another day – another opportunity for him to strike again. And yes, they're talking about a serial killer – already. A serial killer, for Christ's sake. Well, it's not happening. Not on my watch.'

Everyone avoids eye contact. 'Not on my watch' is Cig's catchphrase. Verbal tic. For the millionth time, I wonder how he's not aware of it. And I can't believe one of his buddies has never told him. Maybe that would spoil the fun.

'Shaw, Darmody, what did you get from the boyfriend?'

Niamh and I snap to attention.

'Ex-boyfriend,' I say. 'They broke up before Christmas. She finished with him, but he says it was no big deal. We rattled his cage a bit. Says he was in college on the day of the murder. We're going to check the alibis, and Cig – he drives a silver Golf. We've sent Tech to look at it. Do we have an ID yet for the Tibradden girl – woman?'

Cig shakes his head. Beside me, Niamh takes out her notebook, shuffling through the pages.

'We're looking for a lipstick as well – did the search throw up anything? Sounds weird, but we think he cut Mia's hair and put lipstick on her – either that, or she did it herself at some point on that day. I spoke to the technician at the morgue – she named a few brands it could be.'

She points to the photo of Mia pinned to the board.

'Long hair, no make-up on Wednesday morning – and well, anyone who was at the PM will know what she looked like afterwards. Her hair was chopped – a hack job was how Ella described it. Has anyone got anything to add to that?'

Cig considers for a moment, massaging his temple with reddened fingers.

I turn to Scally. 'Have we pulled up the list of registered sex offenders? Maybe –'

Mairéad nods.

'On it – I've two officers checking alibis.'

Larry gets to his feet and sniffs before pointing at the map. He sniffs again before speaking.

'He took them in broad daylight – on a main road.' *Sniff*. 'Surely it'll be on a traffic camera?'

Cig looks at Byrne.

'Anything from the camera footage at the junction?'

'We're tracing all grey and silver cars that went through between twelve thirty and one, in both directions, so that's ongoing. But there's no footage – nothing that shows them getting into a car.'

'I thought we had an eyewitness?'

This is from a new team member, a young woman with red hair who flushes as soon as she speaks, clearly regretting it.

'Good point,' says Niamh, grinning at her. 'But the

eyewitness is the two-year-old daughter who drew a picture of Daddy's car. That's all.'

Something ticks over in my brain – a little whirr, a question. I can't place it.

Byrne pushes back in his chair with a stretch, folding his arms as he sits forward again. He looks like he's been on the lash.

'Daddy's at it with the babysitter. She threatens to tell – end of story?' he says. 'Not the most original but, hey, who am I to judge?'

'Daddy was in court on the day of the murder,' says Niamh. 'The drowned child?'

'That's him ruled out so –' Cig looks disappointed.

There's a general rustling and scraping as people get ready to move out. But Larry is still on his feet.

'Stall it, lads,' he says, holding up a hand like a traffic warden.

'This is the first I'm hearing about "Daddy's car". I'm giving evidence in that case. I was in the CCJ on Wednesday. Your man – our learned colleague Nairn – stepped out for the afternoon. "Doing a plea", or whatever it's called. I remember because – well, it annoys the hell out of me, the way the silks do that. The way they pop out of one court to dip their snouts in another trough.'

That was a long, uninterrupted sentence. We all wait for the sniff, but it doesn't come. He carries on.

'He opened the case all right – explained to the jurors their roles, you know, standard opening and all. But he left his junior to start calling the first witnesses. He wasn't back' – a long pause as he considers – 'I think, yeah, he came in for the last part, at about three thirty.'

Cig chews his lip, ruminating like an ancient bull.

'You've got to get me more info on that,' he says, with a slow head shake. 'It must have been something big to take him out of that one. What time did they break for lunch?' He looks at Larry.

'Court adjourned at twelve.' *Sniff*, finishes Larry, his face asymmetric with irony.

So, he had from twelve till three. The silence stretches as everyone considers this. Cig breaks into it. He's shaking his head.

'I don't like it,' he says. 'I mean, I don't see it as an avenue of enquiry, even with that. He could have' – he shrugs – 'he could have had an extra slice of apple pie after his lunch – he could have been in the jakes. But never mind that. Garda Wilson?'

The newbie almost leaps out of her skin, hearing her name called.

'Inspect— Cig?'

'You'll check the court listings again, see if there's any other case Nairn appeared in on Wednesday.'

'Yes, Cig.' She immediately makes her way to the desk.

'And I need more than a piece of paper from the child. Find out who was driving the car. Get me the make and colour – get me some bloody evidence!'

He checks his phone.

'McCarthy, can you get down to the morgue for the PM results?'

'On it,' replies McCarthy.

'Shaw and Darmody, get back to the Nairns'. Find something. And bring Nairn in.'

That's our cue. We gather our things and start moving out. Cig hasn't finished. He swivels back, fixing Niamh with a glower.

'Weren't you meant to be checking out the tennis coach?' Niamh flushes. Cig puts his hand up to ward off her excuses.

'Do it. Get weaving. And I needn't tell you that we're running out of time.' He turns back to the desk, dismissing us.

33

Laura

We've fallen into our pattern already. I drive. Niamh talks. We've just spent a fruitless half-hour hanging around the tennis club at Bushy Park, trying to find the coach who worked with Mia. Eventually, we got a name of a guy who used to do early-morning sessions, a Brazilian by the name of Felipe Alzes, but he's not here. He left at Christmas. The girl in the café had a photo of him on her phone from a kids' camp he ran. Twenties, tall, good-looking. She was certain he left at Christmas. She dropped him to the airport.

'Do you think it *is* the same guy?'

I'm racking my brain. We've two bodies found in similar circumstances, both bodies dumped in the woods. But we've nothing as yet to link them.

'Shaw!'

'Sorry, what were you saying?' I hadn't heard Niamh.

'Do you think we are looking for a serial killer?'

'I don't know. We have so little – we've got to go back to – we need to know more about the second victim. We've got to see if the victims have something in common. That might shed – I don't know. It'd be a start.'

Niamh checks a text.

'So, Ella, from the mortuary, she managed to narrow it down – the lipstick we're looking for.'

'Oh? And what's that?'

'She gave me a few names – Mac Ruby Woo, Chanel Rouge Allure, Nars Jungle Red and Maybelline Ruby for Me.'

'Justy wears that Chanel one.'

''Course she does. How is Justy?' she says, turning to smile at me. 'Are you and her getting along any better?'

I sigh. I'd forgotten her – for an hour or so of blissful ignorance, I'd forgotten Justy and the fact that, yet again, she's sticking her oar in. Matt says it's me being paranoid and that his mother loves me and she's only trying to help, but – I sigh again.

'A conversation for another day, perhaps?'

'Too right.'

Now it's Niamh's turn to sigh. She starts again.

'Do you know, it – it doesn't make sense, the whole thing about the make-up. Why would Mia cut her hair and put on lipstick? If she was going to go off with someone, let's say she wanted to run away in disguise. I mean, yeah, maybe she would change her appearance for that. But in that case, wouldn't she choose to leave on a different day? With her wallet and her laptop?'

'And not with the kid.' I agree with her. 'She seems – I don't know – don't you reckon she loved the kid? There's no way she'd have let Carly get mixed up in it all – even if she was running away.'

'No.' She's nodding. 'Which leaves another possibility –'

'Do you think she was meeting him for – I don't know – maybe it was a consensual sexual thing?' I say, just throwing it out there. 'They were going to meet and –'

'Again, she could have done that during the morning or anytime on her afternoon off. Plus, Parminter said there was no sign of sexual assault or recent sexual activity,' Niamh goes on, looking at the trees along the Dodder.

'Which brings us back to the fact that –' I stop, let her finish the sentence.

'That she got into a car with someone she trusted – and either he fecking sheared her and plastered her in red lipstick, or he made her do it. And then he killed her.'

We pull up outside the Nairns'.

'Not going to use their drive-thru?' says Niamh, gesturing towards the heavy gate. 'You're right – we might need a quick getaway.'

I laugh, in spite of the anxiety settling in my stomach.

'Hang on,' I say, pulling down the mirror and scooting the driver's seat back so I can check my reflection properly. I find the hairbrush in the glove box and re-do my ponytail so there's no escaped strands. Then I grab my make-up bag and do a quick sweep of powder across my hot cheeks. 'Hormones,' I say.

'Hormones,' she agrees. 'Bastards.'

I turn to face her, sucking in my soft stomach in readiness for – for what?

'Do you know, I saw this nature programme once about how crabs mate,' I say. 'It was terrifying –'

'Eh – right?'

'So, they're clutched in this embrace, facing each other – the male has to prove he's worthy or something, so he's clutching her with all he's got – and then her shell falls off, and he –'

'Does the business?'

'Yeah – fills her up with, you know, the baby crabs or whatever, and then he hangs around for a few days, just a few days, until she grows her new shell.'

'Right,' Niamh says, nodding. 'Gross! And you're saying what, precisely?'

She cocks her head to one side.

'Are you the Mammy crab? And what – Matt pulled away your shell?'

What am I saying?

'Yeah, I'm the Mummy crab and I'm all soft and vulnerable – that's what it feels like. Being at home with the kids and, you know, just being the soft mummy and – look!'

I poke my finger into my baby-weight belly flesh. 'I'm a white blob – a Mammy crab with no shell –'

Niamh's smile is crooked with concern.

'Well, I think we know Matty the Daddy crab will stick around more than a few days, if that's what you're worried about? And' – she makes a wry face, nudges my elbow so my hand moves from my belly – 'and you well know that's just shite. Are you saying you're fat, Laura? Because if –'

'That's not it!'

She shifts in her seat, her hand on the door handle. How can I explain this?

'No – well, I am – but that's not it. I'm saying – maybe I've lost – I suppose I'm saying I'm scared that I – like, what if I can't do this any more? We've to – Cig wants us to bring him in! Are you not shitting yourself over that? I know what he's like, remember? I've given evidence and been questioned by him, and he's' – I actually shiver, remembering his soft voice, the smiling concern as he unpicks your professional reputation. 'He's – it's like a surgical procedure. He pokes and niggles and –'

'Look.' She breathes out, and I know what's coming. 'Let's cool the jets, okay? First off, that's his job, so it's not personal. And second, he might not even be here.'

'He is,' I say, pointing at the silver Audi.

'We're going in,' she says, carrying on as though I hadn't spoken. 'We're going to play it like we always do – softly,

softly. Right now, all we're doing is talking to the little girl. Worry about Nairn later. Let's see if we can get more from her. Your job is to find out from Carly if it was Daddy's actual car they got into. You're going to keep them talking so I can keep looking.'

I gesture an irritated 'for what?' with my fingers.

'What we always look for, Mammy crab – evidence. Lipstick, to be precise.'

You see, I still cared deeply about my mother at that time. We had our little routine — treatments on Sundays and a weekly practice in the studio. I was now the lead. I had brought the old sofa so we could sit and have a drink between the dances, watching ourselves in the wall of mirrors. We made a good couple — so alike and, though I say it myself, so good-looking. The studio was my kingdom. I often stayed overnight, sleeping upstairs on the mezzanine, preparing simple meals in the kitchenette under the stairs. Father's satchel full of medicines was kept in what we called the dressing room — basically a walk-in wardrobe in the right-hand corner. Sometimes, when I remembered the medicine and the blind worm, I couldn't sleep, and I would give myself 5ml. Never more than that.

On the best nights, Mummy would appear dressed in her ballgown, make-up immaculate, hair slicked back, jewels sparkling at her throat, wrists and earlobes, and she would step into my arms. It could have been any night, in any ballroom, in any city. Somewhere glamorous, like Paris or Venice. Time stood still while we waltzed, and we travelled the world.

Mummy was never angry or disappointed when she was dancing. She was something else. She walked towards me, her feet turning out ever so slightly in her Cuban heels, the best angle to show her still-shapely calves, arms in a soft parallel line reaching towards mine. I would intercept her, stretching my left hand towards her right, bringing our palms together and our bodies into alignment, then I slotted my left hand into position along her ribcage and we were set.

Mummy was more than herself. She was Woman — pliant, fragrant, elegant, thrilling. Though she was thinner now and I could feel each rib under my hand, still she captured the beauty of ballroom. I held her close or spun her away — I could dip her so her head almost touched the floor, or I could thrust her from me with the passion of a tango. I was the leader. I was in charge. All it would take was the merest of weight adjustments, or simply to let go of her, and she would collapse on the floor — undignified, inelegant, mortal.

Those were good years. Mummy was still competing — she and Eric were still winning county championships, though they lost out at the provincials — and every night when she came home, I was ready with her tray. I'd adjusted the dose by 5ml, to take account of her weight loss, and it worked perfectly. She was always fast asleep when the time came.

I was working on her heel when it happened. Mummy's eyes were closed and both her hands hung loosely over the armrests of the chair, her crimson fingernails pointing downwards like dripping blood. Her breathing was slow and even and I watched her breasts move under the silk robe — up and down, up and down — the nipples visible through the sheer fabric, lower now and tilted sideways, as though peering around the corner.

I pressed the blade flat against the tough skin. Mummy's other leg was stretched out — it, too, lay in my lap — and it rolled outwards in the tiniest of rotations, bringing with it the edge of her dragon robe, so that I could see to the valley at the top of her legs and a tiny shadow of hair escaping.

I don't know the order in which things happened.

Perhaps I made a sound — a sigh or a moan — or perhaps she felt the movement under her heel, or perhaps the slip of the blade happened first — I don't know. Her hands gripped the armrests and she lurched upright, pulling her legs towards her. I didn't have time to move the blade and it caught the edge of her foot, scoring a red line along which little rubies of blood immediately began to appear.

She screamed at me — dreadful things — hideous words that no mother should ever say to their child.

'You're disgusting — you make me sick — you're vile!'

I thought of the worm, how it burrows its way into the fruit and rots it from within. I thought of the corn I'd been working on — laughing at me because he's safe from the blade for now. I remembered Father and how he waited until the moment came — the moment for the ugly, angry truth — the blind worm thrusting. The only honest thing between them.

And I knew I hated her.

34

Niamh

My hand is kind of frozen on to the door handle of the car. Jaysus! In all the years I've known her, I don't think we've ever had a conversation like that. *What if I can't do this any more?* I think I prefer uptight, keep-your-shit-together Laura. If Laura can think like that – Laura *it's only bloody diesel*, Laura, who has sent down traffickers and dealers, who got the truth out of Jenny and found her low-life stepfather – I've lost count of the cases she's solved and sorted. If she can think like that, none of us is safe.

I can't understand it – you'd think the whole growing a little human inside you and pushing him or her out into the world with the strength of your own bloody contractions – you'd think that would empower you. It should. They should get medals, the mammies. Instead – I don't know – I've seen it with Siobhán, with Laura and, now that I think about it, with my own mam. There's a decline. You see it in the photos – there's no other way of putting it. The laughing young woman on a windswept beach, the cheeky grin of her, arms linked with my two aunties at some seventies yellow-tinged concert, Mam before she was Mam in the county colours – she was a cross-country runner – she's smiling and careless in all the early photos. Even in the photo of the two of them where Mam had just had Siobhán they looked – both of them – they looked like children, enchanted. It's more than ageing.

Is it having kids that does it to you? The worry. Or, in Mam's case, poor Martin. Mam never mentions my little brother, who died when he was three. Of course, he was actually my older brother, or would have been. Even though Rory and I came after him, Martin is forever preserved as the baby of the family, a sturdy, fat-cheeked little fella glimpsed only in the photo behind the door of the good room. The coroner found that it was a tragic accident. He climbed on top of the trailer – it was parked in the yard. Thank God no one was driving it. So, no one is responsible – or everyone is. Daddy says he was always climbing, that you'd need eyes in the back of your head to watch him. That's kids – climbing, running, risking their lives – on a mission to kill themselves. What must it be like, living on the edge of terror like that? That – yeah, you wouldn't get over that in a hurry.

I feel a weird pull then, in my stomach. I'm definitely not myself at the moment. Why am I even thinking all this depressing shite? The strange, twisty sort of wrenching moves upwards to my chest. I miss Mam.

'Come on,' barks Laura, her voice flat – harsher. 'Let's do this.'

Our feet crunch on the designer gravel. As we pass the Audi, Laura checks it.

'Freshly valeted,' she says. 'And no car seat.'

I meet her gaze.

'Good point,' I say.

We stand on the doorstep. In fairness to her, Laura nails the poker face. You'd never guess that two minutes ago she was poking her own belly and confessing to being petrified. But now, it's like she's grown a couple of inches and aged five years. I'm hoping she's got her shit together.

Tom himself opens the door, his face already assembled into a picture of polite hospitality, blank and unreadable.

'Good afternoon, Mr Nairn,' Laura says, crisp and curt.

'Good afternoon, Officers,' he says, 'let's dispense with the misters and titles, shall we? We're all professionals here.' His smile stretches over clenched teeth.

'I'm Detective Garda Laura –'

'I know who you are, Garda Shaw – Laura,' he says. 'And Garda Darmody – Niamh. I believe you questioned my wife and daughter here yesterday.' He looks at each of us in turn. 'And that I've been implicated by the scribblings of my two-year-old. Hah!'

The skin around his eyes crinkles up. The look he's going for is rueful smile, but there's something a bit nervy about it all the same.

'Come in,' he says, stepping aside to usher us in and closing the main door. We stand in the lofty hallway again. 'You know the service starts at five o'clock?' he says, glancing at his watch. 'I don't want to be rude, but –'

'This won't take long,' says Laura, her voice girlish, raised a notch. 'We just want to chat to Carly again –'

'Of course,' he says. 'Come through.'

Rosa and Carly are in the kitchen. It's like a photoshoot for a lifestyle magazine. They're obviously ready for the service. Rosa wears a sheath dress in a dark blue. I'd say Laura will know the designer – all I know is it looks expensive. Draped over the stool is a blue-and-black coat with a fake fur collar – a matching item. The little girl is in a red party dress – the top part is long-sleeved, trimmed at the cuffs and neck with pink and yellow flowers, and the skirt puffs out like a ballerina's tutu, red netting decorated with individual flowers. Her blonde hair falls in a glossy sheet. She's sitting beside Rosa, and they're looking at a book.

Rosa looks up, gives us a terse smile but doesn't get up. Again, I'm struck by the drained look of her, more than the thinness; it's like something is eating away at her. The platinum-blonde bob gleams. Her lips are slicked in the nude shade – I'm guessing the lipstick I saw in the toilet the other day.

'Good afternoon, Rosa,' says Laura. 'This won't take long.'

'Hi,' Rosa's voice is cool.

'I'll be interested to see you in action, Laura,' says Tom, all friendly. 'I'm sure it's an art. Why don't we go into my study?' I glance at Laura to see how that goes down. She sweeps her hair back behind her ears, though it's already tied back, then nods curtly.

'Well, if we could – I'd prefer to be where Carly is most comfortable. Ideally, I'd like Carly to show me her toys.' She smiles at the little girl, hunkering down so she's at eye level. 'Hi, Carly. I see you're reading a story – I love stories. How about you and I – you could choose another story and I'll read it to you? We could let Mummy have a rest and you could show me and Niamh all your books –'

'Oh, I think not,' he says. 'It's far cosier here, don't you think?' He gestures a wide circle, taking us all in.

There's no mistaking his meaning. We're not getting to talk to Carly alone.

Rosa moves further along the sofa and Laura sits down beside Carly. Tom and I sit on either side of the breakfast bar.

'Did you do any more pictures?' says Laura. 'Do you remember the lovely one you did before?'

Carly regards Laura with a frown, trying to see around behind her, scanning the room.

'Tatie?'

Laura shakes her head. 'Oh! Katie – no – Katie couldn't come with me today, but we must – you'll see her another day.'

Laura peers in at the book open on Carly's lap. She points at one of the pictures.

'Look at all those people! Aren't they funny? Tell me what they're doing.'

Carly looks at the page, thinking. Laura points at something.

'What's that man doing?'

Carly mimes an eating gesture.

'Oh, I see!' laughs Laura. 'Yes! He's feeding the animals. And what do you call that animal – the one having his breakfast?'

'Monkey?'

'Yes,' says Laura. 'And what's he having for breakfast?'

I sit quietly, observing Tom and Rosa, who are watching Laura and Carly. Some of the tension has melted away. It's an innocent scene and a little girl is showing pictures in a book. That's all. This is where Laura excels. She sets it up so intricately – the dialogue – the establishing of trust.

'Carly,' she says, sitting forwards, closing the book, 'I just have one more question for you about the day – do you remember the rainy day when you went in the car with Mia?' The girl nods, but she's already looking for another book to show Laura. 'Was there a car seat in it? Did you sit in a car seat?'

Carly shakes her head, and her hand goes to her cheekbone.

'I got hurted,' she says. 'This one,' she says, clambering up between the two women.

Rosa frowns.

'I forgot about that,' she says, looking at me. 'Do you remember I told you she had a bump on her cheek that day? Maybe she fell off the seat?'

They talk on, and I realize that I don't have much time. They'll be heading to the service soon.

'I'll just – I'll just pop to the, eh, bathroom. Excuse me a moment,' I say, on my feet and in the hallway before anyone can object. I close the kitchen door behind me and open then close the door of the downstairs toilet fairly noisily. Then I double back on myself and start taking the stairs in twos, grateful for the fact that the treads are marble tiles, as opposed to creaky wood.

I just need less than a minute in the master bedroom so I can check out Rosa's dressing table. The door is ajar – yes! A lucky break. I edge myself into the room, turning to close the door softly behind me. To my left is the huge bed that faces a bay window. Mirrored wardrobes line the right-hand side of the room, all neatly closed. Matching lockers with glass tops and mirrored doors flank the bed on either side. On one of the lockers a thriller lies face down with a bookmark set into it a few pages from the end. Who does that? The far wall has a doorway set into it – I glimpse shining marble and reckon that's the en suite bathroom. Facing the bed arranged in neat rows across that wall is a series of black-and-white photos. I tiptoe around to get a better look.

Rosa – stunning – in a ballgown. Rosa and Tom at a black-tie event, him all sharp edges and clean lines in the formal suit. A christening photo, with Carly, I'm guessing, in a waterfall of lace. And their wedding photo, of course. They're in some stately pile – it looks like a castle – and the photographer has captured them facing each other, silhouetted in the Gothic doorway. There's another photograph showing a very young Tom in gown and mortar board and a strikingly beautiful woman who must be his mother standing beside him. She looks French, her hair short and dark, swept back to show massive pearl earrings, and she's laughing at something or someone – the photographer, perhaps. Beside her,

Tom looks gangly and awkward, his free hand clasping her elbow as if he's worried she's going to flit away.

Mothers. Of course, I'm hit with another shaft of – I don't know – that cocktail of pain, regret, guilt. I've got to sort things with Mam when I get the chance this time. I hold my breath. From downstairs, I can just about hear them – Laura and Carly. Their voices are light and high.

I tiptoe to the dressing table. It's been tidied. Chunky perfume bottles – all the big brands – are lined up at the rear and there's a china tray with rings and bracelets spread out on it. Dangling from the little tree are more gems: strands of pearls and crystals, some silver and gold necklaces, earrings. Three shallow drawers are set into the front of the table. I pull them out as quietly as I can.

Jaysus! I think, Amber would love this. Foundations, compacts, blushes and brushes, yokes for contouring your face and highlighting it – the whole lot. More than you could ever need. The drawer on the right has stuff for eyes – mascaras, brow kits, eye pencils. So that means the drawer on the left must have –

I freeze, hearing the kitchen door open and voices leak out into the hallway. Footsteps – Tom's – walking with authority across his marbled hall. Shit! Part of being a detective is, yeah, you do find yourself in scary situations. It's not that you don't feel scared. You do. But you make yourself get used to that – you train yourself to ignore it. Okay, so I don't have a warrant and I'm sneaking around, but damn it! I can do this. I try to calm myself.

I hear Tom's voice in the hall.

'We're going to have to leave now, Darmody, or we'll be late for the service. And that's not happening.'

I hear his footsteps once more. He must have turned and gone back into the kitchen. I look at the door into the en suite. Maybe I could pretend I thought that was the toilet? Yeah – not an option.

As quickly and quietly as I can, I cross the bedroom and edge my way out of the room backwards, holding the door so it doesn't get caught by the breeze. From downstairs, I can hear Laura's voice wrapping up. She's thanking Carly. I'm almost at the top of the stairs when I hear Tom's voice behind me. He's midway along the corridor in the shadows, watching me.

'What do you think you're doing, Darmody?'

It was frosty between us for some days, but even the hardest of frosts thaw. When two people live together, hatred is mingled with familiarity and routine, like vinegar in a salad dressing. You wouldn't tolerate it on its own, but it belongs all the same – it earns its place. After a week or two, routine took over. Treatment days resumed. My mother's dance lessons continued. She began to drink more and more, and her spending began to threaten our way of life.

I was in college at this stage, midway through a lacklustre degree in a discipline which bored me, feigning interest and camaraderie with the idiotic young men in my course, all of whom had begun making forays into the world of adult pleasures. Regularly, they'd tease and boast to each other of pints downed and girls fingered.

'We need to get you out on the lash, weirdo! You're almost nineteen, for fuck's sake!'

'He's going to die a virgin, haha.'

'You should get it out of the way before the exams –'

I laughed it off, raising my eyebrows suggestively – wouldn't you *like to know? I was alone so much of the time I'd begun to have whole conversations in my head. Conversations I could control. I didn't care. I'd no interest in the brittle girls on my course, inventing themselves as Bookworm, Party Girl, Model, Sporty Queen or whatever. They left me cold. Mummy was everything – apex and nadir. Her dainty foot in my lap. The glimpse of her face, eyes closed, mouth parted, leaning back against the chair as I rubbed the yielding flesh.*

I was a model son. I went to college, I came home and studied, I worked at weekends for a pittance, yet still she ignored me. She was swept up in her world of dresses, make-up, shoes, taxis, competitions and post-competition celebrations in restaurants and cocktail bars.

The only time she spoke to me was to ask me to contribute to the household income. She expected me to hand over the meagre amount I earned on weekends.

But I didn't see it this way. You see, I'd realized that we were literally sitting on a fortune. A neighbour further along the road had sold their house – smaller than ours and with less garden – for over two million. The property market was soaring, and we were living on an acre of prime Dublin real estate, in a five-bedroomed detached house. I pointed this out to her. I told her that we could sell up for millions and buy a nice bungalow by the sea. We would never have to work – not that there was any danger of my mother working again. But she didn't want to leave her home and her studio.

I said we could build another studio or buy a fancy barn conversion with massive floor space. She said no. She told me to get a well-paying job. I said I'd think about it.

In our own ways, she and I were equally intractable, it occurs to me now.

We went less and less to the studio, but she still needed me for the Sunday treatments. Only I could wield the blade. Only I could massage the cream into her aching calves and her tired legs.

Slowly, her body changed. Where, before, she'd been soft and yielding, now the fibres of muscle began to knit together. I could picture them, the livid red strands bunching close into steely columns, weaving and wrapping themselves around the joints, gobbling up the fat cells, leaving only muscle. Now, when I smoothed the cream on her legs, I felt the power beneath my fingers, firm and tense.

Gone were her teardrop-fat breasts and soft belly. The mound at the apex of her legs began to shrink, no longer rising in a gentle hillock. Her tender neck, always long and elegant, became roped with muscle, each tendon clearly defined. She had the hairdresser chop her hair severely and on dancing nights she slicked it back with two great globs of shining *jelly, her palms smoothing it into her temples. This was a whole new woman. A creature of strength and sinew — hard on the outside. It was as though she, too, had become coated in a tough skin.*

Was that when I first turned away? When I began searching for the softness, the fragility of innocence and hurt?

35

Laura

'Jesus Christ! Did you nearly die?' I stare at Niamh, my mouth open.

'No, but I may well have pissed myself.' She grins at me, her face still pale. 'Do you get a whiff?'

We both burst out laughing. The Nairns have gone to the service – it's up the road in the big church – and we're parked in a side road around the corner. I knew as soon as I saw her in the hallway that he'd caught her.

'What did he say? Christ!'

'He was like, "What do you think you're doing?" So, I just had to play the idiot. I said I just needed to check Mia's room again – is this not Mia's room? Blah blah.'

'Did he buy it?'

'Did he heck? No! Not a bit! He told me that he's run out of patience, that he appreciates we have to cover every angle, that I was in the wrong room, as I well knew, and that we are on the wrong track, and that if anything like that happens again he'll make sure I'm sent to Ballygobackwards till my dying day type thing.'

She gives a regretful grin.

'I didn't get much from Carly.'

'Did she say anything about the car? Anything else?'

I shake my head.

'No, and as you say, his patience was wearing thin by then.

I reckoned it wasn't the time to mention coming into the unit. I bottled. But we need more.'

She taps her finger against her lip, considering something.

'Right, they'll be safely tucked up in the church for the next half-hour, so can you – can we just head back there for two ticks?'

I switch on the engine and turn the car around, driving the few hundred metres back to the Nairns'. They've left their gates open. The Audi is gone, but Rosa's nifty little Fiat is still parked in front of the house.

'I saw something on the way in,' says Niamh. 'Wait there – it's better if it's just me.'

I watch her stride across the gravel and around the far side of Rosa's car. She hunkers down out of sight. I wait. A car passes and the driver looks curiously at me. I nod and smile. I'm aware, suddenly, that I haven't thought about the kids in a few hours. As soon as I'm aware of the thought, a throb begins in my boobs. No! The plan was to find fifteen minutes to nip home and give Noah a feed –

'I bloody knew it!' squeals Niamh. 'I knew it! This is so bloody weird!'

She's clutching a small plastic zippy bag with a square of paper stapled on to the front.

'What's that?'

'This,' she crows, 'is a lipstick that the dry-cleaners found in the pocket of our favourite barrister's suit. I spotted the dry-cleaning bag in Rosa's car on the way in. Always worth checking and – fecking bingo! What do you think?'

'How did you get into her car?'

'I'm too cool for school, girleen,' she chants, delighted with herself. 'I spotted it on the way in and popped the locks on the way out – Mammy's keys were in the hall.'

I don't know. I'm finding it hard to concentrate, aware that any minute now the milk will start. Don't think about it.

'What?' she says. 'The shade is Ruby Woo. This is evidence! We have him *slipped out* of the case.' She emphasizes the phrase Sniff used. 'We have the child saying they went in Daddy's car – and now we have a lipstick.' She sits back. 'That's enough to get him in for questions. Christ! Will ye slow the hell down? What's the rush?' Niamh is gripping the doorhandle again.

'Yeah, but we can't use it! Jesus, Niamh. Unlawful search, blah blah – shit!'

She's staring at me. 'Not you, sorry – I've about ten seconds before the let-down,' I say through gritted teeth. 'I have to get home!'

I pull up at the kerb outside the house and it's as though my boobs recognize my front door, because it starts. I'm bent over, clutching my shirt to my front, which is drenched in seconds.

'Where is he? Can you make Niamh tea? Hi, love –' This last part to Katie. Matt looks bemused. He points upstairs.

'Hi, Niamh, he's aslee—' he starts to say, then drops it. 'Never mind.'

Bloody hell! Noah is fast asleep – the dark lashes barely flutter when I haul him out of the cot and on to my lap. I stroke his cheek with my curled finger, murmuring his name, trying to wake him. The milk throbs. I try and get him to open his mouth, wetting his lips with the milk, but he wrinkles his nose, clenches his eyes tight and turns away.

'Lunchtime, baba.' I jiggle him up and down. 'Come on, baba.'

He wakes all right. But not for food. He wakes angry. Raging that I've woken him. The screams bring Matt up from downstairs. He stands in the doorway watching me hold

Noah a foot away from me, trying to comfort him without drenching him in the milk that's flowing. The worst thing is the look of sympathy on his face.

'I'll just –' he says, walking over to take Noah into his arms. He begins soothing him, gently stroking his back, and goes into the bathroom to get a towel for me. I go to leave the room.

'Ssh,' says Matt, either to me or Noah or both of us. 'You take it easy – I'll go and get you the pump. May as well?'

He's barely halfway down the stairs when Noah's cries subside. I take over where he left off. Sitting on the edge of the single bed which will be Noah's when he's old enough, my boobs leaking into a bath towel, I contemplate the mess I've made of everything. It's okay, I try to calm myself. I'll change my clothes, get a cup of tea, buy some Panadol and get back to work. I can still do this.

Katie has crept upstairs and is eyeing me from the doorway.

'Your hair is all messy,' she says, shaking her head like a disappointed hairdresser when you've cut your own fringe. 'An' your face is red. Why are you crying?'

I dab my tears with the corner of the towel, still clasping it across my boobs.

'I'm not crying,' I say hurriedly, worried I'll traumatize her. 'I – I'm just –' I reach out a hand and she steps in towards me, kissing the top of my head in a reversal of roles.

'Work is hard. Maybe you should just be a mummy,' she says.

I squeeze her into a hug. She's bloody right, I think, my head pounding. There are scores of better detectives who aren't either in tears or leaking milk. Maybe I'm just not cut out for it any more. Niamh and Senan are more than capable of finding this guy. Even the few words I got from Carly, they're worth nothing: a 'nice man' drove the car. What we should be doing – we should be at the church service – seeing if something else turns up. And one of us should attend Parminter's debriefing on the Tibradden case. But I've derailed all of this.

And, if all that wasn't enough, I completely unravelled Matt's day of successful parenting. When we came in, Katie was colouring a picture and Noah was asleep. I've ruined everything.

Matt is back, Noah fast asleep on his shoulder. He holds his fingers to his lips, whispering, 'You go on – there's a cup of tea for you. I'll get him back down.'

I intend to thank him, to smile and give him a special look that shows how much I love him and how great a dad he is. Instead, I open my mouth and out pops an accusation.

'You must have given him a full bottle at two o'clock? Why did you do that?'

It's strange seeing them together. Usually it's the smaller one, on her own. What was that comedy show? Little and Large. *Yes. I watched them at the car — tall and small. Fair and dark. One grinning, one serious-looking. If she'd do something about her hair — it's far too long — she would look quite elegant.*

Mother insisted on the word 'petite' rather than 'small'. Her size was one of the reasons she and Eric had such a successful partnership. It meant that he could lift, twirl, throw, bend and in every way control her on the dance floor, in every style, across every category. No wonder they became divisional and, later, national champions.

I think, now, that it was a mercy for her to quit when she was at the top of her game.

That night — Mummy's last night — I hadn't even gone to bed, and there she was, flinging her bag on the hall table with such force that it bounced against the glass lamp and fell to the floor. Her tray was already assembled for later but, in a stroke of good fortune, I hadn't yet measured out the 15ml or opened Father's satchel. She kicked off her heels and marched into the kitchen with the flat, ugly gait of a toad.

I don't like loud noises and anger, and I hated it when she was like this. I thought about Hal, then, my ghost brother, wishing he was here to help. In the harsh light of the kitchen, I could see where her foundation was sitting in the cracks and crevasses of her skin, like those faint lines that show underground rivers on a map. Some of her lipstick had bled into the skin around her mouth and I could see the vertical lines running from her lip to her nose.

'Eric is retiring,' she snapped, 'and there's no partner for me. So, it looks like I'm retiring as well.'

Her tone was acidic. She took a gulp of wine, draping her upper lip crudely over the top of the glass like a living thing, and slurping it up inside her mouth noisily. As she swallowed, her mouth pressed together, all the lines converging so that it looked like a sphincter. Disgusting.

I watched her drink and listened to her ranting. It seemed obvious to me that the writing was on the wall and that Mummy — at fifty-six — was past her dancing prime. But she didn't see it that way.

I tried to talk to her but, as usual, it was as though I didn't exist. She only wanted to rant. She might just as well have done it alone in the studio in front of the mirror. It certainly wasn't a conversation.

I watched her make her way to the low chair then plonk herself angrily into it — there was no floating the way she used to. I refilled her glass and wordlessly sat at her feet, lifting them on to my lap and pressing my thumbs into the arches.

'I know,' I said in a soft voice. 'I understand.'

She drank some more, gulping and muttering, going over her plans — who she could contact, what other dance club she could compete in. I concentrated on calcaneus and talus, the individual phalanges and the cuboid. Her breathing slowed. She let her head fall back against the seat. I reached for the kit and got to work, selecting the short blade, which fitted neatly inside my palm.

Mummy's heel was cold and rough in my lap. Even the front surface of her foot was leathery, scored with thousands of wrinkles, like the crocodile trim on her most expensive shoes. I switched to an even shorter blade, as I needed to get close. Things needed to change.

I worked steadily on — slicing — shaving. I could see the blind core squatting in the reddened circle of flesh. I longed to prise it out. Mummy was almost asleep, relaxed now, her mouth open slightly.

I changed the angle of the blade. If I did it quickly, I knew I could get him out. (I thought of this disfigurement of flesh as 'he' — a terrorist, a soldier, a fearsome adversary.) I had to go deep — but I was dextrous. I knew I could get the better of him at last.

Prising her toes apart with my left hand, I switched the tools, discarding the short for the long-scooped instrument, the blade a deep 'C' shape. I watched Mummy's emaciated breasts, her grille of chest bones shining under the overhead light, rise and fall, rise and fall, slower and slower — and slower. Then I struck.

At the first cut, she shrieked, snatching her foot away and bolting upright.

'What did you do?'

'Sorry — it's —' I tried to pull her foot towards me, but she was standing already and hobbling over to the kitchen chair.

'You idiot! Christ! Christ,' she repeated, in a new and harsh voice. 'What did I ever do to deserve you? You're — you're not normal — you're sick! You should have been drowned at birth!'

I moved towards her, desperate to make it all right.

'I'm sorry — really — I — would you like me to make you some tea or something? You go upstairs and I'll bring up a tray — see? I have it all ready.'

At this, something hardened in Mummy's face. She stood there, no longer tall and elegant but flat-footed, wizened, meagre. Where was the bounty of her body, her slopes and planes of flesh? We surveyed each other, she trying to focus through the mist of wine.

'I don't want a tray,*' she said, layering meaning on the word, 'and I don't want your treatments either, you sick, loathsome excuse for a man. You're pathetic! You know that, don't you? And you're disgusting.'*

Here, she held up a hand, as though to say anything else would spoil things. As though she hadn't already said the unsayable.

'Don't come near me.'

I waited as she climbed the stairs, the bannisters creaking as she hauled herself upwards. I unlaced my shoes and slipped them off, tiptoed to the stairwell. When Mummy went into the bathroom, I took the stairs in twos and, after turning off the hall light, hid in the shadows outside the bathroom door. The bathroom was on the left at the top of the stairs, its door opening outwards on to the landing. I knew she would go straight to her bedroom after she'd finished, involving three or four steps across the divide. My opportunity would come — swift and brief — in the moment it took her to exit the bathroom. Hal gave me the signal — a thumbs-up and a brotherly grin. It was time. Even Hal was with me. Not Blood Baby — my big brother, Hal.

It was, all things considered, a triumph — especially as I had no time for advance planning and no chemical assistance in the form of medication — apart from the alcohol, which made her clumsy.

And so Mummy, sure-footed, dainty and nimble, fell headlong down the stairs, her trajectory taking her smack into the interior wall that marked the return into the hallway. Still in her dress — still, mercifully, in her full make-up. There would have been questions to answer if she had made her way successfully to the bathroom and taken off her make-up, only to tumble afterwards. An inconsistency that might prove troubling.

As it was, Mummy's death was declared a misadventure. She'd come home late and tipsy from her dancing. She'd had a further half-bottle of wine on her return and then foolishly attempted to climb the stairs in her high heels. The fall itself is not what killed her. The autopsy showed that her spinal cord was snapped at C6 — and she died within minutes.

I tidied up her feet and covered the offending corn with a plaster — Mummy's toes were often covered in this way when she was dancing. Then I replaced her shoe and set the other shoe on the return, as though it had bounced when she caught her foot on the stairs.

I took ten minutes to tidy away the treatment tray and to set the scene for Mummy's solo drinking downstairs. I changed into my pyjamas and even lay in my bed for some minutes, before throwing back the duvet and enacting my discovery of the body and telephoning the guards. I left the handbag flung on the floor. In my statement, I said I thought I'd heard something clatter but that, to my shame, I turned *over and went back to sleep. It must have been over an hour later when I heard her fall.*

I was full of regret, I said. I should have got up to see if she was all right. I cried then – real tears.

Poor Mummy. Father is gone, and now she is too.

Now, there's only me and Hal.

Sunday

36

Laura

We're in the interview suite in the unit, waiting for Nairn. I'm sick with nerves and Niamh's talking at ninety miles an hour, raring to go.

'Nothing at the boyfriend's place,' says Niamh. 'And his lunch buddies from the Buttery, two of them checked out. The other alibi is away – I'll follow it up.'

She shrugs. 'Seems Marcus is off the hook for now – but we didn't really expect anything?' Her voice holds the question.

I shake my head in reply.

'They've dusted his car for prints, crawled all over it for DNA – likewise, nothing that puts Mia in his car. Traces of drugs, mind you – cannabis. That won't please Mammy. Imagine if that was Katie or Noah in a few years – haha!'

I test out my own response, knowing what my mum's reaction would have been to me having anything to do with drugs. She'd have flayed me alive. I try to picture Katie in college, at eighteen or nineteen, with me and Matt in our fifties, but I just can't see it. It's overwhelming, the distance from toddler to young adult. The distance between myself and Matt. Sometimes I worry we're not going to make it to the end of next month, never mind our middle age. And the worst of it is that I think it's my fault. It's like every time I open my mouth to speak, the words that come out are critical, hurtful –

'He should be here in a few,' says Niamh, giving me a sideways look. 'Are you okay?' When I don't answer, she carries on. 'It's just a chat. Take it handy.' She smiles, aware she's doling out my own advice.

I take a steadying breath. I barely slept last night: my brain whirred in rehearsal of today's interview with Nairn, with regrets over Matt and the things I'd said, thoughts of Mia and her heartbroken parents. We'd had a short meeting with them later in the evening, a hurricane swirl of sadness and anger and questions. Who? Why? Then back to who. If not the boyfriend, who? If it's not Nairn, we're talking someone whose path she crossed in other ways. Maybe someone in the language school? The coach?

'Who would do this? Who would do this, Laura?' her mum had asked, over and over. She pronounced my name 'Lour–a', and somehow that made it worse. Like a lament.

'What if he was having an affair with her?' Niamh speculates. 'Or he made a pass at her and she threatened to tell Rosa –'

'The hair? The lipstick?' I say, shaking my head. 'Why would the killer do that to her? What does it mean?'

I just can't picture Nairn doing this.

'Jaysus! I don't know – use a bit of imagination. Maybe it – we don't know what turns his cookies brown, do we? Look at the missus. Immaculate. Groomed to within an inch of her life. Maybe he likes that – or needs that to do the deed –'

'Yeah, but he didn't touch her like that, did he?'

Niamh looks tired. She said she's due a day's leave and I was telling her she should take it – but she wants to postpone till we've got somewhere with this.

'The lipstick in his suit pocket?' she continues.

'Yeah, true,' I say. 'But two things: one, we can't use that in evidence and two, more importantly, motive.' I take yet another sip of water, my mouth dry with anxiety. 'We don't have a motive, do we?'

'Noke,' she says through the twisty plastic hair bobbin clutched between her teeth as she sweeps her mane of hair back into a ponytail. 'But we have the fact that it's usually someone they know, someone with whom they have an intimate relationship. We have him lying to us – he had opportunity – and now, the lipstick. And remember, we have Carly's picture.'

'I just don't see it being Tom Nairn,' I say. 'And you know as well as I do that the picture is worth precisely zero as evidence. Ditto the lipstick. Unless something else comes up from the car – which is not going to happen, let's face it – we don't have enough to charge him.'

Niamh turns to face me, and I'm struck – even more than usual – by her good looks. She's abandoned the jeans and she's wearing a pair of slim-fitting tapered black trousers that finish just above the ankle, with a tailored open-neck shirt in a jade colour. The only concession to comfort, which used to be her priority, is the long knitted cardigan over the top in a shade of grey-green. On her feet are a pair of flat lace-up brogues.

'Are you checking me out or what?' She laughs, seeing me looking.

'No runners?' I say. 'I've just noticed.'

'Ah, Jaysus – I had to up my game with you gone and, you know, there's McArsey to impress.' She grins, lifting the hem of the trousers so I can see her black socks. 'But there's no way either of you are converting me to the pop socks! Don't know how you stand them.' She turns sideways and points towards her stomach. 'Amber has me in training – she's signed us up for dance classes. We've our first session tonight.

And she's keeping an eye on what I eat.' She pauses. 'Do you think I've got thinner?'

She has – and I tell her so. But it's weird: it seems all wrong for Niamh – this is Niamh – to be talking like this.

'Anyway,' she says, setting out her notepad and pens on the desk beside the recording gear, 'just a chat, and we're doing it for the Super. He says not to go easy on him.'

Another lurch of anxiety bubbles up my stomach. Great. And easy for him to say – he doesn't have to do it. Tom Nairn is not going to be easy. A distant door slams and Niamh and I lock eyes.

'I'll go,' she says, heading out the door to escort him from the entrance. 'He hates me anyway.'

She leaves, and I stand up in readiness, glancing at my reflection in the tinted glass of the interior window. At least I look the part today – I've strapped my boobs out of existence and I'm wearing my favourite work shirt, a roomy, tailored one with a stripe that accommodated my bump up to seven months, so it creates the illusion of slimness now. I have it full-on buttoned to the neck. I still haven't had time to get a haircut, so I've gelled it back, added bigger earrings and a sweep of lipstick.

'You're looking good, Mammy,' Niamh had said when I came in earlier. 'I'm sure he'll appreciate it.'

I didn't even bother telling her to shut up.

His face remains devoid of expression as I remind him of his rights and inform him that the interview will be recorded. At the mention of his right to a solicitor, he raises an eyebrow.

'I hardly think that's necessary.' His lips press together in a line. 'Do you?'

Now there's a job I wouldn't want, I think. Nairn's

solicitor. I catch Niamh's eye, reckoning she's thinking the same thing.

Nairn sits on the edge of his chair, his fingers opened out across his knees. Every now and then he pinches his thumb and forefinger together along the crease, as though sharpening the edge. Anxiety? Then he tilts forward, inclining his head as though angling to hear better – as though he's assiduously assisting the police with their enquiries. He's a colourless man; I can't fix on any feature that stands out – he's a series of shifting impressions of medium-ness. Medium height. Medium build. Hair with a medium amount of grey. Regular features. He's definitely out of his comfort zone, though. And he's very pale. Of course, he's usually the one asking the questions. Asking and listening. A tremor – no – a tiny contracture of muscle twitches along his jawline.

'How well did you know Mia as a person?' I say, after the preliminary questions. No confrontation in the air, all very polite.

'Not well,' he says, adding a regretful shake of the head. 'By the time I come home most nights, Carly is in bed and Mia – Mia would be finished for the day. She'd make herself scarce, you know – she'd be in her room or talking to her friends. She watched movies on her laptop – that type of thing. So, no, I didn't know her well at all.'

'And, in your observations of her with Carly – I presume you would see her at weekends, surely? What was – what was your impression of Mia then?'

He smiles, tilting his head to one side in a patronizing gesture.

'We've established I didn't see Mia often. We've established that I didn't know her well. Now, you're asking about weekends. When I answer that I didn't see her much at weekends, are you going to move into asking about bank holidays and religious festivals?' His smile broadens. It's as though he's giving me a tutorial.

'Oh, and just because you add the word "surely", it doesn't mean that it's any more likely. Let's move on.'

'Fine,' I say, feeling a flare of annoyance. 'We'll agree you didn't know her well. But in the context of childcare, let's look at that for a moment. How did she fit in? Do you think it was working out, having an au pair? I presume you and Mrs Nairn would have discussed her, especially in the early days, when she first started working for you – no? Was Mrs Nairn happy with the arrangement?'

Again, the disarming but patronizing smile. He leans forward.

'You're married, aren't you, Laura?'

'I –'

He lifts his hands from his knees and sweeps them back through his hair, sighing. Then he crosses his legs and leans back more comfortably in the chair, arms folded, watching me.

'I only ask because, as a married woman with children, you must be familiar with the distance and, ah – lack of communication – that can infiltrate a marriage – the partnership – following the arrival of children. It's commonplace. Children are expensive and time-consuming. Someone has got to earn the money to afford them. Someone has got to care for them and ensure their safety.'

He's using his hands like the trays of a weighing scales. This hand, children; that hand, money.

'My wife will be the first to tell you that I am never home, sorry – better be factual – rarely home. On weekdays, I will *rarely* be home before eight or nine and, at weekends, I also go into the office. You'll have found the office I rent near the CCJ, I presume?'

I don't reply. Beside me, Niamh's pen moves down her notebook pointing at an address in town. 'Rented flat' is circled. That was going to be a later question. How has it shifted so quickly to this? He's questioning me.

'No matter. If you haven't, I'll give you the address so you can search it.' He smiles. 'And you'll find a fancy-looking desk which turns into a bed – very flash.' He flips up his hands in a gesture of 'what can you do?' 'If I'm in the middle of negotiations or a complex case, I spend the night there. Alone – and no, sorry, no convenient alibis, although there is a coffee shop nearby – the barista there can vouch for my endless coffee runs.'

I open my mouth to speak, desperate to get this back on track, but he sits forward with a burst of energy, hands back on the knees. It occurs to me that he'd prefer to be on his feet, addressing a jury.

'So, let me help you out here, since you seem to be' – he pauses, but only for a split second – 'having difficulties.'

Now he folds his arms and sits back again.

'I did not know Mia well. I had very few interactions with her. I am a busy man and, you will observe, not a young man. I've no doubt that I am lacking in the fatherhood stakes and condemning Carly to years of psychotherapy for absent-father issues.' He gives a wry chuckle. 'Likewise, I'm not an advertisement for the best husband in the world – but that doesn't make me a killer, does it? Does it, Detective?'

He tilts his head, waiting.

'I came in here on a Sunday, of my own free will and on my own time' – his voice underscores the word 'time', making sure I know how valuable that commodity is – 'to help you out. To *assist with your enquiries*. So, come on now – please tell me you have some actual questions!'

I know he's needling me deliberately, but even so I take the bait. I'm raging. A girl is dead – a girl who lived in his house, took care of his child, ate and slept and breathed the same air as them. And he couldn't give a damn. It's a game to him. I steady my breathing, turning pages in my notes as I wait for it to settle.

'Where were you on the afternoon Mia went missing?'

'Now, this is disappointing, Laura,' he says. 'Surely' – he labours the word until it groans – 'surely you checked the court listings. The case has been on every news channel for days!'

I allow him his moment – just a moment – and do a bit of frowning, looking flustered. Then I begin trailing my pen through the lines of script, avoiding looking at him.

'Well, yes, we saw the listings. I'm aware of the case. But, you see, Mr Nairn, the fact is that you were *not* in Court Five from the time the court rose for lunch' – I carry on scrolling, pretending to look for the time – 'at midday. And, when the court readjourned at, let's see, two o'clock, you had slipped out. Your Junior Counsel in the case, he handled everything until you *slipped back* in at three thirty.'

I look directly at him, pen hovering above the page as though I'm eager to record the information.

'Where were you on Wednesday last between twelve and three thirty?'

He inhales as if to speak but doesn't. A beat. It couldn't be this easy, could it?

'We've checked all the court listings, you see, in all the courts. And you weren't in any of them. So, where were you?'

He sighs out the same breath he inhaled moments ago. I wait. Out of the corner of my eye, I see Niamh's hand move towards the lipstick in the plastic evidence bag. I shake my head. There's a big risk if we're going down that route. But either she didn't see the head shake, or she's on her own mission. Before I can stop her, she places the lipstick in its evidence bag on the table between us. Nairn frowns.

'A tube of lipstick – what – what does that have to do with anything? With me?'

I say nothing, because now we've upped the stakes. And he knows it. And now I should be reminding him of his right to a solicitor, repeating the caution. I dither. Seconds pass and, across his features, there's a softening, or maybe a settling. He looks at me sharply and this action brings him clearly into focus. He's decided something. He chops at his knees with the edges of his palms, in a karate-chopping motion, then he presses his hands flat and pushes himself to stand.

'Right,' he says mildly. 'I'm going to overlook the fact that you failed to inform me that the evidence you presented there, in your mind anyway, links me to the offence – so-called evidence, I might add, about which I know absolutely nothing, and which, if you found it in my home, you have obtained through an illegal search. In other words, you are invoking adverse inference without reminding me of my rights not to self-incriminate. If that's the route you're taking, you also have a duty to remind me of my right to a solicitor. Are you really going down that route? Are you going to charge me?'

I'm on my feet too, my palms clammy with a cold sweat. The lipstick is not enough. Carly's drawing is not enough. We have to let him go.

He knocks his knuckles against the desk in a parody of a judge's gavel. *Case dismissed.*

'And so, if you're not going to charge me with anything, and there's nothing further I can assist you with, I'll head on now.'

37

Niamh

'What the actual?' I stare at Laura. 'You had him! He was about to confess!'

She's shaking her head, the fingers of her left hand clamped over her mouth as if she wants to stop herself speaking.

'The lipstick? What the hell?'

I can't understand how it all went pear-shaped so fast, ending up with me stopping the interview and the pair of us running around like headless chickens to escort Nairn out of the unit.

'So, let's arrest him. We'll do it right.' I pace the room, too annoyed to sit.

'It doesn't add up.' Laura's shaking her head. 'He's – I don't know what he's playing at, why he won't tell us where he was when Mia was abducted – but he's sure as hell not about to confess to a murder.'

'Two murders.' I take out my phone and scroll through until I find Parminter's report on the body, which came in while we were with Nairn. 'Severing of spinal column – single blade,' I say. 'Same method. They've ID-ed her through dental records. Kim Zhou, a twenty-four-year-old master's student from UCD. Missing since October. Cig is going to go apeshit –' I stop, because she's clearly not listening.

'We were distracted by the drawing – the car that Carly drew. You know, that's been niggling. I've been going over and over it,' she says, tapping her nails against her thumb, as if she's dying to pick at the skin but won't let herself, 'because it just doesn't make sense.' She looks directly at me.

'Did she say, "Daddy's car" – or "Daddy car"?'

I'm confused.

'What's the difference?'

'When Katie was learning to talk everything big was Daddy and anything smaller was Mummy – you know the way little kids are. And' – she leans forward, her voice rising with mounting realization – 'that could apply to anything – cakes, biscuits, houses. The big ones were Daddy and the smaller ones Mummy. Baby was for the tiniest thing, so, yeah' – she turns to look at me – 'I think I went off on the wrong track there. Maybe she said, "Daddy car", meaning a big car – not a little hatchback like Rosa's Fiat.'

There's a beat of silence. She nods.

'She said, "Daddy car", I'm certain,' she repeats, looking up at me, jaw set.

'It's not him. There's something – we're – we're missing something, someone – someone. It's someone else,' she says softly. 'Not the boyfriend, not Nairn. I really just don't like him for this.'

'Then who?' I sigh.

'I think we need to go back to Mia – to the victimology. For both victims. It's got to be someone else. Someone else whose path crossed Mia's – and the earlier one – Kim? We have two victims, both young, both students. What else have they got in common?'

'And remember the attempted abduction?' I start getting my stuff together, but she's shaking her head.

'McCarthy's on that,' she says. 'Cig asked him –'

'Jesus!' I snap, 'I hadn't forgotten –'

She frowns, puzzled by my reaction.

'Niamh, what's wrong with that? And anyway, I thought you were taking the day off tomorrow. Why would you not let McCarthy do a bit of work on this and take one day – just one day? We have to regroup. We need to go back to basics.'

She's right. I'm being an idiot. Mam and Dad are expecting us. I haven't been home in months. I can't back out now. It's the thought of bringing Amber home. I see her – I see us – driving into the yard and getting out of the car, bringing her in – no, maybe I'll bring her round the front – yeah.

I don't like myself for this. Face it, bitch, I'm scared of what Amber's going to think. How she'll measure Knocknabo against the Vico Road.

'And what about your dance class tonight?'

'It's fine with me, honestly,' I say. 'Amber won't mind. We can do the dance thing another time – it was only for a laugh.'

Laura's sitting with her notes spread out all over the desk. She looks jaded.

'No,' she says. 'Anyway, you told me it was a birthday present for her? So you can't back out. And from what you tell me about her, Amber will definitely mind if you cancel!'

She shuffles the pages together in a sheaf, taking care to place each precisely on top of one another, and looks up at me, deciding something.

'No way, Niamh. You're due your leave – it's one bloody day. And we need to regroup here. Because if it's not Nairn, you know what that means.'

She waits and in the silence my phone buzzes with a text. I don't look at it; we continue staring at each other, neither of us saying the words 'serial killer'. But we're both thinking it. Between us sits the glaring fact that the first few days immediately following a murder are crucial. You've got to get some traction before trails go cold. Day Three is over;

we're into Day Four now. And for Kim, the trail is long cold. We've wasted time and got precisely nothing.

After a moment, she inhales sharply, gathering herself.

'Go home,' she says. 'Try to enjoy one night off. I'll get Cig up to speed.'

She nods towards my phone, reminding me. It's Amber.

Don't forget – (pouting cat emoji) *Be there quarter to? Xxx*

'Go on.' She's frowning. 'One night. I'm going to go home via the crèche, have a look around. It's on my way.'

She stands – decision made.

Having only seen her every now and then through the course of my work, now, it seems, our paths keep crossing. Strange. Hal would say that these things happen for a reason. It's how he's been able to accept his fate. Nature can't be argued with, and neither can fate. Predator and prey. The strong versus the weak.

With my mother gone, I began to grow. It was as though, as long as she was alive — so real and vivid, so full of certainty, so full of her own needs and desires — I was shrivelled and starved by comparison. My grades improved. I began dating — always the most immaculate and elegant of women. I began to hope for a future.

My first was a girl from work. Nuala. She worked in the shop — the new girl they took on to replace Mummy. There already was another one — I can't remember her name — it doesn't matter. She was older and kind of tweedy. On the weekends when I was on, Nuala took over the till and I handled enquiries, taking in prescriptions, directing people to the quiet corner of the shop for consultation with the pharmacist. Nuala was a curvy little thing. She must have been in her late twenties, but she seemed younger than me in so many ways. She wore a full disc of face make-up, the scent of which was what first attracted me — that, and her myriad curves of flesh that fought their way out of her white, popper-button tunic, like so many 8s stacked one on top of one another. She was clean, too — not like the other one, who had an acrid, medicinal smell and a curving black hair on her jawline, of which she was clearly unaware. I pointed it out to her — discreetly, of course.

Nuala stood at the till and I moved beside her, now reaching past her shoulder to pass out a saline nose spray or a balm for chapped lips, now kneeling out of sight beside her, keys in hand, opening the glass cabinets in which the pharmacy-only medications were held. Such a game we played for about a month.

Because of my practice with Mummy, I found it easy to move Nuala about. A press of my warm palm against her lower back as I reached behind her, adding a hesitant 'Excuse me' for effect. A heavy hand on her shoulder — I was easily a foot taller — just enough to demonstrate my strength, the way you'd steady a patient undergoing a painful procedure. A gentle squeeze of her forearm accompanied by a warm 'Thank you, Nuala' when she saved me from a tricky customer. A playful tickle of her rounded ankle while kneeling to take something out of the sliding cupboard.

And then, of course, it was so easy. I'd wait until she was in the middle of serving someone — the more garrulous and pernickety, the better — then I'd take the keys from my lanyard and move behind the counter, nodding a 'Pardon me' at the customer and a knowing look at Nuala. The trick was to do it quickly — to keep the keys rattling with one hand as I slid the glass door across and rummaged about, while the other hand went rogue, encircling her ankle as best I could with thumb and forefinger then slowly, slowly, up and up, my palm curving around the swell of her knee, her inner thigh and all the way to the top.

She wore skirts, so don't say she didn't like it. And the first couple of times, she was wearing tights — but pretty soon, Nuala began to appear bare-legged under her uniform.

The day it happened, David had asked Nuala to lock up — it was a Saturday and he was going to a family barbecue. I left mid-afternoon when my shift ended, but I was waiting outside the back door of the shop when Nuala was about to close. It was like tracking an animal in the bush, and I imagined Hal beside me, his fingers to his lips. 'Wait', he mouthed.

At last, the door opened and there she was. She smiled and stood aside to let me in. I stepped inside and breathed deeply. The empty pharmacy belonged to us. Well, in actual fact, it belonged to me. The night was ours. 'Mating season,' grinned Hal.

The normal lock-up procedure was to clean the surfaces, unplug the electrical items, apart from the fridge, lock all the cabinets and switch off the lights, reversing your way out of the shop as you did so and finishing by pulling down the metal shutter and locking that. That night, the order was reversed. Nuala pulled down the shutter and locked it, then the glass-front door. I waited for her, then switched off the lights and beckoned her towards Father's inner sanctum, the small square dispensary at the back of the shop. I sat her down on the edge of the treatment couch, the padded bench that ran across the back of the room, and her short legs dangled. I ignored the swinging, childish movement and stepped closer to her.

In the harsh strip lighting, her features looked coarser and, I could see now, a little nest of yellow-headed pimples had made their home at the edge of her hairline. I switched off the main light so the room was lit only by the fridge, then I pulled my gaze away and concentrated on her mouth. That was better. Nuala's lips were full and fat — plump pillows of soft flesh. I had an idea. In fact, in that moment of clarity, I knew exactly what I wanted.

I turned from her and moved to one of the make-up stands, selecting the reddest tint I could find — I think it was called Ruby Me or something. I twisted the sleek container, snapping the thin seal of plastic and pulling the ends apart. It had been years since Mummy had let me put on her lipstick for her, but of course I remembered how. With my left hand, I held her face steady, my thumb pressing under her chin, downy skin rising on either side and, with the other, I began to apply the lipstick. I shushed her when she tried to speak, worried that I'd get it on her teeth or over the line. Instinctively, she made her lips into the long boat-shape required. Above her mouth, her eyes darted left and right, the pupils dilated in the dim light, and her breath came in little damp billows, wafting across the fingers of my right hand as I pressed into the yielding flesh. Close up, I could see the tiniest of cracks at the edge of her mouth, silvered with saliva. It glistened.

At that point, I had no idea of the disappointment lurking just minutes away. Here was a young woman — if not a friend, then certainly someone who bore me no ill will — sitting in readiness for — for whatever I wanted. Her bulging chest rose and fell — and at last, she'd stopped swinging her legs. I pressed myself against her knees, enjoying the fact that she could feel me — strong and rigid. I knew what I was going to do. Having applied the lipstick, I would open her tunic at last, and then take off her shoes.

The poppers snapped with a satisfying sound and Nuala's gentle curves were revealed in the dim light. Her breasts, so high and round, perched above two — no, three — rolls of soft flesh. I hadn't even kissed her, and I ignored her as she tried to angle her face into mine, leaning away and stretching my fingers towards her belly, desperate to push them into the shadowy folds.

'Get off!' she said. 'I'm too fat.'

She kicked off her shoes. This was good. I took her feet into my hands and began to caress them. They were damp and soft. Sharply, she drew them away from my hands.

'Don't,' she said. 'It tickles.'

She lay back, hitching her skirt up a couple of inches. Not enough for me to see.

'Now,' she said, nodding at her private area, 'hurry up.'

In ballroom dancing and in nature, the man takes the lead. It's a simple rule and, like all rules, it's there for a reason. Nuala ruined it. With her fumbling and fussing and her endless attempts to kiss me, the strange dance began to fall apart. We raised the back of the couch, but it was too steep and she began to slide down it. The bench was narrow too, and we were in danger of falling off. As it was, Nuala's hip was half off, wedged in against the wall. I knew from tales at school that people do this standing up, or leaning over tables, and so I tried to get her upright. Hal told me to grab her from behind, but she wasn't having any of it.

With an impatient sigh, she drew her heels up towards her buttocks and, in an ugly movement, opened them to either side — the way you'd pin down the pages of a tightly bound book. I felt Father's presence then — which was not a surprise, given where we were — and I remembered suddenly, in a flood, it seemed, all the messes of the female body. And here they were: beads of sweat on Nuala's upper lip and in between *her breasts, saliva mixed with phlegm and remnants of the afternoon chocolate biscuit lurked in her mouth. I became convinced that the little tear I'd seen at the edge of her lip was a cold-sore and I shuddered at the thought of the virus making contact with any part of me.*

I no longer wanted to explore the folds and crevasses of her flesh — a yeasty scent rose from her — there could be fungal infections in those soft pink folds. Worst of all was the prospect of what lurked under her skirt. I couldn't believe that I'd wanted to — to enter that realm.

Nuala mistook my hesitation for the anxiety of a virgin. She propped herself on an elbow and reached towards my crotch, pulling me towards her by my belt. Ever dextrous, she undid both it and the fly, and began rummaging in my underwear.

Her face fell, and a look — a hideous look of sympathy and understanding and, yes — humour — rose into her features.

'Never mind,' she said. 'First time is a killer.'

The coroner ruled that Nuala died by suicide. She was found on the following Monday morning, laid out neatly along the couch, empty containers of tablets littering the floor beside her, a thin paste of ground-up tablets made to look like vomit peeping out of her mouth like a speech bubble. All those weeks of administering Father's morphine had proved useful and, when I left by the back door, locking it with Father's key, I made sure to bring the empty vial with me. The other one was inconsolable — or so I heard — I had exams and couldn't attend the funeral.

A change came over me after that. Maybe I, too, was developing a hard skin. When you don't care what people think of you, the world opens up like a flower. I've seen this first-hand. Being thought of as kind, considerate or nice counts for nothing and gets you precisely nowhere. You need to set that aside in order to achieve your goals. Once you do that, I'm telling you — it's a whole different world. Different rules. 'Kill or be killed,' says Hal. How right he is.

I kept the lipstick. The scent alone gets me hard.

38

Niamh

It's five minutes to closing time and I'm in the queue for the only bloody till open in the hardware store. Jaysus! You think they'd open another! There are three – no, four – people ahead of me, and another five or six behind. The fine weather has everyone buying bedding plants and deck stain. Why would they not be taking it easy on a Sunday evening? What's so important about your man's pack of sandpaper, or your woman with the tin of pink paint? On the side of the tin, there's a picture of a rustic wooden shed, painted pink, with a bench and flowers and a little pink watering can beside it. I look at the purchaser. Malnourished in the true meaning of the word – overweight and out of shape, with rolling knees and ankles constantly under pressure from the mass above them. She's wheezing a bit – I'm thinking she was lucky to escape Covid – yet she's clutching the tin and yakking away to the woman on the till. They're both raving over her choice of colour, her smartness in buying a ticket to the dream – to the neatly tended garden and the little pink shed.

I don't know what's wrong with me – I'm not myself, I know that much. I feel like everything I do is wrong – or about to be wrong. Instead of going straight back to the flat, I told Amber I'd meet her in town – the dance classes are in a studio on Foley Street – so that I could nip into Homebase and pick up the swallows' nesting boxes for Dorothy. They come mounted on boards with the fixings and stuff, so it should be easy enough to put them up. I reckoned ten minutes would see me in and out of the shop, then twenty-five minutes to get into town and find parking – I'd easily make it by a quarter to seven. Not at this flipping rate.

I sigh. Hurry the heck up! Pink shed and till woman are still chatting. I hear a chuckle behind me and turn to see an old fella eyeing my would-be purchases. I've three boxes. On a whim, I picked one up for Dad. The old fella nods in the direction of the boxes.

'Expecting a crowd, are you?'

I laugh, feeling a bit ridiculous.

'Well, I –'

He holds up a leathery palm.

'Ah no! You're right, you don't want to keep them birds waiting.' He laughs again, a wet, rumbling sound rolling like distant thunder in his chest. 'They're probably years on the housing list, heh-heh! They'll be fairly narky if you keep them hanging about – heh-heh!'

He takes a moment to enjoy his own joke, turning to the couple behind him to see how it went down.

'If only it were that simple' – the woman nods at the boxes, leaning in to press her hand on the old man's forearm – 'for the humans.'

There's a chorus of agreement.

I inhale deeply. Get it together, Niamh. Cool the jets. What's your panic?

'Too right,' I say, stepping up to the till.

I'm literally parking the car outside the dance studio when my phone pings with an incoming message.

Where are you?

What's your panic, Niamh?

Well, that's the answer, I realize. I'm shit scared of being late for Amber. It's got to the point that I'm terrified of displeasing her. Not that she'll do anything, it's – it's just that life's so much easier if I give her what she wants. And I'm nervous about the trip home. Anyway, I'm here now and it's not even seven. I thumb a reply of two hearts and a chef's kiss emoji and head into the studio.

An hour later we're laughing, comparing our blisters and aching muscles with the rest of the group during our five-minute water break. Our instructors – stunning short-haired blonde Karina and her stubbled, ponytailed partner, Kris – have pummelled us through an introduction to ballroom that was less like dancing and more like boot camp. Of the three other couples in the group, only one are doing it for fun; the others are preparing their wedding routines. Amber is loving this. She's in her element, dazzling and cute and so quick to master the steps. As the only same-sex couple in the class, we have a bit of novelty value too.

Who knew it was so difficult? We covered a whole raft of moves and I feel I have them, but my mind is a whirl of box step, triple step, forward-side-together, back-side-together. I've to keep my posture in alignment, hold my elbow up, support Amber and *don't forget to smile!* This is chanted every few minutes by Karina. Obviously, I dance the man's part – which, no surprise there, involves me stepping forwards first. Lady has to move back – on the back foot from the get-go.

It's worth it to see Amber's face. Flushed and pretty, she's in a floaty skirt and little strappy shoes from which her bare toes peep their pink, pearly nails. An image of poor Mia's tattered feet flashes into my mind in graphic detail – like when the movie you're watching freezes. I shake my head to clear it.

After the class, we exchange phone numbers with the other couples and Amber volunteers to set up a Facebook group so we can keep in touch. Karina is doing another class in two weeks, and we all vow to be there.

On the pavement beside the car, Amber throws her arms around my neck and kicks up her heels, hanging there briefly.

'That was sooooo fun!' she squeals. 'Thank you for my birthday pressie! And' – she steps away from me to observe me better – 'you were really good too! I thought you'd be rubbish!'

I pop the locks on the car and move to the driver's side.

'Eh, thanks?'

She throws her overnight bag on to the seat and gets in, settling in, already reaching to set up her iPod.

'I'll have you know I'm a shagging top athlete.' I laugh. 'I played for my county, for Christ's sake! I should be able to learn a few moves.'

'Oh, but that's just' – she flaps her fingers about as though flicking water off – 'GAA-stuff.' She laughs. 'And anyway, it was aeons ago – back in the mists of time, haha. No.' She nods, turning to look directly at me and prodding my belly with her bony little finger. 'You were definitely out of shape when I met you, but look here' – prod-prod into my thigh – 'and here' – prod into the ribs – 'you're definitely shaping up. Well done you.' She smiles, turning back to look at the road and taking a sip of her isotonic drink, 'and well done me! Now – how long till we're there?'

39

Laura

The bang on my car window makes me nearly leap out of my skin. I put the cardboard cup of tea into the holder and wind down the window – although something about Justy, in her green quilted Barbour jacket, makes me feel I shouldn't be seated when speaking to her, that I should hop out of the car and snap to attention, throw in a Girl Guide salute for good measure.

'Caught!' She's laughing. 'And there I was, feeling sorry for you, thinking you were stuck home with the two children, and instead, you're having a sneaky solo coffee at' – here, she checks her rose-gold-plated Omega watch – 'six thirty on a Sunday evening.'

'Haha,' I say, with as much warmth as I can muster. 'It's tea, actually.'

'And what have you done with my son? Have you got him in the apron getting the dinner ready?'

She laughs, a hooting laugh that only goes with a certain type of woman. As always with Justy, I don't know if she's getting at me or if I'm being paranoid.

'He's at home, haha, yes – he probably is – he's probably getting their tea into them now. He's great.'

She looks sharply at me, her eyes glittering like stones in reflected light from the streetlamp. I'm parked in one of the spaces facing the road, my back to the hall which is home to Tippy Toes.

'Well, what *are* you doing?' she says, adjusting her scarf against the chill. It's almost dark. 'Are you all right? I'm on my way to book club supper.' She points at the nearby junction leading on to a road lined with large, comfortable and well-maintained homes, each one more desirable than the previous one. I can just picture book club taking place in the wonderful extension, seated around the ten-foot-long hand-carved table made of reclaimed timber. 'I thought I'd walk down for a bit of exercise. One of the girls will give me a lift home later. Are you all right?' she repeats.

Now's as good a time as any, I think. Matt obviously hasn't told her.

'I'm back at work,' I say. 'And I'm just having a look around here. This' – I point at the large bay-windowed building – 'is where she – the au pair – was on her way home from.'

'From here? Good God! From here? From Tippy Toes – where Katie goes to school?' She twists her head from side to side as though expecting to see a killer lurking behind the parked cars or in the shadows at the corner of the old stone walls. 'Lord! I hadn't heard that. Nor had I heard you're back at work. We'll let that go for the moment. Are you telling me there's a – a killer – watching the school my granddaughter attends?'

A gust of wind catches her hair, lifting the carefully arranged and beautifully coloured layers upwards, as though she is sinking underwater. Her skull is revealed, bony and shadowed, perched on top of her thin neck.

'No,' I say, wondering which bit of information to address first, the phrase 'We'll let that go' shimmering in my brain. 'I'm – I'm trying to retrace her footsteps. I thought I'd park here and finish my tea, then have a little gander about.'

I point to my cup of tea, as though providing evidence. 'I'll be home before they go to bed.'

I decide not to add that it's unlikely the killer has any interest in children – that he put the little girl out rather than take her. Justy will think I'm making a case for him.

She stares at me.

'I really don't understand you,' she says, smoothing her hair and fastening the popper at the base of her throat.

'Do you enjoy this?' She shakes her head.

I'm angry, suddenly. When is she going to stop interfering? She herself worked when Matt was small.

'You went back to work, Justy – after you had Matt! You told me you did. Surely you understand –'

'Good God! That was completely different – and we had a live-in nanny. Plus' – she's gathering momentum now – 'my job was regular hours, in daylight, in a nice, warm office – and there was no personal risk involved.'

Again, she looks all around, casting her eyes towards the shadows, checking for danger. The hall is over a hundred years old, a red-brick and mock-Tudor combination built to commemorate the men from the area who served and died in the Great War. The Montessori school uses the three large rooms at the back, and local groups share the main hall, which, judging from the strains of music, old-fashioned and orchestral, and the lights, must be in use at the moment. I cast my eyes back towards my stressed mother-in-law.

'Are you safe, Laura, that's what I'm asking – and all right, yes, if you're going to push me on this, I'll say yes. It *is* different. There are jobs you go back to when you have children and there are jobs you don't. There.'

She pushes her hands into her pockets, shoulders hunched.

'I'd understand – no, I do understand your – your dedication. But you're a mother of two small children, Laura. Surely to God there's an easier way for you to – to keep your hand in, as it were – and to be a mother? I – I could put a word – discreetly, of course – in the right ear?'

We both know that she's already done exactly this and she's only looking for retrospective permission.

'Please, Justy. I – I know you mean well. But please, please, can you let me choose my own path?'

I've never spoken to her like this before, but I can't stop myself. It's flooding out.

'I can't be like you – I can't be this perfect daughter-in-law, I'm doing my best as I am. And I –'

She stiffens, takes a step backwards. And before I finish, she's holding her hand up to stop me.

'Sorry I spoke, Laura,' she says, tears shining in her eyes. 'And you're right. I know it's not my place – I'm interfering. And I promised I wouldn't. I try not to. Really I do.'

She reaches in the car window, giving my shoulder an awkward pat.

'Just be careful,' she says, turning away.

I watch her until she's out of sight, her words running through my head, the image of her tear-filled eyes seared into my brain. And I feel so guilty. I wish – here we go – but for the zillionth time, I wish my own mum was alive. She'd have been such a great foil to Justy – so full of fun. She'd probably have been in the hall there behind me playing Bingo or badminton or listening to old-time waltzes or whatever it is that they're doing now.

Justy is – she's the opposite. Not exactly stern, but serious and sort of rigorous. Well, she's too late. The decision is made. I take a last sip of tea. It's cold. Matt will be getting them to bed and it's better if I don't disturb that. This is where I belong. Pulling my coat closed, I get out of the car and start walking down towards the bridge where Mia would have walked every day with Carly. It's a route I drive often enough, but there's a laneway and a small group of houses set under the bridge which you'd drive past without noticing. The only way to see them properly is on foot. I fire off a message to Niamh – *Checking out Mia's route* – and speed up my pace. The road is quiet and only a few dog-walkers dot the path – one couple walking a giant brown-and-tan dog who looks as though he'd far rather be left alone to sleep. In the distance, I spot marathon-running man – not running; he's standing alone at the entrance to the walkway. Maybe he just needs to be outdoors – maybe he has stress at home or work and he just likes to get out. He seems far less threatening when I don't have the kids with me. Funny, that.

It occurs to me that I haven't been having intrusive thoughts. I haven't been imagining ever worse scenarios in which the kids are harmed or killed. I've done a day's work – okay, the interview with Nairn was a mess, but still. Maybe I'm getting better. I pull up my hood against the chill. Ten minutes, I tell myself. Fifteen, max.

They're completely in the dark — the gardaí. There's no way they'll find any evidence on the body. That's the beauty of planning and being careful. As my mother used to say — if a thing's worth doing, it's worth doing well. Poor Mummy. I thought of everything — every single thing. They have no clues. They simply have no clues.

Hal says you need patience to be a skilled tracker. I know how to wait. Once or twice a year is all I allowed myself at first. After Nuala, the next ones took place abroad — three in France and one in Spain. The Spanish one is what made the au pair so appealing. My first Spanish dancer. On the continent, if you pick a busy tourist spot, you will discover, within an hour of your arrival, the choicest beauties the region has to offer. They will be pouring your drinks, young and friendly, an apron tied around their little waist, perhaps, or a T-shirt, stretched tight over the soft breast flesh. Or they may be vacuuming your room, their curves hidden in a tunic, or waiting to take your dinner order, returning to the table balancing your plate in the crook of a curved elbow.

A letter from the pharmacy stating that the vials of morphine I carry are for my personal end-of-life care has proved acceptable at Customs, and it means that they do not suffer. A final dance.

Because, of course, I must hold them in my arms. I must press my jaw against their face and breathe in the smell of powder, lipstick and sweat. I must take them for a spin in a last dance for me — and for Mummy. For each of them, a new lipstick. Which I keep. A small memento.

It's more difficult here — back home. Before the au pair, there was the screaming one that got away. It makes me so angry to think of her — I'd misjudged her strength; I see that now. And the jogger — knitted together in strands of muscle. A disappointment. And the student — timid, hysterical. Another disappointment.

But the au pair I enjoyed beyond my expectations. So sweet — so friendly in her halting way. On Thursdays, I would arrive a full forty minutes before my class and wait outside the hall. No one ever recognized me from the shop — possibly because there are two other pharmacies in this area. Who is going to trek the extra mile to mine? Or perhaps I've fully mastered the art of what Hal calls blending into the background. Like a hunter.

When Mia arrived, her dark eyes gleamed — I liked to think — with a special flare of friendship for me. It was perfect — at that hour of the day, parents and grandparents tended to arrive singly. There were very few au pairs and no hanging about to talk. They'd ring the bell to announce themselves, then pick up the child and leave. Sometimes Mia texted or spoke on her phone. Occasionally, she would be laughing. And when she did, a tremor ran through her body so that you could see her laughter ripple in the flesh at the base of her spine, a little quivering. We would nod hello as she buzzed the intercom. And when the child came out, she'd turn away, kneeling to tend to the zip or the schoolbag or the untied shoelace. They would say goodbye to the nice man who has a little granddaughter called Lily — aged three. Yes, I played a youthful grandfather — a necessary sacrifice of pride — in order to gain her trust. I had neglected to give her my name, though I knew hers. I remained, for ever, the Nice Man. I knew she walked the mile from Clonchapel Drive to the school twice a day with the girl.

How I longed for Mia, over weeks that grew into months. But I was patient. 'Steady,' Hal would say. 'It will be worth it in the end.' One day, a friendly 'Hi' in passing, no time to stop. The next perhaps a brief pause and mention of the weather or of Lily's progress. Lily often had a cold and for three weeks was poorly with a chest infection.

I prepared the studio. I found a car seat in a skip. The fastener was broken — but no one's going to notice that. And I waited for a rainy day and an opportunity.

By twenty-five past twelve on that Wednesday, the rain was teeming down. From the cut-through, I watched Mia run in the gates of the hall to do the pick-up. Then, I timed it so I appeared to be walking from the bus stop towards my car a couple of minutes later.

'Mia! Would you like me to drop you home?' I said, huddled into my raincoat, with the hood up.

'It's pouring! Great Irish weather, eh? My car's parked just down there. I live nearby.'

I began walking away, as though expecting them to follow. 'Come on,' I said, 'the child is drenched, and I was going to take the car out anyway and head to the shops — I've to get a few things.'

She hesitated, but the little girl was whingeing.

'That's how Lily picked up the last cold,' I added. Something shifted in her face, and I knew she was mine.

'We're almost there,' I said, not letting myself check they were still following.

I stayed ahead of them until we were down on the path. I took my keys out of my pocket and clicked so they could see the garage door opening at the end of the lane. Nothing to worry about.

My neighbours' homes back on to this lane and they were seldom about at that hour, but even so I checked the upstairs windows to ensure that we weren't being observed.

The little girl was splashing in the puddles, chattering. They came into the shelter of the garage and the door began to lower automatically.

'Oops!' I said. 'Quick — hop in before it closes!'

This next part had to be done quickly. 'In you get, princess,' I said, holding the car door open for the little girl. She clambered inside and I slammed the door.

'Oh, I forgot. Lily's booster seat is in the boot — can you get it?' I said, clicking the button so the boot sprang open. Mia had been about to get in, but she stepped back.

'Sure,' she said, moving towards the rear of the car. She bent in, trying to see. I'd made certain the interior light wasn't working. In two *silent steps, I stood behind her and plunged the needle into her upper thigh – a large dose I had prepared in solution for injection and left on the shelf behind the car. Benzodiazepine is so widely available nowadays I felt it prudent to save the morphine for later.*

She cried out and I held her firmly, both of us leaning into the boot, one hand clamped over her mouth, the other pressing against her throat in a chokehold. Crude – but necessary. Ten seconds, thirty – a minute – until she slumped forwards into the car and all that was needed was for me to lift her legs and fold her in. A petite build, Mia.

I closed the boot and got into the car. In the mirror, I could see the child looking this way and that, trying to find Mia. It was almost comical.

Paedophiles disgust me. It is both morally wrong and repugnant, the idea of touching those small, unformed bodies. I needed to get rid of the child as soon as possible – but it couldn't be too close to home.

'Sit!' I said, as though training a dog. She did, although she whined and cried Mia's name for the next few minutes and, of course, she didn't put the seatbelt on, so she slipped down behind the passenger seat. I didn't stop. We were nearly there. I pulled into the laneway – empty, as I knew it would be at this time of day – stopped at the verge about halfway along and told her to get out. I had gloves in readiness, but she obeyed without having to be moved or touched by me.

'Don't move,' I said. 'Wait for Mia.'

During the drive home, I was aware of the keenest sense of anticipation. I felt Hal's presence. And Mummy's, too, of course. Perhaps this is what Mummy felt before taking to the dance floor – when she spent the entire afternoon in preparation. I drove into the garage, cut the engine and waited as the door closed. The ensuing silence was one of the most profound experiences of my life. The engine ticked softly as I walked around to open the boot.

Here she was – all mine. I wasted no time hauling her out and carrying her up the steps into the studio, laying her out on the sofa and carefully – so carefully and gently – removing her clothes and shoes. I draped Mummy's silk robe across her body, not wanting her to get cold.

All was ready – Mummy's dress was hanging from a rail, her make-up bag, scissors and the hair products laid out on a fresh towel. I filled a basin with warm water, adding a liberal squirt of almond blossom oil.

'Time for your treatments, Mia,' I said, lifting her dainty feet into my lap.

After Mia's treatments, when her hair was gelled in place and the jewels sparkled at her throat, I put Mummy's dress on her, flipping her over to lean across my lap as I did up the zip, then gently setting her upright on the sofa with her ankles neatly crossed. Two hours had passed since the injection, and I was worried it might wear off. At one point, she opened her eyes and gazed at me, as though trying to figure out a puzzle or recall an item on a shopping list. 'Ssh,' I whispered, my finger at my lips.

At last, it was time for the lipstick. How soft her lips under my fingers as I applied it. I stretched the skin wide, the way I'd seen Mummy do it countless times, and smiled at her in reply to her sleepy grin.

And then she was ready. In my arms she hung like a melting gold statue, draped against me, pliant and soft, delectably heavy, completely in my power. Her head rested against my chest and I held her tight. We took the closed position with full body contact. The Man leading.

She coughed when I tried to give her a drink and I was worried she might vomit.

'Last treatment,' I told her, bending to kiss her lips. 'Lie still.'

I thought of Father then, on his knees, ministering to Mummy, like some kind of penitential pilgrim. And Mummy lying back, eyes closed, knees apart.

'This will be very quick, I promise,' I said, lifting her for the last time into my arms, the blade ready.

And it was. I made sure.

The weight of her in my arms afterwards is something I will remember for ever. She was mine to the end – mine as she drew her final breath in my arms, her eyes searching mine, seeing me completely.

Mine.

After I had showered and put on the protective clothing I washed her naked body for the last time, removing any trace of our contact. Wearing gloves, I reapplied the lipstick and make-up – she had to look lovely for her final rest. Then, I wrapped her in the plastic sheet, carried her to the car and drove to the spot I'd chosen. Our final dance. So easy.

My intention had been to wait a few more weeks – perhaps even a month or two – before indulging myself again. Have some patience, Hal says. And yet. Opportunity has struck.

She is walking along the riverbank. This is not in itself strange. There's a narrow path from where you emerge from the tunnel. It curves around the corner site – occupied by my house – and brings you along the river, all the way down to the next bridge. There, too, one can choose whether to take the path under the bridge or walk up a few steps on to the main road and cross at the bridge. In this way, you can follow the Dodder the whole way to Ballsbridge.

It's a pleasant walk, and many choose it on a fine morning or sunny afternoon. But here, it's dark and overgrown, overshadowed by the steep riverbank on one side, where the long back gardens of the big houses sweep down to the river. Even in summer, it is always in shade.

What is strange is that it is almost dark, and that she is alone.

Hal and I watch her from the corner window. She's small and slim, bundled into a warm coat with the hood up. It frames a heart-shaped face, pale and ghostly – she's younger than I first thought. A lock of dark hair edges forward from under the hood and she tucks it back. As she approaches, I see her look over her shoulder – she feels the gaze, but she's looking behind her. Wrong way. She's walking towards me – in another twenty paces, she'll be here.

I scan the laneway. It's dark and empty. Fifteen paces – ten. It's too easy. It's all ready. Hal turns to me, one finger against his lips.

'Don't make a sound,' he whispers. 'Hunters must be totally silent.'

I tiptoe down the stairs and open the door, ready.

40

Niamh

'You're looking well,' says Mam, nodding approvingly at me.

'Isn't she, though?' says Amber, turning to admire me, as though I'm her personal project – which, in fairness, I am.

The drive took less than two hours, so there's time for a cup of tea before bed. Mam has it all set out when we walk in – cups and saucers, the whole thing. We came in the back after all – I copped myself on – and they'd obviously heard us drive into the yard. They were both on their feet and, just for a moment, it looked as though Mam was going to go for the hug, but then she stepped back. I got the full hug from Dad – the air nearly squeezed out of your lungs when he clasps his arms around you and pulls you towards him. And, as usual, I'm swept in the tide of memory that his smell – and the smell of home – evokes. It's like every fight and make-up, every Sunday fry and every rainy afternoon, homework and helping out, yelling and laughing – a whole childhood is swept into that hug.

Mam is still standing back a little, watching. If she's surprised by Amber – if she's not what she was expecting, for whatever reason – she hides it well.

'You're very welcome,' she says, extending her hand to Amber, pressing her own on top of the handshake, then releasing it and turning to clasp me in an awkward shoulder-to-shoulder embrace – two little pats on my back and it's over.

Amber is in full-on performance mode, confident of her place, oohing and aahing at our ancient dresser in the kitchen, at the range, the scrubbed table.

'But this is all so on trend,' she says, laughing. 'I swear, I saw a dresser like that in a vintage shop on Francis Street – do you remember, Niamh? Oh, no. I wasn't with you when I saw it – oh well, anyway – the guy was looking for two grand. Two grand! And that's before painting it.'

She turns to Mam. 'Your house is gorgeous, Martina,' she says.

I'm thinking you can't get round Mam that easily and that she's not much of a one for home decor, but she smiles at Amber, flushing a little in pleased embarrassment.

Dad is rummaging in the press, looking for biscuits. He plonks a pack of chocolate digestives on the table and Mam begins setting them out on the plate.

'Oh, please! Don't bother on my account – and anyway,' says Amber, rummaging in her bucket-bag, an enormous leather creation that's so soft I tell her it's made of cow foetuses. (Did she just say '*annie*way'? Is she seriously putting on our accent?) With a flourish, she pulls out a fancy-looking box of cakes wrapped in cellophane and creamy tissue, tied with a cream-and-red striped ribbon.

'I brought these – they're Bakewells – although, as we're both off the sugar, I don't know *what* I was thinking of.'

She turns to me. 'Don't worry, I bought some for Dorothy as well.'

Mam accepts the box and makes a great show of unwrapping it, like it's a holy mystery. As though she's unworthy of such luxury.

'What a treat!' she says.

Amber's full of chat about the dance class, how much fun it was – how mysterious and glamorous our teachers are. Her eyes shine, and I watch her reflected in my parents' eyes – a bright star.

'Can't believe you got that one on a dance floor,' says Mam, nodding towards me. 'Her sister did the ballet classes, and she could have done them as well, if she'd wanted, although –' She breaks off.

'I know!' grins Amber. 'I couldn't believe it either. I'd like to have seen her at the ballet, mind you – that would be a sight.'

There's a beat of silence and, in it, I think, *Great. Now there's a pair of them.*

'Did you ever see one of her matches?' says Dad. 'Have you seen her play?' He gives me a little wink. 'Poetry in motion on the pitch.'

He looks tired, I think – and old. He's wearing the fleece Siobhán and I got him about ten years ago – when fleeces were new. The North Face is written on the upper chest. For some reason, I think of McArsey and his mountainy gear. Maybe Dad is the man he wants to be – ancient and mountainy, hewn out of granite – instead of pale and priestly, like something from under a rock. It strikes me that I know nothing of McArsey's background – only that he annoys the crap out of me.

'How's work going?' Mam is speaking to me. 'What did Laura have?'

I sigh, realizing as I do so that this is a new habit – the sigh before answering a question. What's that about?

'She had a boy – Noah. He's nine months now.'

I wait for her to comment on the name, but she doesn't. Mam loves Laura – doubly sainted by fecking motherhood and straightness. And thinness – the triple crown.

'And work – it's grand,' I say. 'Well, busy, you know – and we're on this case.'

'Desperate,' says Mam.

'They're saying she must have known her killer,' says Amber. 'Like, she got into the car with him willingly and –'

She stops when I get up suddenly and move to the sink, tipping the half cup of tea down the drain, my anger visible in the jerky movements.

'Sorry,' she says, wounded and tragic-looking. 'I just read that –'

'Half of the stuff you read about murder, missing people – all that stuff – it's made up to make the reader feel better,' I say, bitterness in my tone. 'Victim-blaming or, you know, othering, trying to make it seem like somehow they walked into their own fate, that they brought it on themselves. So that the reader – you, in this case – so you think, *That won't happen to me. I wouldn't be out that late, I wouldn't go there alone, I wouldn't get in that car* – whatever.'

I'm aware of my parents' embarrassed silence, witnesses to my reprimanding of my girlfriend. This shouldn't be done in front of them.

'Sorry,' I say, 'rant over – haha.'

I move towards her, putting my hand on her shoulder awkwardly, feeling her anger in the set of the bones. Mam begins clearing the tea things off the table, embarrassed at the touch or the words, I don't know which.

'Everyone's very tired,' she says. She looks pointedly at Dad. 'We'll get on up so. Leave you to it. Goodnight.'

Dad gets to his feet and pulls me into another hug on his way past.

'Great to have you home, love,' he mutters somewhere above my ear. 'Sleep well.'

I sit down beside Amber, reckoning I'd better make it right now, before we go upstairs. As I do so, I feel my mobile in my pocket. Shit, Laura texted earlier, while we were in the dance class, but I didn't read it. Yeah – there's no way I can look at it now. I need to sort things out with Amber before she kicks off. Her voice carries, and the twin bedroom is next door to Mam and Dad's. I pull her against me. She's studying the markings on the wooden table, head bowed.

'Sorry about that,' I say. 'I'm not narky at you – I'm just narky.' I squeeze her little shoulder. She tosses her head and shifts her gaze an inch further along, saying nothing. Right so.

'I'm just tired after – after the dance class,' I say, peering up at her, trying to make eye contact. 'Like, it's all right for you, with all your natural talent and all, but I had to concentrate very hard, for hours and hours. I'm fair exhausted.'

She's still not looking at me, but she nudges against me – *go on*.

'You're an amazing dancer – I'd no idea,' I say, 'and you look so cute in your skirt, though, of course, you're way too skinny.'

Still nothing.

'I'm pure lucky to have you – in *fear*ness, you're a goddess, Amber Kenny, no doubt about that.'

I put my hand on her knee, feeling the shape of her thigh underneath the light fabric of the skirt. I press my thumb into the muscle, cupping the front of her leg and tracing a column of movement all the way to her top of her thighs, letting my fingers graze across the front of her lap. She sits very still. I draw my hand back along the route and repeat the movement, this time putting my hand underneath the skirt – on her bare skin. A plume of goosebumps shivers under my hand. Her upper body tilts towards mine and she rests her head on my shoulder.

I carry on with the same movement – sweep and graze, sweep and graze – until I feel her begin to respond. She anticipates the graze now, pushing herself against my fingers. I'm in an awkward position, sideways on to her, reaching. My shoulder's killing me, but I don't change position.

Amber comes with a sudden lurch, burying her face into my chest and slumping against me, and it occurs to me that this is just how it is with Amber. I'm always reaching. I always will be reaching.

Later, I lie in my childhood bed, listening to her soft breathing from the bed beside me, absorbing the weight of the Tipperary darkness and silence, feeling it like a thick blanket over the house. It's like being in a time warp, this room. Siobhán did it up herself – I didn't get to have an opinion; although she let me help with the rag-rolling. Rag-rolling! Feck's sake. I should come home and do it up over a weekend, paint over all that shite. I can't sleep. I'm exhausted and it's well after midnight, but I'm in that weird state of heightened awareness where your thoughts are whirling about, never settling on anything. I finally got to check my phone when Amber fell asleep – I was sure I'd glimpsed a text coming in from Laura. But there's nothing. The cover is shite here, especially in this part of the house with the thick walls, so maybe there's a problem with it getting through.

I wonder if Laura turned up anything in Clonchapel. I wonder how it'll go tomorrow at the language school. Should we consider Nairn completely out of the picture? I know Laura's not convinced, but he never told us – he never explained the lipstick – and I still think that could be something. And McArsey – did anything turn up with the journalist? Maybe I should go back first thing. What was I thinking, stepping out of the case for a day?

I sit up, annoyed with myself for being here, annoyed at the thought of McArsey, at the thought of him hanging about, muscling in on our case. Why did Laura have to agree to it? It'd be just like him to use what we get and claim it for his own. He's fast-tracking to inspector, no mistake. A chink of light from the landing is sliding in under the door and, as I tie up my hair, which is also annoying me, my stomach growls. Oh, yeah – and I'm bloody starving. That's why I can't sleep.

I look across at Amber. She's moved on to her back and her head is turned to the side, one hand lying by her face, fingers curled in complete relaxation. She looks like a child, the dark lashes shadowing her cheeks, the little chin and soft lips. It's not that she looks like a child, I realize. She looks like an actress playing a child. *Sleeping Child* is what it looks like.

I grab my phone and get out of bed, avoiding the creaking floorboard in the middle of the room. My old dressing gown is hanging on the door – Penny's best – bright turquoise and patterned with monkeys. I pull it round me, rolling the neck up high, enjoying the feeling of comfort, the smell of the fabric conditioner Mam always uses.

Muscle memory gets me along the hallway and down the stairs without a single creak or sound. The handle of the kitchen door tends to stick, so I use two hands to rotate it and, after pushing it open and entering, I turn and close it softly with both hands. For a moment, I stand, my eyes adjusting to the shadows. It's warm – the range never goes out – and a beam of moonlight lights the counter, peering in under the blind. The clock above the range ticks – it always had a weird tick, with its own little echo: *tick-tick*.

I breathe deeply, realizing that this moment is the first time I've been alone – properly alone – in – in what feels like months. I mean, I'm alone often enough at work – in the car, in the shops or whatever – and it's not like I ever felt the need to be alone before. It's more a feeling of owning this moment, of not having to justify it or account for it. That's it. Since Amber, I realize, it's like every moment must be shared or accounted for.

Have I sat in my own kitchen, watched a movie or faffed about, sorting stuff? Have I done anything at all alone? I used to chill out, listening to Dorothy's footsteps on the floor above, content with being by myself. I was busier, I suppose. I was knackered after the coaching and – yeah, I miss the coaching too. A year ago, I was coaching and hanging out and having fun. But I've been cutting back on the coaching – Amber says it eats into our time together. And work – even though we were crazy busy, I was loving it. Why is it that's all changed? Why do I feel like I'm kind of being eroded?

As I reach to get the Weetabix out of the press I have to grab hold of my pyjama bottoms because they're slipping off. I tie them tighter and, while the milk heats in the microwave, I rub my palm over my hip bone and across to the other side, wonderingly. There's a hollow, then a rise and then another hollow. I have bloody hip bones! My first thought is how pleased Amber will be – and then I stop.

Do I want hip bones? Am I any happier now I have hip bones? What the hell do I want?

While the milk is heating I check my phone again. Nothing. I've no message from Laura and only one bar of coverage. Weird. I'm sitting at the kitchen table eating my third Weetabix and hot milk when the door opens and Dad comes in.

'Jesus! You gave me a fright, Dad! I didn't hear you.'

He grins like a boy, delighted with his sneakiness.

'Did I wake you? I thought I was really quiet –'

He shakes his head.

'Sure, I wasn't asleep, pet. It was the quietness of your creeping that brought me down.'

'How did you know it was me? It could have been Amber.'

He looks at me as if the thought is ridiculous.

'You think I don't know your step?'

He considers my Weetabix – nods in approval. 'Sure, I would know the sound of each one of my children on the stairs and, anyway, you have a crick in your ankle when you walk. Or click. Whatever it's called, I knew it was you.' He pulls a chair out and sits opposite me, zipping up the collar on the same fleece he was wearing earlier, now serving as a dressing gown.

'No one can accuse you of fast fashion anyway,' I say with a grin. An upward tilt of the chin is the reply I get.

'Well –'

The word hangs in the air – ghost endings which might follow it hang there too: *What's up? What's wrong? How are you really?*

'Ah, it's a bit of everything, Dad. The case, the tiredness, the –' I stop, not ready to discuss the whole Amber situation with him.

'How's the new flat?' he says. 'How did the move go? I know you were worried about the landlord living above you.'

Jesus, I think. That was almost ten months ago. A lifetime.

'Great – I love it. Dorothy's – the landlord, I suppose, but I don't think of her like that – she's so kind. You'd love her. She must be mid-eighties and she's like a spring chicken, up ladders and gadding about. Oh!' I stop, remembering the nesting boxes. 'Don't let me forget. I brought you a present – you and Mam.'

I tell him the Power-Hosing of the Nests saga and he draws his hand from his forehead to his chin, laughing into his palm. I spot the glint of a tear scribble down his cheek.

I smile.

'Will they come back?'

He's nodding.

'I don't see why not. Put them up first thing,' he says, 'when you get home.'

We both let the word sit. He's right. This is no longer home. The thought hits me that, at thirty-four, it's time I made my own home. I sigh.

'It's – I'm just a bit overwhelmed, I suppose.' I look up at him. 'Decisions to make, work, this case –' I pause, pushing the bowl away from me and leaning my elbows on the table. Now my stomach is bursting.

'Are you not enjoying the work? You used to love it – what's happened?'

'I do – I mean, I think I still do. And at least, now Laura's back, I'm not partnered with McArsey any more.'

The corners of Dad's mouth twitch upwards.

'What's he done on you?'

'Nothing,' I say, realizing I'm just being ridiculous. 'It's like I'm having a fecking mid-life crisis. I just –' I sigh, annoyed with myself. 'Ah, it's fine, Dad. I just have to grow up and sort stuff.' I smile at him, hating myself for the extra lines of concern I see etched into his features. He worries about me.

Again, he nods, sitting back in the chair and folding his arms across his stomach.

'Did I ever tell you about the time I went to help Fennessy? He was clearing the top field of trees and all? Few years back, now. Sure, you were probably small.'

I shake my head – no, don't think I've heard this one.

'No matter. Well, you know where they are, don't you? The Fennessys. Over by Cloughjordan. Anyway –' He sits forward, as if to make himself accelerate. 'Anyway, he needed my help with the clearing. I have – you know I have a tooth bar on the front-end loader? So, I said I'd come up and give him a hand.'

'Go on,' I say, not wanting him to start explaining tractor parts.

'So, Fennessy is up in the field a few hours ahead of me. I'd – I don't know – I'd some jobs to do and stuff, so I went up later by the back road to the field. And when I get there, the gate is open and I see him up the far end of the field, working away, and I'm about to drive through when I see a boulder – a big yoke – smack in the middle of the gateway. So, I cut the engine and I hop down out of the cab to have a look. I look up at Michael – Fennessy – and he can't see me, he's powering away at the far side. And this was before phones.' He grins. 'Back in pre-history, haha.'

I smile, enjoying the moment – Dad cracking jokes.

'So, what did you do?'

'Well, of course I set to,' he says. 'Right away. Rolled up my sleeves and heaved the brute over to the ditch, out of the way of the gate. And I'm thinking to myself of the ragging I'll give him, how he owes me a fair few pints and all that – clapping myself on the back, don't you know.'

'And?'

Dad sits back once more, crossing his legs at the ankles in symmetry with his folded arms.

'And then I climbed back up into the tractor and drove through the gate – only, I didn't drive through. I got stuck. I hadn't realized how deep the rut was and my right wheel went right down into it and stuck completely. It took four of us and a whole load of shoving to get me out, later on.'

He sits forward now, laying his hand flat on the table and smoothing it with his palm – a habit he has – like he's stroking the wood. It makes a soft, swishing sound.

'Thing is, as Fennessy never tired of telling me after, thing is, the boulder was meant to be there. He'd put it there, hadn't he? What I should have done is set my wheel against it, the right tyre up against the boulder, and driven straight over it. Fennessy had put it there to keep his tractor from dropping down into the ditch.'

He looks right at me, and I'm pinned for a moment – in the strength of everything between us – the history of our family, little Martin, Mam's sorrow, his pain. My whole life is frozen in his watery eyes, just for a moment.

'I wish I could help you, pet,' he says. 'But all I know is what I learned that day – sometimes you just have to keep going, straight over the –'

'Yeh,' I nod, 'the boulder. Thanks.' I lift his hand up – it's heavy and shiny with hard work and age. I hold it against my cheek, leaning against it.

'Thanks, Dad.'

'And go easy on McCarthy, the poor fella. There's many a young lad would have gone off the rails with the money he got – and who could blame him?'

'What?'

'Ah, you're too young to remember – it was way back – anyway, his mam and dad were killed in a car accident and McCarthy – what's his first name again?'

'Senan.'

'Yes, right.' He nods. 'I should have remembered that. Same as his da. Senan was only sixteen, or maybe seventeen, and there were three younger than him at home. But he kept it all together for them – kept the family home an' all. Fair play to him.'

'Jesus! Poor McArsey!' And I asked him if he'd won the Lotto.

We say our good nights for the second time and I go back to bed. I'm tired in a different way now, weary and kind of drained. I fall asleep quickly, in that way when you're aware how great it is that you're falling asleep. And in that state, a piece of puzzle slots into place. It's been niggling all evening – since the class. Since we learned the box step, with its forward-side-close and back-side-close – Karina showed us a diagram of the pattern we make on the floor. She drew it out in marker, on a big sheet of paper.

'If your shoes are dipped in paint,' she'd said, 'it would look like this.'

The zigzags of the waltz. Familiar zigzags. The pattern looked like the tracks I saw at the Featherbed. The tracks at the place where the killer dragged Mia around, before dumping her lifeless body on the ground.

Other pieces begin to slot into place. The hair – the lipstick – the glamour. It's something or someone to do with ballroom dancing. The killer waltzed Mia to her grave.

Monday

41

Niamh

Where the hell is Laura? I call her number again and leave another voicemail.

'Laura! Pick up! We're looking for someone who does ballroom dancing. The marks on the ground are a floor pattern – I'm certain! Ring me as soon as you get this. I'll –'

I get cut off. Shite! There's nothing else for it, I realize – I'm going to have to cut the visit short and get back to Dublin. I get up. Amber must be downstairs already. She's left our overnight bag propped open on what Siobhán and I called the Leaving Cert desk. There was only one quiet place to study in our house, so whoever's turn it was for the Leaving got to use this desk. Even though Rory was the last, it must have been returned to our room. I pad across the floor in my bare feet, the carpet threadbare in parts and crunchy with old stains in others. I hope Amber didn't notice – I'm remembering the smooth marble flooring throughout her house; underfloor-heated. Oh God, I think. When will I stop this?

I can't believe I fell asleep and slept through till now. How did I not hear the cows? The milking? As soon as I'd made the connection about the dancing, I left messages for Laura and waited for her to ring me. But the Last Seen time was still the same and I must have fallen into a deeper sleep. It's almost nine now – hell! She'd said she would check out the language school today, so maybe she's in a meeting with them and has the phone off?

Amber packed the bag. And she's left my clothes draped across the top – a sweet and helpful gesture. That's what I tell myself. It *is* thoughtful. And I do like the clothes, a pair of grey, high-waisted jeans and a little white jumper – weekend casual. She's obviously thought about it, knowing I wouldn't want to be in work clothes – well, the new Niamh work clothes. Her shower things are stuffed into a washbag, drops of water glistening on the cap. So, she obviously showered and dressed and the whole lot while I was asleep.

I haven't got time for a shower – I do a quick deodorant and talc job and start getting dressed. I've got one foot into the skinny jeans, as far as the ankle, when I change my mind and go to the sliding wardrobe in the corner. Yes, I think. Comfort.

I grab an old pair of blue jeans and a faded grey T-shirt softened and stretched by a thousand washes and over it I pull my worn dark green hoody. The jeans hang loosely at my hips – I left them behind as they'd never fitted properly – and here they are, done up and loose. The neat lace-ups which would have looked perfect with the grey jeans chosen by Amber look ludicrous against the frayed ends of the pair I'm wearing. So, I have another rummage and – yes! My ancient runners are still here! Tiny bit mouldy – but so what. On the way downstairs, I nip into the bathroom and wash my face and teeth, then make my way downstairs, bracing myself for Amber's disappointment. It will go nicely with Mam's.

They're in the kitchen, and I must have managed my silent descent because they're chatting away, unaware that I'm just outside the door.

'And your people are from Dublin?' Mam's saying.

'Yep, Mom is in Dalkey. Dad is mostly in the apartment in Foxrock. They're separated.'

'I'm sorry to hear that,' says Mam, clearly embarrassed by the full disclosure.

'Oh, it's fine – they get on very well. It was a long time ago. I was nineteen.'

I can just picture Mam figuring out what age Amber is – if nineteen is described as a long time ago. Tea is poured into a cup and I hear toast being buttered.

'And you're happy in Dublin now, with –'

'With Niamh – yes!' Amber's gushing, in full flow. 'Niamh's so lovely – she – when we met, I'd just been through a bad break-up and – oh! I was a mess. An absolute *total* mess! I suppose I was just so inexperienced and, so *young* and everything, and Niamh – well, you know how kind she is, and she took me under her wing and –'

'I see,' says Mam. 'That's nice.'

Her voice is cold.

'Anyway' – there it is, again – 'now it's my turn to look after her,' Amber carries on, her voice light. 'I have her eating all the right things and, you know – looking after herself. Before I arrived, do you know, she really didn't look after herself. At all! But I think health and nutrition are so important –'

I can't listen to any more.

'Morning,' I say, stepping into the kitchen. They both look at me – it's like the scene in those westerns when the bad cowboy pushes his way through the saloon doors. Amber is sitting with her legs tucked up underneath her on the old wooden carver normally used by Dad. She's wearing a knitted fluffy cardigan, striped in ice-cream shades of mint, pink and yellow, and blue jeans with distressed knees on top of which kitten's faces have been embroidered. On her feet are pink fluffy socks. Her eyes are bright and her blonde hair brighter still. She looks about twelve. I don't know what Mam's expression was before, but it's unreadable now – like she's measuring me. Amber's face draws in on itself as she takes in my outfit, pulled by invisible threads of disappointment.

'I have to get back to Dublin, Mam. Sorry. Something's come up.'

Amber holds the frown, her body unmoving, while Mam begins clearing the plates. She makes no attempt to help – in fact, she sort of pushes her plate into Mam's hand, without looking at her, as though Mam was a waitress.

'But we just got here, Nimmi – it's your day *off*!'

'I'm sorry, but I can't get hold of Laura. I need to ring – there's calls I need to make, and I can do it on the way.'

Mam gets the cloth and begins wiping away the toast crumbs, then she fills the kettle and puts it back on the range.

'You'll have a cup of tea before you go,' she says – a statement, not a question.

'Thanks, yeh, and I'll nip up to see Daddy. Where is he?'

She nods.

'Up above.'

That means the 'office' – a Portakabin tacked on to the far corner of the yard.

'Thanks so much for the breakfast, Martina,' says Amber, recovering her composure and unfolding herself from the chair. 'It was yummy. I'll just go and change.'

Of course. Amber can't return to Dublin in 'weekend casual'. *Yummy*. I wonder what they had. Mam is a no-nonsense cook – food is food. I thought they had toast.

She leaves the room, and it's just me and Mam. Our eyes meet. Hers are tired – I've never known a day when she didn't look tired – and there are grooves – not lines, grooves – radiating from their corners. In photos before she was married, she was blonde. But Mam has been grey since – well – all of my childhood. With a tiny shift of understanding, I realize she probably went grey in the years following Martin's death. She's wearing the cotton trousers from M&S she favours – she has them in three colours – and a swirly-patterned top in shades of maroon and green. For warmth, she has her old navy cardigan.

'Sit,' she says, nodding at the chair and taking the teapot over to make a fresh brew. 'I'll bring it over.'

I sit, bracing myself for the talk I know is coming, cursing Amber for how she made it seem. Like I – took advantage of her or something. This will be the final straw for Mam. She'll have added it to her catalogue of disappointment in me.

She plonks a mug – the one with a duck and Siobhán's name hand-painted on it – in front of me and passes me the milk and sugar. She fills her own cup and sits down, leaving an empty chair between us. We hear Amber tramping about upstairs. The sound galvanizes her.

'Niamh –'

'Mam –' I'm suddenly desperate not to hear what she's going to say. 'Mam, I know – I know I'm not – I know it's hard for you, all of this. And I know you're – oh –' I set down the mug and look her square in the eyes. 'We both know I'm a disappointment to you –'

She sits forward urgently.

'Niamh!' Her voice is harsh. 'Stop. Hold your whist, will you? For once, just for once, will you listen to me? You need to listen.' She clasps her hands together, squeezing. 'I need to tell you – I've been wanting to tell you that I'm sorry. For months. I've been thinking about it and – I'm the one who's sorry. I was no use to you at all when you, you know – when you told us – when you came out.'

I almost laugh – 'came out' sounds ludicrous from Mam's lips.

'But –'

'I – I see it now,' she says, nodding. 'It took a long time, I'll grant you, but – it doesn't matter, does it? Now that I understand? I'm sorry.'

She sits back, releasing her hands and letting them fall to her lap. We hear the bathroom door close, and Mam looks up at me, as if scared we're going to run out of time.

'You are a great kid. You always were – and you didn't have it easy, being born after –' She doesn't say his name. 'I was broken-hearted,' she nods, as though acknowledging something to herself.

'My life – ah – it's like, it was like my life was over. And I had to close – I closed off part of myself. I see that now. And then you came along and you – and this is it – this is what I have to say to you' – she grabs my hand and squeezes hard – 'you were like a tornado!' She smiles. 'You're a great kid, and I'm proud of you. I am. And that' – she tilts her head towards the door, towards Amber's footsteps – 'that little wan – well. If she's what you want – if she's *who* you want – fine. All well and good. But you know what, love?' Mam releases my hand and sits back, patting my knee in a kind of farewell as she does so. 'You're worth ten of her. She's in the halfpenny place compared to you. And she's bloody lucky to have you. And you're the only one who can't see it.'

A kind of rushing sound fills my head at her words, and I try to process what Mam means – what this means. *Mammy loves me and she – she thinks I'm –* somewhere in my head six-year-old me is stuck at 'Mammy loves me.'

It has never once occurred to me that I'm a good match for Amber. I realize – yeah – I'm – I'm flattered by Amber's interest in me. How someone like her could choose someone like me.

Mam's lined, gnarled hand with its swollen joints and chapped skin rests on my knee. I think about telling her how much I love her and how much it means to me, what she just told me. I think about telling her about the tattoo.

When I was eighteen, my school buddy Shauna and I went to Dublin and got tattoos. She got a dragon and I got a little blue tractor on my hip with Martin's dates across the bottom: *21.1.84–19.5.87*. I never told Mam and Dad, and I think about telling her now. How Martin is real to me, though I never met him. How my heart breaks for her. But I don't. She pats my knee. Takes a crumpled tissue from her sleeve and blows her nose.

42

Niamh

'Can you see if you can get a signal?'

Amber takes the phone reluctantly and places it in her lap. She's still pissed off at having to go back to Dublin. At me, for deciding to go back to work.

'You were *meant* to be taking a day off,' she'd said, waiting for me to carry our case downstairs, her arms folded across her chest. 'One day, Niamh – just one day.'

In the yard as we say our goodbyes she hugs Mam then draws back, shaking her head at the strain of dealing with me. 'I wish we could have stayed longer, Martina, but she's a workaholic, your daughter, isn't she?'

Mam's tight smile says it all.

'You'll need to hold it up,' I say, concentrating on the zigzag bends of the land that leads on to the main road. 'The wall blocks everything.'

She transfers the phone into her left hand and holds it up against the window, resting her elbow on her other hand, which she's folded across her chest – sort of half arms crossed position. Half a huff.

'I'm sorry,' I say again, for what must be the tenth time. 'I'd no choice, Amber. I – I shouldn't have taken the day off in the first place, not in the middle of this case, and not – even if I did take a day off, I should have stayed in Dublin. Where at least there's a decent signal.'

'Kenneth says you always have a choice,' she says in a small voice.

Bloody Kenneth! She's been seeing him since before we were together. Sometimes Kenneth says stuff I agree with but, other times, I think he hasn't a bloody clue. Or rather, I think, what's the point of going to therapy if you're just going to pluck the statements you agree with from the hundreds of other ideas and use them to – use them against your partner.

I turn on to the link road, a long, straight stretch that leads on to the roundabout.

'Anything?' I look over at the phone, trying to see if any texts have come in.

'Niamh!' she squeals, as we bump against the uneven surface of the ditch. 'Watch what you're doing!'

'Sorry – I'll – here, I'll pull over,' I say, looking for a space. At that moment, the phone starts to ring. That'll be Laura. At last – thank Christ!

Amber answers the call and switches it to speaker. It's not Laura. It's McArsey.

'Darmody, can you talk?'

'Yeah, hi, Mc— hi, Senan. I'm on my way back to Dublin from home. I've been trying to –'

'Has Cig called you? Did you hear?'

'No, he hasn't – or he could have, but the signal's crap at home and –'

He cuts across me, his voice bleak. 'There's been another one – a murder.'

'Christ! Who – where? Christ! Same guy? Same thing?'

The call begins to break up. I hear McArsey's voice in patches.

'. . . took her . . . rough ground . . . Outside . . .'

Feck's sake!

'Can you hear me? Senan, you're breaking up, can you hear me?'

We're on the motorway. I realize I'm breaking the speed limit, but I'm going to need to floor it. I'll go straight.

'Senan, text me the location, yeah? Send me the pin? I'll go straight to the –'

That's when my body realizes something before my brain. There's a cold, lurching bolt through my core, and my stomach drops like a stone with dread – Laura.

Laura.

'Listen! Senan! Have you seen Laura? Have you been in contact with her?'

Only a roar of static by way of reply.

I'm only barely aware of Amber, shifting in the seat beside me as I speed over the bumps and potholes.

'What is it?' Her voice is injured, like I'm personally responsible for the road surface. 'Why are you driving like you're trying to kill us both?'

'They've found another –' I say, gripping the wheel so my tendons pop like cables. 'Another body. And I haven't heard – Laura went to check the route last night, and –'

Fractured light from between the trees zebra-stripes its way into the car, like some kind of strobe-light torture, glaring bright and disorientating. Something about the set of her body – Amber's head turned away so I can't see her expression – she's studiously looking out the window.

'All right,' she says, deciding something. 'Maybe she's okay, though. Maybe she texted you and I might have –'

She turns to face me, and now I'm the one that can't look at her. I could kill her.

'You deleted my message?' My voice is steady – way, way steadier than the thumping of rage in my heart.

'I thought – you needed a night *off*,' she whines. 'I thought it was just work –'

'What time was it? What did she say? Where was she?'

Silence.

'Where *was* she? For Christ's sake, what did her text say?'

'I didn't read it properly,' she says, like that's a good thing. Like she wouldn't stoop so low. 'Something about checking Mia's route.'

I can't speak.

In that instant, something dies. And a terrible dread is born.

'*Gardaí at Seskin West have appealed for information after the body of a young woman was discovered in rough ground near the entrance to Tibradden by a passing motorist earlier this morning. The identity of the woman is not being disclosed at present. The body has been removed to the city mortuary. A post-mortem is being conducted by the state pathologist, Dr Leo Parminter.*

'*Superintendent Shane Murtagh, who is leading the investigation, has called for anyone with information to come forward. Gardaí are asking anyone who may have seen anything unusual or suspicious in the last seven days in the area, or in the vicinity of the Military Road, to contact Seskin West Garda Station or call the Garda Confidential Line on 1800-666-111.*'

I switch it off. Who cares? I knew as soon as I held her that she was of no consequence. One of those forgotten — no, not forgotten — one of those invisible women that no one cares about. In fact, when I set her down and looked at her properly, I almost didn't bother. Her hair was lank and she was unkempt — dowdy. Like I say, a mercy. I probably didn't even need the excuse of calling her over to the doorway to help me with my cracked phone. It occurs to me now that maybe she was begging, or selling something — that she would have knocked on the door anyway.

No matter. I pride myself that I did a good job with her treatments. She was bathed in the lavender wash — I wasn't going to waste the almond milk on her — and I took the time to wash and comb her hair. A musty, unkempt smell rose from her body — from the area at the top of her legs. It persisted even after I'd washed her completely, and I found it offputting, troubling. Perhaps she was ill. I shudder to think.

Her skin was sallow — I didn't bother with foundation — but the crimson lipstick was a revelation. Her mouth, which I'd realized too late was small and mean, filled with tiny greyish teeth, became reborn into a thing of beauty in that dark colour. I took pride in that.

She didn't speak. She didn't cry. She never got the chance. The sedative took hold immediately, sending her right under. So much so that her breathing slowed right down and I was worried she'd be gone before I got the chance to hold her. Hmmm . . . perhaps I should start weighing them first so I don't make that mistake again.

I put her dirty clothes into the black bag with the others — I must take care of that — and moved back to the couch to look at her, trying to decide which of Mummy's dresses she would wear. She was no goddess. The bare light threw shadowy angles at her hips and shoulders, and a pinkish scar ran across her lower stomach, at the line of her panties. I wondered if she'd had a C-section. A weak specimen — and Hal agreed with me.

Her feet were white and small, devoid of corns, although she had matching blisters on her heels from her grubby trainers, which she wore without socks. In the end, though, I didn't even bother with the dress. She was almost gone — her feet and hands tinged with blue — even before the dance.

I'd underestimated her, though. I'd thought it would be nothing, the moment she passed. As I say, I thought she was already gone. But in actual fact, it was beautiful. She stiffened when she felt the blade, throwing her head back and opening her dark eyes wide to stare at me — rigid — just for a second. I drove it through, and she gasped. Such a gasp! Then her head fell back, her body drooped, and she was gone.

Poor Mummy. She really did suffer with her feet, and it occurs to me now that it was unnecessary. If she'd bought her shoes a half-size larger, perhaps? Or if she'd contemplated wearing a pair of comfy trainers when she was in the shop? I look at these girls — not a corn in sight, their soft little toes unblemished, and I miss poor Mummy even more.

I will have to burn the clothing, I realize. My original plan had been to wash the clothes by hand in hot water, then chop them up and bring them in batches to the recycling bank in the village. But I see now that cameras have been installed to catch those filthy scum who dump their soiled duvets and grubby cast-offs into the clothing banks. The last time I looked, there was a poster of a soiled nappy with a line through it. What lowlife would do that?

I make a cup of coffee and take it up to the mezzanine. I sit on the stool in the corner, like a child — the way I did on those Sunday afternoons — peering through the crack in the wood, remembering. Father on his knees, worshipping. The thickening as the blood gathers — the drive onwards. The blind worm making its laborious journey to the heart of the apple — now raised, now flat — raised, flat.

I relax my grip — it's not working. Perhaps I should — I think about pouring myself 25ml and trying again — perhaps. But I stay where I am.

In the silence, I hear Mummy's voice. 'You're pathetic. Disgusting.' And in my head, I'm the blind worm. I'm the blind worm, but I'm wearing Father's white coat and I rise up, up and up and up, until I tower over her, the fallen goddess beneath me. And her long, pale legs fall apart, and she opens her eyes at last, and she sees me.

You see, the thing is, I've been a coward. It's been too easy. I need a challenge. I need to be like Hal, strong and brave. I need a lioness.

43

Laura

I'm in the doorway of the language school, finishing up a dead-end conversation with the boss, Hannah, when my second mobile rings.

'I have to take this – sorry,' I say, holding up a hand in farewell and walking down the steps, looking for somewhere out of the wind to take the call. It's the Super. I duck into a corner facing Stephen's Green, watching the endless procession of people coming in and out of the park gates, while he yells. 'Another murder! That's three, for God's sake! The press are going apeshit at the thought of a serial killer! What the hell are we playing at? What the hell happened with Nairn? When are we going to make arrests?'

I'd taken a call from Senan earlier, as I was walking up the steps of the school, and he'd filled me in on the latest – the naked body, the lipstick.

'Did he cut her hair?'

'She'd short hair – slicked back,' he'd said. 'So, it's a possibility.'

We left it that he'd get in touch with Niamh, and I'd see if there was anything useful to be found at the college. Shit – I should have checked in with Cig. Save myself an irate Super on the line. One guy – three murders. There's no doubt in my mind now that we're looking for a serial killer. They've got to be linked.

'I reckon they've got to be the same guy,' Senan had said,

'and the attempted abduction. The journalist who covered it – you know, the one in Old Bawn – she said the guy was wearing PPE, gloves – the whole shebang. He tried to get her into the boot of his car.'

'Can we talk to the victim again?'

'I'm looking into the details. Tallaght are going to pull the file for me.'

'Great, and –'

'But don't get your hopes up,' he'd interrupted. 'She couldn't remember anything. Only that she was screaming when he tried to get hold of her. Then he stuck a syringe into the side of her thigh and she lost consciousness.'

'How did she get away?'

'The screaming panicked him and he took off – left her on the ground.'

'Anyone get a reg number?'

'Too dark – too fast – take your pick,' he said.

Cig's yelling, I can take. It's all bluster and noise. You know that, underneath it all, he's just trying to light a fire under you – like a hockey coach. But the Super is different. Normally urbane and soft-spoken, it's deeply shocking to find yourself at the other end of Murtagh's temper. I'd better go back. He wants a meeting this afternoon, ahead of a press briefing. Sighing, I check my personal phone, listen again to Niamh's message about the dance-floor pattern thing. That is nuts. I wonder if she was maybe on the lash last night at home. At that precise moment, she calls.

'Hi there, I was just –'

'Laura! Christ! What the actual? Where the hell were you? Jesus Christ! Laura!'

'Eh – what's going on? Are you okay?'

'Am I okay, she says. What about you? I'm okay. I'm driving up from home and thinking that I'm going to see your fecking cold dead body laid out on Parminter's slab – that's how okay I am! Fuck! Laura! Why didn't you answer your phone? Did you get my message?'

'Jesus – wow! Okay – but – sorry, okay? Why – how would I be expected to know you would think that?'

'Because you, you texted me – you said you were going to check out Mia's route. And it was dark and you were on your own and –'

'Okay,' I say, 'but if I hadn't come home, Matt would have started ringing people and –' I stop, aware that I'm making it worse. 'I'm sorry,' I say. 'I was leaving you alone for a day. I wasn't going to text you or message or anything so you could have a day off –'

There's a long silence, and I realize she can't hear me. 'Niamh?' I wait. 'Hello?'

'Anyway,' she says, and I hear the vibration of the road surface, 'I'm on my way back. I'm heading into town – I've to drop Amber home and I'm going to call to Karina.'

'Who's Karina?'

'She's a dance teacher. Where are you?'

'Stephen's Green.'

'Oh, that's – right. That's something. Stay there – in town. Meet you – can you get to Foley Street, the dance studio? Meet you there at twelve?'

I park around the corner from Foley Street but, instead of going straight into the studio, I sit in the car, trying to collect my thoughts – resisting the urge to call Sylvia and see how it's going at home with the kids. She'll have dropped Katie to school by now and Noah will be – Christ! Did I ask Matt to explain to Sylvia about Noah's bottle – to water it down a bit?

I pick up my phone, find Sylvia's number. I'll just ring and see how the school run went. The familiar racing begins in my chest at the thought of Katie outside – out in the world – clambering into Sylvia's car and being driven to school. Or maybe they walked – it's a nice morning. Jesus! I think with a lurch, what if that creepy guy is there again, down near the kiosk? He's always hanging around, the wannabe marathon runner with that water-pack thing strapped to his back, but I've never actually seen him running. What if he offers to help Sylvia with the buggy, like he did with me before? It was all I could do not to shudder when he spoke to me. And I saw him again by the park when I walked Mia's route last night.

A new thought grips me. Worse. Maybe he's stalking us – maybe, oh Christ – maybe that's our killer? Or no – a different one. One who's into kids. I can't believe I ignored him. What if he – what if he's after Katie? And we're off. I'm sweating now – the familiar panic. I've got to ring Sylvia. The urge to ring her, to tell her to stay indoors, to hold Katie's hand, not to let her out of her sight – it's overwhelming. I try to breathe – to do the tapping. You are not ringing home, I tell myself. This is a compulsion and you are not giving in to it.

These are only thoughts – fears are only thoughts. Why am I still like this? It's only in the last few months, since Noah was born, that I've been able to cope with Katie going off with other people – and the other people consist of her father and granny. I've turned down playdates and trips to the zoo. I've turned down Kay's offer to mind her at home while I do the shopping. Would it be so terrible for Katie to spend forty minutes with Kay? Why do I think only I can mind her properly? Or is that what I think? Is it maybe that it's my need, not hers? Is it that I can't face the world without my children beside me?

Face it, I think, when was I happiest? When we were in lockdown and me on maternity leave, the three of us and Noah in the womb, confined to the four walls of home.

The realization brings with it depressing clarity. Why did I think I was getting better? Matt's right – I've just shifted the anxieties around.

Mostly, the angrier Matt is, the less he says, but last night he was on a roll. And I sat there, guilt-ridden, miserable and hating myself for what I've done to him. He'd had a boyish look, right up until recently, but somewhere along the line it's gone – along with the sense of fun, the rugby trips and lads' golf outings, the few pints after work on a Friday. He reports for duty instead, on a daily basis, like I'm the duty sergeant in charge of the roster. Face it. I've put him through hell.

'This is the last time I'm going to say this,' he'd said, calmly stuffing the holiday brochures into the green bin. Because, even in the middle of an argument, Matt's a man who cares about recycling. It's why I want to hate him. Yeah. And it's why I love him.

'I'm happy for you if you want to go back to work, really, Laura, I am. You're amazing at your job. You've worked hard to get where you are – I don't, for one second, honestly – I don't want you to think you've to stay at home with the kids, and certainly not on my account. But –'

Here, he'd moved away from me, moving to stand by the fireplace, as if he needed space for what was coming next.

'But you need to decide what is going to make *you* happy, Laura. Because from what I've seen, *nothing* makes you happy! Nothing I do, nothing you do can beat your anxiety. You stay at home, you're unhappy and stressed. You go to work, you're unhappy and stressed.'

'Thanks!' I'd spat the word angrily. 'I'm an impossible bitch. Glad we cleared that up.'

I went to get a glass of water, intending on heading to bed. I hate arguing.

'I'm not going to fight – I really don't want to argue with you, Matt.' I picked up the glass and moved to the door.

He blew out a sigh through clenched teeth.

'This is part of it, Laura. The nonsense – the lies you tell yourself – that's what has you the way you are! Why can't you sit down – talk to me? Let's talk it through. We don't have to argue. For once, can you not do that thing where you refuse to talk about it – the whole acting thing? The lying?'

He pulls out a chair and sits, gesturing for me to do the same.

Panic begins to bubble – the tiny spheres at the edges of the saucepan. Soon it will become a roiling, scalding torrent. I don't want to do this now.

'So, it's me,' I say stubbornly. 'I'm at fault. Is that it?'

'No, you're not at fault. You're –' He pauses, and I leap into the gap.

'Sick! That's what you want to say. That's what it suits you to think, isn't it? Makes it easier. I knew it! You love me when I'm an injured little bird and you're taking care of me. That's when I'm easy to love. Not the reality. Well, I'm sorry that real, live, angry, mad Laura's not good enough for you!'

I'm sitting at the far end of the table, my hand still on the water glass. I watch a drip make its way down, down, on to the table, and I want to – I want oblivion. I want – if there was a way of silencing your brain and still functioning, I'd take it. Just an hour without the tormentor in my head. Or maybe it would be better for them all – Matt, Katie, little Noah – if it just ended. If – I just want silence. Oblivion.

Matt says nothing. He stretches a long arm across the faded wood of the kitchen table, resting his palm over my wrist. Underneath our hands, the bare wood is patterned with thousands of spidery, narrow black lines, like someone traced the whorls with a fine mapping pen. A wedding present from Dermot and Justy. Spalted beech, the black lines formed by a fungus.

'You're wrong about that,' Matt whispers, addressing my

wrist. 'I love real Laura. Always have.' He shrugs, like *What can I say?* 'Real, live, angry, mad – all of the above. Every little bit.' He clasps hold of my wrist and turns it over, tracing a thumb along the veins. He looks up. *Every little bit.*

'What do you want, Laura? Seriously. What do you want from me – us – our life together? I'm trying. I swear to God –'

'Matt – so am I, and –'

He holds his finger to his lips, motioning for me to wait, to hush.

'I know. I know. We both are. But the difference is this. I'm not – I'm not the one – I'm not fighting you, Laura. I want whatever you do – whatever makes you happy. When are you going to realize that you're at war with yourself?'

He shrugs, sitting back and letting his hand fall away from my wrist. Suddenly, I'm cold.

'You deserve to be happy, Laura. What happened to you in the past – the rape' – he leans towards me, puts his smooth palm against my cheek – 'we've got to face it. We've, both of us, we've got to be brave enough to talk about it. And the anxiety – and everything that's going on for you. We can't hide it. You can't hide it – or you shouldn't. Not from me.'

He's looking at me, directly into my eyes, and I feel my anger waver and shrivel, and it's like fainting, because, if the rage goes, if the anger steps out of the way, then there's nothing to stop the pain. My breathing quickens. The word 'sullied' sneaks into my brain. Old and tattered and dirty.

I can't tell him. Anger is all I have. It's the only thing keeping me upright.

'I've put that behind me,' I say. 'I've said all I need to say about it. I have the kids and you, and – I want – I just want –'

My throat constricts around the unspoken words. I want the pain to go away. And the fear. That above all.

'What do you want, Laura?' he says.

44

Laura

I'm still sitting in the car outside the dance school. A small victory. I've resisted the compulsion to check on the kids. On the footpath outside, a group of dusty sparrows is pecking at the remains of a roll. I watch them, trying to focus my thoughts, to breathe. I tell myself it's going to be okay. A magpie swoops down and the smaller birds fly off. It stabs at the roll, malevolent, as though enjoying a kill. That's bad luck, I think. A magpie – a single magpie. I actually say the charm that's meant to undo its bad luck: *Good morning, Your Worship.* I whisper it. And then I recognize it for the compulsion it is. Back to square one.

'May I help you?'

The girl on reception looks up from the laptop with an open smile. I glimpse a tongue-stud. Her lower lip is pierced also; a silver stud is perfectly centred between the gap in her front teeth when she smiles. From the inner edges of her nostrils peep two more buds of silver. I find myself wondering if they're attached and threaded through. But how would you do that?

She's short-haired or, rather, her hair looks shorn – the dark locks zigzag in line with her jawline – and slim, with a dancer's body hidden under various T-shirts. I think how pretty she'd be without the piercings, wondering if she'll regret them when she's forty, and am seized by horror at myself the second I think it. I've turned into Justy – making judgements. And worse, I'm betraying her – betraying all of us. What was that book title? *Women Don't Owe You Pretty* or something? Why should she be pretty? What even is pretty? Why is it any of my business if she's pretty?

'Are you here for a class?'

The girl is waiting. I tell her who I am and ask about Karina.

'Oh, she's teaching the professional class right now,' says the girl, nodding towards the large clock on the wall beside us. 'Ballet – in studio two. Up two flights of stairs on the right. They're almost finished. You can watch the last five minutes if you like.'

'I'll go on up then, thanks,' I say, heading towards the door to the stairwell.

'Oh, can you sign in, please?' She points to the large notebook, ruled for the date, time of arrival and exit and name given. Excellent.

'Does everyone have to sign in?' I ask her, filling in the details.

She nods. 'Yes.'

'And do they?'

She considers this.

'Pretty much. We police it – haha – yeah, I think they all sign in. Sometimes a person might forget when they're going out, but –' The sentence peters out. 'Do you need to look at it?'

I shake my head, already on my way upstairs.

'Not at the moment,' I say. Not until we know who we're looking for.

Upstairs, I peer in through the window at the class in progress, mesmerized. This isn't ballet, is it? There isn't a pink shoe in sight. Some of my friends in school did ballet, and I remember the talk of shows and exams. I was into the hockey – the thought of all that fuss, the big skirts and the pink tights and ribbons, stressed me out. Actually, it wasn't that – it's more like it took place in a country I didn't belong to, where people went skiing twice a year and their parents golfed. They spoke a different language, these girls. These moneyed, highlighted girls, destined for postcodes with even numbers less than ten. Destined for careers that involved screens and paperwork in airy offices filled with glass. Like Justy – or like the woman Justy wishes her son had married.

She brought me to a ballet once. It was the year we were married, and Justy declared that we should have a girls' trip. So, we taxied into town and had an early meal in one of the restaurants beside the Bord Gáis theatre, which had recently opened. All I remember is that it was long and there were an awful lot of big white dresses. The set was beautiful – I remember twinkling lights, as if you were looking at a village at dusk – and the music, it was thrilling. I could feel it in my chest. But I couldn't make out what was happening, what it was meant to be telling me.

A couple of feet away from me, inside the studio, there's about fifteen dancers – mostly women, though I count four guys. Karina – blonde and chic in a black tracksuit with leopard-print stripes along the legs and arms – has her back to me, watching them and calling out what I presume are the names of the moves. They're wearing an assortment of T-shirts and track bottoms, vest tops, shorts. Some are standing around the edges of the room, waiting for their turn to do their bit across the expanse of floor. I can see by the sheen of sweat on bodies and dark patches on clothes that they've been training hard. Three female dancers are travelling across the width of the room with a combination of small steps that gather speed and lead into a sequence of leaps that render them airborne. I see muscle and bone, strength and beauty. I see the human body defying the limits of the human body. If you got in their way – if you stepped in front of them – they'd smash into you with the force of a small truck.

I'm hit with a longing to be like them. To feel that freedom again. They look so free. I think of all the ways our bodies – women's bodies – are constrained and punished. Bras with wire and hooks, being zipped into tight skirts, buttoned into high-waisted jeans where heaven help you if a bit of flesh slips over the top. *Muffin top, spare tyre, bingo wings, flab, wobbly bits*. The hideous words for unwanted flesh, even if that extra flesh is post-natal. Giant nursing bras with eight hooks and five-inch elastic. The control pants and tights that squash you into smoothness like some class of wetsuit. Even the word 'control' – does anyone ever talk about controlling the male body? Like, what's going to happen if we lose control?

They're bursting with power, these dancers. Fierce. Bulletproof. They're the ones in control.

I think of Katie being like that when she's older. Being brave enough to take up that much space, having access to that freedom. That would be something to give her. And I wonder when I last felt like that. When I owned my body. Myself. When I respected its power. When I was fierce and strong.

Before the rape. Yeah.

45

Laura

By the time Niamh arrives, flushed and angry-looking, I've located Karina and we're sitting at a table in the empty foyer.

'I remember you from last night,' Karina says to her, smiling. 'I didn't know you were police – on a case?'

'Hah! Nor did I,' Niamh says. 'And I wasn't – at that stage. I was just at my first dance class. Hi, Karina.'

The foyer is an airy room with a high ceiling, bounded on two sides by walls of glass. Niamh spreads the sketches out on the coffee table.

'This is why I was late,' she says to me. 'Byrne did them out – based on the footage from the drone.'

She turns to Karina, pointing at a page which shows a series of straight lines and shaded blobs.

'This is a tracing of marks we found on the ground at a' – she pauses – 'in a car park – well, an area of open ground, near a car park. The circles are footsteps, and we think –' Again, she hesitates. 'What I'm wondering is – is it possible these lines here are tracks, like a floor pattern of a dance?' Karina looks at the sketch and then up at Niamh. 'If, say, a man was lifting her – the woman – instead of her stepping and taking her own weight – what I need to know is, could these be tracks of a man – a bigger person – sort of dragging around a – maybe an unconscious person?'

There's a silence as the three of us consider this. Karina pales; her right hand drifts to her mouth and stays there.

'When I got home last night, after your class and what you told us about the floor pattern – it's – it was just a thought.' Niamh sits back. She has dark shadows under her eyes and she's wearing jeans and a hoody. Like old times, except she's lost her shape. The clothes hang loosely on her, baggy and formless. She doesn't look well.

We both watch Karina studying the sketch. There's a long silence. Then Niamh shrugs.

'It was worth a try,' she says to me. 'Maybe I'm way off –' She reaches towards the page. 'Thanks, anyway, Karina – thanks for your time.'

But Karina presses her hand on to the page and with a neat, manicured fingernail begins to trace the pattern.

'If he starts here and he goes – this is the line of dance – here.' She looks up at Niamh, her eyes lit, then back down at the sheet of paper. 'The man steps on his right, and he – you can see here it goes *step, side, close*, then again *step, side, close*.' She poises the tip of her fingernail on the page. 'And this could be – it's not very clear because Lady is not on her feet, but it could be – I think it's a lockstep, *one two three four*, and then here, you can see this big circle?' We both lean in, watching as she twirls two fingers on the spot. 'This could be the spin turn before he – he finishes or – the track finishes here?'

In the sunny room, blonde, beautiful Karina holds her fingers in position on a sheet of paper, unknowingly marking exactly where Mia's dead body was found.

'I think he ends the dance here,' she says. She sits back in the chair, pushing her fringe back into the clip. 'A quickstep,' she says. 'The man was doing a quickstep.'

We face each other across the table in the little café on Talbot Street. Niamh's having a mug of tea, which I'm eyeing jealously. I'm on the third day of giving up breastfeeding, so I'm cutting down my fluid intake. Lactation cessation, they call it, like you can cease, just like that. As with everything to do with babies and motherhood and being a woman, there's a zillion different theories on how you do it. Some say drink less fluids – great: so you're dehydrated as well as in agony with throbbing tits. Or take B vitamins or stick cabbage leaves down your bra or bind your breasts.

'Can't believe I'm the one making you eat something,' I say, gesturing towards the oat biscuit she has in front of her – untouched. She does a half-hearted laugh, then takes a big swig of her tea.

'Ouch! Christ, that's hot!'

'Smooth,' I say. 'Listen, I'm sorry I didn't reply to your texts – I didn't check my phone. I made an effort, you know, when I came home last night. I tried to switch off – literally. You know – and *be present in the moment*' – I make the air quotes – 'with Matt and the kids. That's why I didn't message you. I thought one night of phone silence wouldn't kill us. Both of us need to take a break every now and again.'

'You're grand,' she says, pouring more milk into the mug.

'Yeah, I was just panicking – on edge, you know. I hate the fact that we've no idea – that he's out there – somewhere, like – he's so close and we haven't a fecking clue who he is or what we're looking for. Three victims. Christ!'

Again, she sighs. 'I know you say look at the victim, but seriously, what do we know about him? The bastard.'

'The earlier woman was young too.'

'Yeah, we know he likes young women. Doesn't exactly narrow it down, does it?' Her tone is bitter. 'I've asked Byrne to make sure he gets overhead shots of the drag marks from this one as well.'

Now, it's my turn to sigh.

'He's had at least a few months of ballroom dancing

classes, so we know he has some disposable income. We know he's got to be strong – to get the girl in and out of the boot and haul her around. We don't know where he lives, but we know he has a car and that he was somewhere near Tippy Toes Montessori last Wednesday.' I shake my head, wishing we'd more to go on.

'We never did get an answer from Nairn about the lipstick, you know,' she says, stirring her coffee.

'I know. But –' I don't finish the sentence. We both know it's moved on since then.

'Carly said he was a "nice man" – isn't that what she said? It makes sense that he must have come across as nice – you know, trustworthy? Or Mia wouldn't have gone with him in the first place.'

She reaches for the handle of the mug but doesn't drink.

'So, for Mia's killer, we're looking for a nice, respectable, trustworthy-looking man in the Clonchapel slash Terenure area last Wednesday,' she says.

'Who had – already got to know her,' I say, halting. 'It's got to be someone Mia trusted on sight.'

'Yeah, and who has done some ballroom dancing lessons. What about the language school? Any leads there? Maybe a tutor or something with a thing for young students?' says Niamh.

I tell her the language school turned up precisely zero.

We sit in silence for a few minutes. I think – or try to think clearly, to home in on the piece I'm searching for, but it's no use. Cig says sometimes you need to wait till the blood goes round again. I tilt my head, considering the image of a sad-looking Niamh in front of me, and change the subject.

'How did it go, anyway? Bringing Amber back home?'

She sighs from the depths.

'Yeah, not great, but –' She stops, seeming to think of something. 'It was good to see Mam and Dad.'

'How are they?'

'Grand.' She nods, as though trying to convince herself of what she's just said. 'Look – feck it' – she sits forward, bringing the mug to her mouth and trying again – 'never mind that. Let's follow the dancing. What next for fricking Flatley?'

'That's Irish dancing –' I start to say, stopping at her eye-roll.

'Karina said we're looking for someone with a reasonable amount of dance experience, didn't she? Was it two or three terms of classes, can you remember?'

I think back to the conversation.

'She said you'd cover quickstep after box step and triple step – um –' I check my notes, where I'd written, 'Cha cha 1 x triple step 1 x rock step.'

I take out my phone and open the search app.

'At least it's a guy – narrows it down a bit,' I say, attempting to cheer her up.

'What are you doing?'

'Looking up ballroom classes in the South Dublin area,' I say. 'He had to learn it somewhere.'

Her phone buzzes and she reads a text.

'That's McArsey – Senan,' she amends. 'He's heading into the post-mortem on the latest. Cig asked him to –'

I frown at her – this is weird. She called him Senan.

'*Senan?*'

'Ah, yeah. I've to stop calling him McArsey. It's just I found out some stuff, you know. When I was home Dad filled me in on his backstory,' she says, her brows drawn together.

'The crash?'

'You knew? Why didn't you tell me, instead of letting me walk around like a thundering bitch hating his guts?'

'I –' I throw my hands up, mystified. 'I thought he – I thought you knew. Everybody knows! Why do you think – how do you think he's got a house and he's in the unit and he's like, next up for sergeant?'

'You thought I knew his – his tragic past and that I still ripped the piss out of him every chance I got?'

I nod. She looks crestfallen.

'You're nice to everyone,' I tell her. 'No, that's not true – you rip the piss out of everyone equally.' I shrug. 'I wasn't sure – I didn't even notice, to tell you the truth. What's wrong?'

'Ah, nothing,' she says. 'I – nothing.'

'*Annie*way,' I mimic her, 'he's annoying as shite, as you'd say yourself.'

Her biscuit stays uneaten while she makes a call to Byrne.

'Still no name for the girl,' she says, ending the call and putting her phone back in her pocket. I check mine. It's just after one thirty, and the body was found this morning. If his modus operandi was the same as before, he'll have taken her yesterday, or maybe even earlier. The fact that no one has come forward yet, looking for her, raises questions – maybe she's a tourist travelling alone, or a runaway. An asylum seeker – homeless – trafficked?

'They're checking the missing-persons list, contacting the refuges, the homeless charities. But nobody so far knows who the hell she is,' Niamh says, her voice flat, and I know we're both thinking the same thing. What does it say about us, that a young woman is abducted and killed and no one has noticed? Are there two types of people – ones who matter and ones who don't?

There's a beat of silence during which I rummage around, looking for something to lift us – we're meant to be a team. And usually there's an energy between us – that's what I've missed – that's what I thought I was coming back to – Niamh's energy. Instead, it's like we've both lost our way. We're wading in a mire of mud, feet dragging. No leads. No evidence – or no real evidence. The thought of trying to find this guy looms into the skyline, blocking all the light.

A niggling truth prods at me, like a piece of metal against a filling – hot, sharp, nerve pain.

All this time, you piggybacked on Niamh's energy, it tells me. It wasn't a partnership – she was carrying you. Look what happens when she stops.

'Come on,' I say, standing up and gathering my things together. 'We've got to try. I'm going to call ballroom teachers. You – link up with your friend Senan after Parminter's finished.'

She nods. Tries to summon a bit of energy.

'Right you be,' she says. It's the smile she tries to muster that worries me. What has happened?

Of course, I see Mummy still, especially when I'm dancing. Thursday and Friday nights from 7 p.m. sharp in the hall, though we never start until at least a quarter past. Thursdays are for beginners and Fridays for improvers. Anita likes me to attend both because men are scarce. And so I like to get there early – I help Laurence set up the chairs while Anita busies herself with the music, setting out the CDs in a row along the tall windowsill running across the top of the room. Laurence must be seventy-five if he's a day – and the rumour is that Anita's ten years older. He's dapper, with a Clark Gable moustache and trousers creased blade-sharp. She twists her white hair up in a fancy clip and, like Mummy, always wears a beautiful gown or a sparkly top with a full skirt.

Anita and Laurence were crowned Irish Amateur Champions over and over – they talk about the competitions at the teabreak and the characters on the Dublin dance scene and the good old days of trips to Brighton for competitions. Once, they even mentioned Elizabeth and Eric – Mummy and her partner – and I longed to say who I was and talk about her with people who knew her in her prime. But I stayed quiet. I keep Mummy to myself. They don't know a thing about me – only that I live nearby and I love to dance.

Anita and Laurence say I'm their star pupil – waltz, tango, quickstep, cha cha – even the foxtrot. I've mastered them all. And so, I hold those middle-aged bosomy women in the small of their frumpy lumpy backs, trying not to think about the purple thread veins that carpet their flabby thighs or the spider veins sprinkled on their crêpe-paper chests, or the rhinoceros skin around their elbows and vast, enormous knees. I refuse to consider their unattended shins, like stubbled fields, and the reddened welts of giant underpants pressing into their greywhite stomach flesh. And their ravaged, calloused feet. They disgust me. Ancient lizards – lazy, blinking – thinking they've earned their place in the sun.

But I hold them firmly and I look over the top of their wiry heads, into the air behind them, looking for her. And sometimes – just sometimes – I can see Mummy, and I long for her to see me. The lights shine on her gleaming hair, catching the emerald that dangles from her earlobe. Her skin seems lit from within, gold and cream, a shimmer of silver on her cheekbones and the red, red curves of her soft lips. Her eyes are closed, and she leans back.

And I'm the man. I lead.

46

Niamh

Parminter is tilting forwards over his shiny shoes, nosing into the beam of sunlight like one of those wading birds you see standing in the river, scouring the water for fish. Then he rocks backwards on his heels, repeating the movement over and over as he goes through the findings. The post-mortem is finished. McArsey – Senan – got the end of it, and I just arrived. We're standing in the corridor outside the viewing room in the mortuary.

'Your colleague will fill you in on the PM, no doubt,' he says, looking at each of us in turn.

'I will, Doctor,' says McArsey – I can't think of him as Senan – I just can't. His tone pure arse-lickey, as ever. Like he thinks Parminter is the Pope or something. I shake my head, like I could rid myself of the thought that way. And I'd better wise up – he's back on the case, clearly. So that's that. So much for Cig getting rid of him.

'Any luck with the ID?' I say, wondering about her family – who she was and what twists of life brought her to end up on Parminter's slab.

'Her name is Nicole. Ruhama contacted us,' says McArsey. 'They were working with her; she'd been attending one of their mobile units in town in recent months. She was – her best friend, a Lithuanian girl, sounded the alarm. Ruhama tracked down her parents. She was from Sligo originally.'

'Where was she living, do we know?' I say, though I already know the answer. She'll have been squatting somewhere, or sleeping rough, or maybe, if she's 'lucky', in a hostel.

McArsey looks up from his notes.

'She'd a tent by the canal,' he says. 'Her friend said she'd been homeless for two years at least – feeding her habit – you know.'

Parminter leans in.

'Preliminary results show benzodiazepines, but we don't know the levels and there were traces of other drugs.'

'And it's definitely the same guy?'

'I would be ninety-nine point nine per cent sure of that,' says Parminter, nodding. 'Same modus – the single deep stab severing the spinal cord; same absence of DNA evidence, the body having been sterilized afterwards.'

'What about the bruising on the body?' I cut across him. 'Like with Mia, you know, the bruises under her arm and across her ribs – we think he holds them as though he's dancing with them, like a ballroom hold.'

McArsey is looking at me like I've six heads, but Parminter is thinking. He tilts forwards suddenly – it's like the heron spotted a fish.

'Yes,' he says. 'Actually, that would explain the perimortem bruising under the armpits and – I couldn't understand why there were finger marks, each finger and the thumb spread wide across the side of the victim's body – but that would make sense.'

He reaches his long arms forwards as though embracing an invisible dance partner, the thumb and fingers of his right hand splayed and clawed, pressing against flesh and bone that aren't there.

He rocks backwards, letting his hands fall to his sides.

'How curious.'

'And the other one, Kim? The one he buried? Were there marks – bruises – in the same place as on Mia and Nicole?'

Parminter hesitates – he's looking at me as though weighing something up.

'With an actively decaying body – post bloating stage, you understand – much of the skin will be loose and grey-blue in colour. And so, no, I did not find the same bruising.'

He walks us towards the entrance hall, turns.

'You've spoken to Dr Fallon about the organic material on the feet, yes? She believes it to be wood splinters.'

I shake my head. Danni Fallon is one of the top techies at the lab, a brilliant scientist and regular expert witness. A year ago, she helped us put away a major drug dealer by linking the mud found on one of the holdalls to mud from a dried-up puddle near his home in Malaga. It contained pollen grains from a plant that grows only in that area. Dainty and blonde, behind the girlie facade is a Rottweiler, determined to catch her quarry. I haven't met a guard that doesn't revere her, or a defence barrister who doesn't fear her testimony.

'Pollen?' I say. 'That's her area?'

'Organic material of all types,' he says. 'Pollen, spores, fibres, fungal remains' – he pauses – 'and the insects that feed on them. She gave me a courtesy call and filled me in. I believe she sent the file to your team. Have you not seen it yet?'

McArsey is hanging his head in shame at not having seen whatever the doctor wanted him to see.

'The splinters in the feet were identified as being from a maple floor – maple is a hardwood, used in –'

'Dance floors?'

He nods at me, pleased.

'And she noted the presence of a worm feeding on the

skin around where the toenails had been. This worm was previously known to feed only on decaying wood.'

McArsey and I lock eyes – it's like a game of chicken. I will myself not to throw up the coffee I had with Laura. He looks like he's having a similar struggle. Parminter's features light up with the ghost of a smile.

'*And* she found samples of a semi-aquatic plant – colloquially, it's called Parrots-Feather.'

'Do we know where it grows?' McArsey recovers first, his pen poised in readiness.

'I don't, but Dr Fallon will,' he says. 'Though she did mention rivers and streams. It's an invasive species.'

We stand separated by my car, talking across it. McArsey's pale ginger eyelashes blink as a gust of wind blasts into his face. His eyes water.

'Where's Shaw?' he says. 'Will she –'

'Checking out dance teachers in the Clonchapel area,' I say, 'so we should –'

'I'll contact Dr Fallon, will I?' he says, already jingling his car keys in anticipation. 'See if we can find anything about the pondweed.'

'Yeah,' I say, glad not to have to start reading through reams of info on aquatic plants. 'That's more your type of thing, pondweed –' I stop. 'Sorry, Senan,' I say, reddening. Fecking force of habit. 'I'm only messing with ya.'

He gives me a pitying smile and the corners of his mouth curve upwards, framing his pink-tinged nose. Maybe it's his looks, I think, hating myself. Maybe I simply don't like his pale pinky vibe and I'm just being lookist.

'You're grand,' he says, like I'm flirting with him. Argh!

'Okay so, I'll –' I'd been about to tell him that I was going to get back to the unit, ahead of the meeting, but my phone rings. Dorothy. Jaysus! Why's Dorothy ringing?

I nod at McArsey, getting into the car out of the wind, mouthing, *Got to take this.*

'Hi, Dorothy!' I say, remembering the swallows' nest boxes still waiting to be put up. Shit! Why hadn't I made time to do that?

'Is everything okay?'

'I think you'd better come home straight away,' she says, her voice serious. 'I'm worried about Amber.'

47

Laura

A WhatsApp image from my friend Christine slides across my phone as I switch it to Silent. Mallorcan sunshine beams down on a dazzling blue swimming pool and empty deckchair.

Sun lounger with your name on it! Mid June for Fortieth Fun!

Christine has been sending me this pic for the past three months, reckoning, rightly, that it will take some work to convince me to leave the kids and head over there for her fortieth. I'll have to reply soon. Standing on Rosa's chilly doorstep, it looks pretty tempting. She's invited us both – she adores Matt. We could laze by the pool, walk into the town for late-summer-evening suppers in the town square, read books beside that very pool. What the hell is stopping me? Other people work *and* take holidays *and* go for weekends away. I've got to get a grip. There's nothing wrong with me. I've no excuse. It's another thing I hate about myself.

I push my hair back behind my ears and straighten my shoulders before ringing Rosa's doorbell. The breeze whips across the drive, dislodging a shower of cherry blossom from the tree by the gate, and the little blooms fall like snow on to the tulips and hyacinths someone has planted in a circle at the tree's base. On either side of the front door, bay trees stand guard like sentries. It is such an impressive house. Like Justy's. Like the home Matt grew up in. Am I jealous? I don't know – actually. I really don't know. I think I recognize in Rosa, when she comes to open the door, something of the same imposter syndrome that I felt in the early years with Matt — that still haunts me, if I'm honest.

I plaster a bright smile on my face and brace myself. Maybe I shouldn't have come, but I have to try one last time with Carly — if Rosa will let me. She's pale and drawn, and her eyes are lined with red. She's wearing a fawn-coloured thick roll-neck jumper — cashmere — and black trousers. She's not pleased to see me.

'Mrs Nairn — Rosa,' I say. 'Look, I know we didn't get off to the right start the other day, but —'

'It's fine,' she says wearily, ushering me in. 'Come in.'

I kick off my shoes and put them in the basket, then follow Rosa, padding in my stockinged feet into the kitchen. Carly is sitting on the couch at the far end of the room with a vast array of teddies and dolls around her and a plate of what looks like slices of apple and biscuits. She's watching TV and completely engrossed.

On the kitchen island sits a half-full glass of wine, a mobile phone and the newspaper open at the court pages. Rosa points to the paper.

'At least that's over,' she says, pointing to an article about the child who was drowned. 'So sad. Not guilty by reason of insanity. That poor, poor woman.'

She picks up her wine glass, cradling it in her long, bony fingers. I notice that her engagement ring is askew, the stone hanging downwards, as if her fingers have got thin.

'Would you like some wine? I know it's the middle of the day, but —'

'No, thanks,' I say, shaking my head. 'But, hey, I'm not judging you, Rosa. You've been through the mill. I — I hope you don't mind — is it okay — would you mind if I just try to talk to Carly one last time about the car?'

She sips her wine, nods.

'Tom told me everything,' she says.

I'm stunned. What does that mean? Has he confessed? Or is she talking about the fact that we interviewed him?

'I see,' I nod, encouraging her. 'Go on.'

'Like, there I was, thinking he was having an affair and that he was going to leave me – us – and go off with some young one, and' – she takes another sip and places the glass unsteadily on the marble counter – 'and in actual fact, in – actual – fact' – she repeats the phrase, pausing between each word – 'he's sick.'

She looks directly at me, her lips clamped shut while she struggles for composure. Her chin puckers with the effort.

'And I've been – I feel like I've been such a bitch, because I knew he was lying to me. I knew it. And I was so angry, and I hated him, and I was resenting him, too, and all the time – all the time, he was lying, but he was lying to protect me. Do you know, I'd even – I even suspected him and Mia! I mean, I don't know when he'd have got the chance, and he was being so secretive but – but when Carly said the thing about his car, just for a tiny second – it crossed my mind.'

She looks at me – through me – tears trembling in the corners of her eyes.

'And now I'm left with all those feelings – the anger and the guilt – and new ones, like what will I do and how will I watch him die.'

I saw a piece on the news not long ago where some artist arranged it so that as soon as his piece of art or painting or whatever was bought and paid for, it self-destructed. It disappeared into a shredder or something. Looking at Rosa Nairn, I feel the same thing. She was so carefully put together – so beautiful and perfect – and she's literally shredding, dissolving, in front of me. Tears spill from her eyes and she brushes them away with the back of her hand. I reach out to place my hand on her arm, but she moves away, shaking her head.

'Do you ever wish –' She stops and picks up the glass once more, looking directly at me.

'Do you ever wonder when the lying starts? You're married, you have kids, Laura – you must know what it's like. Like, when, when does it happen that we stop being honest with each other and the distance starts to creep in? You stand there on your wedding day and you make all these promises, and you have all your hopes and dreams, like a pair of idiots – like children. And you haven't a bloody clue, have you? None of us have a clue, do we?' She gulps her wine, answers her own question. 'I hadn't, anyway. I hadn't a notion what it would be like. Promising to live to the end of your days with someone you hardly know.'

'I'm so sorry, Rosa,' I say, still playing for time. 'We'd no idea that Tom was – was ill. And –'

'I suppose I should thank you that at least it's out in the open.' She tries a wry laugh, but it turns into a sob. 'He only told me because you had him in for questioning and you – or was it the other one – Niamh – one of you found out that he wasn't in court on Wednesday, when Mia disappeared.'

'Yes.' I nod. 'We knew –'

'You knew bloody nothing!'

Her voice is bitter, tinged with anger. She scrunches the tissue into a ball and meets my gaze, a defiant set to her chin.

'But now I – I know that he's not cheating on me and he's not a bloody murderer. He's just a middle-aged man with a particularly nasty cancer and he was seeing the oncologist at the time poor Mia –' Her voice cracks and she gives up trying to speak, taking a swig of her wine. 'He's in the Blackrock Clinic – I'll give you his number, if you like.'

'I'm so sorry,' I say, meaning it. We sit in silence for a few moments, then she seems to decide something. She nods towards Carly.

'You'll need to turn the TV off,' she says, 'or she won't take in a word you say. She's obsessed with that show.'

'Thanks,' I say, beginning to make my way towards the living-room area.

'Oh – and he told me you were asking about lipstick?'

I turn back towards her.

'Tom wouldn't remember – that was from a charity ball we attended, way back. I didn't bring a bag, I just put my lipstick in his pocket. It was months ago,' she says, shaking her head. 'But it was mine. Seriously. Can you cross Tom off your bloody suspect list and give him – us – some peace?' The words hang in the quiet of her designer kitchen.

Half an hour later – at three o'clock – I pull into the lay-by beside the new bridge into Bushy Park, hoping to gather my thoughts in the silence. I got very little from Carly, and what I did get contradicted what she'd said earlier. 'No Mia,' she kept saying. I'd asked her what she meant – did she mean that Mia wasn't in the car? – but she clammed up. She's just too young to remember. I have to leave it. I sigh and sit back in the seat.

It's very quiet. Most of the older kids will still be in school and the younger ones gone home or on their way there. Poor Rosa Nairn – not a phrase I thought I'd be saying. A quiet Monday afternoon. A woman returning from her dog walk pops the boot and her elderly dog – a wire-haired terrier, maybe – gamely makes as if to leap in. Just for a second, anxiety blankets her face and she throws up her hands – Wait! Wait! – before gathering the creature into her arms and lifting it up. She sees me watching and smiles a sad little smile.

Okay, I think. We'll go back to the dance angle. I take out

my phone and start a search for ballroom dancing lessons. There's a school in Ballsbridge, one in Rathgar, another in Harold's Cross, specializing in salsa as well. Who knew there were so many? I keep having a feeling that I'm missing something – it's like I know it's staring me in the face. Mia and Carly – or at least Carly – got into a car with someone near here. All that's between me and the school is a corner of parkland and the big crossroads. Someone Mia trusted – a man – maybe a parent or grandparent at the school? Suddenly, I remember the older dad I saw waiting near the school. The guy with the shiny shoes. He disappeared inside when I was talking to Joanne. I never saw him emerge with a child.

My heart begins to race – but just as quickly the certainty subsides. There's no connection to the dance aspect. And what about the latest victim – Nicole? We don't know where he took her from, but she mostly worked the area by the canal, a good two miles away.

My phone rings as I'm scrolling through details of a ballroom dance school in Harold's Cross. It's Matt.

'Everything's fine,' he starts, knowing that I'll already have had the first lurch of panic. 'Just calling to see how you are –' He hesitates, and I can picture him frowning, thumbing his new glasses back into place. Since he's started wearing them, he's got a couple of new tics – that one, and one where he slides his hand down over his mouth, thumb under his chin and forefinger curved across his lips, as though trapping the words inside. Like he's worried he'll say something wrong. And I know it's because of me – that I've made him like this. I'm about to tell him that I'm okay – I'm reminding myself that he's not trying to handle me, he's not checking up on me, that things are improving, when he cuts across me, his voice suggestive.

'And how are you after your seeing-to last night?'

I laugh, in spite of myself. This is brave. After the talk, we went to bed early last night – and together. We had what we call Old Married People Sex, where pyjama bottoms in Matt's case and a Dunnes Best maternity nightdress in mine, remained in place. My boobs are still so sore and full of milk I was worried they'd start to leak, so we did it with two pillows across my chest. Matt couldn't even see my face.

'I quite liked that,' he'd grinned afterwards, like he was being naughty. 'It was an improvement – ow!'

I'd thumped him, and we giggled, petrified of waking the kids. When Matt fell asleep beside me, I lay there observing the tiniest shift in perception – a mini lifting of spirits. I felt my body, tired and sore though it was, was telling me something. You're alive. You're living. And it hurts. Get used to it.

'I'm fine,' I say.

'You certainly are,' he replies, the smile still in his voice. My breathing calms and a small knot unravels somewhere inside. Maybe it will be okay between us, I think. Maybe Rosa is right about the lying and the distance. I just have to be careful not to let it happen to us. If I try really hard, maybe we'll get through this and I'll be able to do what I do and still be a half-decent wife and mother. Good enough – isn't that what they tell us to aim for? Not perfection.

'Have you spoken to Sylvia?'

'No.' There's pride in my voice. 'I decided to let them at it – they'll be grand.'

'Great. Of course they will,' he says.

'I'm in Clonchapel,' I say. 'I might even see them if she takes them out for a walk. I'm parked outside Bushy Park, googling ballroom dance schools, for the case. But there's loads of them – more than you'd think. I'd no idea there were –'

'You checked out the one in the hall, I presume?' he interrupts. 'I'm sure there was a ballroom class going on there – do you remember? No, actually, you weren't there. It was when you were in hospital, having Noah. Mum was looking after Katie, but that day she had something on and Katie stayed late in the crèche. I picked her up on the way home from work, about half six or so.'

'What? The hall where Tippy Toes is? Yes! Of course, that's it! What day of the week, can you remember?'

'Um, let me see. I could work it out –'

'No, it's fine –' I cut him off. 'Doesn't matter. That's great – thanks, Matt! That's it! I'll go – I've got to go.'

I hang up and get out of the car, zipping up my coat. There's no point in driving up to the hall – they rent out the parking spaces to local businesses during the week, so I won't get parking. I do the quick check – ID, phone, torch, gun and handset – then breathe deeply and set off, deciding to go through the park as opposed to around by the road.

On the way, I start composing a text to Niamh but then abandon it. I'll wait till I have some more details. I stuff the phone into my pocket and cross the bridge.

I'm standing in behind the wall at the kissing gate. It's called a kissing gate not because you are meant to kiss at it — although they do. I've seen them, the teenagers that come to Bushy in their gangs, wearing their hormones in stripes of acne and loud laughs and those stupid giggles of girls. I watch from the corner — they never look around. People never look around when they come in here. They follow the path towards the little waterfall and the steps and on up to the top road. Or they — the teenagers — shove each other into the wall, kissing like they are actually eating food from inside each other's faces, and they rub each other up down up down. Disgusting. And Mia — I saw her once in here, doing the same thing. She let him hold her breast and he bent his head to lick it.

I am tired of pretending. I am tired of being invisible — of being the weak little brother. I have the blade in my hand and it's dark down here. There's no one about. And here she comes — I saw her get out of the car. She's pretty — dark, wavy hair falls on to her shoulders and she's walking along by the river. I know who she is. She comes into the shop quite a bit. She has problems sleeping. I've seen her with her little girl, and I've seen her with the tall one. Little and large. She's little. She puts her phone in her pocket — it's a deep pocket — good. She's not tall and she walks well, upright and straight. She doesn't see me in the shadows, and I wait until she's almost past me before I step out.

I use the classic hold — arm bent behind her back. You can steer them anywhere like this. With the other hand I press the blade under the base of her skull.

'Feel that? Don't struggle,' I whisper in her ear. 'Don't scream, or you'll be dead before the sound leaves your mouth.'

I shuffle-bundle her in front of me through the dark tunnel and she tries to move, but I dig the blade in — just the tip. The tip is enough. Down and down we go — no one is about and I know she's going to fight — I only have a moment. I can feel her searching the dark for help. I keep hold of her wrist. With the other hand I swap the blade for the syringe. She shouts — I stab the syringe into the bare skin on her neck — into the muscle. I grab her towards me like we're long-lost lovers, my hand over her mouth. I stuff her head into my shoulder, pressing with all my weight so her screams are muffled. She struggles. She fights and we do a strange, shuffling dance — certainly no move I've ever seen. This is messy. This is risky. I — we could have been seen — her screams may have been heard. Blood races through my veins. I'm alive in a way I feel I've never been before. I'm hunting. It should take effect within two minutes. 'Come on,' Hal urges. 'Don't let her go! Hold fast!'

At last, she slumps against me, her knees buckling. I carry her the last few metres — my partner and my prize. The garage door is activated and there's a judder of metal as it settles in the frame when it bangs closed.

There's a moment of complete and utter silence. Another. One more. No shouts or running feet. There's no one here. No one's coming.

No Mummy. No Hal.

Just us.

48

Niamh

I see the note taped to the door before I've even cut the engine. A flimsy blue Post-it does back-flips against the door knocker – up and over, up and over – fluttering in the breeze. Something inside me drops with a whoosh – so sudden and so strong I look down to see if I've wet myself. My hands are blocks of ice and they're shaking as I pull down the note.

Do not enter, she's written.
Call the police.

I fucking am the fucking police, I think. Is this a joke? I'm trying to get the key into the lock, but it's slipping and tapping around the place. I'm picturing Amber hanging from the beam in the sitting room, the buckle of her Ralph Lauren belt digging into her soft neck; or Amber lying on the bed, naked and dead, sightless eyes reproaching me; or slumped in the shower in a pool of her own blood. She could do it! She's so – she's so fucking young and dumb she could –

The door opens from inside, and I'm looking at Dorothy's concerned face.

'It's all right,' she says. 'She's not here – I – I hope you don't mind – but I didn't want you to have to face – whatever it was – alone, so I came down through the house.'

She steps back into the small hallway, opening her arms

and pulling me into a swift, bony hug. She smells of mothballs and medicated soap.

Relief sweeps through me. I hug her back, then pull away, walking into our flat. It looks like we've been robbed. Cushions and rugs from the sofa are strewn across the floor. There are feathers everywhere, and the TV is on mute, a daytime TV show flickering across the screen. The Ikea bookcase we assembled together has been tipped over, its contents – a few recent bestsellers and a handful of fancy candles – vomited from underneath. The diffuser I gave her for Christmas has been thrown against the fireplace and smashed. I set it upright, though it's too late – the water has leaked on to the carpet.

'I'm so sorry,' I say, turning to Dorothy.

'Oh, for goodness' sake!' she snaps. 'Don't worry about that! What do you think – what happened?'

I haven't been into the bedroom yet – or the bathroom. Dorothy sees me looking behind her.

'She's not here,' she says, 'and she didn't wreck – I mean, the rest is okay –' She motions for me to follow and we walk into the bedroom. Every drawer is pulled out of the chest and the built-in wardrobe doors are gaping open. The top shelf is empty – which means she's taken her suitcase and moved out.

In silence, we walk back into the living room and begin straightening up – folding rugs, picking up books and candles, cushions and magazines. I get the bin from the kitchen and dump the smashed diffuser and the butchered cushions that used to read 'Mrs & Mrs'. A thought occurs to me – her keys – and I step into the little hall to check the status of the birdhouse. Status is that the birdhouse is no more. She's reefed it off the wall and smashed it. I find myself picturing her rage – it would take a fair bit of effort to break the wooden cube – but she managed it. Fair play.

Dorothy is sitting perched on the end of the couch with a small stack of blankets folded neatly in her lap.

'I take it you two were a couple?' she says.

'Ah – yes –' I start to gabble, embarrassed. I'd never told Dorothy – not to – not because I was ashamed or anything, I just didn't want to offend her, I suppose, and I –

'Oh, for goodness' sake! I knew you were gay.' She smiles. 'What I'm asking you is were you – did you think –' She pauses, lets out a breath and starts again. 'What I'm asking is were you exclusive as a couple? Because – well –'

'What?' I say, sitting down beside her, wondering what I'm going to hear. 'What, Dorothy?'

'Look, it's none of my business, and I'm only telling you this so that you have all the facts, all right?'

I nod.

'Amber often had visitors – one visitor in particular – when you were – it was always when you were at work. She'd park in your space.'

I'm shaking my head, nonplussed.

'As I say, it wasn't my business and so I wasn't keeping track. But it did seem strange that she never called when you were here. Maybe – does she have an older sister?'

'What does she look like?' I say, shaking my head. 'No – no sisters.'

'Mid-thirties, shortish – dark hair worn over to one side.' She mimes that asymmetric haircut – like Karina's. 'Wears colourful scarves and those – you know the chunky black boots young women wear a lot nowadays? Sorry – I'm sure I'm getting this all wrong – it could be perfectly innocent.'

'No – you're fine,' I say. 'I think I know who that is.' Caoileann ('pronounced Keelin, Niamh!') – director of the pilot that Amber was in. I sigh.

'I was out for lunch, but when I came back, I knew one of

you must be downstairs – she'd everything on: the TV, music – blaring. So, I went into the kitchen, you know, to let you get on with it, I suppose. Loud music is not going to kill me, and you never play it at night. But then' – she stops, turning to look at me – 'after a while – about a half-hour or so – it all went quiet. I came out the front, looked over and saw the note on the door and –'

'Here we are,' I finish. 'Thanks, Dorothy, and I'm so sorry to have you – that you got dragged into this. We – I told her I thought we should cool it, just for a few weeks. That was earlier – this morning in the car – we were driving back from home because of this case, you know? And yeah, maybe my timing wasn't great, because she was pretty pissed off – you could call it – raging, I suppose. And I didn't have time to sort it out or discuss it or anything. I just dropped her here and –' I stop, feeling the familiar shame of how badly I treated Amber.

'I should have –'

Dorothy looks at me, her head tilted to one side. A feather is stuck in her hair. I don't mention it.

'You're a very kind person, Niamh,' she says. 'It's the first thing I noticed about you. And I don't think you should start handwringing over this, if you don't mind me saying.' She pats my knee. 'It's been my experience that there are some people in this world who you simply cannot please – nothing is ever enough for them – and you can destroy yourself, running around trying to please them. That's all I'll say.'

She looks at me.

'You did your best,' she says, nodding at the tears threatening to spill from my eyes as though giving them permission. 'Move on.'

'I like that one, Dorothy,' I say, feeling the tears fall and wiping them away in one sweep. 'I'll keep it – "You did your best – move on." That'll be my new motto.'

'Good.' She smiles. Then her expression changes – she's looking at the TV behind me.

'That's your case, isn't it?'

I turn to look at the TV, scanning the room to find the remote. Dorothy hands it to me, and I turn up the volume. It's the press conference – Cig, the Super and Feeney are taking their places in front of a bank of microphones, the gaggle of photographers and journalists arrayed in front of them. No sign of Laura – although she usually keeps out of the limelight, so I wouldn't necessarily expect her to be there.

'Yes – thanks.'

We sit in silence, watching.

49

Laura

It's dark and I'm lying down no I'm floating but it's not the water and I want to open my eyes but they're already open. He's looking at me and he's wearing – is this real? – I'm maybe I'm having the baby. He's wearing a white coat and he's the doctor but he's not the right doctor. I close my eyes and open them again to see if he's real. And now he's floating too. He floated right by me and he's touching me, but I can't feel it. I can't feel my legs and my body but he's touching them and lifting bits of me, moving me around.

It must be the baby. I had a baby. I had – I had Katie and she's so little and I see her face and her hair is tied in bunches she did it herself and one bunch is over her eyes and I'm crying tears tears tears rolling down into my ears. I want to shake them out and I need to move my head to tip them out first one then the other but I can't. I can't move anything – not my head not my hand not my legs. I will cry and I'm going to cry out and yell and Matt will wake me because I have Matt beside me and he's moving my body and he's taking off my clothes but it's not Matt. That's not right it's someone else it's the doctor but I'm only – this is dreaming and I feel sick. I'm feeling and I'm going to be sick and now I remember – I have the baby I have had have had I have another baby at home and it's not home here. I have a little boy baby and he's he's – he's the boy from the ark and we are I am floating on a wide wide sea and I'm looking down and I see me lying there and my baby Noah and the ark and my baby is beside me and I'm feeding him and I'm crying but I can feel him beside me and I'm crying

50

Niamh

'Look, I'm sure this is absolutely no assistance whatsoever,' says Dorothy, 'and I don't want to waste your time, but –'

I take a last swig of tea – she'd insisted I have something before heading back to link up with Laura – and tip the dregs into the sink. The uneaten Bakewell slice sits in the box, neither of us mentioning that it must be the gift from Amber.

'Never a waste of time,' I say. 'You never know what can give you a lead. Shoot.'

'They mentioned a single stab wound – that in both cases the girl died from a single stab wound, yes?'

I nod. Murtagh had obviously decided to reveal that nugget of info – maybe hoping to lead to recovery of the weapon.

'A long time ago – I mean, I'm talking about the nineties – before I had the shop here, I worked in a pharmacy over in Clonchapel. And the son of the previous owners used to work there – he was in college, so it was weekend work for him. And I remember – well, I remember him for a few reasons. He was – strange. One tended to avoid him. Well, I tended to keep away from him – I found him creepy. Anyway, one day a woman came in looking for chloroform. She said her cat had had a litter of kittens – five or six – and she'd never be able to find homes for them and that the kindest thing to do would be to "put them to sleep", she called it. We knew this woman. She lived locally and was a regular – highly strung – and I could just, I could well imagine her putting the kittens in a biscuit tin – that's how she was going to do it, she said – and chloroforming them to death.'

'Jaysus!'

'Well, the boss – David – he told her we couldn't do that and that we didn't sell chloroform. He told her to ring the DSPCA or the cat protection society or someone like that, but he' – she shivers, remembering it – 'Whittle – that was his name – can't remember his first name, no matter. He went over to the rack where we kept items for pedicures and suchlike, and he came back with a – with one of the knives you use to pare down corns, you know? They're like scalpels. I don't think you can buy them any more, actually. But he came over, holding this, and said something to the effect that she should stab them in the neck – in the back of the neck, as this would sever their spinal cord.'

Dorothy looks up at me.

'I mean, it's probably nothing at all. Just a creepy young man a long time ago. But I do still remember him – his face. Plus, there was a tragedy in the shop – one of the girls working there took an overdose – in the shop itself, over a weekend. And he was very strange about it. I –'

She waves her hand up by her ear as though brushing away cobwebs. 'Forgive me – this is probably – I'm wasting your time. You go on.'

'No,' I say slowly. 'Maybe not. The area is right, for a start, Dorothy. And you've given me a name. Whittle.' I take my phone out, ready to search the name. 'Whittle,' I repeat. 'Can you describe him?'

She narrows her eyes, considering.

'I can't remember much – dark hair – well, it was then, and tallish, I think.' She pauses, frowning.

'He was very touchy-feely, if you know what I mean. Not

with me, but with Nuala, the girl who killed herself. And sometimes even with customers. He'd – it was as though he'd find an excuse to touch them – tap their arms, take their elbows and steer them to where he wanted them to go.' She shivers. 'The father died and left him the shop, but he never took it on full time.' Her brows knitted together. 'I don't know what he went on to do. He was still working there on weekends when I left. He'd have to be in his forties or fifties now. His mother – well, you'd be too young to remember, but she was Elizabeth Whittle – such a glamorous woman, even then. She'd been a champion dancer –'

I freeze.

'Ballroom?' I say, like I need confirmation.

She nods.

'The parents lived in one of those big houses on Clonchapel Park – you know the ones?'

Adrenalin races through me.

'What number?'

I grab hold of Dorothy in a hug that nearly breaks her, then set her aside and sprint towards the door.

'Oof! No idea. It's big, though – I think I heard they built apartments in the –'

'You're pure fucking magic, Dorothy!' I yell, racing out the door. 'Magic!'

This one is going to be the best — I know it. I dealt with the phone first, removing the SIM card and destroying it. I dumped the phone into the weir — it only took five minutes. While she had her nap. And it gave me time to let the excitement build. Yes. She watches her figure, like Mummy. I used to think the phrase meant Mummy went to the studio in the mornings when I was in school, perhaps, or at night when I was asleep — and I pictured her in her bra and half-slip, walking the length of the studio, watching herself in the mirror. She wore the half-slip because of static.

Father explained static to me when I was very young. I remember the morning, the sunlight in the kitchen and Mummy sitting at the table in her robe. It was before her treatments and she was soft and sleepy — no make-up and her hair tousled in little waves. He rubbed a piece of cloth along over a plastic comb — fast up and down, up and down — then he held the comb above Mummy's hair. Her hair rose up like a crown, wafting in the sunlight.

So funny that I should think of this now. Poor Mummy.

I take my time before I start, because she is very pretty. For this one, I am using the morphine as I did in the early days. Another end-of-life pack came in for disposal and so I was able to measure it exactly with fresh product. This is something Hal knows nothing of — my area of expertise, I tell him. I need enough for a sedative effect, for total compliance and total relaxation of the muscles — but not so much that her breathing is affected. It will wear off — but not yet.

I find myself nodding in approval — exactly like Mummy would — when I see what she's wearing. She's wearing a grey business suit and proper leather court shoes in black. Even though it's a trouser suit, I can see that it's cut well, although it's all bunched up at her hip. So I open the button and that's when I see it, the reason for the bunched fabric. She is wearing a holster — a gun holster. This beautiful young woman, all soft and feminine, is carrying a gun.

I sit back as though I've been stung. I wasn't expecting this. I've seen her at the shop with her children. Why on earth would she have a gun? Well, well, well. The gun is black and chunky. It reminds me of the wooden spoon Mummy used to threaten me with — thick and ugly. This changes everything. This makes me very angry. What would Hal do? I wonder. Hal was no stranger to guns.

I take hold of it. It sits snug inside my palm. Neat and cold. I raise it as though I'm going to shoot, pointing towards the door. 'Don't you dare,' I say. 'I wouldn't try it if I were you.'

I turn back to the job in hand, carefully pulling off her jacket, her shoes, the trousers. Underneath the trousers, she is wearing pop socks — disgusting things. I let them fall to the floor, where they lie like used condoms, shrivelled.

She makes a tiny movement and her breathing changes. Quickly, I reach for another vial. I don't want to give too much but, clearly, I have work to do. The hair alone will take ten minutes and I want to get the make-up right.

'Ssh,' I whisper, pressing the needle flat against her thigh and reaching to stroke her dark hair. 'Ssh. You relax now.'

51

Niamh

A missed call from Laura. No message. And nothing from Amber. Should I ring her? I'm pure raging. That note! I don't know what I would have done – Christ! What would it have been like to come home later tonight, alone and in the dark, and to find that? She didn't know Dorothy would find it – only for Dorothy I'd have been completely alone, thinking what I was going to find, dreading it, guilt and terror drenching me. The anger drops, and ice replaces it.

Fuck you, Amber. And your 'Kenneth says' and your pilot and – yeah – Caoileann-pronounced-Keelin is welcome to you.

Fuck you and the fucking horse you rode in on.

The anger feels good – justified. With a lurch of relief, I realize I'm so tired of apologizing to her, of coming up short. I did my best. Move bloody on. At least that's over.

Monday-evening rush hour starts early. It's not the returning from office rush, it's the school pick-ups from the suburbs rush of mammies – mummies – mostly, and in some cases fifth and sixth years with their own cars.

It's just gone four thirty when I pull up outside the house. It's the sixth one in a row of Victorian red-bricks along the right-hand side of leafy Clonchapel Park – easy to spot because of the block of fancy apartments in what must have been the garden. The house itself is still standing. It yells pure privilege – as far from Mam and Dad's ramshackle stone farmhouse as it's possible to be. Black-tiled rooves slice at different angles, describing the areas of luxury underneath: porch and entrance hall, front bedroom with large bay window, reception room, leading to extension, leading to conservatory, and double-height garage with room for a fecking yacht – a small one. I lean back in my seat, following the line of the roof to a little creature – like a strange lizard – placed at the tip of the roof, beside the stack of four chimneys. That's what I mean. A lizard guarding your house. Who does that?

Laura's phone goes straight to message: 'The number you have dialled cannot be reached.' I try the handset. Nothing. I sigh. Where could she have got to? I don't want to go in without her but it's a lead where we haven't had any leads.

I make my decision and get out of the car, walking in through the black iron gate and up to the front door. I may as well do a spot of house-to-house. The porch is set into a black-and-white tiled archway, large enough to be a room in its own right. Wisteria and roses, well tended, curve over the arch. I ring the bell.

Silence yawns at me. I try to peer through the wavy glass set into the door but all I can make out is a long hallway with light at the end – a sort of tunnel. Leaving the porch, I walk around the right-hand side of the house, along the narrow corridor, but come up against a thick wooden gate which blocks entrance to the back. It's about two metres tall and pretty sturdy. I turn back on myself, heading to the other side, to where the apartments are.

It looks as though they were built in what was a side garden, to the left of the parking area, which is still there. A large square building made of the same red brick, it squats beside the main house. It, too, has narrow passageways on either side, which must lead to rear access. There's a matching black-and-white tiled entrance porch here too, with two banks of intercoms. I press number one. No reply. I press a few more. It seems that if you want to live on Clonchapel Park, you need to be out earning the cash. Finally, number seven answers. I show my ID and the guy says he'll be with me in a minute.

I check my phone again to see if Laura has got in touch. Nada.

Ten minutes later, I'm down by the river, standing in a laneway, looking up at the same apartment block, which can just be seen through the trees. Sleepy-looking bloke from number seven – shift work at a lab, he tells me – said that, as far as he knew, the original owners of the house and land are long gone, but that the garden used to back on to the river all right. He brings me to the landing on the first floor which looks out over the back and points downwards, into a clump of trees. I can just make out a low, flat-roofed building and a grey twist of what must be the Dodder in front of it. I thank him and give him my card then waste no time getting down here on to the lane.

I pull in about halfway down and get out. The buildings on my right back on to the lane. I count three – no, four – back gardens and gates. Ahead of me, just where the laneway sweeps around in front of the river, there's a garage with a steel door and, tacked on to it, the flat-roofed building I'd spotted from the apartments. To the left of the door and high up, almost at ceiling height, there's a bank of windows set horizontally into the plaster. Unless he goes upstairs, the resident would have no view out the front.

I walk towards the garage, looking either side, not sure what I'm looking for. It's kind of creepy here, in the shadow of the trees. You're close to the river all right, but it's the dark part of the river – this building is tucked into the darkest corner. It's obviously a catch-all area for rubbish too – a couple of thin plastic bags, a crumpled newspaper and various empty plastic bottles chase each other in scuffles caused by the latest gust of wind. But the area in front of the –

My phone rings, interrupting my train of thought.

'McCarthy?'

'Where are you, Darmody?' he snaps.

'I'm in a laneway below – at the back of Clonchapel Park. I've got a name – Whittle – as a possible suspect worth checking out. Where are you?' I say, continuing my progress along the front of the garage and the building beside it. Two steps lead up to the doorway – they've recently been swept.

'Back at the unit,' he says, 'and before that, I was in Trinity College, talking with Dr Fallon. I've a location for the pondweed. Apparently, it's very common at the edge of the Dodder, especially in shaded areas.'

'It's pretty shady here,' I say.

'At the water's edge – it grows in water.'

'Hmm,' I say, turning to look at the river – about two metres away and behind a boundary wall.

'I presume Shaw is with you?' says McArsey.

'No,' I say. 'I've been trying to get her.'

'So have I – I was expecting a call from her. She was meant to get back to me on the dance schools –'

'She hasn't been in touch with you either? Shit.' A scrawl of anxiety crawls over my skin, like someone ran a fingernail along my spine. 'Unless she's gone home?' I say, hoping for a harmless explanation.

'Shaw's car –' says McArsey.

I realize he's speaking to me and try to focus.

'I've tracked it. She's not at home. Her car, it's parked a bit further upriver – near the bridge. Do you know where I mean?'

'I know it,' I say. Between here and the bridge the path

snakes through a tunnel. Not a pleasant part of the park. I don't like this at all. Shit. 'I'm on it. I'll head up there now.'

'Let me know when you find her,' he continues. 'And bear in mind that she's not up to speed in terms of professional development. Her last firearms training session was almost three years ago. So even if she has her weapon –'

I'm not letting him finish that sentence. *Don't make it worse!* my mind is screeching.

'I'll take it from here,' I say, ending the call and sprinting back towards my car.

It's all going wrong. I've done her hair and smoothed it all back with the gel, but she doesn't look right. It makes her look young and a bit like a boy. Maybe when I put on the lipstick. Or maybe I need to take off the shirt, because it's a shirt with a collar, like a man would wear. I look along the length of her body, at her legs and feet – pale and cold to the touch. There's a long scar that runs beside her left knee and it doesn't look right and I wonder how she got it. It could be a stab wound, I think, or a dog bite, but it's too narrow and straight to be a dog bite. You can see the marks of the stitches on either side of –

I stop. This is not working. There's nothing to be gained by looking at her scar. I wish she didn't have it, though. I need to think of Mummy. I take a deep breath, reaching my hands out to touch the swell of her breasts through the fabric of the shirt. I think of Mummy in work, all buttoned up in her dress or blouse. I think of the half-slip and the big bra with the criss-cross strapping and her full breasts straining at the edges, where skin meets elastic. The little bulge of flesh.

I stroke down the length of her torso, shoulder to hip, collar bone to the little rise of stomach, pleasantly soft under my hands. This is better. This is like Mummy on treatment days, and the dragon robe and the soft softness underneath. I start to unbutton the shirt, her breasts warm – hot, even – under my touch. One, two, three –

I freeze. Beneath my cupped palms I feel a surge of heat, followed by a pulsing, throbbing dampness. I jerk my hands away – frozen in the air as though someone had yelled, 'Hands up!' Her shirt is sticking to her breasts and her breasts are leaking, circles of wet fabric blooming larger and larger, until they're like those massive flowers, fat and swollen after rain. I stare, and as I do, the fabric glistens — drenched — tiny beads of moisture trembling, then rolling away. Disgusted, I stand up.

What was I thinking? This is not how it's meant to be. This is like — this is a joke — a trick. I hear Mummy laughing at me. Laughing at me for choosing the wrong one. Even Hal would laugh.

'She's ready to feed her young,' he'd say. 'That's nature.'

Disgusting.

I take another step backwards then rush to the bathroom, nausea rising. I think I'm going to be sick. Imagine if I'd — imagine if it had happened when I was — without the barrier of the shirt — I heave, but nothing comes out.

I run the hot tap and wash my hands the surgeon way, soaping in between the fingers and all around the thumb — anywhere that could have been touched by the milk. I take a breath and smooth back my hair, eyes locked with my reflection in the mirror. My jaw is strong and my face is calm. In dancing, you must always look the part. Never show your nerves. It's important to present a strong and confident appearance. The audience needs to know that you're in charge.

I hold my own gaze. I'm trying to get back to — I want it all to be right. I'm in charge. I'm the man. But, instead, I hear Mummy.

'You're a mess. You're pathetic. You can do nothing right.'

I want Hal to hit her for me. We could do it together. Forget the dancing, we could just hit her and slap her mean mouth and punch her face in so she never says stuff like that again. She would never hit Hal.

I straighten up. I turn my head to check my jaw — is it strong like Hal's? I fix my lab coat and straighten the collar. I do that thing where you shove your arms forward fast, jerkily, so your cuffs pop out from under the sleeves of the coat. There! That's it. Posture is important. I stand up even straighter and stride back into the studio like I'm walking on stage. There'll be no dancing tonight, I realize. I have to get rid of this mess.

I stand at the side of the couch and look at her and I feel nothing — only a cold, cold rage. A small trail of saliva glistens at the edge of her *mouth and grey lines of streaked foundation stretch from the corners of her eyes into her ears. She's not even worth the lipstick. I look around for something to throw over her, to cover the stains of secretion on her chest, then I drag her into the dressing room, out of sight. She can stay there. Father was right. They're disgusting. A nursery between open sewers. Excretions, secretions, moisture, detritus. Skin flakes and stubble, fungus and rot. I'll get rid of her tonight when it's dark.*

52

Niamh

I'm in full-on panic mode about Laura. If McArsey's right and her car is parked up near the bridge – shit. Where the hell is she? Where was she going? Why is she not answering her phone?

I call her number again as I'm driving past Ely's Arch, where Jenny was found. Laura basically went AWOL on the fourth day of that investigation, discharging the girl from the psych ward without permission and bringing her to the tower. Laura, usually so risk averse, was completely out of control. Could she have done something similar? Or – and I don't even want to think it – but what if he's got her?

With a sudden lurch of 'Duh!', I realize Cig must be using Senan to keep an eye on things. He'll have said something like 'No shitstorms – not on my watch.' Setting up his little maneen to keep an eye on us. But thank Christ he did.

I take the lower road along the edge of the river, trying to make myself slow down for the ramps. A small group of photographers clusters together at the edge of the walkway, like paparazzi, zoom lenses and expensive-looking cameras trained on a patch of thicket on the far side of the water. I slow, rolling down the window and catching the eye of one of them, a slim woman dressed in black with a black beanie hat pulled down over her long hair. I nod in the direction of the spot and she comes over towards the car. The logo on the beanie reads 'Dodder Photographer'.

'How's things? Matt Damon doing a spot of river swimming?'

'Even more rare.' She gives a little grin. 'We're trying to get the kingfisher. There.' She points at the spot, then turns back to me. 'But the light's gone now anyway, so —'

I don't have time for this.

'Listen, have you been here all afternoon?' I wave on the car that has pulled up behind me. 'I'm looking for someone — dark-haired woman, late thirties, short? She maybe came down this way in the last couple of hours?'

The woman considers for a couple of seconds, then shakes her head.

'I — I don't think so,' she says uncertainly, 'although we're all so obsessed with the bird' — an apologetic shrug — 'she could have passed this way and I wouldn't have noticed. Sorry. But you know about the tunnel?' she says, pointing. 'So, there's a tunnel under the main road, down there. You can go either way, but if you go through the tunnel, you don't have to cross the road.'

'Thanks.' I pull away sharply and take the ramps at sixty. There's Laura's car. I abandon mine parallel to hers and do a quick circuit. There's a water flask in the footwell on the passenger side, and a crumpled tissue in the pocket of the driver's side door. Apart from those, nothing.

I run across the bridge, pausing at the place where Katie and I dropped our sticks into the river a few days ago, and I force myself to slow down, to think.

A sudden shadow looms overhead, accompanied by a rushing sound. I jump, startled. A heron is in flight — weirdly angular and gangly, its bony claws not quite tucked into its body – following the course of the Dodder. I watch until it passes the bend in the river and disappears out of sight. Okay. I'm going to check the tunnel and the path. And after that?

I don't know.

I have to find her.

I saw her earlier, of course. I was watching from the landing. She's tall, with long hair falling in waves to her shoulders. The hair is a brown-gold colour, not dark like Mummy's. Her face is beautiful — pale and creamy-complexioned and very light eyes. Feline. Leonine. Mummy would not approve of her outfit — you can't even call it that. She's very casually dressed, in jeans, a baggy top and an army-green hooded coat over the top. She's wearing lace-up runners. Runners. And yet there's an energy to her — there's something extra in the way she moves. She was on the phone, but she paced across the space in front of the studio like a golden lioness in too small a cage. She seemed to get angry and she got into her car and drove away. With her went something of mine — longing would be too strong a word, but I felt a sort of regret. Yes. A worthy adversary — because, of course, I know now she must be a guard as well. And I know she's looking for the other one.

Hal's adventures — and Roger — of course. Poor Roger, always trying to keep up. Hal and Roger's adventures grew ever more risky and dangerous. They battled dastardly villains. They fought against insurmountable odds. One time they nearly starved on an island. It's strange how it's all coming back to me now. Their battles. 'H' is for Hal and 'H' is for Hercules. Maybe your name has to begin with 'H' if you're going to be a hero. 'H' for hero as well. 'P' for pathetic. And puny. And punishment.

When Mummy shouted, her face livid, the vein above her eyebrow pulsing with poison — when she screamed and dragged me to the bathroom to show me the splashes of urine I'd left around the toilet, I thought of Hal and how he would be hard as steel. When she pressed my face into the bookshelf or the wall, bending my arm behind me until I thought my shoulder bone would snap, I screwed my eyes tight shut and imagined Hal watching from the undergrowth, waiting to strike. When she slapped my head and I thought I felt my brain shift inside my skull and my ears rang with a hot pain, I didn't cry. Hal says never to show weakness. He says I must do my exercises every day. And he is right. I do my callanetics because Hal says exercise fixes broken things. It makes me stronger. He says you find what hurts and hurt it more. He told me that one day I would get my chance. He was right.

'Preparation is key,' says Hal.

I have made myself useful in preparation – because, of course, I knew the other one would come back. They're always together. She's a worthy opponent. I have examined the weapon – it's a Sig 229 – and I've seen a video with the slide lock and the lever you pull down – the cocker, or maybe it's a de-cocker. And, like I said – it feels just right in my palm.

And here she is. Back again. She slams her car door. I take my hand out of my pocket and make my way downstairs. I am Hal. I am hard and dangerous. I am taller than her and stronger. I will show her who's in charge.

She knocks on the door.

53

Niamh

The door is opened by a guy in his late forties — maybe early fifties. He's tallish and well built with a jutting lower jaw. Dark hair going grey at the temples, a kind of guy in a coffee-ad vibe — sort of fake. There's something off in his expression, but I can't work it out — a disconnect between the expression in his eyes and what comes out of his mouth. He's wearing suit trousers and a white shirt, like he's giving me the impression that I disturbed him working from home, like he was on a conference call or something.

'May I help you?'

He tilts his head enquiringly.

I show my ID and introduce myself. He nods, as though I'm confirming something he already knows.

'We're making house-to-house enquiries,' I say, 'in relation to the abduction and murder of the two young women recently.'

He nods quickly, repeatedly.

'Yes, yes, I heard about that on the news. Dreadful.'

He takes a step back, allowing the door to open a bit further. To his right, I can see a staircase and, behind him, I can see that the hall opens out into a large square room, bounded on one side by a wall of mirrors. My hand goes to my belt and I edge backwards. I'll need to call this in and get back-up. But I hesitate. He's smiling. Like he's pleased by my reaction. And I just know something's off. A perfumey smell is overlaid on top of something medical — like disinfectant.

'I'll give you my card,' I say, reaching to my pocket. 'You can call if you think of any – anything.'

'Why don't you come in, Detective?' he says. 'We can talk. I may have information – yes. I'm sure I do.'

My head tells me to get away – get back-up.

I step inside.

I have two plans. This is how ready I am. I am always one step ahead and I am always the lead. I saw in her eyes — they're green, and they shine as though there's a light inside them — I saw her hesitate and move away. This tells me that she's scared. Darmody, her name is. Darmody is scared, so I will calm her with my voice, like Roger did with the nervous animals. I'll make her tea and the 5ml or maybe 15ml — because she's almost as tall as me — the 15ml will be in the tea. Tasteless. Job done. That is the first plan.

The second plan is only a back-up plan. It will come into play if she puts her hand into her pocket or anywhere near it. The gun is in my pocket.

'Take a seat,' I say, pointing to the couch along the far wall. 'I've just made tea — you'll have a cup,' I say — an instruction, not a question. The man leads. The hunter. She walks towards the couch and sits. I can clearly see her every movement in the mirror while I pour the tea. I bring the cup over to her and she takes it, thereby keeping one of her hands occupied. I sit on the kitchen chair opposite her.

'You said you had information,' Darmody says, not drinking her tea.

I sip my tea, to encourage her to do the same. I nod.

'Yes — I — I heard that the girl, the babysitter, I heard she got into a car with someone. Well, I think I saw — I may have seen that.'

Why is she not drinking? She's sitting on the edge of the couch as though she's ready to leap up at any moment. Her eyes dart to and fro, scanning the room.

'What did you see?'

I wish her jumper wasn't so baggy. I can't see her waist or the shape of her breasts. I wonder how she will feel in my arms. I wonder about her stomach – her hips. She's almost as tall as me. A handsome pair. I feel the gathering, the thick feeling. I think about what it would be like to see her face thrown back and the green eyes closed. I think of her stretched out along the couch like a goddess. Like Mummy. We can do this, me and Hal. We will show her.

'What did you see?' she repeats, leaning forward to put her untouched cup of tea on the floor. There's a clunking sound as it hits the wood – sprung maple, the best type for dancing. And then – then everything changes and I realize it might have to be plan two.

Because – beside the cup, half hidden under the couch, is one of those sock things – a pop sock. She spots it and her mouth drops. She gets to her feet, but I'm also on my feet.

I draw my weapon and with my other hand I open the door to the dressing room so she can see the other one, slumped in the corner. I step one leg in the doorway, gun trained on the sleeping one.

'Laura!' she cries, and it sounds false. 'You f—' She's going for her gun and so I slide the lock and the Sig makes its cocking sound. I point it at the head of the other one, but I keep looking at Darmody.

'Shut up!' I yell, but I don't like that. I sound like a kid. I step closer towards her friend – Laura.

'Here's what's going to happen, Darmody,' I say. And I can be Hal. My voice is steady and I am holding her with my eyes. No one is laughing now. 'You're going to take your weapon out – and your phone. You're going to empty your pockets slowly and put everything on the floor. Everything. If you move – if you do anything sudden – I will put a bullet in her brain.'

She hesitates.

'Do it!' I yell.

She takes her phone and keys out of her pocket and puts them on the floor. She's wearing a belt thing with the gun and other items on it and I watch while she unbuckles the clasp and lowers it to the floor.

'Now your shoes,' I say.

She heel-toes them off and I feel Mummy's anger. I would have got the wooden spoon for that.

'The rest,' I say, and it's brilliant. I'm Hal and I'm in charge. I am the lead.

She shrugs off her jacket and pulls her jumper over her head.

'Throw them on top of the pile,' I say. 'Now kick the whole lot behind you – under the sofa.'

'This is not a good idea,' she says. 'Paul – that's your name, isn't it?' *For a moment I'm dumbstruck. How does she know my name?*

'I looked you up,' she's saying. 'I wanted to talk to you about dancing – ballroom. I'm learning it. I heard that your mum was a champion back in the day.'

She's stopped moving. Now she's standing in her socks and jeans, with just a light vest top over her bra. The top is yellow and so is the bra. Something glints at the edge of her hip pocket. I laugh.

'Take your jeans off and then put those on yourself,' I say, nodding at the handcuffs. 'Do it.'

She pulls down the jeans and I can see her – I can see it cross her mind to dive on top of me, like a rugby tackle. But I'm too smart for that. I take aim and give the other one a hard kick in the stomach. She groans but sinks back into oblivion almost immediately.

'Before you get to me, she'll be dead,' I say. 'Don't even think about it.'

Darmody takes off her jeans and, slowly, like it's killing her, she puts the first cuff on herself.

'Now move over there.' *I nod towards the ballet barre along the end wall.* 'Attach it to the bracket there.'

When Mummy took off her heels, she sank down, and I remember the surge of disappointment that washed over me. It meant the magic was gone. At the end, she moved like a toad or a waddling corgi, ugly and splay-footed. I watch Darmody walk to the end of the room – even in her socks, she is beautiful. The long legs, the straight back. A lioness – prowling. I just want her to shut up.

'You could let her go,' Darmody is saying. *'Please, she's no use to you. Let her go.'*

'Let me see you've done it properly,' I yell. She raises both hands and pulls; they're attached to one of the barre supports.

'I've done it. Listen now – just listen to me, Paul.' She's gabbling, watching me come closer. *'You can still walk away – you hear me? If you – you have to think this through – you don't want to do anything you might regret –'*

I stop a few feet away from her. Still she's talking. Then she sees me looking.

'I'm interested in coming out of this alive,' she says. And I can tell that is true. *'I'll – I'll do whatever it is you want – if you let Laura go, I'll do whatever you tell me to.'*

She tosses her hair to get it away from her face and looks up at me, her head lowered.

'What do you want me to do?' she says.

You see, Mummy? I can show them who's master. I check our reflection in the mirror to see what it looks like. I see a tall, strong man holding a gun and a scared girl in her underwear, begging. She thought she was so smart. Now who's pathetic?

54

Laura

I hear voices. Niamh. Niamh is here. Where is she? My eyes are swimming – it's like when you're trying to wake up from a dream and you're opening your eyes but still the dream rolls on. My head is jammed in a corner and I see a window up very high with a bluey-purple slice of sky. Dusk, or maybe early morning. I scrabble through my brain, rooting for scraps – for anything that will help me assemble the jigsaw. Where am I? What's happening? But my body is slow, slow, slow and sore. I'm so cold. I twist my head the other way – away from the window – and it hurts my neck, but I know I have to do it. I know something very bad is happening. There's a black bin bag on that side of me and there's piles of clothes – some on the floor, some fancy dresses hanging on a rack.

I see shoes tucked into the corner under the rack, pairs and pairs of fancy ladies' high heels in jewel colours – red, emerald, sapphire. I blink and blink but they're still there. My eye travels up above the bright bright shoes to a counter all laid out with what looks like medicines – syringes and bottles and little glass vials. And lipsticks. Dozens of them. They're reflected in the mirror behind them – and then I think I must be backstage at a theatre – could that be right? The mirror has light bulbs around it in a big square.

What is this place and why – I move my hand and it weighs a ton. I lift my thousand-ton hand on to my hip and drag it up my body, feeling my way, trying to find out what has happened. My shirt is soaking wet. Am I bleeding? Am I shot? I have such a pain in my stomach. I'm shot and – he thinks – he – the man who –

I turn my head again, towards the black bag and the pile of clothes. A slash of blood-red catches my eye and it's like my body knows before I do that it's Mia's skirt – the red corduroy one from the press photo. It's like she just stepped out of it. And it's tiny. The sight of it, beside what must be her black tights, flaccid and devoid of shape, cast aside in a pretzel of lifeless rags, chills me to my core. This is where Mia died. And the others. And now, we are here. Niamh. Me.

There's a shuffling of pieces and a settling, a kind of creeping horror as I realize that I've been taken by the killer. The man who killed Mia and – and –

Carefully, I tilt my head and look down along my own body. My shirt is ripped and my lower half is bare, except for my pants. The shirt feels soaked but – but there's no blood. It – it must be milk. I try – I concentrate as hard as I can and try to move my toes and a tiny movement happens before I flop back, exhausted.

I think of my baby. I remember Noah and I remember Katie and Matt and I remember who I am and feel a howl of grief begin to gather – for the fact that I might never see them again. And they'll have to grow up without me. And Niamh – Niamh! I hear her voice but I can't hear what she's saying and she's my best friend and I realize she's come for me – she found me and now she's the one in trouble. He's – she's out there with him and now he's got her and I want to weep because it's my fault she's here. It's all my fault.

But I need to – I strain my ears – I know that voice. His voice. I'm sure I recognize it. Images try to scribble themselves together in my brain – a man and he's old – not old – no, but he's older than me. I see a snatch of a jaw and stubble, dark hair receding, strands of grey – oh! It's so frustrating this piecemeal jigsaw of memory, this drugged body with limbs that weigh a thousand tons.

I lie back for a second, trying to slow my breathing. I'm panting little, short breaths. The door of the room is part closed and – thank Christ – I realize he's forgotten about me, that I'm with the rubbish. Half the room is rubbish and I'm discarded. He's finished with me for now and he's dealing with Niamh. And I don't know where my gun is, and I'm too weak to bloody stand. I can barely move my head.

I'm too weak, too useless, too pathetic, to do anything about it. What was I thinking? Coming back to the unit. Coming back as Niamh's partner. I'm – I'm worse than useless. I'm a liability.

I should have stayed at home and let the others – other people with skills and talents and bravery – people – whole people – people who don't have OCD clawing at them. Those are the people you want as your partner – at your side in a crisis. Not a stupid, neurotic, over-thinking, clueless mammy who somehow manages to make even a simple job into mission impossible. I despise myself.

Tears slide into my ears, and I let them. I try to move my hand. Nothing.

55

Niamh

You think you know yourself – that you know what you'll be like in a crisis. In training, on the pitch, at the scene of murders and accidents, I've been pretty calm. I go to a quiet place inside my mind and it all slows down. I've had blades pointed at me and, once, a fricking crossbow, and I didn't panic. I suppose because I didn't really think this was it – that this was my moment. But now – this is different. This guy, he looks like he's capable – scratch that – I *know* what he's capable of.

Is he buying it? I try to get into his mindset. He's into his strength, their weakness. He drags them around – maybe if I try to talk to him about the dancing? Yeah, you bloody idiot, I think. He kills them first – before he dances. He drags them around afterwards. He's a strong-looking bloke too. He's got maybe two stone on me – certainly one – and he's a couple of inches taller. Not much – but that gives him a longer reach of arm.

He's staring, though. His eyes rove all over me, skeetering about the place over my tits and crotch, my thighs. I've got to buy time.

'We – we could have – we could do whatever you like,' I try again. The words splat on to the ground between us like the cowshite they are. He's not buying it.

He reaches into his pocket and pulls out a knife – like a scalpel or a knife you'd use for cutting carpet. My stomach pitches. I scramble myself into the wall, as if I could pass through it. My knee twitches upwards – self-protection or trying to knee him away, I don't know. He laughs.

'Stay still,' he says softly. 'If you stay still I won't hurt you.'

'Please – you need –'

There's a ripping sound and I'm yanked away from the wall by his hand on the front of my top. He nicked it with the blade and then pulled, ripping it in two. He steps back. I stand there in knickers and bra, the vest-top dangling from either shoulder, open. I see him look at my boobs. I brace myself in case he's going to do the same with the rest of my clothes and then there's a beat of silence.

He's looking at the tattoo – at Martin's tractor on my hip bone. I follow his gaze, seeing him notice the wheel of the tractor. Martin's dates are hidden below the waistband of my pants.

'I had a brother,' I say. 'That's for him.' My voice shakes. Not for little Martin, who I never knew – for Mam and Dad. I have this picture – clear as anything – of them walking behind my coffin back home, on their way to the graveyard with another of their children. I'm so angry at myself, that I've cocked this up – that they'll bury two of their children in their own lifetime.

'He died when he was three.'

I look at him – really look at him. If he's going to kill me, he can at least – I can at least make sure he bloody knows who I am. He's still holding the gun and it's still pointing at me. He walks to the far end of the room and puts down the blade, then he turns back to me. He's shaking his head and frowning.

'My name is Niamh – his was Martin and he would have been my big brother. I never knew him,' I say, my words tumbling faster, faster. 'I have a big sister, Siobhán, and two other brothers, Rory and Tom. I'm a garda – you know that, of course you do – and I swear to you –' I feel a tear splash against my bare stomach, though I didn't know I was crying. I don't cry. I never bloody cry. 'I swear to you – you don't have to do this. You – if you think about it –'

'Shut up!' he roars, so loud and so shrill it's more like a scream. Like he's being tortured. He puts a hand up beside his head and turns away, stumbling towards the kitchen area. I hear him clattering about in a drawer, his back to me, then he turns and I see he's holding a length of masking tape and a pair of scissors. He's left the gun down in the kitchen.

I pull as hard as I can against the bracket, the movement tearing at my shoulder muscles. Did I just imagine it? Did it move? I try again but, in a second, he's shouldered me against the wall, slapped the tape across my mouth and is pressing his forearm against my throat.

I can't breathe. I can't breathe.

Mummy is laughing. Her head is thrown back, but it's not the good way, with her eyes closed. She's sitting over by the music on the high stool, swinging her leg. Her legs are crossed under the big skirt and her bare legs shine under the lights. The top leg is the one she's swinging, and the foot of that leg is half out of her shoe. I can see her naked arch – the pale arch of her foot – and I want to run my nail along it so her toes clench and then I want to run the blade along it so the red beads pop up like a bracelet.

At least the girl – the lioness – is silent. She's slid down the wall and her legs are splayed out like a puppet; her head lolls against her chest and a curtain of her golden mane hangs over her face so you can't see her.

'Do it,' says Hal. 'You could do it now. It's only nature.'

'He'll never do it!' laughs Mummy. 'He's pathetic!'

I will decide. I can make my own decisions and I don't have to listen to Mummy. Poor Mummy. Bitch Mummy who is dead.

The scissors make a crunching sound snipping through her hair, like crrroosh, crroosh. *I grab the tub of gel – quick before she wakes – and slide all her hair back down the nape of her neck. It looks all wrong – the tape across her mouth means I can't put the lipstick on but –*

I stand up and go to get the syringe. I can't think straight. She's not meant to have the big X over her mouth and she's not meant to have the blue tractor for her brother drawn on her body so you can't forget him and you can't ignore him. How can I – I can't put the blue tractor out of my mind. I will know it's there and he'll be there. I am calling Hal. He'll know what to do. He would cut it out with a blade, yes.

I could just do it now – with the blade – before she wakes up. I put the syringe down. I pick it up again.

That's when I hear Mummy laughing and I know she's watching. She's sitting on the high stool and her elbow is resting on the back of the seat so her breasts are arranged wide and high, displayed on a shelf. I can't see Hal. Where's Hal?

And that's when I see Blood Baby. He's crawling out from under Mummy's skirt. He's slick with blood and his tiny hands leave red prints along her bare skin. He opens his mouth in a wide grin and blood is sticking on his teeth and dripping.

56

Laura

Come on – come on – I hear Katie's voice and I come to with a start. That's what she yells when she's up and ready for the day and Matt and I are still in bed. *Come on! Come on, Muma!* I don't know if minutes or hours have passed. My head is thumping. It feels as though it's been filled with molten lava, like the worst hangover multiplied by a thousand where every movement brings a blinding surge of pain. Now, I feel a stabbing pain in my chest – a broken rib? But that's – that tells me I can feel more than before. I lift my arm. Lower it. I think – I think I can move my legs. Can I? I've got to move! It can't end like this.

Why can't I hear anything from outside the door? I can't hear him. I can't hear Niamh. That thought is like an icy dagger plunged into my core. Niamh. For Niamh. For Matt and Katie and Noah. For all of them. And the voice in my head is saying *every little bit, every little bit.* Because nothing matters, only them. The people I love. Every little bit. I've got to move. Slowly, I heave myself over on to my front and slowly, slowly – why am I so slow? I turn so I'm facing the door, inching along in a desperate crawl that's all I can manage without knocking things over and drawing attention to myself.

At last, I reach the door and, through the crack, I can see Niamh in the far corner – she's on the ground, handcuffed to the rail on the wall, her arms over her head. I can't tell if he's drugged her. I don't think so because he's pacing – his back to me, but I can see that he's holding a syringe. Shit.

I hoosh myself along another couple of inches so I'm right at the edge of the door. I can see most of the room reflected in the mirror opposite – the tattered sofa with the pile of Niamh's clothes underneath, the door of this dressing room ajar, blocking any sight of me. Closest to me is one of Niamh's trainers and her jeans and – my heart starts whamming in my chest – her holster and gun. I pinch myself. I'm still woozy – I wonder if I'm hallucinating and I close and reopen my eyes. It's there.

A sudden movement makes me pull my head back in again, scrunching my eyes closed as if that's going to stop him seeing me. But he can't see me. He's facing the other way, his back still towards me, dark hair edging along the collar of a white jacket as he hunkers down in front of her. He's dressed as though he's a doctor. The white coat. A lab coat. What the hell? It's him –

It comes to me the way a lift sometimes jolts as it arrives on the chosen floor. With a weighty thud. The older dad. The shiny shoes! I've been face to face with him. Maybe several times, because I realize – yes – he's the guy from the pharmacy. Same guy! Oh my God. That's him. Carly's words hang in the air. The nice man.

Shit – he's reaching towards Niamh and I'm straining to see what he's doing – he's cutting her hair. Her head is lolling about and he's pulling her by the shoulder. She's so floppy. Maybe he's already – oh Christ!

He's muttering. He turns to look over his right shoulder, towards the music stand, and that's when I see his face clearly. No doubt about it. He stands up and strides the length of the room – towards the far end.

I wait. I don't know what – I don't know how much I can

trust my body to do what I tell it. I can't afford to move unless I can be sure he's looking the other way. But there it is, the Sig, less than a metre away. If I pull the runner towards me, it's on top of the jeans and the belt is attached – so if I can reach the runner there's a chance of getting the whole lot. Or I could make a dash for it – but I can't see my gun, I realize. And if he hasn't bothered to take Niamh's, that means he could have already got hold of mine. I try to think clearly, to remember our training. Assess risk. Consider tactics.

He's still holding the syringe, meaning the risk is he's about to drug Niamh. If he hasn't already – no. No, it looks like he's deciding something. He's going to do it. Okay, that won't kill her, but it will knock her out and it'll all be down to me. There's a chance she can get out of the handcuffs – maybe –

'Shut up!' he yells – to no one – or someone only he can see.

He paces the length of the room. He's muttering and crying. Niamh's head jerks up and she looks around her. I breathe. At least she's conscious. He's cut off all her hair and gelled it back. The sight causes a surge of bile from my stomach. It's as though he's gutted her – prepared her for sacrifice. She looks like the others. He passes out of my line of vision and I hear his footsteps – those shoes – pacing up and down along the wooden floor.

Focus! Christ! I try to focus. I have to get hold of Niamh's gun. That's what I have to do. I'll need to – to disable him before he can get to the other gun. I don't see any other way. There won't be time for negotiation. I'm barely able to drag myself across the floor, and Niamh's handcuffed, so tackling him is out. I don't even know if my legs are working, but at least movement has come back to my arms and upper body. I have to get hold of the gun.

Suddenly, he seems to decide something. I hear his steps.

He walks to the other end of the room and then reappears, standing a couple of feet in front of Niamh, his back to me. He's put away the syringe and, in his right hand, he's holding the knife.

Niamh's hands are cuffed to the rail above her, and she's slumped over. I once saw a dead pig – the door was open to the back of the butcher's shop and it was like a glimpse into hell: chunks of flesh, great white slabs of flesh that looked human – pale and purplish. The butcher released the pig from a steel hook and caught it against his body, ready to begin the butchery. As the creature slumped over, the two curtains of flesh moved aside so I could see the ribs – like the vaulted ceiling of a cathedral – curved in all their beauty.

Niamh tries to straighten. She lifts her head. I see her try to set her shoulders, to brace her centre. But it's her jawline that does it. She raises her chin so her neck elongates, and she's – she looks at him. She looks right at him, trying to focus. And she's so brave and she's staring him down. And she would die for me. I know it at a visceral level. I know this.

57

Niamh

The pain in my throat – he's crushed my windpipe. And I – my head is freezing and it feels wet. Is it bleeding? I catch sight of myself in the mirror and see what he's done. My hair! Then I see him on one knee beside me now, ready with the blade.

'Sit still!' he yells.

I'm screaming through the masking tape and I'm filled with a surge of fury – I'm raging for my mam and dad. No way are they – no way are they going to bury another child – and Siobhán and the kids and my brothers and my team and – Laura! Oh Christ! He'll kill Laura after me!

Not Laura! And I was meant to save her and I've messed it up. The thought scalds like boiling oil and I realize I'm not going down without a fight. Not on my watch. And I want to cry because I thought of Cig's favourite 'not on my watch' and I can't even tell Laura. And this is my watch. This is my watch and I've messed it up, and that's when I see behind him, over his shoulder, a small movement at the door of the dressing room. Laura?

It is – oh, thank Christ! I force myself to tear my eyes away from her and look back at him, and I'm trying to think – what's her plan? She's going for my gun but she won't have a clear shot here – he's right in front of me and already he's hunkering down with the blade. If I stand up – no – then he'll stand up. He's a broader target hunkered down, unless I –

I bend my knees up and scootch myself back in against the wall. He's watching. Even now, with the blade in his hand, he can't help himself. His eyes are pulled to my crotch like I've a giant magnet stuffed in my knickers. Fucking men! Fucking, fucking men! I want to say what is the fucking mystery, you big fucking –

I let my left leg fall gently towards the floor and his eyes follow. He takes a step closer. That's when I kick out at his knee with my right heel – as hard as I can – bracing myself against the wall behind me and using the bracket to pull myself upwards. His leg gives way and he crumples over, but he's not down and – and Laura's still half hidden by the door, frozen.

And that's when I hear McArsey. That's when McArsey's voice is beamed into the building because somehow – somehow McArsey is outside and he's got a fucking megaphone.

58

Laura

I shuffle back behind the door, the Sig in my hand. No! We could have – I was about to turn the gun on him – Niamh had created space. I'd have had a clear shot and now – McCarthy's outside.

'Mr Whittle,' he's saying, like he's canvassing for an election, 'armed gardaí are outside your home. You need to come outside with your hands up. You will not be harmed. We want to resolve this situation peacefully.'

I daren't make eye contact with Niamh. Shit! Shit! Shit! No! What if he decides to kill us all? I scrunch my eyes closed, trying to think. Think. Think. We had this. I was almost there. I'd have given him a chance to surrender peacefully, and I'd have had a clear shot. And now McCarthy is here and he's going to – I could weep, thinking of the whole protocol. He'll have to wait for the negotiation team and the ERU – unless they're there already.

'You will not be harmed,' says McCarthy, his voice ringing with feedback from the loudspeaker.

'No, no, no, this is not –' the guy half sobs.

I edge a little further back inside the room and peer through the crack. I see him stumble towards the far end. He's limping and dragging one leg. Then I hear a clatter of something metal and the unmistakable sound of the Sig being cocked.

I get to my knees and then my hunkers, testing my muscles. Can I do this? I stand up behind the door then catch sight of Niamh. She makes the tiniest movement with her eyes. *No.*

'Mummy is not poor Mummy,' says Hal. 'Why could you never see that? She hated you. She laughed at you. She was always laughing at you, but you couldn't see it. You and Father. Idiots.'

I look over at Mummy on the stool to see if he's telling the truth. She's not looking at me because her head is back and grinning. Blood Baby is sitting on her lap and he's holding her breast like Baby Jesus in those paintings, except his hand is red with blood.

I want to say, 'Shut up, Hal, that's a lie,' but Hal is my big brother. And I need his help because now I'm being hunted. Hal knows about hunting.

The lioness hurt me and I will punish her, but first I must kill the hunter. Hal says get on to higher ground. Move!

And so I climb the stairs to the mezzanine, up high like the savannah. And it hurts my knee so badly and I don't think I'll dance again and I hear Mummy laughing. And she says, 'Who cares?'

They can't see me up here, but I can see them, and he said armed guards but there's only him and two normal gardaí and everyone knows they don't have guns. And they've put tape around my house, and that's going to look very messy. There's a garda car and the door is open and I see the guy with the gun and he goes to put the loudspeaker thing in the car, then he turns back and he has his gun trained on the door of my house. He can't see me up here.

Plan two, no, this is plan three. Plan three is me and Hal on a hunt. And I will do the kill shot and then I'll bag the lioness.

'Wait,' says Hal, 'until you can see the whites of his eyes.'

He's right, because it's dusk and you need to be sure. Armed garda guy is waiting a few metres away from my front door.

'Target at seven o'clock,' says Hal. *'Breathe in. Then out. And before you breathe in again – shoot.'*

I suck in a big long breath and it helps with the pain. I wait.

And then I shoot.

59

Niamh

Two shots exchanged! The sound of breaking glass. Jesus Christ! My eyes lock with Laura's. She comes out from behind the door and I nod, *Go go go,* my eyes signalling the corner under the stairs. He's moved back from the window. He dropped to the floor when it shattered. I can't see him over the gallery rail. Could McArsey have got him? Did – was that McArsey shooting? Maybe – maybe McArsey – God! I can't believe McArsey fired! Against every rule – every hostage situation, every protocol, everything we ever learned!

There are about two seconds of silence, and I'm hoping – could McArsey have actually hit him?

And then Whittle stands up, outlined against the light like an actor on stage, standing on the balcony. He's still holding the gun, and he's grinning.

'Hal! I got him! Did you see? Hal?'

Laura edges out from the shadowy area below the gallery and flattens herself against the front of the staircase, creeping along towards the bottom step.

Christ! My stomach lurches. He got Mc— he got Senan!

Whittle turns to his left. It's like he's talking to someone. He's delighted. Proud. He looks all around the room, like he's receiving applause from spectators gathered below, and then I see his gaze land on me. His face closes. His mouth turns into a thin line of pencil. I keep my eyes locked on his, willing him not to notice Laura creeping up the staircase to his right.

And then he tilts his head as though he's listening to something or someone. The pencil line stretches into a wide, upturned curve. The biggest smile I've ever seen. He raises the gun in both hands and points it at me.

And that's when Laura shoots.

Two shots in quick succession.

60

Laura

It's hard to think over his screaming and the yells of Niamh shouting at the team outside that he's down and to get in here and the thumping of my swollen brain. I'm beyond nausea, beyond exhaustion. My hands are shaking and I'm clutching the gun in two hands, aiming it at his head. He's writhing on the ground, squirming at the pain of his knees. There's broken glass all over the carpet by the window. I spot the gun sitting in the middle of it and, trying not to step on the glass in my bare feet, I shove it backwards and out of his reach. I cast around for something to tie him with in this weird viewing platform-cum-gallery. There's a small sofa and a little table, a bookcase containing what look like dance trophies and medals, and – yes! That will do. I spot an old-fashioned satchel-type briefcase with long straps and a handle attached by clips at either end.

I resist the urge to look out the window to see what happened to Senan and to sprint downstairs to untie Niamh.

'I am arresting you on suspicion of murder and abduction.' I place my foot in the centre of his back, forcing him face down into the carpet while I bind his wrists with the strap. And my brain is reeling because – because – because here it is, the nightmare, and I'm –

'You are not obliged to say anything unless you wish to do so, but anything you do say will be taken down in writing and may be given in evidence against you.'

Niamh is yelling – screaming or cheering – from below, and there's a thudding in my chest like it's terror, but maybe it's joy – relief – triumph. All the fears – the terrors conjured up by my brain are nothing to this – and – I force myself back. Concentrate. Contain the situation.

When he's securely tied I pick up the second gun and hobble downstairs, my legs shaking more with every step. In the hallway, I'm about to open the door but think better of it. I can hear by the engines that the armed units are here – but we're not out of the woods yet. I realize no one's safe. They don't know what's going on inside. What if someone is trigger-happy or –

'The radio!' yells Niamh, reading my mind. 'Beside my jeans.'

I find it and make the call.

'You're safe to come in,' I say. 'Suspect is disarmed and secured.'

I find the key to the cuffs and get them off. Then I hold out my hand to her. Words refuse to come. Niamh grabs my hand and I help her haul herself upright. Her hand is warm and dry. Mine is freezing. One of us is shaking. I don't know which.

We huddle together like that, trembling – our hands clutched together. Then she puts her arm around my shoulders. I curve mine around her waist. My forehead rests against her chest, her chin on top of my head. We stay like that.

Epilogue

Two weeks later

Niamh

'In fairness, you surprised me, McCarthy!' I say, tapping McArsey's bony shin through the hospital bedclothes. 'Never had you down as Rambo. Thank Christ you were wearing the vest and he only got your shoulder. Now – are you going to open them chocolates I brought you or what?'

He casts a pained expression at Laura, like he's asking her to put some manners on me. Or maybe it's because I said 'only' about his shoulder. Whittle's bullet shattered the shoulder joint and collar bone. It'll be a while and a fair few operations before he's back to normal.

'I mean it – it's good to know you've got my back, like.' I grin at Laura. 'Isn't it?'

'Sure is.' She smiles.

'How did you get that shot?' McArsey is shaking his head in wonder. Laura had done the impossible – got two bullets into the suspect without managing to kill him in the process. She'd gone for the knees.

She frowns and I know she feels bad.

'Jaysus, Laura! Stop looking like someone pissed in your cornflakes! You did what you had to do!' I look to McArsey for support. 'Didn't she?'

'Too right,' he says. 'Great shot, Shaw. And I know – I know I shouldn't have fired,' he says. 'I should have waited for the ERU. Cig will –'

'Ah! Don't mind Cig – no matter what you did, he'd say it was the wrong thing, the narky bollix,' I say. 'He's –'

There's a shift in the atmosphere and, across the bed from me, I see Laura smirking.

'He's behind me, isn't he?'

'Hi, Cig,' says Laura. 'Come in.'

Cig comes in, preceded by his belly. I swear to God I don't know why he does that fasting thing. As soon as he loses the belly and goes back to normal eating it appears on top of his trousers like a lost dog at the back door. Behind Cig is the new recruit – the red-haired little one. She walks over to the bed in three hurried steps and bends to hug McArsey, trying not to get caught up in his sling.

McArsey sees me looking.

'My niece,' he says.

Oh.

He smiles his patronizing smile and I wonder if he's letting me know I'm still in with a chance. For Christ's sake.

We're all a bit embarrassed, in fairness, standing around McArsey's bed with him in his pjs. Cig looks so out of place – it's like when you're little and you see your teacher down at the shops or somewhere and you can't believe she exists outside the classroom. Same with Cig's worn and battered face. It belongs in the unit.

'Nice work, lads,' he says. 'And it looks like we'll be able to get him for the others – Kim and Nicole. And a twenty-year-old case – girl in the pharmacy where he worked. He faked her suicide.'

He sighs a world-weary, criminal-weary, life-weary sigh, and I feel like hugging him. Dorothy must have gone in to talk to them about her time in the pharmacy. Good woman.

'He's in the high-security unit over in Dundrum for now. Until the trial.'

'Well, he won't be getting out of there anytime soon, Cig,' I say. 'We got him.' And then I chance it – 'On your watch.'

Laura busies herself tidying up the chocolates, her eyes sliding away from mine. McArsey turns a snort into a cough, wincing at the pain.

Ten minutes later, we're standing by Laura's car in the hospital car park. It's warm – very warm for the end of March – and the breeze from the mountains has a summery feel to it.

'Do you want to come over and see the kids?' says Laura. 'Matt has taken the day off and we're meeting at the playground beside the castle.'

I shake my head.

'No, thanks.' I point to my shopping bag, weighed down by bags of sugar, ground almonds, a jar of jam and a pound of butter. 'I've my first lesson with Dorothy. We're making Bakewells – I'll save you some. And then I've to put up nest boxes before the swallows feck off and move somewhere else.'

She smiles, moving her hand to sweep her hair behind her ear, although her short crop means there's nothing to sweep. It's so bright I can see clouds scudding across the sky reflected in her pupils. There's a lightness to her face. The shadows – the haunted look – for the first time in an age, her features are open. The fear is gone.

The breeze lifts my own hair and I notice – again – the lack of it. My neck is freezing. In fairness, it's way quicker to dry.

'Okay, great,' she says, popping the locks on her car and getting in.

I pat two little pats on the car roof and walk away. She reverses out of the space and pulls alongside me, lowering the window.

'See you Monday.' Laura grins.

'You will indeed.' I grin back.

Laura

I spot them at the entrance to the playground. Noah is strapped on to Matt's chest in the baby sling, conked out. Above him, Katie sits on his shoulders, swinging her legs with excitement, one hand clutching a fistful of Matt's hair for balance, the other waving what looks like a soggy piece of toast in my direction.

'Mumaaaa!' she yells. 'We're here! We waited for you!'

Matt's face splits into his creased grin – scores of lines around his eyes, each of them telling me he sees me, he loves me. Inside my guts, I feel a quickening, and it's all I can do not to sprint the hundred yards to meet them. And then – and then I think – *Run to them, you stupid idiot. You bloody love them.*

I run. My cracked rib twinges, but faintly. Much fainter now. And Katie squeals to get down and Matt sets her down just as I reach them and we have a family hug and it doesn't matter that it wakes Noah and he starts to grizzle. It doesn't matter.

Katie has to go on everything in this playground in a particular order, starting with the swing. She sits on the big-girl swing, somehow managing to eat her toast, which I see now Matt has cut in the shape of a heart – she's big into heart- or butterfly-shaped toast – and Noah swings gently, wedged into the bucket swing next to her.

Matt and I stand behind them, side by side, ready to catch or push them higher. Whatever is required. I look at him and

I notice how much older he looks – the thinning hair, the etched brow. I know that I've caused those lines, that what happened to me both recently and in the past has caused him so much pain and stress. But he hums a little tune, one of Katie's school songs, and I laugh, because that's exactly what his dad does. How like his dad he is now.

I look at him and I can't believe my luck. A fierce, raw strength races through me. It burns – embers from ashes – a thing forged in flames. It's as strong as anger, but purer, brighter. A burning phoenix of power.

'Matt, a while ago, you asked me a question and – you asked me what I want.'

He stops humming, turns to look at me.

'I did.'

'Well, I know the answer now. I want it all. You – this – work – Niamh. Every bit of it.'

He grins. His eyes crease. He pulls me closer.

'Of course you do,' he says into my hair. 'Every little bit.'

Every. Little. Bit.

Yeah.

Acknowledgements

Sincere thanks for guidance, friendship and double doses of faith to my agent Faith O'Grady and to all the team at Lisa Richards.

For helping chisel this story into a recognizable shape while saving me from my worst excesses, massive thanks to amazing editor Patricia Deevy. I am so lucky to have your wisdom, insight and general brilliance never far away. Likewise, I am so grateful to Sarah Day and Natalie Wall for their skilled editing and to Cliona Lewis, Carrie Anderson, Issy Hanrahan, Laura Dermody, Louise Farrell and Sorcha Judge, for their excellent scheming.

To both Penguin teams – Sandycove and Random House – thanks for getting this book out into the world. Thanks also to the librarians and booksellers and the readers who keep us all going.

To Paul Brennan, thank you for hours of your time helping me work out how to use pharmacy medications for nefarious purposes. In particular, thank you for letting me use your name for my killer!

To Danni Cummins, Mary Fallon and Deasún McNally I renew my heartfelt thanks for information regarding the work of the Gardaí – and this time, massive thanks also to Lana Cotter. And yep – all mistakes are entirely my own.

I am so grateful to Conor Devally for answering a barrage of legal questions with patience, humour and the charm for which his profession is known. Don't worry that I've only used a fraction of what we discussed – I have plans.

To pathologist Dr Marie Cassidy, thank you most sincerely for your prompt and informative reply to my queries and for always being ready to talk forensics with crime writers. Everyone who hasn't already, do read Dr Cassidy's brilliant book *Beyond the Tape*.

As usual, I've mined relatives and friends for their knowledge of psychiatric medicine. As well as sibs, thank you Erina Fahy and Zoë Acheson for your help with social psychology.

Teachers, tutors and writing friends both recent and from way back, thank you for your inspiration, guidance and encouragement. Past and current students from school and ballet worlds, I have learned so much more from you than I ever managed to teach – thank you.

Thank you to the happy throng of Irish writers who have welcomed me so warmly and generously into their midst and said nice things about me on book jackets.

To my sisterhood and brotherhood of friends and dear in-laws – I can't list you all because of the ranking problems. Thank you. I love you all. You know who you are.

To my wonderful siblings, forged by our feral childhood in the wilds of Rathmichael – or maybe that was just the sixties? Keith, Adrienne and Conor, I love you, guys. Thank you.

To my non-dancing husband Angus, who has been in step with me since prehistory, thank you for always dancing at weddings. And for everything else.

To our daughters, Jess and Sara, who have made sense of the chaos, thank you.

And to you, dear reader, a final heartfelt thanks for reading this book.